Alburquerque

ALBURQUERQUE

◆◆◆◆◆◆◆◆◆◆◆◆◆◆◆◆◆◆◆◆◆◆◆◆◆◆

Rudolfo Anaya

◆◆◆◆◆◆◆◆◆◆◆◆◆

University of New Mexico Press
Albuquerque

◆◆◆◆◆◆◆

All characters and events in this novel are fictional.
Any likenesses to real people and occurrences are purely coincidental.

Library of Congress Cataloging—in—Publication Data
Anaya, Rudolfo A.
Alburquerque / by Rudolfo Anaya. — 1st ed.
p.   cm.
ISBN 0–8263–1359–0
I. Title.
PS351.N27A79   1992
813'.54—dc20   91-43597
CIP

In April of 1880 the railroad reached la Villa de Alburquerque in New Mexico. Legend says the Anglo stationmaster couldn't pronounce the first 'r' in "Albur," so he dropped it as he painted the station sign for the city. This novel restores the original spelling, Alburquerque.

RUDOLFO ANAYA

Alburquerque

1 Ben Chávez walked into Jack's Cantina and ordered a beer at the bar. April was already warm, and the air conditioning felt good. The image in the mirror smiled back, showing a row of even teeth in a brown face. The dark hair was graying around the temples. Hitting forty isn't bad, he thought, as he took his beer and found an empty booth. He sipped and enjoyed the cool, bitter taste of draft beer.

It was Friday afternoon and the bar was packed with university students, local patrons, and a few professors. Things don't change much, Ben thought as he leaned back into the well-polished vinyl seat of the booth.

He was teaching a writing class at the university just up the street, and today after class some of the students had invited him to an uptown bar. Ben declined. If he was going to have a beer on his way home, he preferred Jack's. The old bar on Central Avenue had been a favorite place for a long time.

Sooner or later everyone passes through the doors of Jack's Cantina, Ben thought, from the winos who hung around the blood donor center to the downtown bigshots. The place had been around a long time and its booths were worn, but it was comfortable. For Ben, it was a friendly wateringhole. He felt the tension generated by student questions drain away as he enjoyed his beer.

He was working on a story, thinking of writing something about the current political situation. The mayor's race was heating up. Frank Dominic, an old high school friend, was running. He wanted to be governor, but he hadn't played hardball in New Mexico politics, so he planned to get experience as mayor. That meant he had to beat the incumbent Marisa Martínez, a thirty-year-old attorney. She had called Ben a few weeks ago to ask for his support, and Ben was sure Dominic would be calling soon.

In the meantime Cynthia lay dying in St. Joseph's Hospital; the cancer was winning the battle. He sighed. There wasn't anything he could do about it. Nada. Death came even in springtime. Maybe that's why he had declined his students' invitation; he wanted to be alone. He felt tired, and he knew it wasn't the job. The thought of Cynthia dying had worn him down. He had been to see her, and the woman lying on the bed was no longer the young woman he once knew. Time had come between them, and now her death was about to seal the separation.

He scribbled a note on the bar napkin in front of him. Maybe he should write her story, not the story of the political struggle that was going to tear the city apart. Cynthia is dying, that's what mattered. It was a story he had never told, and maybe its time had come.

As he wrote, an old nemesis from high school appeared at his booth.

"Ben, cómo 'stás, vato?" the big man said. He slapped Ben on the back. Not a friendly gesture.

Ben looked up. Fat Bernie. Fat Bernie was king of the pool table in the back room. He also ran drugs in the student ghetto that lay along the university's south side. They had gone to high school together, and because they were from different barrios, their gangs had fought, big-time rumbles after football games or dances.

"Okay, Bernie. You?"

"Just earning a living," Bernie shrugged. "Come on, let's play a little eight ball."

Ben shook his head. He hadn't played pool in a long time, and Bernie played for high stakes. Besides, he didn't like Bernie.

"Come on," Bernie insisted. "You used to play at Okie's. Remember?" Bernie laughed. He was fat and dark as he loomed over the writer, a shadow from the past.

Ben remembered. He had played a lot of pool when he was a student at the university, but that was another time, another world. He had played Bernie and beaten him, and Bernie had never forgotten.

"Come on, one game, five bucks," Bernie kept bugging him, drawing the attention of the other people in the bar. "I'll give you a handicap. I'll tie one hand behind my back!" Bernie roared. His buddy, a simian character in pachuco dress, emerged from the crowd to laugh with him. Chango was Bernie's compa in the drug game they played. Everybody knew.

"Es gallina," Chango sneered. He looked at Ben with evil eyes.

Chicken, Ben thought. I was never chicken. We knocked the hell of out you, Chango. Remember? Nobody called him chicken.

"Okay," Ben slid out of the booth. "Come on, Bernie, let's see how good you really are."

Bernie led the way into the back room, and Chango laughed. They were loaded with dope money and high on a few snorts.

A buzz filled the air, heads turned, and some of the workers drinking at the bar followed the players into the back room. Some of the men knew Ben had played once. They watched as he slapped five twenties on the table and picked out a cue stick.

Bernie cleared his throat. A hundred bucks a game? Most of the guys shot for beer money. Beads of sweat broke out on Bernie's forehead. He felt the wad of money in his pocket then looked at Chango. Chango smiled, "Chingalo."

They rolled up their sleeves and played. Ben's instinct was to go easy at first, let the sucker win a few, then raise the bets. But Bernie and Chango had ticked off something in him, an anger that had lain dormant. Old scores he thought were dead and settled from his youth.

It was like going to a cockfight in Bernalillo or Belen. You go thinking you're not going to get involved, but the flurry of the cocks and blood spilling excite everyone, and soon you're betting, soon you're in the game.

He planned to put Bernie away as fast as possible. He hated bullies, and these two had bullied him all the way through high school. He let Bernie take the first game, upped the bet, then ran the table on the next three.

Afternoon turned to late afternoon. The pool room grew crowded as other players and customers gathered to watch the game. The word filtered out quickly: Ben Chavéz was giving Bernie a hard time on the table. Silent Ben Chavéz, who just wrote books and was always courteous when he dropped by for a beer, could play pool. And Bernie had the reputation for being one of the best players in the city.

But now Bernie was sweating and puffing. He hadn't expected a tight game, and he sure as hell didn't want to lose to Ben Chavéz. He kept digging into his pocket, and in a couple of hours he was over a thousand into the wad of money he owed his boss. The man who supplied him with dope would not wait to be paid. He cursed and looked at Ben. Pure luck, but the sonofabitch was running hot. Too hot. Bernie stomped, changed from beer to shots of tequila, changed his cue stick, and still Ben ran table after table.

An hour later Bernie knew he had taken a beating. Sweat dripped from him as he leaned exhausted against the table. He looked at Chango. His partner had covered bets on the side, but that had only increased their losses. Lady Luck, la Señora dressed in white lace, followed Ben around the table. Today I am with you, she whispered, but playing pool ain't like writing a story. Tomorrow no one may care when you finish the poem.

Ben smiled. Suerte was fickle, he knew, but he had been given a gift early in life. Lady Luck was always by his side.

Do something, Bernie's scowl said, but Chango was sweating, too. In a few hours they had to deliver the Friday night take, and they were going to be short.

Only Ben Chavéz remained cool. He hadn't played eight ball in a long time, but the skill was still there. He was enjoying beating Bernie. He felt high, in charge of things. He could still shoot a good game, and that pleased him.

"Last game, Bernie," Ben smiled, "then I'm looking for new competition." He and those around the table laughed. He had two balls to run. He leaned over the table, stroked the cue stick, and as he did he accidentally touched the eight ball with the back end of his cue stick. It was a mistake Bernie and Chango had been waiting for.

"Hey! Hustle!" Chango cried, grabbed Ben and spun him around.

"Accident," Ben tried to explain as he pushed Chango back, but Bernie had already charged. He swung his cue stick and the blow glanced across Ben's forehead.

Stunned, Ben fell back. He cursed himself for the stupid move. Anger overwhelmed him as he struggled to his feet.

"Okay, Bernie, you asked for it!" He swung back. No sonofabitch was going to hit him and get away with it. It was like old times. Somebody pushed and you pushed back—that was the rule of the barrio.

"You hustled!" Chango shouted and pulled a switchblade. The crowd drew back. Chango moved in slowly. "You asked for it, ese."

Ben shook his head to clear the cobwebs. Ah damn, a knife. Same old story. Why couldn't he fight with his fists?

"Put the knife away," he heard himself say.

"Yeah, put the knife away," someone repeated. Chango turned to see a big Indian step forward.

"Stay outta this, Joe!" Bernie shouted.

He knew Joe Calabasa, an ex-Nam vet who drank his afternoon beer at Jack's. Next to him stood Abrán González, a former Golden Gloves boxer.

"Stay out!" Chango yelled at Joe. That was his big mistake. Joe kicked out and Chango's knife went flying. In the same motion he hit Chango with a crushing blow that sent the man sprawling over the pool table, blood gushing from his mouth.

Bernie came in with a cue stick, but Abrán stopped him with a left jab, then a short right that split the fat man's lip. The fight was over. Tony, the bartender, came pushing through the crowd, shouting "Break it up! Break it up!"

"It's okay," Joe said. Nobody was going to jump in for Bernie.

Bernie and Chango knew they were beaten. They backed away. "Sonofabitch started it!" Bernie cursed.

"I don't care who started it," Tony threatened. "No fighting here! Move on out!"

Bernie pulled Chango away, and nursing their wounds they left the bar.

Joe Calabasa turned to Ben. "You okay?"

"Get him a drink," the bartender said, and Angel the waitress hurried to the bar. "Clear the room, folks, just a little argument. It's all over. All over." He looked at Ben. "You okay?"

Ben Chavéz nodded. "I'm okay."

The writer looked at Joe Calabasa, then at the young man with him. Abrán González. A handsome kid. His eyes were a light brown, the color of his curly hair.

"Abrán," he said. His hand trembled when he took the handkerchief the kid offered him.

"You know my name?"

Ben pressed the handkerchief to his wound. "Everybody knows you. You were Golden Gloves champ."

Abrán smiled; a couple of men returning to their tables slapped him on the back. Others congratulated Ben on the game as they went back into the bar to drink and talk about the fight. Ben drank the shot of Jack Daniel's that Angel offered him. It eased the pain.

"And thanks, Joe. . ." Ben looked at Joe and tried to remember where they had met.

"Calabasa. From Santo Domingo. I took a class with you a few years ago."

"That's it. I can't remember plots, but I never forget a face," Ben smiled. He shook Joe's hand then Abrán's. "You saved my life."

"Nah. But you better see a doctor," Joe said.

"Ah, it's nothing. I'll get home, be okay," Ben answered.

They walked with him out the door into the bright afternoon light. A spring windstorm was sweeping over the city, raising dust. In the neighborhood behind the bar the tall elm trees were already green with seed clusters. Somewhere in the apartments nearby a woman called a child, and a screen door banged. In the parking lot someone had run over a snake that had come out of a garden with the warmth of spring. Two winos had stopped to look at the mess.

"Okay?" Abrán asked.

"Feel like I have rubber knees," Ben said, catching a glimpse of the dead snake. The wind swirled dust in his eyes, and he thought of the snake dance at Zuni. The snake had awakened to spring and come into the light to meet its death; it was not a good omen.

"We can drive you home, Mr. Chavéz," Joe volunteered.

"Or the hospital," Abrán added.

"Ben, call me Ben. This? It's nothing. You should have seen some of the high school fights I was in. Blood and broken bones all over the place. And we're still alive. It's not bleeding. I could use a ride home. . . ."

"Can do," Joe said. "Abrán can drive your car, I'll follow."

They helped him into his car and Ben told Abrán to follow Central Avenue across town to the West Mesa.

"I was stupid," he said. His head throbbed. "I haven't been in a fight since I was in high school. What am I going to tell the wife?" They drove in silence. "It was a good one," he smiled. "You know what they say, Dios cuida a los niños y los borrachos. He also takes care of writers," he added.

They crossed the Río Grande and Ben looked out across the river bosque. The cottonwoods were sprouting buds, a light tinge of green in the otherwise dusty afternoon. The windstorms came with spring, the souls of the dead rode the wind. Most people grew nervous and unsettled with wind; Ben listened to its cry.

"I built my home on the West Mesa so I could watch the sun rise in the morning," Ben said. "From there I watch the city. A man never runs out of stories to tell when he has a city like this."

Abrán listened politely as Ben talked. He had never thought about the life of a writer, although as a first-year student at the university he was enjoying the literature class he was taking. It was his favorite subject, and he never tired of analyzing the novels he read for class. But he had never met a writer. The man took what were the ordinary events in life and created stories. He listened closely as Ben Chavéz talked about his past, and he sensed the man was struggling with a problem, something he needed to resolve.

He drove into the driveway, and he and Joe walked Ben to the front door. "I want you to come in," Ben kept insisting. "Meet my wife. She's going to be upset. Come in." He called and his wife, a slim, attractive woman, appeared. "Elena, mi amor, these are my friends, Joe and Abrán."

She greeted the two young men. "What happened?" she asked. Ben was still holding Abrán's handkerchief to his forehead.

"It's nothing, a small cut," he tried to explain as she looked at the wound.

"A bruise, but you should see a doctor."

"For this? It's nothing. A bandage, that's all I need. Look, it stopped bleeding."

"Okay," she said, "but it's going to leave a scar."

"The scars of life," he said and looked at Abrán and Joe. Something about the incident had released more than adrenaline. He felt he was destined to meet the two young men, but he didn't know why.

"All right," she agreed. "Go in the study, I'll bring the bandages."

"Follow me," he said and led Abrán and Joe past the dining area and down a set of stairs. His study contained a desk, a typewriter, a word processor, files, and shelves stacked thick with books. Along the top of a bookshelf sat an array of plaster saints.

"My santos," he explained as he offered them chairs. "They have delivered me home once again. Gracias a Dios y las kachinas."

"Nice place," Joe said as he looked through the bookshelves.

"It is," Ben answered. "I have peace and quiet here. Look around. Can I get you a drink?"

"No, not for me," Abrán said.

He watched Abrán, taking in the boy's face. His fine sculptured nose hadn't been damaged by the years of boxing, and the gaze in his eyes was still innocent.

"I want to thank you," Ben said.

"No problem," Abrán answered. "Bernie had it coming."

Joe had made his way around a bookshelf to look at a large painting on the wall. It was the scene of a matanza, the butchering of hogs for winter meat. It was so vivid in detail and color that the people in it seemed alive. He was about to ask Ben about the painting when Ben's wife reappeared.

"It's a clean cut," she said as she cleaned the wound. "It will be bruised awhile."

Ben handed Abrán the handkerchief he had borrowed.

"I can wash it," Ben's wife said.

"No, no trouble," Abrán said. "We have to go."

"I want to thank you," she said. She shook their hands and wished there was something she could give them.

"Stay and eat with us," she invited.

"Thanks, but my mother is waiting," Abrán explained. "She promised us a big supper."

"If you hadn't been there Chango would have cut me in thirteen pieces and fed me to the ducks at Tingley Beach," Ben thanked them.

"Glad to help," Joe said.

"We better get going," Abrán said. "It was an honor to meet you, Ben. And you," he said to Elena.

"Come again and stay longer," Ben said as he walked them to the door. "Adiós," he waved.

He stood there and watched them drive away. He felt the pain of the headache, but it was a surface pain, something he knew would eventually go away. The pain inside was not as temporary. Cynthia was dying, and there was nothing he could do, nothing except begin the story that came to him at Jack's.

Each small event in life has a meaning, he thought, each event connects us to the web of life. Strands of the past return to haunt us; the past is never dead.

Troubled by the sudden turn of the afternoon, he went to the terrace to sit and watch the sun set over the city. The wind had died down, as it usually did in late afternoon. The apricot trees had already flowered; if there was no late freeze there would be fruit, the golden fruit of early summer. The first purple buds had also appeared on the lilac bushes that lined one side of his garden. When they bloomed, spring would change to summer, and the passion of summer would flood the valley. Spring was the time of transition, the time of awakening.

His wife brought him an herbal tea and they sat together, looking out across the valley.

"Nice young men," she said.

"Yes," he answered, and he thought of the other two young men who were characters in the epic poem he was writing. He had to finish the poem because now he had a new story forming and ready to come alive.

He gazed across the Río Grande Valley, mesmerized by the wide horizon in front of him. River, mountain, and the valley that held the oasis of the city.

The river was a serpent winding its way south. It was carrying the snowmelt of the northern mountains of Taos, the mountains of the Sangre de Cristo. Normally he could sit for hours and watch the rich glow of the setting sun light up the valley and clothe the Sandías in mauve majesty, but the clarity of light that came with dusk did not comfort him today. He got up and went to his desk to write. Old themes, he thought, have to be resolved. Cynthia was dying.

2 Abrán and Joe drove south on Atrisco toward Central, then across the old Tingley Beach road. Tingley Beach was a large pond which ran parallel to the deep acequia on the east side of the Río Grande. On the north side of the irrigation canal spread the Country Club golf course and beyond that were the homes of the once prestigious old neighborhood.

Tingley Beach had been the city's first swimming hole. It was built during the term of the late 1930s mayor, Clyde Tingley, so the name had stuck. It was the only lake of any size in the city. In the forties and fifties the city swarmed to Tingley Beach on Sunday afternoons, but when the polio epidemics swept the country, its use as the local swimming hole was prohibited. Municipal pools were built in the fifties and now the beach was a winter fishing hole. Ducks lived there year-round, and withered elm trees lined the dry, sandy banks.

In every kind of weather, fishermen plied the stagnant waters, lovers came to sit at the tables on the sandy banks, and joggers ran along trails by the side of the beach. Today there was a family enjoying the first warm day of spring.

"If they build the big aquatic park the city is planning, la raza gets pushed out," Joe said. "My grandfather used to tell me the city was going to grow. 'Just don't let them get the pueblo land,' he said. If you give up your land, you die. The developers have built clear up to the Sandías. Now they're buying up the downtown barrios."

"What's left?" Abrán asked.

"The river land. 'Water is blood,' my grandpa said, and now they need the blood to keep building."

"The conservancy won't let them," Abrán said.

"Don't believe it, bro. See in the paper where Dominic is running for mayor? He cooked up a big water scheme. Gonna take the river right downtown. When men with money want to do something like that, the laws bend for them."

Abrán nodded. Joe was right. "What did you think of Ben Chávez?"

"He's okay. Sure as hell should never have gotten in a game with Bernie."

"You had a class with him?"

"Yeah, when I first started at the university. I thought I wanted to be a writer. Write about my grandfather, the way he lived. It was no good, Nam was too close."

Abrán turned toward the barrio.

"Hey, where you going?"

"Home. The jefita's got supper waiting."

"Can't, bro. Not tonight."

"Come on, I told her after we ran we'd be hungry. She's expecting us."

They had jogged around Roosevelt Park, then stopped at Jack's for a beer. Joe sometimes went home with him after they ran. Today was special, Abrán thought. He had gone into the fight instinctively to help Joe, and when he had time to reflect, he realized he still had the quickness in his hands.

"I can't. Drop me off at the bus depot."

"Meeting someone?"

"I want to send a letter to my mom. My cousin is picking up his rides about now."

There was a sadness in his voice, something Abrán seldom heard from his friend. Joe was tough. He had survived Nam and he had survived life in the streets after the war. Now he was catching up on the years he had lost. He lived in an apartment near the university and he was taking classes, but Abrán knew that the real issue Joe had to deal with was whether or not to return to the pueblo.

"The men of the pueblo will be out cleaning the acequias," Joe said. "They need help. My old man will spread out his corn and calabaza seeds like they were gold coins. Almost time to plant."

Abrán knew Joe needed the pueblo, he needed to be back in its circle, but he was afraid to return and take the ghosts of Nam with him.

"I'd like to see Bea," Joe said. "When I first got back, I thought I was okay. Had my uniform on, spit shine. I was drinking, but so was everybody. First night I took her out, I drank a lot. I guess I wanted to tell her about Nam, but when I tried I went crazy. I took it out on her. I don't ever want to do that again."

Joe grew silent, immersed in his own thoughts, and Abrán respected the silence. Abrán knew a little about the kind of pain Joe was carrying. He remembered the death of his friend, Junior Gómez. Gunner they used to call him, because when they were kids he imitated the sound of a submachine gun when they played war. Junior was with Abrán in Golden Gloves all the way through their senior year. Then one afternoon, after a sparring session, Junior died. He went home with a headache and died that night, and Abrán had blamed himself. The coaches tried to tell him it was an accident, but the death of his best friend haunted Abrán. He put away the gloves and the dreams of turning pro, finished high school, and escaped to Los Angeles for two years. During those years he tried to cut himself away from the past. He called only his mother, Sara, and he lost touch with the old gang. Still, Junior haunted him.

He also remembered the death of Ramiro, his father. He was six when the old man died, and that memory was not as poignant. Yet there were times when he remembered things Ramiro had told him, and the warmth and earth smell of the old man.

Twice, death had changed Abrán's life.

He sighed as he pulled up in front of the bus depot. "There's Sonny," Abrán said and nodded at the pickup in front of them.

"Yeah," Joe said. "I'll call you Monday. Tell your mom to save me some tortillas."

"Take care," Abrán waved, but he waited. Maybe Joe would change his mind.

The man standing at the truck door turned and watched Joe get out of the car. "Hey, Joe, you ugly Indian, have a beer."

"Hey, Sonny," Joe took the beer and nodded at the guys sitting in the camper. A couple of San Felipe boys who worked with Sonny.

"We're going dancin' in Algodones," one of them said.

"Goin' kick ass with our Cochití cousins," the other added. They laughed.

"Come on," Sonny said, "lez go, cousin."

Joe turned and looked at Abrán. Go on, Joe, Abrán wanted to call to him. Go home. You've been away too long. And Joe, who had stepped close to the truck and now had Sonny's arm around his shoulder as they drank beer, wanted to go home. He wanted to crawl into the camper and drink and sing all the way home. He wanted to envelop himself in the smell in the camper, the smell of men who had sweated and worked hard all day.

"Come on, Joe, let's haul ass," one of them said.

"We gotta go, Joe," Sonny said. "You comin'?"

Joe shook his head. "Nah. I got things to do here. Take this to my mom, huh." He handed Sonny the letter.

"Sure," Sonny said, "but you're gonna miss a good dance."

"See you, Joe."

"Don't take any Indian nickels."

"Watch out for them white girls!"

They called and laughed as Sonny burned rubber out into the traffic. A car honked; the driver cursed.

Joe turned and looked at Abrán. He had waited, hoping Joe would change his mind, but Joe waved and walked off down the street. Abrán pulled away, a bitter taste in his mouth. He didn't like it when he couldn't understand Joe, when Joe went into one of his moods. He's going to drink this weekend, Abrán thought. Dream of the pueblo and drink.

He had met Joe in a PE class at the university. They began to run together, talk about other classes, and they became good friends. Joe was older; he knew the world. He became, in a sense, the father Abrán didn't have. Abrán knew when Joe was in a drinking mood, when he needed to escape the demons that had entered his soul in Nam.

Abrán turned south on Fourth into the Barelas barrio and home. Dusk was settling over the neighborhood. He pulled into his driveway, then stopped at the door and paused to break a sprig of yellow forsythia for his mother.

When he entered, the aroma of food filled his nostrils. Chile, beans, potatoes frying, hot tortillas. "Mamá!" he called. Always Mamá or jefita. He never called her by her name, Sara. She was in her late fifties and proud, she said, to be old-fashioned. Dinners were important, and they centered around her son. I cook for you to please you, she said. Your father was like that, the evening meal was special. It was a time for family to be together.

"Sorry I'm late," he said as he picked up the mail at the telephone table and entered the kitchen. The envelope had a St. Joseph Hospital return address. A bill? he wondered.

"Mi'jo, I'm glad to see you," his mother smiled as she turned from the salad she was mixing to kiss him. He handed her the flowers. "For the salad?" she smiled.

"For you. I met Ben Chávez, the writer. Joe and I dropped in for a beer at Jack's. And there was a fight, not bad, just . . ."

"A fight?"

"Not bad. An argument. The writer—"

"What writer?" she asked, wiping her hands and putting the sprig of forsythia in a glass of water on the windowsill. The geranium was still blooming bright red, but the forsythia made her realize spring had arrived. She would have Abrán turn the soil in the flower bed. And the trim around the house needed painting.

Abrán opened the letter. "Do we owe St. Joe's?"

"No, not that I know. So, tell me about the writer."

"He got in a game of pool with a bad character. . ." his voice trailed off as he read the letter. When he finished he looked up at her. A dark, penetrating look. He was looking for himself in her. She felt her heart skip a beat, and the fear she had lived with since Abrán became her son surfaced. It had come. The letter she had feared for so long had come.

"There's a mistake," he said softly and looked at the envelope again, then at the letter.

"What does it say?" she asked, her knees weak, her mouth dry. He had looked at her and did not recognize himself. Santo Niño de Atocha, it was bound to happen. She had always known it would happen, hadn't she told herself? She knew that one day he would look at her and not see his reflection, and she would have to tell him that she and her husband, Ramiro, had adopted him as a child. He was given to them, and they were made to take a vow never to tell Abrán about his past.

With trembling hands she took the letter. Cynthia Johnson. The pain in her heart grew sharper.

"Sit," he said and he quickly got her a glass of water. She had glanced at the letter and grown pale. He held the glass to her trembling hands and she sipped.

"It's not for me," he said. "A mistake." His voice seemed so far away. Would she lose him? Why was this woman writing now?

"She says she's my mother," he said, then repeated, "a mistake."

"No," Sara shook her head. "Not a mistake." Her voice broke, she felt tears in her eyes. "Ay, hijito, hijito," she cried.

He put his arms around her. "Who is she? Why does she call herself my mother?"

He should know the truth. One day he had to know the truth, and if the Johnson woman had broken the vow of silence, now was the time. Sara González had to tell her son she was not his mother. She had promised her husband that when the time came she would tell Abrán.

"There's got to be a mistake. I'll go over to the hospital in the morning—"

"No. Not a mistake," she gasped and wiped her eyes with her apron. She looked into his eyes. She had to be strong, she could not hide the truth from him. "I want you to know I have always loved you," she whispered.

"I know that," Abrán answered, feeling empty inside. The woman who wrote the letter said she was his mother, and when he looked at Sara he knew it was true. It was his turn to feel the shock; his stomach turned and tightened. Sara was not his mother, and Ramiro was not his father. Perhaps he had always known this, but never faced it. He loved them too much, and their love for him was the love of a true father and mother.

"And I love you," he said and held her hands, and felt their strength. "There's a mistake. . . ."

"We adopted you. But we loved you like our son, our own blood."

"Adopted?" The word rang hollow and wrenched his soul. The vague dreams of his identity suddenly became a disturbing reality. The light color of his skin, his eyes, his features that were not the features of this woman he called Mother.

You resemble your father, she had told him when he asked, but he remembered his father as a short, dark man. His skin was the color of the earth. Yes, I resemble my father, he agreed, and because he didn't want to trouble her, he asked no more. But in the barrio there were whispers. The old people called him güerito.

"The woman who wrote the letter is your mother."

He shook his head, turned and looked at the letter again. Cynthia Johnson. The artist? The daughter of the well-known banker? It couldn't be. Somebody was playing a cruel joke. He was Abrán González, he had always been Abrán González. His mother was sitting in front of him, her name was Sara.

"Adopted?" he heard himself say again, and Sara's eyes told him the world he once knew was slipping away. To steady himself he reached out and touched his mother's hand.

"You were given to us, mi'jito," she said and held his hands tightly. She did not want to let him go. She had raised him, she knew his soul, but he was not of her blood. What would Ramiro say? Tell the boy the truth. She needed Ramiro's strength now that she felt so weak and useless.

"Ramiro worked for the family of el señor Johnson. From the time we came from Guadalupe, he worked for them as the gardener. For a while I worked, cleaning the house. We knew the family; we knew Cynthia from the time she was born."

She took another drink of water and looked into Abrán's eyes. The pain was as much his as hers. Would the truth separate them? She braced herself and continued.

"The girl grew. Cynthia. Cindy, the kids used to call her. When she was in high school she became pregnant. You see, they are rich, they did not want the child."

Me, Abrán thought. They didn't want me. I am that woman's child, the unwanted baby.

"I would not lie to you, my son. It hurts me to tell you this."

"Go on," he said. He felt bruised, as if he had taken a beating, as if he had just come in from a long, tiring journey.

"Cynthia's father wanted the girl to have an abortion, but the girl resisted. You were born, and you were given to us."

"But you've never said anything," he groaned. His life had been a lie, and the woman he had called Mother was part of that lie.

"We couldn't," she grasped him. "Don't you see, we gave our word that we would never reveal the truth. El señor Johnson is a very rich man. He made us promise that we would never say anything."

"And my father?" he asked. "Who is he?"

There was a long silence, then Sara sighed. "We never knew," she said. "But Cynthia is your mother. Your blood."

He looked again at the letter. "She's dying. Cancer."

"That is why she wants to see you."

"All these years," he shook his head.

She reached out and touched his cheek. "Don't be harsh on me, mi'jito. We did what we had to do. We promised to raise you as best we could. Ramiro and I didn't have children; we were hungry for children! And don't be harsh on the woman who is your mother. She provided for you."

"I should have known, I should have asked."

"There was nothing to tell you. We took a vow, and until now the woman has never contacted us."

"She sent money?"

"Yes. We had enough, Ramiro always worked. After he died she made sure we had what we needed. She was always generous."

"Ah, damn, jefita!" Abrán cried, a sob escaping with the pain he felt. "I don't know what to say." He rose and looked out the kitchen window. Night had settled on the barrio. His mother rose to remove the food from the stove.

Where do I belong, Abrán wondered.

"I have to see her," he said.

"Yes," Sara nodded. "She needs you."

"I'll go right away."

"Eat first."

"Can't."

She understood. "I wish I could have made this easier," she said, hugging him. "You are still my son."

"I always will be," he answered and tried to smile. He kissed her forehead and went out the door into the night. But now his world was different. In the night shadows there lurked a sense of danger. Who am I? he asked, and he did not know the answer.

My world has changed, he thought as he drove up the dark barrio street. That morning he had gone to classes, then hit the books. In the afternoon he called Joe and they jogged. Then the chance meeting with the writer, the fight, and finally the letter. In a short time the world was a very different place, and he was a man with a clouded past. How could this woman be his mother? And who was his father? He felt anger building inside, and he cursed the crumpled letter he held in his hand.

He, Abrán, had been born into the world an orphan, unwanted. What did he owe this woman? Nothing, he owed her nothing. Sara was his mother, she had raised him, he loved her. And Ramiro was his father. The old man with the smell of earth and sweat was the face he remembered as Father.

But old, nagging questions now made sense. Sara was now in her fifties. You were born late in our lives, she said once. Una bendición de Dios. He was fair-skinned, so he learned to smile when the old people in the barrio called him güerito, and he learned to fight when the dark-skinned Mexican kids made fun of him. "You're not Mexican, güero," they teased, and that barb hurt more than anything. He learned to take on the tough kids, and he grew skillful with his fists.

"I'll show you I'm Mexican," was his battle cry, and he cursed with the best barrio Spanish he knew and went in swinging. He grew tough, and by the time he was in middle school they no longer teased. He had become intensely proud of his Mexicanness by having to prove it, and during those crucial years of puberty he became the leader of a gang called Los Gatos.

Los Gatos, he remembered. We did some crazy things. At eighteen Paco wound up in the pen for distributing marijuana, and Ricky died of an overdose when he was a senior in high school. That had made Abrán snap. He didn't need the stupid things they were doing, the drinking on weekends and partying. They had not thought about death until Ricky died. Abrán grew up that year, and he turned all his energy into boxing. His old coach, Rudy Sánchez, took him under his wing and made a boxer out of him.

Two of the guys, Pollo and Jimmy, had married right out of high school, so they remained in the barrio. He saw them from time to time, but less and less as their families grew. He was the only one from the gang who tried college. Boxing had taught him discipline, and it had given him direction. But it was really Sara's guidance that focused him on a meaningful future.

Sara was the only mother he knew. She lived her life for him. She was his mother, not Cynthia Johnson, not the woman who lay dying in the hospital.

He was deep in thought when an old woman ran in front of his car. He slammed on the brakes and skidded to a stop. He saw her clearly, her wild hair flowing around the wrinkled face, the eyes wild and dark, the lips open in a scream that filled the night. La Llorona, he thought, the wailing woman of the barrio.

He felt a chill of adrenaline; his fingers clasped the steering wheel. Then the creature stepped into the headlights and he recognized doña Tules.

He breathed a sigh of relief and got out of the car; she stepped back into the shadows. Had he hit her? Why did she curse him? He had heard a lot of stories about doña Tules, how she roamed the streets at night and frightened the kids of the barrio. She really was a Llorona, but a flesh-and-blood one. She always appeared along this stretch of dirt road, because, as the story went, it was the road between the church and her shack near the river. People said she came out late at night to cry at the steps of the church where she was jilted long ago.

Sara said not to believe what people said about doña Tules. She was a kind soul, she had suffered much in life. She had lived alone so long that she had visions. She knew how to heal people, and she went to the church to light candles to the Virgin, not to cry.

"Doña Tules?" Abrán asked. "Are you all right?"

"Abrán de la Sara?" she asked hoarsely.

She was standing in the shadows, pointing at him. Dressed in a dirty and tattered gown, she drew close. Thank God he hadn't hit her, he breathed in relief.

"Sí," he answered.

"Your mother is dying, and you are being born," she said. Her words sent a chill through Abrán.

"Come to me when you want to know the truth."

"What truth?" he asked.

"Tú eres tú," she said, and pointed a thin finger at him. Then she turned and fled. A long drawn-out cry filled the night around Abrán, chilling his blood anew.

"Doña Tules!" he called. Crazy old woman. What did she mean, Tú eres tú? Is that what he heard? You are you? Or did she say Tu-er-to? Blind? He shook his head and got back in the car. He looked into the shadows, but she was gone. He shivered and felt a cold sweat on his body.

Had he really seen her? It wasn't a ghost, it was a woman, he was sure he had seen her. Doña Tules who lived alone and wandered the back alleys of the barrio; the barrio's bag lady of the night. What did she mean?

"Who is la Llorona?" he had asked Sara when he was a child. "We, the mothers of the world, are the crying women, because we cry when our children suffer," Sara had answered. "Every woman is a Llorona."

He shook his head, got back in the car, and turned the ignition with trembling hands. In the rearview mirror he saw a swirling red light appear. A cop car cruising the barrio. He didn't feel like explaining, so he eased forward. There was no pursuit, the red light turned a corner and was gone. Maybe that's what he had heard, the cop's siren?

At Central he stopped for a light. He would ask Sara what the old woman meant. Sara was one of the few women in the barrio doña Tules would visit. Once or twice a year she came by to have coffee. She drank in silence, took the clothes Sara had saved for her, and that was it.

A car honked and Abrán drove on, turning into the Central Avenue artery and joining the stream of the cruisers and lowriders celebrating Friday night. Here he was just one more child of the city, anonymous, not the child of Cynthia Johnson, not the troubled Abrán anguishing over what being her son meant. He flowed with the loud music and shouts of the kids in their customized cars. In their rite of spring he forgot for a moment the weight he carried, but when he turned toward the hospital he was Abrán again, Abrán being born into a new life.

The point was now persistent; the woman dying of cancer at St. Joe's was his mother. Would his father be there?

It was long after visiting hours, and the dark corridors were deserted. At the nurses' station he explained he had come to see Cynthia Johnson. The two nurses glanced at each other, the older nodded and the younger one said, "Come with me." Her name tag read Lucinda Córdova.

"What's your relationship to the patient?" she asked as she led him down the quiet hallway.

"I'm her son," he answered. The words sounded strange.

"Her son?" the nurse asked.

"Yes," he answered.

She stopped at a door and turned to look at him. "You know she's dying." Abrán nodded. Her eyes were kind, she was trying to prepare him. But what was he supposed to feel about the dying woman? He didn't even know her.

"She can barely speak," she explained. "She may not recognize you." She paused. "Are you ready?"

He nodded and they entered the room.

"Let's see if she's awake. . . ."

They entered the dark room. A bedside lamp cast a dim light on the thin, shrunken figure on the bed. The cancer had been victorious; it had eaten away at the flesh and the spirit, leaving a frail body gasping for breath. Abrán approached, looked at the face of Cynthia Johnson. In spite of the ravages of the disease it was a handsome face, the face of a once-attractive woman.

The nurse leaned and whispered in the woman's ear. "Ms. Johnson? Are you awake? Cynthia? Can you hear me? Someone to see you. Your son." She looked at Abrán.

"Abrán," he said.

"Abrán. Your son."

Cynthia's eyelids fluttered, her eyes opened. She had been dreaming that she was painting a picture in which a bright figure dressed in white appeared. The figure glowed and moved; the sound of a drum filled the air.

The nurse was the figure in the painting, the angel of death. Perhaps the figure was doña Sebastiana, the skeleton of death of the old Hispanos of the valley. Perhaps she came dressed in white after all. La muerte, death, her sister. She saw the bony hand outstretched and Cynthia reached out to take it.

She had painted the figure of death once, doña Sebastiana in her cart, a bow and arrow her hands. But she had painted la Muerte in white silk with lace and bows, and she had put bright lipstick on death's lips. The old penitentes of the morada where Cynthia left the painting laughed and said it looked like la Comadre was going dancing. Death was going dancing, they said and laughed.

"Abrán," the figure said again.

My son. Abrán, she tried to whisper. He stood next to the figure in white. He had come at last. Come closer, come closer, let me hold you in my arms. But the shadow of death was too strong. You don't deserve your son, la Muerte said, you must die alone.

"Give me a few minutes with my son, comadre," she struggled to say.

"She's trying to speak," the nurse whispered.

Abrán was glad the nurse had stayed with him. He didn't know if he could face the dying woman alone. His mother. He wanted to feel some emotion, but what? He reached out and held her hands. They were cool.

She felt his touch and responded. A smile appeared at the edges of her lips, and the pain that had burned in her chest was gone. Yes, it was Abrán, her child. The nurse turned on a light and it flooded his face, like an angel glowing with life, like the face of his father when they were young.

She struggled to rise. You don't know how many times I've driven past your home with hopes of catching sight of you, and how many times I've been in the audience when you boxed and wished I could tell you who I was. I sat in the audience when you graduated from high school, and I cried, I cried. What a cruel bargain my father made, the vow of silence. There is no greater punishment than silence.

"Abrán," she whispered. My son, my blood, forgive me, forgive the years of silence. Come, let me hold you so I can die in peace. Forgive me.

"She said your name," the nurse whispered, smiled.

"She recognizes me," Abrán nodded, and he too smiled.

Yes, she looked into his eyes and saw herself reflected. He had some of her features, some of his father's features. It was like seeing her lover again. What a beautiful child their love had made, the love that was not allowed to flourish.

My son. Your hands are so warm on mine. Forgive me, I am dying, I am already dead. I died the day I was separated from you, twenty-one years ago. I had only one love in life, your father. Go to him now. Find him and tell him I asked his forgiveness also. Go before it's too late.

She coughed, a cough born in the shriveled lungs ravaged by the cancer. Abrán instinctively reached for his handkerchief and touched it to her lips. Only after he dabbed the blood at the edge of her lips did he realize the handkerchief was spotted with the writer's blood. He put it back in his pocket and took the towel Lucinda offered.

"Abrán," Cynthia said again, clutching tightly at his hand, but now the smile was lost in the cloud of pain that covered her face.

"My father?" he whispered in her ear, leaning close as he had seen the nurse do. He touched her forehead lightly and whispered the question.

"Abrán," she repeated. She looked again into his eyes, saw the face of the young boy who had fathered Abrán. My love and I will live together in Abrán.

Her eyelids fluttered and she let out a deep sigh. She turned and took the hand of the angel of death, content that she had seen her son before she died. Her hands clasped Abrán's, then released.

Lucinda quickly reached for her wrist, felt the pulse weaken, then grow still. "She's dead," she said.

He nodded. He had felt the breath leave the body, the skin become cold. He had known her only a few, short moments, and now she was dead. He felt anger; he felt cheated. It wasn't right!

The nurse pulled out a chair for him and he sat silently. Conflicting emotions swept through him; love and grief mixed with anger. He had found his mother, the mother who brought him into the world, and she was dead. Why had she kept the secret so long?

Around him Lucinda and another nurse arranged the bed and drew a sheet over Cynthia's body. A doctor was called in to pronounce her legally dead and sign the death certificate. While they waited for him, Lucinda explained that the old doctor had taken an interest in the case.

"He's retired, but he comes every day. He used to practice at Lovelace. He and Cynthia's mother visit, but Cynthia's father has never been here." Her voice trailed. "The doctor brings her flowers. He confers with her other doctor. They say it gives him something to do, but I think it's more than that. He has a real love for her."

The old doctor arrived and stood at the side of Cynthia's bed. When he finished his quiet vigil he signed the death certificate. Lucinda introduced Abrán.

There were tears in the old man's eyes when he embraced Abrán. "She was a beautiful woman," he struggled to speak, but emotion choked him. He shook his head, embraced Abrán again, mumbled "I'm sorry," and left.

Abrán sat all night by Cynthia's side; the night of her death also became the night of her wake. Lucinda stayed with him. It was proper, she told herself, to sit with the dead and pray for the departing soul. In the village of Córdova, where she grew up, wakes were still held at the home of the deceased. People came to pray all night and be with the family during its time of grief. The penitentes sang the old alabados and prayed the rosary. Death became a presence shared.

Here, a person who died in the hospital was delivered straight to the mortuary. Sometime later there was a service, then the burial. Death was kept at a distance. So she stayed with Abrán in the room with the dead woman.

Lucinda looked at him from time to time. Why had he not come before, and why did she feel drawn to him? Was it pity? No, she'd seen enough of death, she knew enough of grief. His eyes. She had looked in his eyes and felt more than concern, more than shared grief.

When the sun's first light began to enter the room, he stood and stretched. "Thanks for staying," Abrán said. The dark of night and the presence of death had woven a bond between them. They had shared the death of his mother.

"I've known Cynthia for a month. We became friends. I wanted to stay."

"You see a lot of death," he said.

She nodded.

"You say only her mother came to visit?"

"Yes."

"No husband, no man?"

"She wasn't married."

Not married? Why were Sara and Ramiro bound to a vow of silence? Who was his father?

"You're wondering about me?" Abrán asked.

Lucinda looked into his eyes. She had seen long, protracted illness by cancer do strange things to families. Cynthia had not mentioned Abrán until she knew she was dying. Then she had the doctor write him two days ago. Cynthia was Anglo, but Abrán wasn't, Lucinda thought as she looked at the features of the young man. Maybe half Anglo, but his father had to be Mexican.

"I never knew her," he cleared his throat. "I didn't know her as my mother. I didn't know she was my mother until last night."

Lucinda reached across and touched his hand. She felt his pain. "I'm sorry," she said.

Abrán called Sara. He didn't want her to worry. She, too, had not slept but she told him to do whatever needed to be done. She was fine; she would wait. "Be strong, my son," she said. It was her way of telling him she loved him, and that she understood what he had to do.

Abrán stood at the window as the sun exploded over the crest of the Sandía Mountains. He sipped the coffee Lucinda had brought him and watched the blinding, brilliant disc rise over Tijeras Canyon. It was returning north, renewing the valley. Joe would be getting up to say a prayer to the sun. Abrán prayed that his mother's soul have a peaceful journey.

As he stood there, Abrán remembered Ramiro's words. The sun is the source of life. The trees, plants, and flowers—without Tata Sol, they do not grow. The gardener with the dark skin had taught him much in those six years. Then he was suddenly gone, senselessly struck down by a drunk driver. How much more did the man have to teach him about the ways of his ancestors? Ramiro and Sara were proud people, a pride they instilled in him. "Puro indio," Ramiro used to say when he described himself. "Pray to the sun each morning, my son."

But now what? The woman whose blood he carried was Anglo. But he had always been Mexican, a Chicano. His father was Mexican, he was sure. What was he now? Half Anglo, half Mexican.

"Abrán," Lucinda said and drew him from his thoughts. He turned to see a woman enter the room. She was in her late sixties, maybe seventy, Abrán guessed. She was short and stocky with dark hair, a handsome woman. She reminded Abrán of the women from the northern part of the state, the slightly oval face with high cheekbones, green eyes, and jet-black hair. She carried herself with poise and assurance. She had an energy within that was subdued only by the grief she felt.

She went straight to the bed and gently pulled away the sheet from Cynthia's face. A cry filled the room, startling even Lucinda, who went to the door and closed it. It was a painful cry, a keening in the bright sun. The sobs shook the woman as she cried over Cynthia's body.

"Cindy," she repeated, "Cindy. My daughter, my child. We sinned against you."

She cried for her daughter and for the years of separation from her. Those twenty-one years they had met only rarely, and then in secret, at hurried lunches or at gallery openings. They spoke briefly, like strangers, always fearful her husband, Walter, would find out. Fearful of the vow he imposed on them.

Now the vow seemed empty, and the time they could have had together wasted. She rose, wiped away her tears, and straightened her dress. Then she turned and looked at Abrán. "We have sinned against you, too," she said.

She went to Abrán and embraced him. A new wave of grief came, and she asked forgiveness, as Cynthia had asked forgiveness. "It is you we have wronged," she cried. "Oh, it is so good to see you face-to-face, to touch you. But why did we have to wait so long? Why did we have to be united by death?"

Abrán didn't know how to answer. He had never seen the woman before, but he tried to comfort her. This was his mother's mother.

"I'm sorry," she said. "I thought I would be prepared. I knew she was dying, but still the end is not easy. How did you know?"

"She had the doctor write him," Lucinda explained.

"I'm glad. She made her peace. Did you get here before she died?"

"Yes, she recognized me," Abrán said.

"God is great," she said. "God forgives." She looked closely at him. "I am your grandmother," she said, "Vera Johnson. Cynthia's mother. You, too, must be forgiving. You must forgive us all."

"What is there to forgive?" Abrán answered. "I know so little."

"It isn't a pleasant story," Vera sighed.

"Cynthia fell in love with a young man when she was in high school. She got pregnant. The young man, who is your father, was Mexican. A boy from the barrio. My husband had built all his hopes on Cynthia, he wanted her to carry on the family business, and when he found out about the love affair he decided that she couldn't have the child. He wanted her to have an abortion. He insisted. Cindy and I fought back, and finally he agreed to let her have the baby. You," she said, looking at Abrán. So many of Cynthia's features were his.

"She could have the baby, he said, but we would have to put you up for adoption. And we would promise never to see you or speak to you again. You see, a promise of silence for life. We had no choice, we agreed. He made an arrangement with Ramiro and Sara to adopt the child, and they, too, were sworn to secrecy. They had no children, so they were glad to take you, and they agreed never to tell you." She reached out to hold his hands.

"Then who was my father?" Abrán asked.

"I don't know," Vera shook her head.

"You don't know?" Anger rose in him. He took her by the shoulders, and his voice was harsh. "What do you mean you don't know?"

"I never knew," Vera cried. "Walter covered up everything. He wanted us to pretend that you had never been born, that you didn't exist. The kids at school knew Cynthia was pregnant."

"Which kids?"

"Cynthia's friends. I don't know, it was long ago."

"Was there a birth certificate?" Lucinda asked.

"Don't you see what I'm trying to tell you? Walter took care of everything. You were born, and you were gone. We never saw you. Cynthia came home from the clinic alone."

Abrán shook his head and turned away. The shock left him weak, trembling. The anger turned on Walter Johnson, the man who had denied him his parents.

"Your husband knows!"

"I don't think so. He went to the school when we first learned Cynthia was pregnant. He wanted to know who the boy was. I don't know what he was going to do; he was full of anger. He could have killed the boy. When he returned he was like an empty shell. He sat in his study, saying nothing for a long time. Then he told me that he had forced the principal to march in Cynthia's friends, the boys she knew. The boy who might be responsible. A girl helped, I think her name was Gloria. She lived in Barelas; Cynthia knew her. When the kids were in the office, Walter discovered they were all Mexican kids. He realized the boy who got Cynthia pregnant was Mexican. The principal had a grin on his face, he said. He thought that's the way it would be the rest of his life, his business colleagues laughing at him.

Walter Johnson's daughter had lain with a Mexican kid and had a baby, they would laugh. He decided you were never to be part of us."

"He must know my father's name," Abrán insisted.

"No," Vera shook her head. "After that visit to the school it didn't matter. Walter needed to pretend it never happened, he tried to make us forget you completely. And he found the way to force us. You were to live only if we gave you up."

"I'll talk to him," Abrán said.

"He won't speak to you," Vera sighed. "Don't you see, to him you're dead. You never existed!"

"But I do exist!" Abrán exploded, the anger he had kept in check suddenly poured out. "I am here! I am alive! He can't take that away from me. He must tell me who I am! I'll force him! Damn him! Damn all of you!" He turned and looked at the body of his dead mother.

"Damn her! I'm not her son, I'm Abrán González, Sara's son! You mean nothing to me!"

Vera trembled. "Hate me if you must, but don't hate her. She was a child, she didn't know how to fight her father. I should have known better." Her tears flowed again.

"Abrán, it's not her fault," Lucinda said, trying to calm him, but inside she felt the same confusion and anger. A terrible hoax had been played on Abrán. She looked at Vera and tried to understand how a woman could do what she had done.

"It is my fault," Vera nodded. "I was weak. I believed Walter, believed that all our work and fortune had to be kept in the family, believed he was doing the right thing. I know what prejudice is like. It can destroy a person. I convinced myself that you would be better off with Ramiro and Sara. A terrible sin. I can only ask your forgiveness. What's done is done."

Abrán took a deep breath. Someday he would have to forgive her, and his mother, but not today. Today was a day of anguish and pain and anger. He thought of Sara. When Ramiro died, she had comforted him. When his friend Junior died, she was by his side. He didn't need the dead woman and her mother; he had Sara. The only bitterness left from the ordeal was that he wouldn't know his father.

"I'll find him," he whispered. The promise was a vow to God. He would find his father.

"She left you this," Vera said and fumbled in her purse for a small book. "Her diary. She wanted you to have it."

He took the book. Embossed in gold was her name, Cynthia Johnson. He opened to the first page and read the instructions for her funeral. There was to be a cremation and the ashes buried in the South Valley.

Reading the burial wishes of his mother to Vera and Lucinda calmed him. Together they made the plans: a small memorial service for her friends, then they would take the ashes to the South Valley.

"Do you know the place?" Vera asked.

"I can find it," Abrán answered.

Later, when the body was wheeled out, he followed it to the mortuary van. Cynthia had requested he bury her, and he would. That was the only connection he would have with her. She had brought him into the world, so he would bury her according to her wishes.

Outside they stood in silence while the van pulled away. Near the entrance two large lilac bushes were in full bloom, protected and warmed by the southern exposure. A Mexican worker tilled the soil around the bush.

Vera had called the funeral home. The ashes would be delivered in two days. It seemed so simple once life was done.

Vera turned to Abrán. "You're all I have left," she said, and before she burst out crying again she hugged him and hurried away.

He turned to Lucinda. "Thanks for staying."

"I'm glad I could help," she smiled.

"If you can, will you come to the burial?" he asked.

"Yes. I want to. I feel I knew her."

"You knew her better than I did."

"She didn't talk much, she never complained. There was a lot of pain, but she learned how to channel it as well as anybody ever learns."

"Can I call you? I want to know what you knew about her."

"Yes, call." She scribbled her number for him.

He embraced her and looked into her face. A lovely face with warm, dark eyes.

"I'll call," he promised.

3 Over a cup of hot coffee he told Sara everything. She listened patiently, rising only to refill his coffee cup. She had tried to get him to eat, but he couldn't.

"That's what I know," he said when he finished the story. "Now I have to find my father," he added with such intensity that Sara's eyes filled with tears. She had listened carefully, noting the change that had come over Abrán. Su hijito, her little one, was no longer her little boy. He was a grown man sitting in front of her; the events of the night had changed him. He had become a man.

She shook her head sadly. "We knew nothing. Mr. Johnson came and told us Ramiro would always have work with him. But we must never tell you about your mother. We agreed. Don't you see, we had no children. You were a blessing, a child we could raise, love, someone to complete our family. We tried to protect you."

"Protect me? From him?"

"He's a powerful man, mi'jito. We were only workers. We had you, and that's all that mattered. We went back to Guadalupe. I told my neighbors my sister was pregnant. We were going to help. When we returned we said you were my sister's son. She was sick and we had adopted you. It was a normal thing to do."

"You never knew the man who was my father?" Abrán asked.

"We knew nothing. The boy must have been from the barrio, that's why el señor Johnson was so angry. Your mother—forgive me, it is difficult for me to call Cynthia your mother."

"You're my mother," he assured her and reached across to touch her hand. "The only one I've ever known."

She smiled at him. "It's hard for a woman to share her son. Very hard. I wish things had been different."

"Yes," he agreed and rose. He felt exhausted. "Someone has to know his name," he said. "I'm going to see Walter Johnson."

"No," Sara shook her head and held his arm. "You're tired, you haven't slept. It's not good."

"Why?"

"Let the past stay buried. Stay here with me, we can be happy as we were before all this."

"I am your son," he said and held her in an abrazo. "But I have to know, do you understand? I have to know."

Yes, he had to know, but she was afraid for him. What would he find? In these matters, the past was better left a secret. She did not want him to be hurt.

"Cuídate," she said. Be careful.

"I'll be okay," he kissed her. "Be back in awhile."

The ride from the Barelas barrio to the old Country Club district took him only five minutes. He drove from one of the poorest barrios in the city into one of the wealthiest neighborhoods. People of the barrio went to work in the homes of the Country Club area or at the golf course, but one didn't cross to socialize. Mexicans stayed in the barrio, and the Anglos came to the barrio only to eat Mexican food at the cafes. One didn't cross to date Anglo girls, Abrán thought. Not now, not then.

His mother had crossed, and the young man who was his father had crossed. And they suffered the punishment of the old prejudices, prejudices which still existed. The city was still split. The Anglos lived in the Heights, the Chicanos along the valley. The line between Barelas and the Country Club was a microcosm of the city. One didn't have to go to El Paso and cross to Juarez to understand the idea of border.

The old rules of division must have been even stricter twenty years ago, Abrán thought as he drove into the streets of the Country Club area. He was a child of this border, a child of the line that separated white and brown. La raza called people like him 'coyote.'

Abrán laughed. "Okay, if I'm going to be a coyote at least I'm going to know my father."

The home of Walter Johnson was easy to find. It was the biggest and most pretentious in the neighborhood. It towered over the other houses, a castle rising above the trees. It was situated in a pleasant street lined with tall elms and flowering redbud trees. Lilacs were profuse along its walkway. Sculptured evergreens and pines framed the house, an abode of power.

Ramiro worked here, Abrán thought, as he stood before the Johnson house. What irony! He had planted some of these trees, and in return he was paid with a child. Now the child returned a man to ask the grandfather for the truth.

Grandfather? The word made him uneasy. He rang and a maid answered, a woman Abrán recognized from the barrio. She led him to the study, where Walter Johnson waited. He sat erect behind his desk. Silver-haired, tall, imposing, he was a man who had built a fortune from sand. He had come from the midwest during the depression, a lunger dying of tuberculosis. He recovered, bought land on the East Mesa, and sold it after the war. He had then built a bank and became the richest man in the state, a man whose holding company controlled a good part of the region.

He stared stoically at Abrán. There was no kindness in his eyes. He had talked to Vera, he knew Cynthia had died, but for him this was not a grandchild returning home. This was a ghost from the past. To succeed in business Walter Johnson had had to bury many ghosts. The formula was simple: He used money to bury them, and they stayed put. But now this bastard child had returned. The boy probably wanted money. He would give him money and get rid of him. The sin of his daughter would remain a secret, because in the act of becoming pregnant she had defiled his dreams. She had destroyed the dynasty he envisioned.

"Mr. Johnson?"

Walter Johnson nodded.

"I'm Abrán. Cynthia's son."

Abrán, Johnson thought, Spanish for Abraham. That was Vera's doing.

"What do you want?" he asked. If the boy asked for a reasonable amount, he might deal, but he wouldn't be blackmailed.

"She died last night."

Walter Johnson stiffened. "What do you want?" he repeated.

"I found out about her last night. I need to talk to you."

"Do you want money?" he asked Abrán, and he saw the color rise in the young man's face.

"I didn't come for money. I want to know about my father. Do you know his name?"

The father, Johnson thought, he wants to know about his father. So Cynthia didn't tell him. For a moment he felt a tinge of pity. The boy had never known his father.

"What did Cynthia say?"

"She died a few minutes after I got there. She spoke my name, but that was all. I wouldn't bother you, but I have to know!" Abrán said forcefully.

Walter Johnson stood and walked around the side of the desk. He looked into the boy's eyes. It was his daughter's son, all right. Twenty-one years after the deed. He was a handsome young man, and had things been different, perhaps today he would be calling Abrán his grandson. But it was too late to forgive.

"I can't help you," he said.

"Why?"

"I never knew your father."

"But you went to the principal, you asked for the names. Don't lie to me!" Abrán clenched his fists.

Johnson checked his impulse to strike out. He felt anger at Cynthia for having reopened old wounds.

"Don't say I lie, boy! I'm telling you the truth! I never knew your father! I didn't want to know," he added. He turned and went to the window. The principal had brought in a bunch of Mexican kids, that's all he remembered. Cynthia had gotten pregnant by a Mexican boy from the barrio.

"I didn't want to know," he whispered.

"Is there any way of finding out?" Abrán pleaded. Anger would only antagonize the old man. He wanted the name of his father bad enough to beg Walter Johnson.

"The past is best left buried," Johnson answered. "Forget you are Cynthia's son—"

"Before she died she wanted me to know. I can't forget that. And I can't forget I have a father who might still be alive," Abrán insisted.

"Did she give you anything?" he asked. If Cynthia left him any of her paintings, the kid would be well off.

"Her diary."

"A diary. Any names in it?"

"No."

"Then there's no way to know," Johnson said.

"There has to be," Abrán said.

Johnson shook his head, turned, and looked at Abrán. What if I had done things differently? he thought. No, no need to think that way. He knew well the old prejudices. All his life he would have heard his peers whisper behind his back. Vera should have known, damn it, she should have known. Her Jewish blood had cost them enough agony, hadn't it? But no, Vera wanted to keep the little bastard. Something about a woman changes as soon as a baby comes into the picture. She wanted to keep it; she sided with Cindy.

"There is no name. I'm sorry, I can't help you." He touched the buzzer on his desk and the maid appeared at the door. "What else did you come for?" Johnson asked.

Abrán glared at the old man. It was because of Johnson that he had been made an orphan. He wanted no part of anything the old man offered. The anger he had felt at Vera that morning rose again.

"I want only my father's name, nothing else," Abrán said. He felt contempt for the old man, and Walter Johnson sensed it.

"If it's money—" he suggested.

"Shove it," Abrán said, and walked out of the room.

Walter Johnson frowned. Something in the boy's movements reminded him of Cynthia. Damn the past, he thought. Why doesn't it stay buried? He returned to his desk to finish drafting the letter to Senator Culson. Frank Dominic was pouring a lot of money into Santa Fé to get a casino gambling bill passed, and Walter Johnson needed to know where the U.S. senator stood.

But Abrán had disturbed his composure. He spun his chair and looked out the window. Across the lawn the boy was getting into his car. Did I make a mistake? he thought. He cursed his wife. If Vera had not been barren those early years of their marriage, things might have turned out differently.

They had wanted a family, but there were long, vacant years until Cynthia was born. He remembered the boys at the bank and at the Rotary slapping him on the back when the baby was born. Walter Johnson has sired a daughter, they said, an heir. He gave the biggest party the town had ever seen. Friends came from all over to Cynthia's baptism. Those were happy times.

Even the early years had been good. The Depression and TB had brought him to New Mexico. The doctor in Chicago said he needed desert air or he would die, so he had put everything he owned into a small suitcase and bought a one-way ticket for California. He was almost dead by the time he got to Albuquerque. He was coughing up blood. It was spring, windy, and the Indians were selling jewelry along the portal when he stepped off the train at the old Alvarado station.

Sweating profusely, he had started across the street to have one last cold beer before he died. Half-way across he fainted. Old don Manuel Armijo, the owner of the First Street Cantina, picked him out of the dust.

Don Manuel still tells the story how he picked me up and took me upstairs to one of his hotel rooms to die, Johnson thought. The train went on to California, and I stayed in Albuquerque to die.

Vera was an orphan don Manuel and his wife had raised. The Mexicans have a great love for children, he thought. If they take somebody in, he becomes family.

Vera helped drag him upstairs, took his clothes off, and gave him his first bath in a week. She was the only one who wasn't afraid of the TB. She had claimed the man dying of tuberculosis, and if she hadn't, he would have died.

Months later, after he recovered and was working for don Manuel and sleeping with Vera, he learned Vera had a Jewish past. She went to church at Saint Mary's, and was as religious as any of her comadres in the neighborhood, but the rumors came to him that she was Jewish. "Judía," the men who drank at the bar whispered in Spanish.

He asked don Manuel and the old man told him Vera's story. "Yes, she is a Jew, from the old Jews who came with the Spaniards. Los marranos. They became Catholics, but they were Jews. The people knew. I will show you," he said, and led Johnson up to the attic where he uncovered a dusty old trunk. It contained Vera's family records. The only thing she had in life were the papers in that trunk, wisps of history dating back four centuries, all written in old Spanish script. She had a bloodline an arm long, but it was Jewish. There in the depths of the trunk lay the worn and brittle record of the originator of the blood line, a Jewish sailor who converted to Catholicism in order to start a new life in the New World.

Don Manuel read the sailor's testament, the paper of the man's conversion, attested to by the Inquisition bishops. The man had renounced his heritage in order to stay alive. Then he caught the first boat sailing out of Cádiz, a man sailing to the New World with new papers, a reborn Catholic, the stamp of the cross blotting out the Star of David.

Don Manuel said he was sorry he had to tell me Vera was a Jew, Johnson mused. He thought I would leave Vera, but I laughed at him.

Hell, Vera and I were both outcasts. She because she had Jewish blood, and I because I claimed no bloodline. I was intrigued by her past, intrigued by that one sailor who gave up everything to come to the Americas. Right there was the history of the Americas. A man who gave up everything to start a new life.

Walter Johnson identified with that Jewish sailor sailing from the port of Cádiz four hundred years earlier. The only difference was that Johnson arrived from the dregs of Chicago. Each had given up his past to create a new life, each had given up his heritage.

What heritage? Johnson laughed. My father was a man who couldn't read or write. He spent twelve hours a day mired in the blood of the stockyards. My mother took in laundry for us to exist. I survived by leaving. I never looked back, and I never thought about my family again.

He remembered awakening in the small room on the top floor of don Manuel's cantina.

"¿Cómo te llamas?" Vera had asked.

He made up a name. "Walter," he said in his fever, because some of the hobos on the train had been smoking Sir Walter Raleigh tobacco and joking about being knights on the road to California.

"Walter Johnson," he had baptized himself.

"I am Elvira," she had smiled.

Names, I need names, anything that will point the way to my father, Abrán thought as he sat in his car in front of Johnson's house. He opened the glove compartment, where he had tossed the diary when he left the hospital. He riffled through it again, looking for dates and names, but there was nothing.

Disappointed, he drove home.

"You have to rest," Sara cautioned when he entered their house.

"I'll rest," he assured her. In his room he scanned the diary again. There were poems, entries on ideas for paintings, and philosophical musings on the nature of art. When he came to the description of a matanza, Abrán thought he had found the answer. She wrote about the young man she loved and described in detail the matanza they had attended. But she never used his name. "Mi árabe," she called him. "Moro de mi corazón," she said in another passage.

Finding no clues in the diary dashed his hopes, and exhaustion took hold. Abrán fell into a troubled sleep. Voices called to him; the faces of men appeared. As each shadow of a man appeared Abrán reached out, but the figure would disappear. They taunted and called until he found himself running, reaching out, calling for his father. Then he fell into a dark void. The only thing that saved him was Lucinda's outstretched arms.

La Llorona is the mother of Abrán, Lucinda sang, and her cry rose like a whirlwind. Abrán awoke gasping for breath.

Sara bent over him and touched his arm. "Abrán."

He sat up, sweating, catching his breath.

"A bad dream." She sat beside him, put her arm around him, and stroked his hair.

"Estoy bien," he said. Outside the sounds of kids playing baseball filtered through the window. "What time is it?"

"Five. There's a phone call. I came to call you."

He went to the phone. It was Vera, calling to tell him that everything was arranged for the cremation. The paper would carry a notice of the services. Was there anything he needed? She mentioned nothing of his visit to Walter Johnson.

"No, I don't need anything," he said and thanked her.

"Who?" Sara asked.

"Cynthia's mother. Vera."

"Elvira. I remember her. She's a good woman."

"She's made the arrangements for the cremation."

"Cremation? Ay, Dios mío. No rosary? How can they bury her without a velorio, some prayers. I will pray for her. I will offer the stations of the cross for her. What did the señor Johnson say?"

"He said he doesn't know."

She looked at her son and felt a sadness. It would have been better for the whole thing to remain a secret. She could see the change in him, she felt his pain.

"It's not right," she shook her head and touched his cheek.

"I'll be okay," he smiled. "I feel rested." He went to the window and looked at the kids playing in the street. He remembered the days he had spent playing ball, but it seemed so long ago.

"Go slow, my son. All this is new; it doesn't have to be solved in one day."

"I'll go slow," he smiled. "What a life, huh, jefita?"

"Sí," she smiled, "qué vida, pero es todo lo que tenemos. We must use it wisely. If only. . ." She thought of her husband.

"What?"

"Nada." She looked at him. "You remind me of Ramiro. He was a good man. He always took care of business, always on time. Now you have to take care of this."

Suddenly Abrán felt like jogging, and for the first time in a long time he felt like hitting the bag. Foster's Gym would be closed, but he really wanted to spar. He needed to get the tension out of his bones.

"I'll call Joe, see if he wants to run."

"Good," Vera smiled.

Joe was home. "Nah, I didn't drink last night," he said. "I walked around a lot, then I hit the books. You?"

"See you in five minutes," Abrán said. He couldn't tell him on the phone. "Don't wait for me," he said to Sara. "We'll get some pizza at Jack's."

"No fights," she smiled as he kissed her on the forehead.

"I promise," he smiled back.

God knows what the future will bring, she thought as she stood at the door and waved good-bye. "Cuídate. Qué dios te bendiga."

Joe had a small apartment in the student ghetto; he was waiting when Abrán drove up. They greeted each other, then in silence they put on their shoes and sweatshirts and began their run. Joe sensed his friend had something to talk about, but it had to wait until the time was right. They ran in silence around the park.

"That was good," Abrán said when they finished.

"You really pushed," Joe said, breathing hard. He looked at Abrán. The kid had run with intensity, sparring as he went, jabbing at shadows.

"Beer?"

"Two or three."

They drove to Jack's. "Seems like a long time since we were here," Abrán said as they guzzled their first beer. He looked around. He had never noticed the men at the bar before, he and Joe kept to themselves, but now he found himself staring at their faces. He was looking for the one face in the crowd. Would he recognize it when he saw it?

"What's up?" Joe asked.

Abrán shook his head and told Joe what had happened. Joe listened patiently. What the kid had been through since yesterday was a heavy trip. Those things one takes for granted had changed for Abrán, created a new reality.

Before Joe met Abrán, he was drinking every weekend, alone. Running together and talking about classes had been good for Joe, a solid friendship had developed. Now as he looked across the table at the kid, he saw a new person. Joe sensed the urgency in Abrán's voice.

Cynthia Johnson, Joe thought, damn, the whole world knew her. Now she was dead and Abrán wanted to know about his father. Who was the man? Where was he? It wasn't going to be easy for Abrán. But how could Joe help his friend when he couldn't help himself? The bottle was still an easy way out when he had to face reality. He was afraid to drive the thirty miles up the road to the pueblo.

Nam had separated him from his own father and from the old men of the pueblo. His father, Encarnación Calabasa, was a Santo Domingo man, heavyset, handsome. He was strict in the old ways, he sat on the pueblo council, and he farmed. He knew how to grow corn, chile, and squash. Squash and summer, that was his identity. He had married a Mexican woman, Spanish, the Indians called them, from Peña Blanca. Flor Montoya became Flor de Calabasa.

Pollen, rub pollen on her thighs, the old wisdom said. Wash in the water of the river. Go visit the kachina Santo Niño over there in Chimayó and pray and you will have lots of kids. In the end they had one child, Joe. Half Santo Domingo man, half Mexican from Peña Blanca.

"We're both coyotes," he joked, and Abrán smiled. He finished his glass and ordered a new round.

"Half-and-half, damn!" Abrán cleared his throat. He didn't want to be half Anglo, he wanted to be the person he was before he read Cynthia's letter.

"Don't feel so bad," Joe kidded. "The kids at school used to make fun of me because I was half Indian and half Spanish. Lots of fights. The Indian kids would call me half-breed, and when we went to visit my mother's family in Peña Blanca, they called me coyote. Nobody likes a coyote," he grinned and drank.

He was trying to cheer Abrán, but the difference was that he knew his father. His father had always been there. The Calabasa family had been Santo Domingo people since the beginning of the world. They lived at the center of the earth, according to their legends. That was stability. And Joe's father was a man of love. To love his earth was as important as loving the woman who would bear his children. His family expected him to marry a pueblo woman, but when he saw Flor, they fell in love. There was little need for words, he asked her to come and live with him in the pueblo and she came. They knew it wouldn't be easy. It was never easy to bring outsiders into the pueblo, it was never forgotten in the memory of the people. Joe Calabasa, the people would say, Oh, the son of the woman from Peña Blanca? Carny's boy? The way they said "the woman from Peña Blanca" meant she was not a Santo Domingo woman.

Still, the two ways of life commingled in Joe, and it had been a good life, especially when his grandfather was alive.

You are special, his grandfather used to tell him. He had raised Joe to be a leader of the people, a good man. He took Joe with him to Alburquerque when he went to sell his summer produce in the barrios. You have to learn the white man's way, he told him, or you get run over. He taught Joe about the people of the Río Grande, told him the history of his pueblo, and how the Spaniards came, and later the Anglos. They want land and water, he said, it is that simple. Never give your land away, be proud you are a Santo Domingo man.

Now, he couldn't return to the pueblo of his grandfather. He had learned too much of the white man's way. "Now what?" Joe asked Abrán.

"I'm going to read the diary again, carefully. Maybe there's something I missed. Monday I'll head over to the library, look through the old newspapers." He shrugged. "Am I different, Joe?"

Joe smiled. "Hell, kid, every day changes a man. You just got handed a heavy dose. Go slow."

"That's what my jefita said, but the more I think about it the more I need to know. If I just had something to go on."

"I felt that way when I got back from Nam," Joe said. "I guess I still do."

"Nam," Abrán said. "Now *that* was heavy." He looked at Joe's left arm. The deep, pink scar was his badge from that war.

"This," Joe said, "is a good reminder. You know, we grunts drank and smoked dope together, and that should have made us tight, but it didn't. Hell, we always knew our buddy could be the next to buy the farm. It made us cautious. We were out there hunting Charlie, and that changed us. After a while you couldn't trust anyone. We sure as hell didn't trust Charlie, and we didn't trust his women or kids.

"When I was a kid I used to hunt deer up in the Jémez with my father. Big mule bucks. When my lieutenant found out I could shoot, he made me point man. Or maybe it was 'cause I was brown, and so when Charlie saw me coming he was going to think a split second before he opened up. I was gung-ho. Shit, I was a dumb kid just out of school. Every fucking little Chicanito or Indian dreams of being a Marine, so there I was, point man, killing commies. We did some bad things, Abrán. Toked up, we began to believe the lie, lied to ourselves. The worst lie I told myself was that I was up in the Jémez hunting when I squeezed the trigger.

"See, when you go on the hunt it's special. You have hunting medicine. A fetish. You get the strength from that animal by praying, same as the Catholics pray to the saints. When you hunt the deer you say a prayer so when you get the deer it's understood that he dies to feed the pueblo. You accept the gift of life, you don't take life. When you bring the deer into the pueblo you offer it cornmeal, so it is a friend. Its spirit will be in peace. The spirit of the deer is important, but it wasn't in Nam."

"What happened?" Abrán asked.

"The day I took my hit? There had just been an air strike, we were mopping up. Not expecting any trouble. Hell, we had just bombed the hell out of the area. We were going in to count bodies. That's what we figured.

"I could smell a fire burning, and I thought, even after an air strike a hungry farmer has to eat. Think of it, the U.S. Air Force dropping hundred pounders and tearing up the fuckin' jungle, and when it's over they come out, curse the planes, and start supper. That's life, qué no?

"The old man who shot me, maybe he'd had enough, so he set up a decoy. Just like a buck will send the does ahead to check out a meadow, the old man sent the girl. Young and beautiful. I saw her only for a moment, and the minute I did, 'decoy' buzzed in the back of my mind, but too late. I felt the sting, heard the shot. My arm was torn and bleeding.

"I didn't feel the pain at first, I was so pissed off. The sonofabitch had used an old trick and I had fallen for it. I swore I was going to kill the motherfucker. So I started crawling up the ditch, circling around him. He saw me fall and he expected me to stay put, but if I could come around on him I was going to blow his head off. Behind me the squad had taken cover. I heard the Lieutenant calling, 'Chief.' That's what he called me, Chief. I think even in the end he didn't know my name. They knew I'd get the zapper, but they didn't know I'd taken a hit.

"Man, the jungle got real quiet. I could imagine the women in the village hiding the minute they heard the shot, grabbing their bambinos and holding them close to quiet them, like the Indians did long ago when the U.S. Cavalry came down to skirmish. I could even smell the rice cooking.

"I was bleeding bad, my left arm burning like mad, but I swore if I got around Charlie I was going to zap him. I knew where he was. Just like an old buck, he had frozen in the brush, waiting for me to lift my head. He thought he'd gotten me. I peered over the bank and there he was. He moved, slowly, toward me. He thought he got me, so he was going to run back to his village, sit around the fire and tell a story about the big GI he brought down. I braced my rifle on a log and waited for the bushes to part.

"He moved quietly, slowly. I begin to squeeze real soft on the trigger, but hell, when he came out of the bush I saw he was an old man. An old, thin man carrying one of those old French rifles. I held the bead on his head. I was sweating, feeling weak from the hit, but I saw him so clearly it was like looking into the eyes of my grandfather. Something happened. There was one thin hair left on the squeeze, but I couldn't finish it.

"See, when I was a boy hunting up in the Jémez, my old man taught me a song. A chant for the deer. And that's what happened. I let go of the trigger and started to sing, real soft. The old man looked up, knew I had him dead. He froze. He listened.

"Come, brother deer, give your life to my people. Let me take your breath of life so my village can live. Let me take you to the table of the old men and women. The winter will be long and cold, share your life with us.

"Then the old man starting singing. A song in Vietnamese. Maybe a song of death. He knew I'd taken his shot and he was expecting to take mine.

"Sonofabitch probably never heard of Lenin or Marx. Maybe he'd seen a picture of Ho and heard the liberation propaganda on radio, but he was just an old farmer taking care of his village. He was an old buck taking care of his does. He was fed up with the bombing and the napalm, and so he dragged out that old rifle and took a shot at the first grunt he saw.

"In his wrinkled face I saw the face of my grandfather, the old men of Santo Domingo Pueblo. Warriors. That's what he was, a warrior, singing, preparing to die. In his face I saw the face of my people.

"I lowered my rifle. The old man looked surprised. I stood and threw my rifle into the ditch. I couldn't kill him. It would've been wrong, the old man wasn't a deer, he was a man, like the old men of my pueblo. He was protecting his village. We just stood there, looking at each other. Then the old man bowed and disappeared into the brush.

"My heart was beating real hard, like a strong drum. Our songs had filled the space between us. Now the jungle was silent again. I dropped to my knees. It was peaceful, the killing was finished. I would never go into the bush again. I was about to pass out, but my head was clear. Maybe the old man was a shaman; he had brought me out of the nightmare. Maybe he had to shoot me to wake me up, to remind me a farmer needs strong arms to farm.

"From deep in the jungle I heard a cry, the cry of a warrior. I guess if there is such a thing as a cry of coup in Vietnamese, that was it. He had protected his village, touched me on the field of battle.

"I answered his call, a cry of the battle ending. I felt like a water buffalo that had suddenly freed itself from the mud. Nam was the quagmire, and I was free. The old man had liberated me.

"My rifle sank into the mud, my blood drained into the dirty water. I knew I was never going back there again.

"'Chief,' the lieutenant called. 'Whaz happenin?'

"'I took a hit,' I shouted back. 'All clear.'

"They came out of hiding. They couldn't believe I'd taken a shot. They looked at my bloody arm and shook their heads.

"'Where's your rifle, Chief?' the lieutenant asked.

"It was gone, covered by the mud. We buried our best there, buried love and friendship. There's going to be blood oozing from the fields of Nam for a long time. Our blood. You can taste it in the rice. But I was done with it."

Joe paused, grew quiet. "I've never told that story before."

"It's important," Abrán answered. "You ought to write the story down. Just like it is."

"Or have old Ben Chávez write it," Joe smiled. "Wonder if he's feeling any pain?"

"Yesterday."

"Seems like a long time to you, don't it?"

"A long time," Abrán nodded.

"When a man has a vision, it changes time," Joe said. "What happened to you is like a vision. You have to sort it out, find its meaning."

"Yeah."

"And the lady? Lucinda? You seemed impressed by her."

"I am. I'm going to call her."

Joe smiled. "A good sign," he said, "the patient is alive. Look, I'll help any way I can."

"Thanks," Abrán raised his beer glass in a toast.

4 Sunday morning he called Lucinda and invited her for a drive. She volunteered to make sandwiches and suggested Sandía Crest. "Let's see how spring looks up there," she said. "I grew up in the North, I miss the mountains."

For Abrán the mountain east of the city was a familiar landmark. The Sandías rose five thousand feet above the valley floor, a rugged blue outline that reminded some of a giant turtle facing northwest. The huge granite face of the mountain was the most dramatic feature of the landscape. At sunset it was bathed in shades of mauve, and thus the name Sandía, the Spanish word for watermelon.

Lucinda had an apartment near Martíneztown, a barrio just northeast of the downtown area. Her place was small but comfortable, and near St. Joseph's Hospital, where she worked. The apartment was built of old terrones, earth clods cut years ago from the valley topsoil. The two-foot-thick walls conserved the heat in winter and the coolness in summer.

"Some yuppies would give a fortune for your adobe," Abrán kidded her when he saw where she lived.

"Yes, if I could transplant it to Santa Fé, I could retire." She handed him the picnic basket and he touched her hand.

"I'm glad to see you," he smiled. Their eyes met. He guessed it was her dark eyes which first attracted him to her, along with the sincerity he saw in the beauty of her face. She wore her dark hair loose. She smiled, and for a moment they stood touching, allowing the warmth to flow between them, then they ran laughing to the car and drove out of the city and east into Tijeras Canyon. The day was brilliant and clear, the mountain air scented with the fragrance of pines.

"Did you get some rest?" she asked as they drove toward the crest.

"Some," he answered.

"There was a strong wind last night," she said, "a lot of energy in the air. I couldn't sleep. I thought you might be asking yourself a lot of questions."

He had felt the storm, and he heard the voices. All night long Cynthia called his name, and doña Tules's cryptic comment kept repeating itself in the fury of the wind.

"I read my mother's diary," he explained, and told her about his visit to Walter Johnson.

"I'm finding out a lot of things I didn't know. Cynthia sent money to Sara. She used to tell me it was social security and insurance from Ramiro. Looking back I see it wasn't easy for Sara to raise me. Maybe I always knew I wasn't her son, knew I was different. I never really knew why I felt I had to prove myself; now I understand."

"You were different. Did the kids call you coyote?"

"Yeah. The rough kids, the cholos. You're not Chicano, they said, and so I had to fight a few to be accepted. After that I ran with the gang. I did a lot of crazy things. Going into boxing was the only thing that saved me. I boxed two years and dropped the gang. After high school I took off for L.A. and worked a couple of years. I needed to get away."

"From?"

"My best friend, Junior. We grew up together, ran in the gang together, joined the boxing club together. He was good. People say I should have gone pro, but he was the gifted one. Man, he could box. Junior had a girl, they were really tight. Planned to marry. Two weeks before graduation she returned his ring. It broke him up. That afternoon he wanted to spar with me. He was angry, he needed to let off steam, so I said okay. But Junior was more than angry. He came at me hard, we were in the gym alone, so we had a real bout. Ten, fifteen solid minutes we hit each other. It was a stupid thing to do."

Abrán's voice broke. He remembered the afternoon clearly, and how he had tried to get Junior to slow up. When Junior didn't, he fought back.

"That night he died."

"And you blamed yourself?"

"He had an old scar from a concussion. The coach tried to make it easy on me, but yeah, I blamed myself."

She reached across and held his hand. He looked at her and smiled. He had called her because he wanted to be with her, and her touch told him she felt the same.

"And you?" he asked.

"I got out of high school and went into nursing school. When I was a little girl I was very close to an old woman in the village. She's a curandera, so I picked up my love of healing from her. My father was attacked by a bear when I was about nine. They sewed him up at the hospital, but that's all they could do. When he came home doña Agapita, an old woman who knew about healing, went to work on him. Without her constant therapy he would have lost his arm. I want to learn her remedies before she dies. In the meantime I'm helping people who have cancer, but something else is calling me."

"Home?"

"I'm very close to my family, and to the people up there. My dream is to set up a clinic in Córdova. The people in the mountain villages have to go all the way to Taos for any medical aid."

"It's a great dream," Abrán mused,

"Maybe I just feel time passing. I'm twenty-five."

He laughed. "An old lady."

"Speaking of ladies, do you have one?"

"No," he answered. "I dated a few girls in high school, but it seems when I was in L.A. they all got married."

She laughed with him. "Any plans for the future?"

"Sara wants me to go into medicine."

"We could make a team," she smiled.

Her smile made him feel at ease. He wanted her, but it was more than just having her in bed. A bond had formed between them. He found himself joking with her, and he enjoyed it.

They talked as they wound their way toward the crest of the mountain. He told her about Joe and his classes. When they arrived at the top of the crest they put their jackets on and got out. A cool wind was blowing.

On the mountaintop the wind was a constant, steady breeze from the west. The sky was brilliant and clear; the horizon stretched for miles. They walked to the edge of the crest. Below them lay the Río Grande Valley, an oasis in an otherwise tawny and bare land. In the west rose Mount Taylor.

Joining hands, they felt they were truly on the back of a giant turtle, and the mountain stirred and moved. They walked along the trail, snuggling naturally into each other for protection from the wind. Only a few hardy souls were on the crest, so it was easy to find a deserted ledge from which to view the panorama.

"Makes you feel like flying," Abrán said.

"The mountain is alive," she said and drew closer to him. He put his arm around her, and they sat quietly and enjoyed the view. A herd of wild sheep made its way across a ridge, an eagle soared in and out of a canyon to the left, hunting its noonday meal, and hikers appeared on a segment of the La Luz Trail far below.

The power and kinship Lucinda felt with the mountain were enhanced by Abrán's presence. The energy and beauty of the mountain satisfied her soul; it was something inbred from her childhood in the northern Sangre de Cristo.

Would Abrán like the northern mountains? she wondered. Her family? The man she gave herself to would have to like her father, a strong and sensitive man. She thought of Abrán as a possible mate, and this surprised her. She looked at him and smiled. She knew she was attracted to him from the time he walked into the hospital, but now she felt a new feeling, a desire. No, more than a desire, she told herself, he is the man I have seen in my dreams.

"I want to know more about you," she said.

"What?"

"Everything."

"Not too interesting."

"Let me decide."

"Bueno," he said and took her hands in his. "If you want to."

"I want to."

He looked into her dark, clear eyes. The sharp wind made them brim with tears. He kissed her, a warm tentative kiss at first, then a warm, lasting kiss that left both breathless.

"I have a few days of vacation coming," Lucinda said when he asked her again to be with him at Cynthia's service. "After your mother is buried, maybe you'd like to go up north and visit my family?"

"Sounds serious," he smiled.

"I think it is," she smiled back.

5 Frank Dominic called Ben Chávez and invited him to a party. "Ben," he said in a subdued tone, "did you hear?"

"Yes."

"She's dead, Ben. I feel awful. I'm having a few people over this afternoon, I can't cancel. I loved her, Ben. Loved that woman. She was a genius. Come over, Ben, I'm not up to facing people." He hung up.

Ben held the phone a moment then dropped it in its cradle. Sonofabitch, he thought. Having a party. So much for old friendships. He, Dominic, and Cynthia had gone to school together, and all had gone on to follow their instincts: Cynthia for art, Ben for writing, and Dominic for money. Recently, it was money *and* politics for Dominic. He was aiming to be governor, but he wanted to be mayor first. He wanted to bring in casino gambling and build a Venice on the Río Grande.

"Who was it?" Ben's wife asked.

"Dominic. There's a reception at his place. Want to go?"

"I've got a class this afternoon," Elena answered. She was studying Tarot cards. She loved receptions and meeting new people, but now she was on a personal journey, a path that took her into past lives. She found people like Frank Dominic bland. "Say hello to Frank, but don't make any deals with him," she cautioned.

"I won't," he answered. She knew Dominic well.

He looked to the poem on the computer screen in front of him. He was writing an epic that explored the Mesoamerican mythic elements Chicanos had incorporated into their heritage. Juan and Al, two plain homeboys from the barrio, took a journey into the Aztec past, and what they found, Ben hoped, would help create a new consciousness for the people. A new identity for the downtrodden.

"How's the epic coming?" she asked.

"Juan and Al are breathing," he answered.

"That's good. But you need a break," she counseled. "Go to the reception. Do you good to get out."

He had been thinking about Cynthia all day. Now Dominic. Was he really feeling the pain too? Or did he just want an endorsement for his mayoral campaign? For years Dominic had tried to run City Hall from his office downtown, but that style wasn't working anymore. Marisa Martínez, the young woman who was just completing her term as mayor, was too independent to be controlled by Dominic. She had turned out to be a maverick, her own boss. So Dominic had cooked up a big urban enhancement project. Canals full of Río Grande water. Casinos. A Disneyland on the river. Why not? The city's flaccid economy needed a jolt.

Dominic couldn't get his way with Marisa Martínez, so he decided to run City Hall himself. He had the best lobbyist money could buy working on ramming a legalized gambling bill through the state legislature in Santa Fé. He had been working on the scenario for years, and now things seemed to be falling into place. He was going to put Alburquerque on the map, he bragged. Create a city to rival Las Vegas.

If he could get the casino bill through, it would change the economy of the state. New money would pour in, real wealth in place of the government payrolls the city depended upon. But the conservative cowboys from Little Texas will fight him, Ben thought.

What if Dominic was planning to get the gambling bill only for Alburquerque? The hell with the rest of the state; he would create a gambling haven here. If the Indian pueblos could have their bingo games, Alburquerque could have its casinos. The city was already a little nation-state unto itself, and the rest of the state hated that. Oh, the small-town folks liked to attend the State Fair in the fall, and they liked to shop at Winrock and Coronado malls, but once back home, they complained about the big city and the power it wielded in state politics. Had Dominic managed to put together a coalition that would get him the gambling bill he needed?

We all have a small role to play in his plans, Ben thought. That's the way the sonofabitch thinks. Dominic's no dummy. He's even promising a performing arts center, the cornerstone of his renewal plan. Plans to surround himself with artists and gamblers. The hell with Santa Fé, Dominic had told him the last time they had lunch, Alburquerque should be the mecca for artists in this state. And Ben, I want you to be the art czar.

The builders and pillars of the city, Ben thought, know so little about art, but they need it. They don't want to be thought provincial when they visit New York. They don't like the image of the vulgar redneck. A city acquires character when it creates its own art, and so Dominic had collected Cynthia's work for the lobbies of his Duke City Plaza. Now Dominic had called on his friend the writer, too.

Ben laughed. Art czar? Art crazy. Dominic was crazy. Loco. But between Walter Johnson and Frank Dominic, Dominic was the lesser evil. Johnson had been the cause of enough grief in his life. The man had destroyed his own daughter. But dammit, it did no good to remember. The past was dead, and now Cynthia was dead.

He remembered the day she told him about the baby. The event was etched in his memory. "No one can see him, Benjie," she said, making herself strong so she wouldn't cry. "If I can't, you can't. Promise me, Benjie. Swear to me you won't try. He'll be taken care of. I have to do it this way; I promised Father."

She was the one who had suffered, not him. And what could he do? Nothing. They were kids, they had no say in the arrangement.

He had never forgiven himself, and he had never forgiven Walter

Johnson. The man had robbed him of the most meaningful thing in his life.

Ben picked up the morning paper. "Dominic Squares Off Against Martinez." There was a picture of both on the front page. Marisa Martínez was an intelligent women, and she was beautiful. The Martínez family was one of the old South Valley families. The father had made a fortune by selling tacos and tortillas, first in the barrio in the forties, then, as the Anglo newcomers discovered a taste for Mexican food, he went into the restaurant business.

When Marisa was elected four years ago the race for mayor had been wide open. It included a disc jockey, a city councilman, a car salesman, a Bircher, an attorney, and other malcontents who came out of the woodwork. The Johnson faction backed Joe Dugan, a city councilman, and a man they could control. The Hispanics fought back. Dugan was unacceptable, so they convinced Marisa to run. She enlisted the help of women, and Cynthia Johnson became one of her main backers. New battle lines were drawn, new interest groups developed, and city politics entered a new era.

The campaign left dozens of political casualties; the race had pitted the conservative Anglos against the Hispanic bloc. Old prejudices came out in the open. The Hispanics wanted the office they had never held, and the Anglos resisted. Cynthia Johnson stepped into the fray, and the vote swung to Marisa Martínez. Dominic tried to claim that he had delivered the swing vote, but it was clear he had been checkmated.

Marisa Martínez quickly developed her independent policies and style and went about running the city in her own way. She responded quickly to the needs of the Hispanic community, and they loved her for it. She was also fair, and she gained the respect of various groups in the Anglo community. She moved to patch the wounds of the bitter race that had gained her the mayorship, and people on both sides admired her for that.

"She's always been her own woman," Ben Chávez thought aloud. Dominic should have known he couldn't control her. He reached into his file, the "Movers and Shakers Notebook" he kept on the city políticos, and pulled the one marked Marisa Martínez. She had graduated from UNM law school with distinction. She fell in love with a young man from a large ranching family. There was a brief, tumultuous marriage ruined by the young man's use of drugs. Two years later Marisa found herself alone and working for the D.A. She begin putting drug dealers into jail with a vengeance, and that's how she built her reputation. Her "No Deals for Drug Dealers" campaign helped rally the different constituencies around her.

But now hard economic times choked the city, and if she didn't turn the crunch around, she could be a casualty of the failing economy.

Ben leafed through the file. She had become acquainted with a Japanese banker, Akira Morino, a man whose factories built computer chips superior to the Intel-100 chip. She invited him to Alburquerque and personally led the effort to land Morino's company. Now she wanted to be reelected, and City Hall commentators said she was just months from landing the plant.

Ben Chávez tossed the file back into the drawer. The sadness he had felt since Cynthia's death would not leave him. He turned to his desk and stared at the poem he was writing. It was almost completed, but Dominic's call had interrupted his creative energy. Juan and Al languished on the blank screen.

His thoughts weren't with poetry, they were with politics. He knew Johnson would cut his veins before he let Dominic get hold of City Hall. That's how deep and old their personal hatred went. And Johnson didn't like the idea of four more years of Martínez. If Dominic and Martínez split the Hispanic vote, the situation was perfect for him. He could garner the Anglo vote and slide easily into office.

But a lot of the valley Democrats owed debts to Dominic. Before Martínez came into office, Dominic had worked behind the scenes in City Hall and the state legislature to get them paved roads and a sewage drainage system that solved the flooding caused by summer thunder-showers. Never mind that in the process Dominic increased the value of a new adobe development he was building in the North Valley; he got something done about an old problem.

Dominic also had the North Valley yuppies on his side. These wealthy professionals, who had discovered rural living and the Alburquerque adobe style, had carved out an enclave for themselves. Their Mercedes and BMWs buzzed along Río Grande as they swooped down from their estates to work in the city. They had changed the character of the old Hispanic communities. Dominic's North Valley area had quietly become one of the wealthiest in the city.

Ben looked at the computer monitor. He flipped the switch off and looked at the clock. The day was gone, and he felt the onset of depression that often followed the waste of time. He might as well get drunk with Dominic. But that was all he'd do; he didn't owe the man anything. Sure they had known each other since high school, they grew up in the barrio together. The difference was that Dominic's father had the money to send his son to Georgetown, Ben thought, as he closed his front door and walked to his car.

After his stint in law school, Dominic came back to turn his father's real estate holdings into a fortune. He created the late seventies downtown boom, and he profited from the business expansion because he controlled enough real estate to cut the deals. Now Dominic was running for mayor, Walter Johnson was coming out of the closet and running, and Marisa Martínez had suddenly decided she liked the mayor's seat and she was running. The season of evening cocktail parties for the candidates had arrived, a spring ritual played out every four years. Last week Ben had been at Marisa's party. She lived in the North Valley, half a mile south of Dominic's place. Hers was a modest ranch-style home, not like the ten-acre spread Dominic owned.

"I need the West Mesa," she had said urgently, her breath tinged with lime and tequila. "Johnson's got the Heights, Dominic and I will split the South Valley vote, but nobody knows how you jackrabbits of the West Side are going to vote. What do you want up there? Schools? We can do that."

"We need a bridge across the Río Grande," Ben replied.

"You're out of your mind," she frowned. "Don't even mention the word bridge in the North Valley. The rich folks will hang me. They've bought the valley and they control it, and they sure as hell don't want a bridge running through. Face it, Ben, Albuquerque's becoming two cities, West Side and East. I don't like it, but that's the way it's shaping up."

"Alburquerque is already many cities," Ben reminded her. "South Valley, North Valley, the West Mesa and the Anglos in the Heights. The Blacks on Broadway. The homeless on the streets. Maybe it's too spread out and too different to pull together."

"I can do it, Ben," she pleaded. "The right economic climate will give people jobs, education, a sense of belonging. But I need four more years, I need to bring in the Japanese plant. Morino's ready."

He followed her glance to where the handsome Akira Morino stood with Gloria Dominic. Frank Dominic had no use for Morino, but his very attractive wife was often seen with the man.

"I know I can land him," Marisa smiled, "but I need time."

"You need to get reelected," Ben smiled back.

She sipped her drink. "I love the West Mesa, Ben. The volcanoes and the escarpment are some of the real treasures we have. You know I lobbied hard to get the area preserved as a national park. It's a spiritual place, something we need. I hike up there just to contemplate. The place can purify even the likes of Frank Dominic. I look out across the city and think of the good things we can become. I don't want to see the West Side split away from the city."

Contemplate among the huge, volcanic boulders of the escarpment is what Ben often did. The dark cliffs were filled with petroglyphs. It was a holy place, a place of ancient shrines.

"The old Indians of the valley made pilgrimages up to the petroglyphs," Ben said. "I think they went to gather rattlesnakes there. Snakes to take back to the pueblos to perform the rain dance. Dances for rain, dances for fertility. The old Mexicanos of the valley used to dance the Matachines up there."

"The park service doesn't mention that in their brochures," Marisa answered.

"They don't see the land as sacred. We do," Ben winked.

Marisa sighed. "Where were you when I was looking for someone to get serious with?" she smiled.

Ben knew there was more to her honor than surface beauty; beneath her teasing there was a very serious woman. He wondered if she were involved with anyone. Seven years divorced, young, and handed the mayor's seat in a bloody election, she had tasted power and she wanted more. Her four-year tenure had begun to turn the city around. But the city was changing, the interest groups were more complex, the balancing act was getting harder. It took a smart politician to stay on top, to keep his or her nose out of Río Grande mud. Too many new people in the city, immigrants who didn't know the history of the place, new people who knew nothing of the values of the traditional communities and who often stepped over the old people.

Those with money built walls around their subdivisions, like Tanoan in the Heights; others built expensive adobe homes with wide lawns and a view of the mountains in the valley. They organized carpools to deliver the kids to private schools, and they were great supporters of the City Symphony. They had all the amenities of Southwest living without ever having to meet the natives. Class lines, ethnic lines, Ben thought. Borders in our own backyard.

"What do I have to do?" she had asked.

"Not much you can do. They're going to come after you. It's going to get dirty."

"I don't want that kind of campaign. What can I do?"

"Believe in yourself," he smiled.

"I do," she whispered as she kissed his cheek and moved on, her tall, slim figure awakening desire in the men who turned to greet her. She was the good hostess, Ben had thought as he watched her move away, mixing with her guests, paying special attention to her daddy's old friends because they loved her and they carried hefty checkbooks.

A very attractive woman, Ben thought, and a tough one. She will survive.

His car window was lowered as he drove. The winds had abated and the afternoon was clear and warm. The fields were brown, some just plowed, some flooded with water. The acequias were already flowing, and alfalfa farmers were irrigating.

The drone of desire filled the air, the desire of spring that came with the winds and drove the natives crazy. Or maybe just me, Ben smiled. April is the cruelest month, stirring a hunger from old, moldy winter rot. It happened every year. Some said it was the hot chile they ate, others said it was the Alburquerque water, but for Ben, desire was in the wind.

"We live too near Texas," Ben sighed, "but for that curse God gave us beautiful women."

As he neared Dominic's house, Ben's thoughts turned to the lunch he had had two weeks ago with Frank in the open-air patio of Duke City Plaza. Dominic had put his building right in the middle of downtown Alburquerque. It had a large inner courtyard with fountains and ponds, rivulets lined with concrete, and statues of Spanish conquistadores fording the stream. Tourists came there to take pictures.

"You know why I picked this place?" Dominic had told Ben as they ate. "Because Francisco Vásquez de Coronado camped right here. And De Vargas and Oñate stopped here on their way to Santa Fé. And, get this," his face glowed, "here's where Governor Francisco Cuervo stood when he founded La Villa de Alburquerque in 1706. He was the architect of the new villa! He appointed Captain Martín Hurtado the first alcalde mayor de la Villa de Alburquerque. I know the history, Ben. Those men walked on this earth!" Dominic paused and grew contemplative. "My dad used to call me Francisco," he said sadly. "I should have kept the name. Frank, ah, that's too anglicized. Francisco Dominic, now that has weight to it."

Ben knew Dominic yearned to be a scion of the Spanish conquistadores. Frank grew up with the Mexican kids, learned the language, and fell into the dream that he really was a descendent of one of the old Spanish families. Sure, Dominic's mother was Italian, she came from one of the first families in the city, but Dominic's father had no known ethnic past.

Ben remembered Sergio Dominic as a dark man, a recluse who kept to himself, a cobbler who worked fifteen-hour days. He had married Frank's mother, moved into the Italian neighborhood, and learned her ways. There was never any love between Frank and his father. The old man worked Frank like a slave.

Dominic had built Duke City Plaza, the tallest and largest building in the downtown hub, on the site where his father had his first shoe shop. Old Sergio Dominic built a chain of shoe stores, and quietly bought downtown property. Now Dominic controlled the holdings. The top floor of his building was a penthouse—his office and a second home.

From Duke City Plaza stretched the strands of Dominic's web; there was very little in the city he didn't try to control. But could he pull off the downtown renewal scheme? Or would the personal vendetta against Walter Johnson be his downfall?

Most of the old businessmen in the city knew why Frank Dominic and Walter Johnson hated each other. During the war Johnson had stolen a chunk of prime real estate from old Sergio. They had gone into a deal together and Johnson left the old man holding the bag. It nearly devastated Sergio Dominic. The elder Dominic recovered his wealth, but he instilled in his son the idea of vengeance. He had a fortune hidden in his shop, but still he pushed Dominic relentlessly, made him work for every dime he earned. It drove Frank crazy. He didn't even have a car in high school, couldn't date girls, and therefore hated his father because he thought the old man kept him from Cynthia. He hated his father but he was a slave to the germ of revenge instilled in him by the old man. Sergio Dominic left his only son a strange legacy: millions in land and money, and a desire to destroy Walter Johnson.

What would my grandfather say? Ben thought. Politics is the art of chingando. Chinga aquí, chinga allá, chinga a todos iguales. The art of chingando was very democratic; everybody got screwed. That's what the mayor's race was going to become, a screwing-over. Was it a mistake to get mixed up in the battle?

"My father, don José," Ben remembered his grandfather saying, "was there when el Kearny marched into Las Vegas. The men from Puerto de Luna and Anton Chico and Delia heard the gringo army was coming, so they picked up their pitchforks and shovels and rode to meet it. A couple carried old buffalo guns and a few carried pistols."

The old man would puff on his roll-your-own cigarrillo as he talked. "The people of Las Vegas met in the plaza to get a look at Kearny and the Army of the West. They knew Kearny was going to make a speech; they knew a new era had come to New Mexico with the coming of the gringo. Kearny said, 'I bring the law of the Great White Father in Washington' and don José, may he rest in peace, took aim with his pistol and said 'No me chinges.' He would have shot Kearny off the saddle if his friends had not pulled him away and told him not to waste his bullets."

The old man laughed when he told that story, coughing and spitting out bits of tobacco. "That's when our life changed," the old man would say sadly. "That's when the chingadera began."

My grandfather tried to warn me, Ben thought as he pulled into Dominic's driveway and paused to look at the adobe hacienda. It was a sprawling complex set on ten acres of prize valley land. Behind the house were guest houses, a large swimming pool, and horse stables. The alfalfa fields beyond the yard had been irrigated, and the smell of damp earth filled the air. Lilac bushes lined the gravel driveway. Young kids were parking cars.

Easily a couple hundred people here, Ben thought, as he handed his keys over to the valet and walked to the front door. The party crowd was a mixed bag. Albuquerque-style meant men in dinner jackets and Levi's, the women in the latest fashion with arms and fingers adorned with Indian jewelry. The thick, aggressive crowd spilled outside into the large back patio.

Ben Chávez let himself in the front door and walked into the spacious living area. It was packed with Dominic supporters. He waved at Dominic's wife, who graciously stood and listened to Senator Culson expound as he puffed nervously on a cigarette. He was a Johnson man, but he was smart enough to play both sides in local politics.

Gloria returned his smile and nodded toward the hall. Dominic had not yet joined the party.

Ben wandered down the hall toward the library. The door was ajar. He pushed it and entered. Dominic looked up from a book. He was dressed in Levi's, cowboy shirt, and boots, affecting the good-old-boy attitude. The Frank Dominic at-home look, entertaining the governor, senators, and East Coast bankers. Frank Dominic was an expert at image.

"Benjie, come on in. I've been expecting you." He closed the book and jumped up to welcome him with a slap on the back. "Mi casa es tu casa," he grinned. "A drink?" and without waiting poured him a glassful of brandy. "Have a seat. Heard about the fight. We got in a few of those in high school, remember? God, I remember the rumble between the cowboys and the pachucos from Old Town. Closed down the school, didn't it? My eyes were black for weeks."

"I beat the man at his own game," Ben said and took the glass, "and you know some people, they don't like to be beaten in public."

Frank Dominic cocked his head, suspicious of what Ben Chávez was really saying. Writers were worse than lawyers when it came to speaking between the lines. What the hell did he mean by getting beat in public? Nobody was going to beat Frank Dominic in public, or anywhere else.

"Stay away from people like that, Benjie. They're penny-ante thugs. We need you for better things."

"Yeah," Ben answered sardonically.

"Have you read any into the history of Alburquerque?" he asked as he sipped his drink and lifted the book he had been reading. "Good stuff. You know, there's a little of that Spanish blood in me. And Gloria's family goes way back. Her clan is related to the original Duke of Alburquerque. When the governor of New Mexico, Francisco Cuervo, wrote to the Viceroy Francisco Fernández de la Cueva, Duke of Alburquerque, he was interested in expanding Nuevo México. This place was on the Camino Real, on the Río del Norte, and near Tijeras Canyon so the cibolleros could go hunt buffalo on the plains east of the Sandías."

"Sounds like he did his homework," Ben sipped the brandy. He knew Dominic hadn't invited him to discuss history.

"Francisco Cuervo needed the viceroy's favor to found the town, so he proposed to call it la Villa de Alburquerque de San Francisco Xavier del Bosque. The viceroy in Mexico City was pleased. The viceroy's junta changed the patron saint to San Felipe, and in 1776 Fray Francisco Domínguez replaced that saint with San Felipe de Neri."

Latin *Albus quercus* means 'white oak,' Ben thought as Dominic chattered. The coat of arms of the town in Spain bears a single white oak on a crimson field. Ben knew Dominic had designed a coat of arms around the very same one. "It's on my letterhead, Ben," Dominic had said.

Those who sought the Spanish in their genealogy never ceased to amaze Ben. Did Frank really believe he was related to the old dukes of Alburquerque? The Spanish legacy was a vision that many grasped for, and many a nut in New Mexico had spent his life's earnings trying to find his link to a Spanish family crest. Dreams of blue blood, visions of the Alhambra, and Spanish conquistadores. And Dominic was bitten by the bug. Is that why Dominic married Gloria, to lay claim to a family once related to the family of the Duke of Alburquerque? Or was this royalty bit part of the political package? Use it in the campaign—it would look good on TV and go down well with his North Valley friends.

"You didn't invite me here to discuss your family history," Ben shrugged.

"Cynthia's dead," Dominic said and drank.

Ben Chávez nodded.

"Damn, I've been thinking about her. I loved her, Ben, I really did," he turned and looked out the window. "I wanted to cancel the party, but Gloria said it wouldn't be right. I've got the president of the Chemical Bank of New York here. Business doesn't wait. Cynthia would want us to go on with our lives. We're getting old, Benjie, getting old."

"Cancer doesn't ask about age," Ben shrugged.

"It hurts," Frank Dominic mused.

"Frank Dominic admitting pain?"

"I wanted her, Benjie, I don't mind telling you. And now she's dead," Dominic sighed. "Anyway, her kid has shown up. Did you know there was a kid?"

Ben leaned forward.

"We guessed Cynthia dropped out of high school because she was pregnant, right? Now we know it's true. That summer you were in the hospital, Benjie, she was gone. Not even Gloria knew what was going on. She had a kid. Can you beat that?"

Ben Chávez felt sweat break across his forehead. His hands trembled. He stood, walked to the window, and looked out.

"Did you know, Benjie?" Dominic asked.

Ben Chávez remained silent. Yes, he knew his son lived in the city, breathed the air of the valley, walked the streets, but he could not go to that son and claim him. Cynthia's vow. We gave him up, Benjie, both of us. He remembered her words as clear as if they had just been spoken.

"It's Abrán González, Ben. Can you beat that? He's been right under our noses all along. He's the kid from Barelas who made a name for himself in Golden Gloves. Cynthia's kid, Ben. He's been in the barrio for twenty-one years and none of us knew."

"Abrán," Ben whispered. He felt his voice would break with emotion. He looked across the fields toward the bosque of the river. He yearned to be there, hidden in the tall cottonwoods, holding Cynthia tightly as he had held her so long ago.

"How did you find him?"

"I make it my business to know what goes on in this city, you know that. You also know Vera wouldn't say anything," Dominic answered, "so I went to the doctor who kept showing up in her room. He wrote a letter for Cynthia, and he didn't mind telling me about it. Cynthia wanted to see the kid before she died. It's that simple. Now we know why her father yanked her out of school. She was pregnant. She had the baby and he put the kid up for adoption. Nobody knew, Cynthia never told anyone. Imagine what she went through, Ben."

Abrán! Ben Chávez thought, and felt a pain in his chest. The room swam around him.

"Now the hard question, Ben. Who was the father?"

"Who do you think?" Ben Chávez shuddered.

"I think it was Bob López, the lover of the group. He was screwing all the little Country Club girls—"

"For crying out loud!" Ben Chávez shouted and spun around. "Not Bobby! He's a jerk! Cynthia wasn't like that!"

"Hey, relax, Benjie, I was just thinking aloud. For all I know it could have been you."

Ben Chávez felt his fingers tighten on his glass. "You're crazy," he said.

"Just thinking," Dominic smiled. "Anyway, Abrán's been living with a family. A woman named Sara González. Father's dead. Right in the old barrio. Know what?"

"What?"

"I've got an idea."

Ben was silent.

"I'm going to announce in a few weeks, and I'm going to give a really big party. I'm renting the Convention Center, and bringing in talent from all over. Ben, it's going to be big. The biggest party this fucking city's ever seen. I am going to make an impression on this city that will blow Johnson off the saddle. I can use the kid."

Ben gulped his brandy, but it didn't ease the pain in his chest, it only made it burn. The room was still slowly spinning around him. He had to get out, get fresh air, get to the river.

"What?"

"I'm going to get the kid to box for me. An exhibition fight. I've thought it all out, Ben. A really good exhibition fight will draw people like a magnet. You know, the vote in the valley's going to be crucial, and those folks love a good fight. . . ."

"The Mexicans?"

"Come on, Ben, you know what I mean."

The brandy went sour in his stomach; he was going to throw up. "You can't mix the kid in your politics, Frank! I won't let you!"

"You won't let me? What is this?"

"You only want to splash Cynthia's name around!"

"You don't have a damn thing to say about it!" Dominic shouted back. "I don't want to use him! I'll pay him. Really make it worth his while. Hell, he can turn pro after this! Cut through right to the top. I talked to some guys in Vegas, they agreed to line up Bo Decker. You know what that means to the kid, Ben. Win or lose he's a star. The kid's ready for a title fight."

He felt like hitting Dominic, or choking him until his anger went away. How could he use the kid and Cynthia's name in the game of politics? He clenched his fists.

"You can't do it!" he repeated.

"You've got nothing to say about this, Ben. I'm sorry I told you. I thought it was something I could do for the kid. We have to let him know who we are. We knew Cynthia. It fits into my plans, Ben," Dominic said with finality.

Ben slammed his glass on the table and stalked toward the door. If he stayed he knew he would hit Dominic.

"You going to Cynthia's service?" Dominic called. "We can talk to the kid there."

Ben didn't answer. The man didn't know when to quit. That's why Dominic had called him, to get him involved in the plans he had for the kid. He should have known, he should have known.

He cursed and slammed the door on his way out. He hurried through the house, past the crowd, and out the back. His heart was pounding, his eyes watering. The anger he felt, he knew, was not at Dominic, it was at himself.

There had been a moment of goodness on earth, an Indian summer of innocence. Then winter came, the workers from the barrio went out on strike, and he was caught up in the rumbles on the street. The season of love turned to one of struggle and emptiness. By the time he got out of the hospital, Cynthia had had the baby.

Ben made his way through the patio, past the blaring music of the mariachis. People smiled, nodded, said hello. He passed the swimming pool and walked beyond the rose garden to the stables. Horses turned and whinnied. He continued into the river bosque, where he found a trail beneath the giant, still-bare cottonwoods. The anger he felt made acid of his stomach; he leaned against a tree and vomited. Dominic was a sonofabitch, even his booze was poison. Now he wanted the kid mixed up in his race for mayor. Why? To get back at Cynthia?

"Damn you, Frank!" he cursed and slammed his fist into the rough bark of the trunk. "You no-good sonofabitch! Leave the boy alone! Leave Abrán alone!"

The blow numbed his hand. "Abrán," he whispered. "Oh God, Abrán." He felt alone and afraid. All those years of wondering, and now the truth was before him.

He cradled his bruised, quivering hand in his lap and cried. What did a man have to admit before he could look his son in the eyes? He had to be able to tell his son he wasn't really a coward.

The sun was setting over the West Mesa. It flamed like liquid lava and spread its fire on the western horizon where a windstorm was brewing. Ben leaned his back against the trunk of the tree and sank into the protective arms of its roots. With every deep sob came the memories of the past, and he heard himself calling her name, over and over.

6 The morning of the burial was clear and brisk. The warmth of summer stood poised to envelop the Río Grande Valley, but for now, a mad spring windstorm, or even a late freezing snow, could still sweep down from the north.

Abrán picked up Lucinda and Joe and they drove in silence to the mortuary. Vera had made arrangements for a brief service, but a big crowd was lining up outside the funeral home.

"Old friends," Vera whispered to Abrán as they met at the mortuary. "Gallery owners, other artists. She knew a lot of people."

In the crowd of mourners Abrán noticed Ben Chávez, the mayor, and other political figures. The silent outpouring of grief was evident; Cynthia Johnson had the respect of many people.

Then, a stir in the crowd caught Abrán's attention—Frank Dominic was forcing his way up to the front of the line. "I'm sorry, Vera, really sorry. You know how much Cynthia meant to us," he said, grasping her hand.

Her attention diverted, Vera thanked Dominic, introduced Abrán, and turned to speak to some old friends who had just arrived.

"I knew your mother, kid," Dominic said, taking Abrán's arm. "She was a good friend. I want you to come and see me. For Cynthia's sake, come and see me." He pressed his card into Abrán's hand. "I wrote down the time. I know some things about Cynthia which might interest you," he said as he patted Abrán on the shoulder and slipped away.

Inside the mortuary, the urn with Cynthia's ashes sat on a small table at the front of the chapel. As Abrán and Vera made their way to the front, acquaintances stopped Vera, whispered condolences.

Finally, the two paused in front of the urn and stood in silence. After a few moments, the mortuary director stepped forward and whispered to Vera. Vera shook her head. They would take the urn. The sallow-faced man lifted the container, followed them outside, and solemnly set it in Abrán's car.

"If there's anything I can do," the director whispered.

Vera shook her head. Abrán helped her into his car, and they were off, leaving the crowd behind.

"A lot of people knew her," Lucinda said as they drove away. She reached across the seat and touched Abrán's hand. He smiled, glad that she and Joe could be with him.

Cynthia's instructions about the burial site were very clear. She had left a detailed map. Joe sat in the back seat and navigated. "It's down toward Isleta Pueblo," he said, the small drum his grandfather had left him cradled on his lap. I brought it to sing a chant, he had said.

They followed Isleta Boulevard south until they found the dirt road that turned toward the river. There they crossed the main acequia and followed the canal road until they came to a lightning-scarred cotton-wood described on the map. The bare, white tree blackened at the top was a lone sentinel. Lightning had killed it long ago, but still it stood. Abrán pulled off to the side and parked. It was an isolated setting, close to the boundary of the pueblo land.

"This is it," Joe said. "Now follow the trail into the bosque."

Vera looked at the river forest and shook her head. "Why such a lonely place?" she asked.

"A place she knew," Abrán answered.

Overhead a crow called and flew north. Doves cried from the riverbank, where they had come to drink.

Abrán carried the urn and they followed the faint trail into the brush. Just before they reached the river's edge, the trail opened into a bower. "Cynthia's Bower," it was called on the map. This is where her ashes were to be buried.

"It's peaceful," Lucinda said. "It must have been a special place to her."

"A place of contemplation," Abrán said. Growing up in the barrio meant he had played along the river with his friends. They swam in the summer, walked for miles on the sandbars when the water level was low, and sometimes they fished the deep holes for catfish. The river was a place he knew well, but he had never been this far south.

Through the brush of river willow, russian olive, and tamarisk, they could see the sheen of the river. Swollen with spring run-off, it slithered silently south. Overhead the sky was cobalt blue.

"It's lonely," Vera shivered and dried her eyes. "But her life was lonely. Beneath the wild artist the papers portrayed was a lonely child. God forgive us."

Abrán and Joe quickly dug a hole in the dark earth at the base of a cottonwood, a tree so big its exposed roots were like arms embracing the earth. This tree would hold the ashes of the woman, just as it held the secret of her past. If it could talk it would tell them of the many days she had come here to rest and think. It would whisper to them of the autumn day twenty-one years ago when she came as a young girl to this bower and lay with the boy who was Abrán's father. This resting place for her ashes was also the place of conception.

Abrán and Joe each took a handful of ashes and dropped them into the hole. Vera scooped a handful of damp earth and pressed some of the ashes into the dirt. She dropped the ball into the hole. Abrán scattered the rest of the ashes, handed Vera the urn, then covered the hole. Lucinda found sprigs of green to place over the simple grave.

Joe went off into the bush and returned with a large, flat sandstone rock, which he placed over the burial site. By summer there would be no sign that she rested here, and the large stone would prevent the bosque coyotes from digging up the grave.

When the burial was done they sat in silence on the large roots of the tree. Joe played his drum. The sound of the chant and drum drifted across the muddy waters of the river. It was a sad sound that complemented the sigh of the breeze in the trees, the lonely call of the doves.

"There was a time when she was a child that she was mine," Vera said. "That time was so brief. When she was in school she liked to bring the kids from the barrio over. She felt close to them. Why not, I thought, they were my people. I, too, had grown up in a barrio. I, too, had known poverty. Living where we lived was too confining for her. Once I went to a fiesta in the barrio with her; the sister of a high school friend got married. We had so much fun together. We danced and enjoyed ourselves as we never had before. Those kinds of secrets we had to keep from Walter."

Abrán listened. He felt a peace in the bower, the same peace Cynthia must have felt when she came here. And he felt the presence of his father.

"They were here," he said and looked at Lucinda.

Lucinda understood. "That's why she picked this place," she whispered.

"Whoever he was, she loved him, of that I'm sure," Vera said. "They were young, maybe too young, but isn't that when love is so intense? How soon we forget. I blame myself. If only I had listened to her, guided her, understood what she was feeling. Life for me at her age was only work. I worked to survive, and I wanted the best for her. I thought Walter was right, we had to protect her. She turned to the boy. It was natural."

She paused, and the silence came again, enveloping them. Joe finished his drumming. "A song for her journey," he said.

"That was beautiful, Joe. I can't think of anything she would have liked more," Vera said, standing up. "She painted some of the people from the pueblo, the old people. Maybe in their faces she was trying to find the parents she never had." She shook her head sadly and headed for the car.

"Thanks, Joe," Abrán shook his friend's hand.

"I hadn't played the drum in a long time," Joe said. "Her spirit is here. She has come home."

Abrán nodded. Yes, she had come home, but where did he belong?

"The man Vera introduced me to, that was Frank Dominic. He knew Cynthia. I should see him."

"A powerful man," Joe said.

"A good place to start looking for information." He took Dominic's card from his pocket and glanced at it. He had to follow all leads, and he felt sure Frank Dominic knew something. He would see the man.

On the return to the city, Vera talked about Cynthia, and Abrán learned much about his mother. He realized that Vera was a lonely woman. Her life had centered around her husband. She had believed in him, helped him all those years before Cynthia came. After he disowned Cynthia, Vera was not only lonely but resentful and full of guilt for what they had done.

"Come and see me," she told Abrán when they dropped her at her car. "I want to know you better."

Abrán said he would, but both knew that was not possible. Walter Johnson would not allow it.

◆ ◆ ◆

7 The next day Abrán and Lucinda drove downtown. Dominic's Duke City Plaza loomed above the rest of the downtown landscape. Across the street rose Johnson's bank. From their respective offices, the gossip said, Walter Johnson and Frank Dominic glared at each other.

"I've never been in here," Lucinda said as they stood looking at the main building. It rose dark and shining into the New Mexican sky. For her it was an ominous tower that gave off a bad feeling.

"I remember the lobby. It has some of Cynthia's paintings."

"What used to be here?" Lucinda asked.

"Mostly small businesses."

"He needed the space, so he tore them down. Same thing happened in Santa Fé. People with money came to live the Santa Fé style, they bought the downtown barrios and built hotels, shops, condos. The old residents were swept aside, the people gone," Lucinda said. "If Frank Dominic has his way, the barrio boys will be rowing boats up and down canals that cover the land where they used to live."

Abrán nodded. Dominic could be dangerous.

Lucinda took his arm. "Don't take anything he offers," she warned him.

"He may have known my father. That's all I want," Abrán assured her.

He led her into the spacious lobby of the El Dorado Building, the central skyscraper of Duke City Plaza. The building was a symbol of Dominic's desire to do everything bigger and better than Walter Johnson. The lobby was done in earth and gold tones. From the high ceiling hung a giant, glittering chandelier imported from Italy. Lush, crimson carpets covered the floor. Half a dozen of Cynthia's paintings adorned one wall.

Abrán nodded, "Mira." Indians mounted on ponies swept across the canvas toward a rooster buried in the ground at the center of the painting. The Indian and Mexican bystanders cheered the riders. The painting was intense in color and action. The gaiety of the pueblo fiesta was palpable, but the strength of the painting was, as in all of Cynthia's paintings, in the faces of the people.

"Corrida del gallo," Lucinda said. She had seen the corridas in the small northern villages and pueblos, and she recognized the genius of the woman who captured the spirit of the fiesta.

They stood entranced by the painting, gazing into the soul of the woman they knew so little about, Abrán's mother.

"Mr. González," a man approached, "I am Casimiro, Mr. Dominic's assistant. Please come with me." He turned and led them to the elevator foyer. "Mr. Dominic's expecting you," he said. "You will have time after your conference with Mr. Dominic to view the paintings. Mr. Dominic's collection is the best there is," he smiled.

Casimiro was dressed as impeccably as the office he led them into. "Mr. Dominic will be with you shortly," he said and disappeared.

In Dominic's office the light was muted, the carpets lush beneath their feet. The room was decorated in wood and leather with fine-grained oak furniture and bookshelves. A large desk sat by the wall facing large plate-glass windows. Behind the desk hung a huge wooden plaque on which was engraved the coat of arms of the Duke of Alburquerque. Abrán drew close to read the inscription: Don Francisco

Fernández de la Cueva Enríquez, Tenth Duke of Alburquerque, Viceroy in Mexico City from 1701 to 1708.

Abrán knew his history well enough to know that it was this viceroy to whom then Governor Cuervo y Valdéz of New Mexico had presented the petition attesting to the founding of la Villa de Alburquerque.

Abrán stared at the coat of arms, thinking aloud, "1706." The city of the Duke, or more rightly, the city of Governor Cuervo, had been around a long time.

A large, antiqued trastero housed the bar, and on the walls were shelves of law books. More of Cynthia's paintings filled spaces on the walls. "Incredible," Abrán whistled softly.

A low growl made them turn toward the large windows of the terrace. Two black dobermans bared their fangs and pushed their noses against the glass.

"Don't worry, they only bite if I'm attacked," Dominic said as he entered the room. "Buenos días," he said warmly and shook Abrán's hand. "Glad you could come. Bienvenidos a mi casa. I see you're admiring the coat of arms. What a history this city has, a history which should be known by all. We're all part of it, you know. My wife's family traces its blood back to the Duke. A great man. But we can discuss this later, you're here to see Cynthia's paintings. These smaller ones are special, and no one sees them except good friends."

He led Abrán toward the paintings. "In the small ones I find the intimate Cynthia. Small details of life which escape most of us. Look, here's a fiddle and a bouquet. The same will appear in a large painting of a wedding dance. Exquisite. I tried to buy all I could, I sure as hell didn't want her work to get bought up by rich Texans." He smiled as if they had shared a joke. "I have nothing against Texans, but she was ours."

He placed his hand on Abrán's shoulder as he led them from painting to painting. "Here, her work is appreciated."

"It's beautiful," Lucinda said.

"I paid good money for it," Dominic said. "Top money. I probably know more about Cynthia's work than most art critics. What do you think?"

"I'm impressed," Abrán said. The paintings were vibrant with color and rich in texture, but it was the faces and eyes of the people she painted that held the gaze of the viewer. Deep in the hues of earth and sun colors, the Hispanos she painted came alive. Many New Mexican artists painted hollyhocks and blue doors, but none had captured the old people like Cynthia. She had recorded a time that was passing away.

"She was a genius," Dominic whispered, and moved them along the wall, pointing out the features of each particular painting, explaining when and where they were done.

At the end of the wall there was a nicho. In it rested a small painting that Dominic called "The Lovers."

"This is her most perfect work," he whispered. "And it's among her earliest. She kept it a long time, but when she came back from Europe she was devastated, and broke. The French critics had panned her work."

Abrán was only half listening. He was staring intently at the painting that depicted two nudes in a golden bower. The boy had his back to the viewer. He was brown-skinned, done in a realistic style, but with elements of the classical Greek. His body radiated light. He was reaching down to hand the girl a golden leaf. The blonde girl reclined on a bed of leaves. Her face was aglow with love. There was no doubt that the girl was Cynthia, and the boy was the young man she called "mi árabe" in her diary.

Abrán turned to Lucinda and nodded. It was the bower where they buried her ashes. The boy in the painting was Abrán's father.

"It's her," Abrán said.

"Yes. You see why we loved her. She was a beautiful woman."

"And the boy?"

Dominic shrugged. "She kept him secret. I've asked some of the old classmates who knew Cynthia, but no one knows his name. My wife was her best friend, and she doesn't know. Or if she knows she won't tell. The young man in the painting is probably your father," Dominic said, looking at Abrán.

Abrán nodded. "Sell it to me," he said impulsively.

Dominic laughed softly. "I can't do that."

"Why?" Abrán asked.

"You don't have the money," Dominic said bluntly. "Let me offer you a drink."

Abrán reached out and stopped him. "How much would it take?"

Lucinda saw them measure each other, the physical strength of the young man and the monied power of the older one. Dominic had what Abrán wanted, so the latter was at a disadvantage. Lucinda started to speak, then paused. Was it possible that the young man in the painting was Frank Dominic? She looked at Abrán and then at Dominic. There was a resemblance.

"I wouldn't let go of it, kid," Dominic said as he stepped to the bar. "Sit down, I want to talk to you. What can I offer you?"

"Nothing for me," Abrán declined.

Lucinda shook her head and sat by Abrán. He hadn't invited them just to show the paintings, she knew he wanted something.

"Fine, I'll get to the point," Dominic said. "I knew Cynthia very well. We went to school together. None of us knew about you, but here you are. I want to help you."

"How?" Abrán asked.

"You're gifted, kid. I followed your career when you were in high school. You're the best to come out of Albuquerque High. That's my old school, you know. You make us proud, kid. You should have turned pro after Golden Gloves. You're a natural. I've been talking to some trainers from Foster's Gym, even talked to your old coach Rudy Sánchez. They say you could walk in the ring today and whip Bo Decker. I want to get you a fight!"

"I don't fight," Abrán answered.

"But you're in shape."

"I run, work out a little, but I haven't been in the ring for three years."

"You're in shape, kid. You're ready. You can go pro at the snap of a finger. I'll level with you, I want to own you. I want to set up an exhibition fight right away." He stood and paced nervously. "You know I'm running for mayor. We have a big announcement party planned in a few weeks. I want to do something big, something that's never been done. The fight would fit right in! Blow away the competition, kid. With you in my corner I know I can do it! You're Cynthia Johnson's boy, the Duke City Kid, our own Golden Gloves champ. This will be your first pro fight. I'll put it on cable. They'll love you, kid! Love you!"

His enthusiasm was catching. Abrán glanced at Lucinda. Her eyes said no.

"I don't want a pro fight," he shook his head. "I gave up boxing."

"There was an accident," Dominic said. "I know all about that. Junior Gómez, a gifted fighter, your friend—"

"I'm not fighting," Abrán repeated.

"He wasn't as good as you."

"Junior was better than me," Abrán's voice rose. He thought of Junior and all the times they sparred together, the bus trips they took when they were in Golden Gloves, and Junior's dream of turning pro. Junior wanted a way out of poverty and the barrio, and boxing was his only ticket.

"It was an accident," Dominic insisted. "You can't let one accident hold you up. You've got talent. This city needs someone like you. Tell him," Dominic said and turned to Lucinda.

Lucinda shook her head. She touched Abrán's hand and felt him tremble.

"I don't box," Abrán said, "that's it."

"Hey, you can make fifty thousand for an exhibition bout!" Dominic said. "That ain't peanuts."

"Not interested."

"You don't know what you're saying, kid," Dominic said with a slight break in his voice. He stopped at the bar and poured another brandy. He hadn't expected the kid to say no. What did he want?

"The painting," Dominic turned and smiled.

"No," Lucinda whispered. She looked at Abrán.

The three turned to look at the small painting. It *was* priceless. Abrán rose and went to the nicho. The painting was the only link he had to his past, the only place he could see his father and mother together. In a few weeks he could be in shape to box anyone, he knew that. He had been running regularly, now he only needed to hit the bags, spar, but he was in shape.

"I want it," he thought aloud.

Lucinda stood behind him. She wanted to say no, but she couldn't. It was his decision.

"It can be yours," Dominic nodded.

After a long pause, Abrán shook his head. "It's not for me. Maybe it was meant for my father, but not for me." He turned and looked at Lucinda. It was time to go.

"What do you want, kid?" an exasperated Dominic asked.

"I want to find my father," Abrán answered.

Dominic smiled. So that was it. He should have known. What the hell did the kid know about art? All he wanted was his father.

"I can find him."

"How?"

"I knew her, knew the kids she knew. I was close to Cynthia. My wife was her best friend, kid, so I have an inside track. I'll hire a good detective. I can find your old man, if that's what you want."

"It's what I want," Abrán answered.

"So it's a deal," Dominic grinned. "You go into training and on the night of the fight I deliver your father's name to you." He put out his hand. "What do you say?"

"How can you be so sure?" Lucinda interrupted.

"I'm sure," he smiled. "Frank Dominic is always sure of what he can do. I can find Abrán's father. Trust me."

"If you don't?"

"You don't fight. That's how sure I am. Deal?"

Abrán nodded and they shook hands. "You won't regret this, kid.

This fight's going to open doors for you. I'll even get your old trainer to work with you."

Abrán nodded again. He had broken his promise never to step back into the ring. He hadn't realized until he made the bargain with Dominic how much he needed to know his father.

"It's going to be like old times for you. Leave everything to me. I know this town, I can find anything."

He pressed a button on his desk and Casimiro appeared at the door. "Take good care of this young man," Dominic smiled. "Take good care of yourself, kid. I need you in the ring."

Abrán and Lucinda followed Casimiro out of the office into the elevator. "Here's our number," he said and handed Abrán a card embossed with the Dominic crest.

"I'll call Sánchez and set up the exam with our doctor. Mr. Dominic leaves very little to chance, so he will be checking on your progress."

Abrán held Lucinda's hand as the elevator zoomed down. His mouth was dry, his knees were weak. Had he done the right thing? What did it mean to break a promise?

"If you need anything, call me. Mr. Dominic wants nothing but the training on your mind. That means no women," Casimiro said, looking from Abrán to Lucinda as they left the elevator.

"Thanks for the advice," Abrán answered, and he led Lucinda quickly out of the building. Outside the air was fresh, the afternoon light mellow, the sidewalk full of workers heading home.

"What do you think?" Abrán asked.

Lucinda bit her lip. She didn't like Dominic and she didn't like the bargain Abrán had made, but she felt she had no right to interfere. Finding his father was important to Abrán. As long as he didn't know his father, he would always be searching. She didn't want that for him, not with the way she felt about him.

"I think you should make love to me," she answered.

He looked at her, held her hand as the crowd swirled around them. "You sure?" he asked.

"Yes. I want to make love to you. I want it before that fiend Casimiro and his boss put you in training and you can't have me."

"I'll always want to have you," Abrán answered.

"Always?"

"Yes."

"Then why are we wasting time?" she said resolutely.

He laughed and pulled her into the car, and they sped to her apartment. She opened him a beer when they arrived, turned on some salsa music, and opened the windows. "Stuffy in here," she said.

"Hot," he nodded and sipped the beer.

"I'm going to take a shower," she said.

He watched her walk to her bedroom. He could hear the water running and Lucinda singing as he finished his beer. When she returned, she wore a terry cloth robe. Her hair was wet. She smiled and put her arms around him, and the fresh scent of soap filled his nostrils. He felt his heart pounding as he drew her close.

"Junior's girl?" she asked, "Was she in love with you?"

"You knew," he answered. He had never told anyone.

"I guessed," Lucinda said.

"He thought something had happened between us. When we fought at the gym he wanted to hurt me. He was angry."

"I'm sorry I brought it up," she whispered. "Love me."

He picked her up and carried her into the bedroom.

8 "I'm going to fight," he told Sara the following Sunday.

He had been nervous all day about telling her, and as he stood next to her while she prepared a salad he suddenly blurted out the news.

She paused and looked at him. "You're going to box?"

"Yes. In a few weeks."

"But why?"

He told her about Dominic's offer. She listened, but in the end shook her head. "I feel like Lucinda," she said, "I just don't like it. Isn't there another way? Maybe I could go to Mr. Johnson—"

"No, Mamá! I don't want you to have to beg from that man. If he knows, he won't say anything. Look, it's just one fight."

She knew how much he had suffered when Junior died, and how hard it was for him to go back into the ring, and it was natural for him to want to know his father. But she didn't like his being mixed up with the attorney who was so rich and always in the papers. Being mixed up with the rich could only bring trouble. She didn't like it, but for her son she would bear it without complaint.

"Go and get Lucinda, I'll finish here," she said calmly. He handed her the vegetables he had cut, and washed his hands.

"It's going to be all right, jefita. It's something I have to do." He kissed her.

"I know, I know," she answered. "Go on, the enchiladas will be ready when you return."

He drove to Lucinda's. She was radiant in a white summer dress. She kissed him and whispered, "Tú eres tú. You're all I want."

Sara had prepared red chile enchiladas, beans, and tortillas. For dessert she served sopa, a sweet bread pudding topped with melted cheese. It felt good to have Lucinda in her home. This was what Abrán needed, not the boxing and not the running around and making deals with the big-shot lawyer.

Time was the most valuable ingredient in life, and for Sara it was to be enjoyed with family and friends. She sipped wine and enjoyed the warmth of their company as they ate. Lucinda talked about her life in the mountain village of Córdova. Sara had asked her about her family. Quien es tu familia? was one of the first questions that was always asked. One was known by one's family.

Lucinda told about her father and how he came to be a santero, and she told them about her mother and many of the old customs in the isolated villages of the Sangre de Cristo. She wanted Abrán to visit her family, she said with a glance at Sara. "That would be good for Abrán," Sara agreed. "He's a city boy. He needs to see the villages."

"How about the training?" Lucinda asked.

"I can jog up and down the mountain," Abrán said. "We'll go on Good Friday, come back after Easter. The doctor gave me a physical, said I'm in great shape."

"I knew that," Lucinda teased him.

"He is in good shape," Sara said as she cleaned up the dishes. "He runs every day, he doesn't smoke, but he drinks beer," she said with a mock frown. "Bueno, let's go in the living room. Lucinda, help me get the coffee and sopa. Then I want Abrán to read the beautiful story Cynthia wrote. She was not only an artist, she could write like a poet."

They gathered in the front room for dessert. Abrán flipped through

Cynthia's diary. "This is an old entry, and it's as close as she comes to describing my father. They went to a matanza in the South Valley, near Los Padillas. It was the day they discovered the bower where we buried her ashes. She never mentions his name. She refers to him only as 'mi árabe.'"

"So he is dark," Sara said. A dark and handsome Mexicano was her son's father, an indio like Ramiro, a dark, curly-haired árabe. She looked at her son and admired him. Yes, he would find his father, it was best to believe that. He had been bound by destiny long enough, now he had to break those old ropes and create his own future.

Abrán smiled at his mother. "Yes. Bueno, aquí 'stá."

He read Cynthia's "la matanza," the entry that described the killing of the hogs for winter meat:

It was in the fiestas of the people that I discovered the essence of my people, the Mexican heritage of my mother. Other painters had concentrated on the Indians; I went to the small, out-of-the-way family fiestas of the Mexicanos. There is a chronicle of life in the fiestas, beginning with baptism. La fiesta de bautismo. I painted the padrinos at church as they held the baby over the font for the priest to bless el niño with holy water. In the faces of the padrino and madrina I saw and understood the godparents' role. The padrinos would become the child's second parents, and the familial kinship in the village or in the barrio would be extended. La familia would grow. I painted a scene where the baby was returned from church by the padrinos, the joy of the parents, the song of entriego, the return of the child, the food and drink, the hopeful, gay faces of family and neighbors.

And I painted wedding scenes. Gloria has my favorite. She has the painting that captures the moment when two of the groom's friends grab the bride and stand ready to spirit her away. The bridegroom is caught off-guard, someone is pouring him a glass of champagne. The fiddler is leaning low, playing away, his eyes laughing. The other músicos join in the polka, drawing attention away from the traditional "stealing of the bride."

Fiestas, I loved the fiestas. There is a series: "Spring Planting," "Cleaning the Acequias," "Misa del Gallo," "Los Matachines." I did the Bernalillo Matachines, although my favorite were the Jémez Pueblo Matachines. I painted los hermanos penitentes on Good Friday, the holy communion of Easter Sunday, the little-known dances of Los Abuelos and Los Comanches. I painted a triptych of Los Pastores at the Trampas church one Christmas. And the Christmas Posadas. All the fiestas of life that might die as the viejitos die.

I painted the fiestas of the Río Grande, the fiestas of your people, mi amor, the fiestas my mother used to tell me about when I was a child, because if life had not been so cruel, we would have shared these fiestas.

Do you remember la Matanza in Los Padillas, mi árabe moreno? We were invited by your friend Isidro. His family was having a matanza. We had fallen in love that summer, and suddenly it was October, a more brilliant October I never saw again. The entire river was golden, the álamos had turned the color of fire. Long strings of geese flew south and filled the valley with their call, and we, too, drove south along Isleta. Farmers lined the road, their trucks filled with bushels of green chile, red chile ristras, corn and pumpkins, apples. It was autumn, and the fiesta of the harvest drew people together.

It was my first trip into the South Valley. I was a gringita from the Country Club; I had been protected from the world. But the valley was to become my valley. I would visit the villages of the Río Grande again and again, until the old residents got to know well the sunburned gringa who tramped around with easel, paint, and brushes. I earned their respect. They invited me into their homes, and later they invited me to their fiestas. Their acceptance kept me alive.

The night had been cold, and the thin ice of morning cracked like a fresh apple bitten. The sun rising over Tijeras Canyon melted the frost. Gloria helped, as usual. She picked me up. I told my parents I was spending the day with her. Without her help we could never have had time together. Why did she marry F? What a pity.

The colors of autumn were like a bright colcha, a warm and timeless beauty covering the earth. The sounds carried in the morning air, and all *was vibrant with life before the cold of winter. Oh, if we had only known that the wrath of parents can kill!*

The matanza was beginning when we arrived. Cars and trucks filled the gravel driveway. Family, friends, and neighbors filled the backyard of the old adobe home. Isidro greeted us.

"Just in time," he said and we followed him to the back where the women were serving breakfast. They had set a board over barrels to use as a table, and on it rested the steaming plates of eggs, bacon, potatoes, chile stew, hot tortillas, and coffee. The men were stuffing down the food. Somebody had already called for the first pig to be brought out of the pen. Whiskey bottles were passed around; those who had gotten up early to help the women start the fires and heat the huge vats of lye-water had been drinking for hours.

A very handsome, but very troubled, young man held a rifle in one hand and a bottle of whiskey in the other. Remember Marcos? I will never forget him; he learned a lesson that day. We all did. At the pigpen the frightened sow was being roped and wrestled out.

The women watched; they goaded the men. My mother was a woman of great strength, I always knew, and I saw that same strength in those women of the valley.

"Ya no pueden," they teased the men wrestling with the sow. The worst thing to tell a macho, especially when he's drinking and doing the "bringing the meat home" business. But it was a fiesta, and the teasing was part of it.

"¡Andale! ¡Con ganas!"

"¡Qué ganas, con huevos!"

They laughed; the men cursed and grunted as they lassoed the pig.

"Don't shoot yourself, Marcos!"

"Don't stab yourself, Jerry!" they said to the young man who held the knife.

Isidro told us that Marcos was an attorney in town and Jerry was a computer man at Sandia Labs. Like other young men who had left the valley for a middle-class life in the city, they only returned once in a while to visit the parents and grandparents. Or they returned for the fiestas. They had almost forgotten the old ways, and so the older aunts teased them.

Who remembered the old ways? The old men standing along the adobe wall warming themselves in the morning sun. With them stood don Pedro, Isidro's grandfather, the old patriarch of the clan. These were the vecinos, the neighbors who had worked together all their lives. Men from Los Padillas and Pajarito and Isleta Pueblo. Now they were too old to kill the pigs, so they had handed over the task to their grandsons. They warmed their bones in the morning sun and watched as the young men drank and strutted about in their new shirts and Levi's. Those old men knew the old ways. Maybe it was that day that I vowed to paint them, to preserve their faces and their way of life for posterity. They would all die soon.

"Hispano Gothic," I called the painting I did of those old men. The last patriarchs of the valley. And their women, las viejitas, las jefitas of the large families, stood next to their men and watched. These old men and women remembered the proper way of the fiestas, and so they watched with great patience as their uprooted grandsons struggled to prove their manhood. What a chorus of wisdom and strength shone in their eyes. What will happen to our people when those viejitos are gone? Will our ceremonies disappear from the face of the earth? Is that what drives me to paint them with such urgency?

Time has been like a wind swirling around me, my love, since I last touched you. Time will scatter my paintings, but the seed planted that autumn day will survive. Our seed will grow, but we were not destined to nourish it.

The children were always present at the fiestas, and they were there that day. They laughed and played tag, chased each other, the boys shot baskets through a hoop, a baby nursed at his mother's breast. As the squealing, struggling pig was pulled out of the pen, the children paused to watch. Here was the link between past and future generations, this is how the young would learn the old ways.

Near the fire a large, wood plank was set over two barrels. The dead pig would be hoisted up onto the rough table to be gutted and cleaned. A huge cauldron sat over the hot fire that had been lighted before the sun was up. Boiling water laced with lye let off wisps of steam; a thin scum clouded the surface. When the dead pig was raised onto the plank, it would be covered with gunnysacks and the hot water poured over the sacks. The bristle would be softened and easy to scrape off with knives.

The shouts of the men grew agitated, the sow was big and nervous. The men pulled with ropes, others poked and pushed from behind. "¡Nalgona!" one cursed. The women laughed. "That's the way you like them, Freddie!"

Don Pedro and his compadres watched patiently.

"¡Sonamagon! ¡Pinche! ¡Muevete!" the young men cursed the pig.

"Come on!" Marcos shouted. "A little closer!" He aimed the rifle. He was drunk.

Marcos' wife stood in the circle of people around the pig. She was a Northeast Heights gringa, and she didn't like what they were doing. She wished they hadn't come. Marcos was making a fool of himself, she thought, and he was going to muddy the new boots and Levi's she bought him for the State Fair. Too much pagan ritual in the air for her taste.

"Hold him still," Marcos shouted.

They had frightened the pig, made it nervous, now they couldn't hold the struggling animal that pulled from side to side.

"Watch out, Marcos!"

"He's going to shoot someone!"

"Ramona. Take the gun away," someone said to the oldest aunt. She was in charge of the fire and the cleaning, and tough enough to keep the men in line.

"Marcos?" she called.

"I'm okay," he answered angrily. He threw the empty bottle aside and cocked the rifle.

"No tiene huevos," somebody shouted. Marcos heard. He turned and glared at his cousins, those who had not left the valley.

"Sonofabitches!" he spat. They'd been razzing him all morning, now they came out and said he didn't have the balls to do the job. He was a drugstore cowboy playing at being a macho man. He'd show them.

Then his wife whined. "Marcos, let somebody else do it. You're ruining your boots."

His face grew livid. I painted anger in his eyes, for it was there. Bitch, he wanted to scream, I'll show you.

"Grandpa," Ramona said, and for a moment everyone glanced at don Pedro. Would he stop the charade before someone got hurt? The old man looked at Marcos' father. The father shrugged; it was up to don Pedro to decide.

The old man nodded. Continue. He held up a finger. Make a clean kill with one shot, he said.

"You damn right, daddy-o," Marcos grinned. Somebody handed him a just-opened bottle of Jim Beam and he took a big swig.

"Don't give him any more to drink, he's going to shoot somebody." The women were worried, they had known of matanzas that turned deadly.

The men heaved and pushed the pig in front of Marcos. He aimed, the rifle wavering.

"¡Cuidao!" one man shouted and jumped aside.

"Behind the ear! Behind the ear!"

"Between the eyes!"

"Watch out!"

"He's drunk!"

"Get back!"

The men jumped away from the pig and a deafening explosion filled the air. The baby cried, the children screamed, the crows in the giant cottonwoods by the ditch rose cawing into the air. Dogs barked, and the air echoed with the report of the rifle. The smell of gunpowder filled the clean morning air.

The pig gave a shrill cry and reared up. The bullet had only grazed it. Marcos fired again, wildly, and the second bullet entered above the left shoulder. The sow hit the ground, turning round and round in the dirt, crying shrilly as blood spurted from its wound.

"You missed, cabrón!"

"Shoot!"

"No! The knife!"

The men pulled at the ropes around the pig's feet and held it. But Marcos would not take the knife. The pig's hot blood made him turn away and vomit, the stuff splattering his new boots.

Tío Mateo took the knife and pounced on the screaming sow. He grabbed an ear for leverage then plunged the knife into the throat as hard and deep as he could. The wounded sow thrashed and turned.

"Hol'im! Goddammit hold him!"

The men held, dirtying themselves with mud and blood as the knife found an artery and the blood rushed out. Then the pig grew still. The men got up slowly, covered with filth and blood, wiped their hands on their Levi's and cursed Marcos. They spit out the bitter taste in their mouths and reached for a drink.

Against the wall the old men stood quietly. They shook their heads; it was not good. The frightened children had turned to the women, hiding in folds of skirts. This is not how it should be.

"Pinche marrano," Marcos cursed and kicked the dead pig at his feet. "You sonofbitches didn't hold it," he blamed the men.

"Fuck you," one of the men answered, "you're a lousy shot!"

They faced each other, angry that it had not gone right. They blamed Marcos, he blamed them. None looked at the old men along the wall.

"Bring the other one! I'll show you who's a good shot!" Marcos bragged and wiped the vomit from his mouth. He cocked the rifle.

"Put the gun away, Marcos, you're drunk," tía Ramona said. She was angry, too. She remembered matanzas that were done right, not crazy and dirty like the one she had just seen. She looked at the children; they shouldn't be frightened, they should be learning to value this old custom.

"Stay out of this, tía!" Marcos insisted. "Bring the other pig!" he shouted, waving the rifle. "I'm gonna blow his brains out!"

"No!" a stern voice broke the tension in the air. We turned to see don Pedro step forward, bent with age but resolute. He had stayed out of the argument as long as he could, but now he had to set things right. I think it was the frightened children who compelled him to stop the debacle.

He walked right up to Marcos and looked squarely at his grandson. "Ya no valen ni para matar un marrano," he said.

Marcos and the other men stiffened. It was an insult, and if any other man had said that, there would have been a fight, but this was their grandfather so they swallowed their pride.

Don Pedro, still sinewy and tough, was the patriarch of the family, and respect for elders was still a value in the family. He took the rifle from Marcos.

"You call yourselves men," he said firmly, "and look at this mess. You can't even kill a pig."

His words stung. His sons and grandsons looked at their dirtied clothes and the mess of blood on the ground and knew he was right.

"Ah, come on, Grandpa," one of his grandsons said, "don't take it so serious. We're just killing a pig, it's no big deal, ese."

"It is a big deal," the old man retorted. "It has to be done right."

Marcos' eyes narrowed, but he tried to make amends. "Come on, Grandpa, have a drink. . . ."

"I don't drink with boys," don Pedro answered, a hardness in his voice. He stood unwavering, strong as an old tree of the river.

The silence was deadly. Marcos clenched his jaws in anger.

They were young men full of booze, and the smell of blood had made their own blood boil. I felt something terrible was about to happen.

So did don Pedro's wife, because she stepped forward and put her hand on his arm, trying to coax him back. The arena of blood and drunk young men was no place for an old man. Better to stand with his compadres at the wall and warm his bones in safety. But don Pedro wouldn't budge.

"Okay, Grandpa," Marcos spit out the bile in his mouth. "If you're such a man, why don't you do it."

It was the grandfather's turn to be stung. He looked around and saw the men nod. Yes, if you're such a man, you show us how it's done.

"Grandpa likes to talk," Marcos continued, "but he's too old to cut the mustard."

The young men smiled.

"¿Qué pasa, Grandpa?" a grandson said, and slapped the old man on the back.

"No puede," Marcos snickered. They stood facing each other, Marcos and don Pedro, the young and the old. Their veins bulged with tension, their eyes glared.

The old woman whispered. "Anda, Pedro, vente." Come away, leave *this to the young men. The old man straightened his shoulders, looked at her and smiled. Then he turned to the old compadres who stood along the wall.*

"Secundino," he said softly, "el martillo."

The old man Secundino thought he hadn't heard, then he smiled and nodded. It was the call to the matanza, an old calling, something they knew in their blood, something they had done surely and swiftly all their lives. The right way. He hobbled to the shed and returned with a ten-pound, short-handled sledgehammer.

"Procopio, ponle filo a la navaja," the old man said as he rolled up his sleeves.

"Con mucho gusto," Procopio spat a quick stream of chewing tobacco through yellow-stained teeth and smiled. He took the long knife and began sharpening it on a small whetstone. "Lana sube, lana baja," he whispered as the blade swished back and forth on the stone.

"Compadres," don Pedro whispered, "la marrana." The old men ambled silently but quickly toward the pen.

"Wait, Grandpa," Marcos said, "you don't have to—" But it was too late, the old man's eyes were fixed on the huge sow that the men moved out of the pen by softly clicking their tongues. They needed no ropes to move the pig. Secundino slipped the big hammer into don Pedro's hand. Then Procopio handed don Pedro the sharpened knife, so now the old man balanced the hammer in one hand and the knife in the other.

The young men had only heard these stories, that long ago when rifles and bullets were scarce, the matanza was done like this. Like a bullfighter meeting a bull with just a cape, the old man met the two-hundred-pound pig with just a blade and hammer.

Don Pedro moved in a circle, keeping his eye on the pig as it came closer and closer to him. There was no noise, no ropes, no fast motions to spook the pig, just the circle of men getting smaller.

The compadres smiled and remembered all the years of their lives when they had done this. It was a ceremony, the taking of the animal's life to provide meat for the family. The young men needed to be reminded that it was not sport, it was a tradition as old as the first Hispanos who settled along the river.

This is how we have lived along the river, the viejos said. We have raised generations on this earth along the Río Grande, and we have done it with pride and honor. Each new generation must accept the custom and likewise pass it on.

The air grew still, we stood transfixed. The circle closed in, until the animal was only an arm's length away.

Crows called from the cottonwoods of the river, a dog whined, the wood embers popped, the wisps of steam hissed and rose from the lye-water in the cauldron.

When don Pedro had come face-to-face with the pig, he raised his hammer, and with the speed of a matador, there was a brief glint in the sunlight, the arc of his arm, a dull thud, and the pig jerked back and stiffened. The kill was complete and clean.

It had taken all the old man's strength to make the kill, but he had done it with grace. There was no loud thunder of the rifle, no crying children or barking dogs, just a clean kill. We stood hypnotized as don Pedro dropped to his knees in front of the quivering pig. Two of the men held the pig by the ears as don Pedro plunged the knife into the pig's heart. The blood flowed swiftly.

Tía Ramona stepped forward with a pan to save the hot, gushing blood. Not a drop was wasted. She would mix it with water in a bowl, then slowly stir it with her hand until the thick coagulants were removed and only the pure blood remained. This she would fry with onion and pieces of liver as a blood pudding, a delicacy for the guests.

When don Pedro withdrew the knife it seemed to come out spotless, unbloodied, and his hands were clean. Then the old man stood, and a shudder of fatigue passed through his frail body. He took a deep breath, and then sipped from the tin cup of water his wife handed him. He smiled at her, and when he looked at us, there was a serene beauty in his face. A noble look on the faces of the old men of the clan.

His compadres nodded, slapped him gently on the back. That's the way we used to do it, their nods said.

"Chingao," one of the grandsons exclaimed, breaking the silence.

"Did you see that?"

"Damn, Grandpa."

They moved forward to touch the old man. One handed him a bottle so he could drink. They were filled with admiration. Even Marcos reached out to touch the grandfather, as if to share in the old man's valor.

"You're too old to be killing pigs," his wife scolded. She took his arm, and together they walked back to the safety of the warm adobe wall.

"A man's never too old," he winked, willing to withdraw. Let the young men lift the hog and begin the gutting and cleaning, he would sit with his old vecinos and watch. They had done their duty, they had shown the young people the right way to perform the ceremony.

The pig was gutted and the liver was thrown on the hot coals. When it was baked, the first slice was served on hot tortillas with green chile and offered to don Pedro, a tribute to the old warrior. Then he and the rest of the men ate, drank wine, and talked about the old days when the people of the valley lived in harmony with the earth and their neighbors.

"We will die and all this will pass away," I remember don Pedro saying.

That is why I had to paint. I wanted to preserve the beauty of those moments. That was the gift and the commitment which came to rest in my soul that day. The life and love of the old people opened my eyes, and I wanted to share that gift.

Love filled that entire space of time, the people and the golden colors of the river. Love consumed us, and we thought time would never change. We drove south and walked along the river bosque. There we found our bower. Do you remember, mi amor? The warmth of the brilliant October sun, the love we shared? The beauty of your bronze body was so new and pure that I couldn't get enough of you. That bower became our place of love, it will always be my home. I return there to be with you.

Abrán finished reading and placed the diary on his lap. Sara sighed, and Lucinda's eyes were filled with tears.

"It's beautiful."

"Yes, it is."

"Such a gifted woman," Sara whispered. She looked at Abrán. So this was her son, the child of that woman. Ah well, life is passed on like that, not to own and possess, but to nurture for a while. The woman had given him the gift of life, but she had given Abrán love all these years. Each had offered what she could, and at that instant Sara felt very satisfied and content.

9 Frank Dominic awoke with a grin on his face. On the roof of his home a roadrunner scattered gravel as it walked across; from the alfalfa field the warbling of a meadowlark echoed. Beside him his wife, Gloria, stirred but did not awaken. Quietly he slipped into his sweatsuit and stepped outside onto the patio. In the east the Sandías were a shadow against the bright sun. Damn, it's good to be alive, he thought.

He did a few warm-up exercises, then began his run, a fast jog on the dirt road along the irrigation ditch. With luck Marisa Martínez would be up doing her morning aerobics. His run took him up the road, and when he came to the mayor's house he often paused to watch. From behind the russian olive trees that lined the ditch road he could get a good look at Her Honor. She was an exciting woman, he thought. His current affair was losing its excitement. He needed a new challenge.

He heard the sound of music and slowed down. The bushes were thick along her back fence. It was not a big place, just three acres, so her backyard was close to the canal road. He stared through the bushes, careful not to get pricked by the thorns of the russian olive. She was by the swimming pool; the tape player on the table blasted "Jailhouse Rock."

She went through her routine of stretches and Frank Dominic admired her beauty. What a waste, he thought. She lives alone, sleeps alone. He watched and regretted that he and the mayor were on opposite sides. Politics often made for strange bedfellows, the saying went, and in this case he could only fantasize about the possibilities. The tape ended and Marisa Martínez disappeared into her house. Dominic returned to the trail and walked, slowly, home. Something in what he had just seen depressed him. He was going to have to beat her in the mayoral race, but what he really wanted was to make love to her. She had gained too much power these past four years; he had made a mistake. He knew he couldn't have her in his corner, and he sure as hell couldn't have her in his bed. She had created her own power base, and she would not be bought. She wasn't as strong as Johnson, but she was the incumbent—she held the balance in the race between him and Johnson.

There was only one way to stop her, and that was to get something dirty on her. Find something, or create something. He made a mental note to call Sonny Baca, a young detective who lived in Los Ranchos. He would put Sonny on her trail, day and night, and see what developed.

Gloria had just stepped out of the shower when Dominic entered the bedroom. "How was your run?" she asked.

He looked at his wife. Though she was an attractive woman, there had never really been any love between them. He asked her to marry him the day after Cynthia had laughed at his proposal. This part of his life had been a lie. He and Gloria were never meant for each other. Time had made them a good team, a business partnership.

Why, he wondered, why? He reached out and touched her, she let slip the towel from around her shoulders. He had never made love to Cynthia, and that had gnawed at his insides all those years.

"Great run," he said, drawing Gloria to him. She was surprised. He threw her hard on the bed and stripped his sweatsuit.

"Frank, you're too rough," she protested as his weight pushed down on her. She knew his desire was not for her, but she let herself be used. There was another woman, or women, and it didn't matter anymore.

He finished quickly, rose, and headed for the bathroom. She remained on the bed, her eyes closed, thinking she would have to bathe again. Frank Dominic was already in the shower, singing happily as his mind worked through the possibility of creating a situation for Her Honor. He needed to see his acupuncturist, he remembered as he toweled, get rid of the knot he felt in his gut.

Maybe the timing wasn't right, he thought. Everything had to fall into place in the next few weeks. The politicians in Santa Fé *had* to give him the legalized gambling bill, that was sure. Today he was testifying before the legislative committee considering the gambling bill; at noon he would dine them at the Pink Adobe. Passage of the bill was going to cost, but they would finally see the way: casino gambling in Alburquerque would create a new mecca. Some of the redneck conservatives were holding back; he knew Marvin House, the cowboy attorney, was going to need a kick in the ass. But he wouldn't kick too hard, because good ole Marv had his eyes on the governor's seat, and four years from now Frank Dominic wanted to be governor.

So he had to play his cards right with the cowboys, promise them plenty of homegrown morality and a cut of the business the casino gambling would bring. Dominic was only running for mayor, but as Alburquerque went, so went the state. A lot of people out in the small towns didn't give a damn for Alburquerque and its problems, but they needed the city. If he could get the gambling bill and urban plan through, it would ripple all over the state. Hell, it was going to change the region!

Dominic had already spent a fortune on the urban plan. Than, just as the City Council was about to approve it, Johnson got into the act. Johnson had enough power in City Hall to swing votes and make things tough. Years of planning to divert the river and build the canals could go down the drain. Bad joke, he thought, but he didn't laugh.

He'd take his plan to the people. Yeah, show them the model of the city and let them decide. He was going to put his mayoral announcement party on cable TV, beam it all over the city. Put up screens all over town and let the people see the Duke City Kid beat Bo Decker. The Duke of Alburquerque packs a power punch, he grinned.

He would also call Sonny Baca. Sonny was one of the best detectives in town, an ex-cop who knew City Hall. He was also young and tough. Two years ago he had gone into Mexico and brought back the men who killed the wife of Peter Schwartz, a big car dealer in town. There had been a bungled abduction, then the FBI got into it and spooked the abductors. They killed Peter's wife and fled into Mexico to hide in the Chihuahua mountains. The FBI lost the trail, or they were too chicken to follow the murderers into the godforsaken mountains. Sonny Baca was hired. He sniffed the murderers out like a determined bloodhound.

There wasn't anything Sonny couldn't find. He could locate the kid's father, and if there was anything dirty on Marisa Martínez, he'd find that, too.

Dominic tapped the steering wheel as he sat at the stop light at Río Grande and Central. This was Old Town, La Plaza Vieja, the center of old Alburquerque. The place was an important tourist attraction with its plaza, the old San Felipe de Neri Church, shops and restaurants, and already the Old Town merchants were complaining about Dominic's plan. They claimed they would lose business if the canal system bypassed them. Hell, he would triple their business. Put one of the casinos in the plaza and bring a canal right to it.

The Old Town merchants were no problem, compared to what he was going to have to do to Johnson. He would paint him as a man who disowned his own daughter, a woman the state had loved, and his own grandson, a talented young boxer who had brought the city fame. Johnson could be dragged through the mud and shown to be a man who didn't take care of his own family. How could he take care of the city?

The Hispanics especially were big on familia. It could be made a crucial issue. And Marisa Martínez wasn't married. People wanted a stable family man as mayor, someone who would take care of their problems. They needed the patrón, the man in charge, the man dispensing favors. Jobs, clean streets, education. Dominic had in his plans a Hotel College where kids coming out of high school could learn to run his hotels and casinos. He could do that for the city; he would be the old-fashioned patrón. He would be the new Duke of Alburquerque.

He smiled, then frowned. Marisa Martínez. She was no dummy when it came to dispensing favors. Her picture was in the paper every day. But she was too good; in four years not a piece of dirt had surfaced. Old Patricio Martínez, her daddy, was a wise politician who watched over his daughter. He often accompanied her at the evening receptions, made sure his daughter preserved an aura of innocence.

Shit, Dominic thought, she has to be screwing someone. The image of Marisa Martínez bouncing in bed bothered him.

He burned rubber down Central when the light changed. He reached for his phone. "Casimiro. Make sure the kid is at the meeting Thursday."

He hung up the phone and hummed, enjoying the ride. This is how the Mexican alcaldes of Old Town must have felt as they rode horseback along this trail toward the New Town built when the railroad arrived. The Mexicano and Indian farmers would come to sell their produce and watch the growth of the Anglo town, pausing to survey the Anglo ways, their horses neighing and pawing the air as the first train roared into the city in April of 1880.

The men who were building New Town were there: Franz Huning, don Santiago Baca, Elias Stover, Judge Hazeldine, Werner. Now, one hundred and twelve years later, he, Francisco Dominic, would create the New Alburquerque.

He remembered that it was a gringo stationmaster who had taken the first 'r' out of Alburquerque. Because he couldn't pronounce the "Albur" he dropped the 'r' in a move that symbolized the emasculation of the Mexican way of life. Frank Dominic knew his history, and he realized that beneath the surface of poverty that affected the Hispanics of the valley lay a tremendous potential. If they had someone like the old patrón to lead them, a new alcalde mayor of the city, they would gather around him and approve the ambitious plan he had for the city.

Politics, the people loved to play at politics. Beneath the surface there was a poetry and charm in the language and lifestyle of life of the old Hispanos. The newcomers didn't see it. Every newcomer who arrived in the city ought to learn Spanish. The language of Cervantes! The language in which the history of the city was written.

The sound of Spanish should fill the streets, like it used to when he was a kid running errands for his father downtown, delivering shined shoes to the big bosses of the city. Everybody spoke Spanish then, Dominic thought, that's how I learned it. It was a normal part of growing up; if you didn't know the language, you didn't do business with Old Town.

I love the language and the history more than some of my Mexican friends, he thought, and as he entered his building he exuded the confidence of a man about to tackle the world.

10 Casimiro had insisted: "Wear a suit, preferably dark." Abrán had enough time to rush home from the gym, shower, and get into his only tie and jacket. "Muy guapo," Sara exclaimed when he stepped into the front room.

"Big meeting," he explained, kissed her, and hurried out. Casimiro had said it was important, and for Abrán that meant Dominic had possibly found something. He felt excited, and was rethinking some of the reservations he and Lucinda had had about Dominic.

Abrán wasn't prepared for the turmoil of television crews and newspaper reporters that flocked around him when he walked into Dominic's building. The word had gotten out; the mayor was meeting with Frank Dominic, and Abrán González, the city's former Golden Gloves champion, was to be there.

"Mr. González," a reporter called, "is it true you're turning pro? Does Frank Dominic own you?"

"Have you met Bo Decker?"

"What kind of shape are you in?"

"Why did you leave Golden Gloves?"

Casimiro appeared from out of the crowd and rescued him. "Don't say anything to the press," he said as he led him into a large meeting room. "I received the doctor's report. They say you're in great shape. Sánchez already has you working out, I see."

"I'm running and hitting the bag," Abrán answered.

The large room they entered was packed. At least a hundred people, Abrán figured, but definitely the most influential leaders of the community were present. At the front of the small auditorium stood a large table covered with a sheet. The excitement in the room was high.

"Businessmen and politicians," Casimiro whispered as he led Abrán to a front-row seat. "These men run the city."

Abrán looked around. The people in the room were strangers to him. Most of the audience was male; women were not yet power brokers in the city.

Abrán recognized Ben Chávez sitting in the back of the room. Their eyes met, Abrán waved.

"Kid," Dominic welcomed him at the front of the room. "Glad you could make it. Look," he whispered, "I wanted you to be here to see the show. These people are eager to meet you. I especially want you to meet the mayor. Cynthia did a little politicking for Her Honor when she ran—you know, one of those women's groups. Have a seat, enjoy the show."

Abrán sat and Dominic turned his attention to his guests, personally greeting each person who entered.

Marisa Martínez knew my mother, Abrán thought. He had done a lot of reading in newspaper files at the public library downtown, and he remembered the articles that mentioned Cynthia and Marisa. Maybe Marisa would know something new about his mother.

Abrán heard a stir at the back of the room; he turned to see the mayor enter. Three aides accompanied her. The leaders from the Hispanic Chamber of Commerce had been awaiting her arrival and now they pressed forward to greet her.

Abrán was struck by her beauty. She was tall, with dark hair, flashing eyes, high cheekbones, a clear tan skin, and a warm smile. She had a flair for dress, for meeting men on their territory, and the poise to make them feel at ease. Even surrounded by friends, she seemed to take in the room and note who was there. She glanced through the crowd and saw Abrán, their eyes met, and she smiled. Abrán smiled back.

He could see why men gravitated toward her. She was very attractive, and she had the guts to take on issues. Her fault was, the morning paper kept repeating, that she was too pretty to succeed. The paper had been opposed to Marisa Martínez from the beginning; compliments on her beauty were backhanded slaps. The paper blamed her for the economic slump; it wanted a business leader who could turn the economy around. It was obvious the paper meant Walter Johnson.

Dominic stepped forward and greeted the mayor.

"Marisa, so glad you could come," he smiled.

"How's it going, Frank," she smiled back. "Still jogging?"

Dominic cleared his throat. "Every day. You know everyone here. We have a seat in the front row for you, and someone I want you to meet."

Abrán watched Marisa walk toward him.

"Abrán González," Dominic said. "Her Honor, the mayor."

"Marisa," she said and took Abrán's hand.

"Glad to meet you," he said. Her handshake was firm, warm, but the real communication was in her eyes. Abrán felt a natural attraction to the woman. The pictures in the papers didn't do her justice, he thought.

"Abrán is Cynthia Johnson's son," Dominic said.

Marisa nodded. "I'm sorry about your mother," she said. "She was a great woman, a treasure, not just for her artwork, but because she cared for people. I wouldn't be in office if it weren't for her."

"She helped?"

"Helped! She was one of my key organizers! She knew we needed a change in the city," Marisa said and glanced at Dominic. "She did a painting for my campaign, her only political scene."

"I'd like to see it," Abrán said.

"Come this afternoon," Marisa invited him. "Today is my doing-paperwork-at-home afternoon. I'd love to show it to you. I idolized your mother." She smiled and handed him her card. Her eyes lingered on Abrán. She had been attracted to him when she saw him at the funeral home, but she had thought it was pity. Pity that Cynthia had never mentioned her son. But looking at him now she knew she had been wrong. He was a handsome, rugged young man with a silent charm, and a sincerity she did not often see around City Hall.

"I've put him under contract," Dominic grinned.

"You're turning pro?" she asked. "Why?"

"Not pro, just one fight for Mr. Dominic," Abrán explained.

"I see," Marisa smiled. So Frank had scored early, hired Abrán to do a fight. With his name, it could translate into a lot of political mileage.

She faced Dominic. "All right, Frank, we're all busy. Get this show on the road." The audience laughed. She knew how to goad Dominic.

"Any newspeople in here?" she asked. Casimiro shook his head. None had been allowed in. She glanced around the room and saw Ben Chávez. What the hell was he doing here, she wondered. Ben looked up from his notes and smiled at her.

"So this is off the record," she said. "I hear Frank wants to irrigate his downtown property by changing the course of the river. Frank, we have acequias for the farmland, not for your buildings." The crowd laughed openly. She was sparring with Dominic and landing the first blows.

A flicker of irritation crossed Dominic's face. He had a lot of explaining to do; Marisa Martínez sure as hell wasn't going to hand him the election. And right now, the Japanese deal had put her a few steps ahead.

Reading the crowd's mind Marisa jabbed again. "We don't want to become the laughingstock of the region, Frank. You know we're on the verge of getting Morino's high-tech plant to settle here. If you blow it, we'll hold you responsible."

Her use of the collective 'we' put Dominic on the defensive. Few people could do that and get away with it. Dominic hadn't uttered a word yet, and she had already taken him to task. He motioned for her to take a seat. She shrugged and sat next to Abrán.

"Her Honor is impatient today," Dominic grinned and turned to the audience. "Thank you for joining us, Your Honor, and welcome, ladies and gentlemen. I was going to start by introducing Her Honor, but she's taken care of that."

The men in the audience smiled. Now it was Frank's turn, and they knew he could be deadly.

"You all know each other," Dominic continued, "but I would like to take a moment to introduce a young man some of you know well. Abrán González, Golden Gloves champion a few years ago. The best we ever had."

He motioned for Abrán to stand and when he did the audience applauded.

"Abrán is the son of someone we all knew, Cynthia Johnson."

A murmur swept across the audience. The artistic activities of Cynthia Johnson were well known in the city, so was the split with her father, but never had there been mention of a son. That was Walter Johnson's grandson standing at Dominic's side!

"He's playing politics," Marisa whispered to Abrán as he sat back down. He nodded. Was she warning him to watch out?

"Off the record," Dominic smiled, pleased with the ripple he had created. "Strictly off the record.

"Now, all of you know I'm running, and you know Her Honor is running. I want to be mayor because I love this city. I want to see it grow, I want something new and exciting to happen here. I want to turn the economy around and have this city prosper like no other city in the Southwest. We know the Japanese microchip plant is not our answer. It's peanuts compared to what I have to offer."

The room grew quiet. The plant could bring in billions, enough work for a thousand people to start, according to the mayor's plan. Nothing this big had come to the city since Sandia Labs. It could be the cornerstone of the mayor's term in office, and if she could capture it, she would be governor material. The crowd didn't think it was peanuts.

"First, this legislative session we are going to get a gambling bill through Santa Fé, right Marv?" Dominic looked at Marvin House, the state senator. He squirmed, nodded, and looked nervously at Manny Arroyo, the majority leader. Oh God, Arroyo's worried expression said, it's going to take one hell of a sonofabitching coalition to put this together.

"Off-track betting and a new sports arena," Dominic continued. "A major league football team."

Half the audience nodded eagerly. They had heard the rumor that Dominic was vying for the Dallas Cowboys. The other half shook their heads. They had heard political promises before; they had come for something concrete.

"A super stadium, a lottery, the whole enchilada," Dominic concluded. "I promise you, it can be done."

A buzz swept the room. A gambling bill coming out of Santa Fé was news in a state that allowed only bingo games, and those only on Indian reservations.

"The real test of the gambling bill is how we use it," Dominic said. "Are we prepared to go in with a plan of action which immediately takes advantage of the resources gambling can bring in?" He looked at the mayor and smiled. She had opposed legalized gambling during the last legislative session. The room grew silent again.

A lot of the conservative businessmen in the room opposed gambling. Their jaws tightened, they crossed their arms, and sat back in a gesture that said, show me.

"We have been working on a model of the El Dorado plan. This is a preview; you're the first to see it," Dominic gloated. "You all know Pete Lupkens. Pete, do the honors."

Pete Lupkens, one of the most respected architects in the city, stood up. He motioned and an assistant removed the cover from the scale model at the front of the room. The audience leaned forward, and what they saw made them gasp.

The pattern of the city was clear, but there were new buildings rising where none now existed. Throughout the city ran the canal system, paths of blue. The Albuquerque of the year 2000. A desert Venice with beltways of green, ponds, and small lakes, all interconnected by the waterways that crisscrossed the downtown area. Each businessman looked for his office or shop. To be on a canal meant survival.

Dominic smiled. He saw the looks on their faces and knew he had them.

Lupkens began the explanation. "Designing the city that Mr. Dominic envisions has been one of the most exciting highlights of my career. Not a single Southwest city, to my knowledge, has been designed with so much care. At the core of the model is the diversion of the river. The dam to divert the water will be built at Alameda. We pump the water into the main canal, which follows the railroad tracks. When it reaches the downtown area we let it flow down the main canals into the lakes and ponds. Once the water stabilizes we'll be pumping only enough water to keep the flow clean and fresh. After it's been through our canals it empties into the river again—"

"What's that going to do to the valley farmland, Frank?" Marisa Martínez asked. "And the water table?"

Frank Dominic grinned again. "The only cash crop the Alburquerque valley area has been growing for the past twenty years is alfalfa. Alfalfa to feed horses, and it's a very small cash crop at that! You know it and I know it! In short, agriculture in the city valley area is a thing of the past. Let's use the water to build this concept! Tourists coming to gamble are our new industry. We're going to pass out estimates of income which can be generated, and you'll see that in the first five years the annual income to the city will quadruple."

A surge of excitement passed through the room. Dominic didn't have to say another word. They could see the city in front of them, and it didn't take much imagination to see the profit in the water theme. Here was something that would generate tourism. Dominic had hit on a gold mine.

Pete Lupkens continued. "Once we get the canal structure in, we build the sports stadium. This giant complex here," he pointed, "is completely covered with a dome of this new material I'll explain in a moment. The racetracks line this end, the hotels and casinos are in the middle. The kiddy park occupies this end. The adults can check in, drop off the kids, gamble all day, and not see them until evening."

"We want them to have a good time here, not in Santa Fé," Dominic reminded them.

The men chuckled. Dominic crossed his arms; he felt very satisfied. The crowd had taken the bait, and was eating out of his hand. He looked at Marisa Martínez and saw her complexion had changed. She looked pale, her lips drawn.

"It's all there, down to the last detail," Dominic said triumphantly. "Five years of planning. And everything is in the computer. A child could build it."

Pete Lupkens nodded. "It's an ambitious project, gentlemen. I've never seen one like it."

Marisa Martínez rose to face Dominic. "Where in the hell are you going to get the water, Frank?"

"Río Grande's too thick to drink and to thin to plow," a voice in the crowd added. The men turned to see Manuel Armijo rise. The old, enfeebled politician was one of the last patrónes of the city. The man who had adopted Vera and who had been the padrino at her marriage to Walter Johnson knew the political temperament of the city better than anyone. He was invited to most political events as a matter of courtesy.

"It's a beautiful plan," don Manuel said, his solid frame quaking as he spoke, his stained teeth chewing on a cigar stub. "All the nice, fresh water, the people on the little boats, ah, it's like heaven," he chuckled. "But Frank, there is one problem. The water rights of the Río Grande Basin are sold or tied up in court fights 'til hell freezes. Water rights, Frank, you can't get the water rights."

The bubble burst, the sharp realism returned. Don Manuel was right.

"What little water there is belongs to the pueblos and the Hispanic villages of the norte, and to Texas, and on and on. Frank, you can build a dream on the agua, the blood of the valley, but you can't buy the blood."

Don Manuel finished and sat. The crowd turned back to Dominic to see how he would react. Water rights in New Mexico and in the Southwest were tied up in so many court suits and adjudications that it was impossible to think the scheme would work.

The public utility president rose. "He's right, Frank. I wish I could say I believed in this, God knows the city needs a shot in the arm. A beautiful plan, but you can't get the water." He shook his head sadly.

Marisa Martínez stood and turned to the crowd. "Looks like we're wasting our time, ladies and gentlemen. Frank built the dam but forgot there wasn't water to go with it. If you'll excuse me, folks, I'm a busy woman. I've got a Japanese gentleman waiting who wants to bring real industry to Albuquerque."

"Wait," Dominic motioned. "If you leave now you'll miss the best part." He smiled a disarming smile they all knew well. The mayor looked at her aides, shrugged, and sat. The quiet returned.

"There's water," Dominic smiled. "We wouldn't be wasting our time on the El Dorado project if there wasn't. There's enough water up in the San Juan to flood this valley. We're just not using it properly. If we can bring the San Juan to Cochití Dam, we tap the lake. That new water is what we buy. Then we empty it back into the Río Grande. I assure you, the water we owe Texas under the old covenant will be delivered. We're going to use the water, not consume it."

"But you can't get that much water into Cochití Lake without tapping someone's water rights and being sued," don Manuel said. "The Indian pueblos are not going to let you take one drop."

The men nodded. Water and the right to use it were the most crucial problems for development. The mountains of the north, the high arid plateau, and the desert to the south all depended on the meager Río Grande for existence.

"The pueblos will sell," Dominic said. "We're wrapping up negotiations right now." He turned to Marisa Martínez and smiled. "I have my Japanese connections, too," he smiled. "We have a commitment from a Japanese bank to provide a major part of the financing in exchange for land to build factories, cheap labor, and a new Las Vegas where they can spend their money. The pueblos are dying and the Hispanic villages up north are withering away. This is the last chance they have to revitalize themselves. We are promising each pueblo and each land-grant village a percentage of the casinos right off the top. They also get the first shot at jobs in the casinos."

He paused; another murmur swept through the audience.

"They want to join us," Dominic continued, turning again to Marisa Martínez. "Your Honor, your plan calls for one Japanese plant, I'm not talking about one plant, but dozens. A new silicone valley from Taos to Alburquerque! And the center is here!" He turned and pointed at the scale model.

The silence returned. He was persuasive. Had Frank Dominic finally found a way to buy water rights?

Dominic nodded and two assistants entered with large plastic shells that they placed over parts of the model so the geodesic bubbles enclosed the casino area.

"Pete," Dominic said.

Pete Lupkens cleared his throat. "The bubbles are constructed of a new material which Sandia Labs has been working on for years. . . ."

The men glanced at Steve Rodney, the Sandia Labs representative. He nodded.

"Call it a plastic, it's really a new type of membrane. So elastic and durable it can quite easily cover large areas. With it we can create a controlled environment. The membrane breathes; it actually cools and heats the air within. In the summer a dye circulates in the cells of the membrane and shields out the sun, in winter the dye is removed and the sunlight heats the air. And it's cheap. The cost is to erect the frame of the dome, but the membrane is so light that weight is no problem. It's a proven science," he added. "We can control the color of the light within the Doradosphere, and thus control the mood of the crowd.

With the right colors you can actually get people to gamble more, spend more money."

The audience chuckled, and Dominic smiled. He knew they were impressed.

"Imagine tourists strolling through our streets in the dead of winter or during spring windstorms," Dominic smiled. "The fresh water is constant, the boats take them from casino to casino, or to the art center if that's their preference. The air is sweet, the kids are at playworld. It's all within our grasp, gentlemen."

No one spoke. The men looked at the model, then at Lupkens. They glanced at the Sandia Lab representative. It sounded good, too good.

"The water, Frank?" Marisa spoke again.

Abrán glanced at her and saw how cold her expression had become. Thin lines had appeared around her eyes and the edges of her lips. Abrán wished he could touch her and in some way alleviate the anxiety on her face. Frank Dominic was playing with the crowd like a cat plays with a mouse. And he was still holding something up his sleeve. Abrán realized at that moment that Marisa's political career was at stake. Frank Dominic was closing in.

"The only way to handle the water rights, and ensure water for the future, is to privatize it," Dominic said.

There was a stir in the room.

Dominic turned and nodded at his attorneys. Al Romero stood and faced the audience.

Al Romero came from a well-known New Mexican family, had a degree from Harvard Law School, and had built his reputation, and fortune, by becoming one of a handful of attorneys in the Southwest who specialized in water-rights law. Even the commissioner for public lands called on Al for consultation when lawsuits arose over water, and in New Mexico that was a constant.

Al cleared his throat. "Mr. Dominic has put it in a nutshell. The only way to own enough water rights for a project this size is to do what he has done—form a corporation and buy the water rights."

The crowd leaned forward. Buy the water rights? Buy the Río

Grande Basin? This was Al Romero talking; his father had distinguished himself in Washington. The elder Romero had served with Senator Dennis Chávez, then gone on to serve as ambassador in the foreign service. Al could be trusted, but did he know what the hell he was talking about?

"Government agencies, even the City of Albuquerque, can't buy or control enough rights without the constant legal suits. The pueblos are on the warpath, as all of you know, to carve out all they can get as first-in-place users. The way to go was to form a corporation and deal with anyone who had water to sell. Treat water as a commodity. People understand that. One has to get past the emotional issue. If it's a commodity, then it's for sale. The Hispanic villages and the Indian pueblos will sell what they're not using."

The audience hung on every word. Abrán felt Marisa's hand on his arm. She breathed softly, almost a sigh. Something had gone out of her; she seemed vulnerable. Abrán glanced at her and then at Dominic, who was staring at her, looking for signs of surrender. The minute he saw her sag, he smiled.

"We formed Río Grande Entertainment and it has done the major negotiating. Every pueblo along the river has a contract in hand; they sell their water and they get the percentage Mr. Dominic has already mentioned. I think everyone agrees that the days of the small farmers along the northern Río Grande are a thing of the past. The Indians can retain enough water to raise a few crops, but it's really in their long-term interest to join the RGE plan."

The Hispanics in the audience winced. To give up the water rights of the Hispanic land grants was unthinkable, the Indians selling their water was just as preposterous. Yet Dominic was convinced they all would sell.

"The initial line of credit comes from New York banks," Al Romero continued. "It is, let us say, substantial. And that, of course, is backed by the Tokyo banks. The initial fees go to the Indians when they sign, but what they really get is participation. Frank has been very generous to the Indians, and quite frankly, that's why I know the effort will succeed. Are there any questions?"

"You have enough water," someone mumbled weakly.

Dominic jumped up. "We not only have enough water, we're ready to have a groundbreaking, as soon as I'm mayor," he quipped. Many in the audience nodded their approval. "I want to thank all of you for coming, and to thank the present mayor for giving of her time today," he said turning to Marisa. "We're going to build a new city, gentlemen, the likes of which has not been seen before in this land of enchantment. A new El Dorado, the kind of place the first Spanish conquistadores only dreamed of finding. In the meantime, I would appreciate your confidence. All this will be made public at my announcement."

He turned to face Marisa. She gathered her composure and rose quickly.

"It's ambitious, Frank, but then you always were an ambitious man," she said, a tone of cynicism lingering in the air for all to hear. Dominic smiled and made a slight bow.

"Maybe too ambitious," she repeated the warning. "If it screws up, it's going to be a royal screw. We could be made the laughingstock of the nation, and we don't need that. Not now. In the meantime, I want your group to come in as soon as possible and meet with the city attorneys so we can review the entire project."

Without awaiting an answer she turned to leave, pausing in front of Abrán. "I hope you can come this afternoon," she whispered. Then she was off, her aides trailing behind her.

The room was suddenly clamorous as the men descended on Dominic, congratulating him and patting him on the back.

"This is the biggest, gol-damn project anyone has ever conceived."

"Dammit, man, forget wanting to be mayor, you ought to be running for governor."

"You got my support, Frank. A hundred percent."

The party was over, and an ebullient Frank Dominic bathed in the adulation. Abrán skirted the press of people and caught up with Ben Chávez at the door.

"Mr. Chávez," he greeted the writer.

"Call me Ben," he smiled. He looked into the young man's face. It was Cynthia's face, he should have recognized it long ago. He felt again the wrenching of the afternoon when Dominic told him Abrán was Cynthia's son.

He had not slept well since that day. The novel sparked by Cynthia's death had come pouring out; he was writing day and night, consumed by Cynthia's story. Could he break the vow he had made to Cynthia and greet Abrán as his son? Now as he looked into Abrán's eyes, he recognized himself.

"¿Cómo estás?" he managed to say, and not knowing what else to do, or fearing voice would break, he reached out and embraced Abrán.

"Bien," Abrán answered. He didn't understand the warmth of the man he had met only once.

Ben stood back and looked at him, somewhat embarrassed by the show of emotion. Whatever he felt would have to remain a secret.

"You're looking good," Ben said.

"Started training," Abrán answered.

"That's what I heard."

Ben Chávez looked at the crowd pressed around Dominic and shuddered. "Come on, let's get out of here. I can't stomach Mr. Dominic when it's time to kiss his ring." He took Abrán's arm and they walked through the lobby and out into the street. "We can have a drink at La Posada."

"I'm sorry, I can't. But I'll walk with you."

"Good," Ben smiled. "What did you think of the plan?"

"Ambitious."

"That's Frank Dominic in a word. Ambitious. He's got everything he needs, but he wants more. You be careful with him."

Abrán nodded. That was another warning about Dominic.

"Did you know he wants to be the Duke of Alburquerque?" Ben said as they walked down the sidewalk toward the hotel.

"I've heard some of the people who work for him refer to him as Duke. Thought it was just a nickname."

"No, he's serious. Frank Dominic has hired every genealogist to trace his ancestry back to that Duke. He has the coat of arms of the Duke hanging in his office."

"I've seen it," Abrán said.

"And embossed on his stationery, the side of his car, his necktie, his key ring, etcetera. He's into royalty."

"Can he build the canal system?" Abrán asked.

"Probably not."

"It sounds too big."

"It is," Ben said and stopped. He looked at Abrán and remembered the times he, as a young man, walked the streets of the city. He knew them well. Now he wondered if Abrán knew how to survive in them.

"There's no water," Ben said, "but Dominic's not listening."

"He seems to think the Indian pueblos will sell."

Ben shrugged. "If they do, the way of life they hold sacred will be sacrificed. Once they can't irrigate the fields of maíz, they'll die. Then they'll have to come into Dominic's city to work for minimum wages, make hotel beds, and hold Indian dances in the casinos for the tourists. The minute you become a tourist commodity, you die."

Abrán looked at Ben Chávez. Would it be that bad? he wondered, and why was Ben involved with Frank Dominic if he feared his power?

"What can be done?" he asked.

"It's a rule of this land: la gallina de arriba se caga en la gallina de abajo. Those at the bottom always seem to catch the caca," Ben Chávez said. "We know that, but we forget when people like Dominic hold out their bucks. He offers everybody something."

"Why were you there today?" Abrán asked.

"I'm working on a book," Ben answered. "This is research. Now you have to answer the same question: why were *you* there?"

Abrán felt the jab. Whether Ben Chávez intended the insult or not, he felt it.

I made a deal with Dominic, same as thousands of others have done before or will do in the future, Abrán thought. He has something I need and I took the offer. He realized that his bargain with Dominic was no different from the deals the Indian pueblos would make.

"I—" Abrán stuttered, but Ben Chávez had turned and was walking away, waving, "Cuídate, Abrán. Cuídate."

Be careful. Be careful.

11 Abrán worked out at the gym the rest of the afternoon, but his mind kept drifting to Marisa's invitation. He wanted to see the painting she had, and he wanted to learn more about the mayor's relationship to Cynthia. And, he finally admitted to himself as he showered after his workout, he was intrigued by Her Honor.

"You're slow today," Rudy Sánchez, his trainer, had complained. "Gotta get your mind on the work."

Sánchez was right. Abrán knew Lucinda was out shopping for the planned trip home, and still undecided about Marisa's invitation, he headed to the Frontier restaurant where Joe sometimes had his afternoon coffee. Talking to Joe often helped clarify things.

Luckily, Joe was there. He waved and Abrán grabbed a cup of coffee, then joined his friend at the window booth. Outside, the traffic on Central was heavy, the students thronged by as the last weeks of classes drove them into near-panic.

"So how's it going," Joe greeted him. "Any news?"

Abrán told Joe about the meeting at Dominic's. Joe listened intently. "It won't be the first time someone tries to take pueblo water," he said when Abrán finished. "The pueblos depend on the water. In

Nambé or Jémez, it's all under adjudication. Dominic can't touch pueblo water."

"He promises to cut them in for a share of the pie," Abrán said.

"Some of the políticos in Santa Fé can be bought," Joe cursed, "all it takes is money. But the pueblos won't sell," he insisted. "No way."

"According to Dominic, you don't have a choice, Joe. You start with bingo and wind up selling your water rights; it's a natural progression. You leave the land, don't farm, what's the use of water? That's the way Dominic thinks, and he convinces people."

"We won't sell!" Joe slammed his fist on the table. "Dominic's crazy!"

"Joe, didn't your primos up in Cochití lease some of their land? Leasing mother earth, Joe, and after that selling the water comes naturally. One step at a time."

"Not if I can help it!"

"What are you going to do? Take on the Dominic machine? Take on the development the state wants? The businessmen are dreaming of Japanese plants, rich Arabs, Hong Kong investors, anybody! The men there swallowed it hook, line, and sinker."

"A lot of people promise the pueblos a get-rich scheme, and not a one has worked," Joe shook his head.

Abrán grew quiet. He listened to the song on the jukebox, a Mexican ballad, the story of a man who ran a car full of marijuana up from Mexico. La movida, the hustle of life. Dominic knew about movidas; he was going to hustle the city. Hustle everyone.

"How can you stop it, Joe? He's probably dealing with the pueblo council right now. Maybe the deal's already made."

Joe frowned. Yeah, maybe the deal had already been made. He'd been away from home too long. Maybe it was time to get back to the pueblo and find out what was really going on. He was responsible if the council sold the water.

As they sat in silence and sipped their coffee, Abrán thought of Marisa. Her eyes spoke to him, light brown, deep.

Marisa Martínez was a tough woman, but the tone of her voice had grown soft when she invited him to view the painting. He felt excited when he thought of her. Suddenly he wanted to see her; he decided to go. Although he couldn't explain the urge, the resolution made him feel at ease. He glanced at his watch, and then noticed Joe's troubled look.

"Those guys mean business," Abrán said.

"That fucking Dominic ain't gonna take my water," Joe grumbled. "Not if I can help it."

"Dominic deals with the council," Abrán repeated, "and the council has its own lawyers."

"¡Tío tacos!" Joe swore. "Bad apples!"

Abrán shrugged. "I don't like it either, Joe, but that's who's cutting the deals. If you don't fight the problem, you're part of the problem."

He pulled the card Marisa had given him from his shirt pocket. On Río Grande, he could be there in fifteen minutes.

"Yeah, I'm part of the problem," Joe nodded.

"Dominic figures if you leave the land, you don't need water. So he makes a deal, the pueblo attorneys agree, then it's gone forever."

"And I'm sitting here reading philosophy books," Joe gritted his teeth. "Dreaming of law school. I gotta go," he said.

"Where?" Abrán asked.

"Home," Joe answered, getting up.

"We'll come and see you," Abrán said, silently relieved by his friend's decision.

He watched Joe leave, and for awhile he sat looking out the window at the variety of people moving up and down the sidewalk. Maybe something good would come out of this. If Joe was angry enough to return to the pueblo, the battle wasn't yet lost, it was just beginning. He glanced at his watch. Five. He went to the phone and dialed.

Marisa answered, "I'm expecting you. The swimming pool was just filled. I'll fix a pitcher of margaritas. My recipe. Please come."

"Be right over," he said and hung up the phone. He felt a blast of excitement as he hopped in his car. Something deep inside was drawing him toward the woman, and he let the urge take him.

Abrán hummed as he drove west on Central and then north on Río Grande. He thought of Dominic's grand plan. The man was bent on a wild scheme, all right. A canal system that diverted the river. Alburquerque would become like the old Aztec capital of Tenochtitlán, the precolumbian Mexico City. He wondered if the Aztecs gambled, or if the ball games they played caused as much grief as Dominic's game would bring. He read somewhere that the Aztecs played a prototype of basketball, and the losers of the game were sacrificed to the gods. Duke City Dominic, the city's new chief priest, would sacrifice anyone.

As Abrán pulled up to the mayor's house he saw that Her Honor's mailbox was stenciled with her name: Marisa Martínez. He knew she wasn't married, but other than that he realized he knew very little about her. He walked up her graveled driveway. He was a man from the barrio who only a few weeks ago knew next to nothing about the politics of the city, and now he was knocking on the mayor's door. There was some irony in that, and it made him smile.

Marisa's invitation was like Dominic's deal—it was drawing him out of the shell in which he lived. The two years in Los Angeles had taught him just how protective Sara had been. If Cynthia's letter had changed his life, then let change come. He suddenly felt strong and exuberant about the challenges that had come into his life. Muy macho.

"Tú eres tú," doña Tules had said. That's why he made the deal with Dominic; he wanted to find out who he was. And who knows what Marisa had to offer. Of one thing he was sure: it wasn't just a look at the painting.

The sun was setting, flooding the valley with its radiant light as he knocked on the door, which was ajar. "Hello," he called. "Come in," Marisa's voice answered, "I'm in the back."

He stepped inside, shut the door, and walked into the living area. So this is how the other half lives, he thought. The room was tastefully decorated. The adobe walls wore a soft white coat, a beehive fireplace filled one corner, and warm Navajo blankets were spread on the red brick floor.

"In the patio," Marisa called.

He walked across the room and through the plate glass door that led into the patio. Beyond the pool and patio lay a large lawn and beyond that a tall hedge of wild russian olive trees. Behind the silver-gray of the hedge lay the shimmering green of the river bosque, a stunning frame for the afternoon sunlight that clothed the mountain. The Sandías were on the brink of turning mauve. Overhead a bank of clouds wore a luster of pale apricot.

"I had just started mixing my special potion," Marisa smiled and took his hand. "Welcome. I'm glad you came."

He felt the light and the landscape infused with warmth and softness, the same softness in her voice and eyes. Her lips were a soft red.

"Can I help?" he offered.

"Only to try one," she answered. "This is a special recipe. In the family for years."

The excitement Abrán had felt all afternoon mounted. He shivered when Marisa handed him a glass. She had already been in the pool, and she wore a terry cloth robe over her swimsuit. The slant of light shone on her wet, black hair, as shiny as raven feathers. He took the glass and clinked it against hers.

"Salud. I'm glad you're here," she said. "Look at that sunset." She turned to face the mountain, and as she did, her hand brushed his arm. "Isn't it magnificent? And it's better when it's shared."

He sipped the margarita, tasted the faint touch of salt, the lime juice, the swift warmth of the tequila.

"Normally I work late, so I miss the sunsets. But today is special."

"It's a great view," he smiled.

She looked at him. She had wanted to know him better the moment she had met him, not just because he was Cynthia's son, but because she was lonely. She met a lot of men in her work, some made propositions, very few were tempting. Abrán had awakened a need she had not indulged for a long time. She wanted to make love to the man, and have him make love to her.

"You live alone?" he said.

"Yes. I was married when I was in law school, but it was a disaster. Since then I've put my energy into work."

They stood looking at each other, each feeling the strong attraction that had drawn them together. She took his hand and felt an arousal she hadn't experienced in a long time.

"It's no fun living sola," she said, surprising herself by admitting her loneliness. Her few intimate friends kidded her and said she lived a nun's life. The presence of Abrán, the chemistry between them, told her that was about to change.

"To us," she said. "And the beautiful sunset," she added as she led him to the lounge chairs at the edge of the pool. The mountain was reflected in the softly lapping water, a mauve dappled with blue.

"Sunsets are to be shared," she said.

"What did you think about the meeting this morning?" he asked.

"Dominic is going to ruin this city, I know it in my bones. He only cares for himself." Her voice rose. "I've been working hard to land the Japanese firm, and just when that's about to become a reality, along come the elections and Dominic's crazy plan. The Japs are smart, they're going to stall. We might lose everything."

"And the election?"

"I've enjoyed being mayor. I have a lot of ideas. And I work at it twenty-four hours a day. I have no choice but to fight him. And you?"

Abrán shrugged and sipped his drink. The tension was slowly easing out of his shoulders. Being with Marisa was easy. He looked at her and smiled. Her gaze was open and honest, and she returned his smile. A silent exchange of attraction and need flowed between them.

"I made a deal with Dominic because he knew my mother. He went to school with her, knew her friends. I only found out about her a week ago. . . ."

"That's what I gathered. So not even Dominic knew about you?"

"No, I was a secret 'til the night my mother died."

"When I ran for office she got involved in my campaign. She liked the idea of a woman running for mayor. She didn't like the parties and rallies that are part of the process; she was a loner, but she turned the whole campaign around. She liked people, and they responded to her. We became good friends. Then I was in office and busy. I lost track of her. A few months ago I learned she had cancer. I went to see her. We talked. I'm sorry we had lost track of each other. She was a beautiful person."

"That's what I'm finding out. I made a deal to box for Dominic because he can find my father, find his name, whatever."

"He promised that?" she exclaimed. "He's going to use your name to get mileage out of Cynthia's name. That's Frank Dominic for you, he doesn't miss a chance."

"That's what I'm finding out."

She reached up and touched his cheek, the tips of her fingers warm and sensual. She smiled. "Enough politics. I invited you to get to know you, to relax. . . ."

"And to see the painting."

"We can do that later. It's hanging in my bedroom," she smiled. "Let's swim. I've been in. The water's cold, but invigorating."

She finished her drink and stood. Quickly she slipped off her robe. She wore a two-piece swimsuit that revealed the beauty of her full figure.

"Come on," she invited him, stepping close to him.

"I didn't bring my trunks."

"You don't need trunks," she said, putting her arms around him and kissing him. Her lips were warm, her breath sweet. "I've wanted to do that all day," she smiled, then dove into the water. Her dive shattered the mauve sheen on the water. He saw her emerge midway across the pool where, looking him in the eyes, she discarded her swimsuit. She then turned and stroked strongly to the other end of the pool.

"Come on in. It's great," she called.

He stripped quickly, stood poised on the edge of the pool for a moment, the light of the fading sun shining on his muscular body, then dove. He surfaced and swam quickly to her. She opened her arms to him.

They kissed, a passionate kiss that dissolved any remaining tension they felt. "I want you," she said. "From the time I saw you at Cynthia's service, I wanted you."

"And I want you," he responded. He helped her out of the pool and onto an air mattress.

"I thought at first I was just feeling sorry for you. . . ."

"Why?"

"You looked so sad. So handsome, but sad. I wanted to know why Cynthia never said anything about you."

She held him tight, kissed him again, and felt the warmth of his kisses and body. He responded, his own need overwhelming him.

She moaned and he picked her up and carried her into the house.

In the grove of trees by the fence, Sonny Baca relaxed after watching them disappear into the house. "Damn," he whistled, Her Honor was a fine-looking woman. What the hell does the kid have that I don't? he wondered. Some men are just born lucky.

He laid aside his camera with the telescopic lens and lit a cigarette. He was trying to quit smoking, but moments like this just called for a smoke.

He had taken a lot of clandestine photos in his life, grubby sex shots in dingy motel rooms or of people writhing in the backseats of cars. He thought he was immune, burned out by the quickies of people who got caught playing around and who would settle out of court when his photos were presented in pretrial negotiations. He was a pro, used to all the games people played, but the beauty he had just witnessed told him this case was different.

"Damn," he repeated to himself. Even through the lens of the camera he could feel her passion. And the kid? A handsome stud, all right. But Marisa Martínez' future in politics was in real trouble as soon as he delivered the film to Dominic.

He took another drag of his cigarette and looked at Marisa's house. They wouldn't be coming out again. And he had enough to create a lot of problems for the woman. That's what it was going to be used for, wasn't it? That's what it was always used for. For a moment he thought he should get rid of the film, expose it, throw it in the ditch, let the water dissolve the images of the lovers.

He weighed the thought a moment then shook his head. No, it was his job, he was a professional detective, and he had been hired to do a job.

Let people fuck who they want to fuck, he thought angrily as he turned to leave. He was only doing his job.

12 Frank Dominic propped his feet on his desk and opened the sealed envelope. Fresh, glossy prints slid out and tumbled into his lap, revealing in black and white, Her Honor, the mayor, and Abrán. Dominic's breath caught. His feet dropped to the floor and he leaned forward to study the prints.

"Oh, these are good, they are good," he smacked his lips. "Oh, Lord, these are good."

The prints were in muted light, an artistic rendering of the curves of Marisa Martínez. Damn, it was better than anything he had expected.

"Almost too good," he thought. Art-show quality, he laughed. The city would love to hang these in the Albuquerque Museum. He buzzed his secretary. "Call Sonny Baca."

Yeah, Her Honor in a nude exhibition at the museum. That would cost her the election. When she found out he had the photos in his possession, she would come begging.

In a moment Sonny's voice was on the speaker phone, the husky voice of a man who had not slept all night.

"Yeah?"

"I got the pictures."

"Good, huh."

"Beautiful."

"I had good material." Sonny laughed. "I guess I've fallen for the woman. I almost didn't send them to you."

"They're good," Dominic said as he flipped through the photos again. "You did your job."

"Yeah, and you lost my vote, Frank."

"Your check's in the mail," Dominic said abruptly and flipped the phone off. Sonofabitch! What the hell did he mean, lost my vote. He dropped the photos on his desk and stood, anger written on his face.

The kid had scored, and he didn't deserve her. The woman had class, a kind of quality that went deeper than her physical beauty—she had a nobility. With both the Spanish and Mexican blood in her ancestry, she could probably trace part of her history all the way back to the conquistadores. Where in the hell had he been all these years?

Dominic looked out the windows at the city coming alive in the early morning. He saw the blue canals of his plan, the parks and walkways, the casino doors open twenty-four hours a day, the vitality of an oasis in the desert, not the rangy, hard, scruffy frontier Alburquerque. He would ask the mayor to join forces. Would she? Together they could create the new El Dorado. Together they could replenish the old dreams of the Spanish colonial empire. Nobility. Royalty. Something no other city in the Southwest could claim.

Suddenly he felt weighed down by his life, weighed down by Gloria. He'd been watching Marisa Martínez for years now, and he realized he looked at her as he used to look at Cynthia, from afar, desirous of possessing what did not respond to him.

"Face it, Francisco," he cursed himself, "you want that woman and she doesn't give a damn!"

But why not share the power? There was nothing between him and Gloria anymore. Had there ever been? Divorce was an option, but only in the recesses of his mind. Gloria had helped him create the vision of the new El Dorado; maybe it was Gloria who had the idea of the canals in the first place. There was something psychic in her, some power that brought her strange dreams. Yes, the canals had been her dream to begin with.

But it was men who created cities, he comforted himself, and who thus created history. Immortality. Once you put your name on something it became yours. That's why the Hispanics in the state had such a strong hold in politics: they had founded the region, named the cities, the mountains, the rivers. They never discovered an ounce of gold, only the Indian pueblos, and next to each pueblo they built a town: Las Cruces, Socorro, Alburquerque, Santa Fé, Española, Taos. They had named the towns of the Río Grande Valley since Coronado's entrada in 1540.

Dominic glanced at the newspaper on his desk. Three more people had announced for mayor! The guy from the City Council who ran on a no-smoking-in-public-places platform, a pro-choice feminist, and a jogger who promised to close the downtown streets one day a week so workers could jog to work. On and on it went. One-issue small fry.

It irritated him that every bastard who could get enough signatures on a petition could get on the ballot. The summer on the campaign trail was yet to come, and he would have to sit with all the idiotic candidates at the public forums and argue about a new bridge across the Río Grande, police protection, schools, every little issue—the dull drivel of small minds.

"Excuse me," his secretary interrupted, "but Moises Lippman is here to see you."

Moises Lippman, a Santa Fé attorney who said he represented Cynthia's estate, had called yesterday. Dominic had felt nervous about the possible complications Moises could bring.

"Yeah, send him in," Dominic said, picking up the photos and slipping them back into the envelope.

Moises Lippman was a small man who wore boots, a bolo tie with a chunk of turquoise in it, thick glasses, a cowboy hat, and a pleasant smile. He knew a lot of Santa Fé artists and writers, and he represented some of the best in the state. He had argued the O'Keeffe case, a multimillion-dollar suit that catapulted him into national limelight.

The *Wall Street Journal* even had done a short piece on him. Now he was mostly representing Hollywood movie stars and directors who were buying homes in the Santa Fé foothills. But he continued to represent the local writers and artists. Dominic knew, Moises Lippman was no dope.

"Moises, it's good to see you," Dominic greeted him with a firm handshake and motioned to a chair. "Been a long time, we should have lunch next time I'm in Santa Fé."

"You're a busy man, Frank," Moises smiled. "You're splashed all over the paper. I'll try not to take up much of your time."

"Hey, if it has to do with Cynthia, I have time. You know we were tight."

"Yes, tight." Moises nodded. He knew about the gang. Cynthia had told him about the five or six kids who had gone through school together. Of them, Frank Dominic was the most arrogant, Cynthia the real genius. She was smart enough to know not to use Dominic as her lawyer.

"I'll get to the point. Cynthia left a will—"

Dominic leaned forward. "A will?" Why hadn't he anticipated this? She had houses, property, probably some paintings.

"You drew it up?"

"Yes. A few months before she died. I'd like to get this done as soon as possible. As executor—"

"Executor?" Dominic interrupted. The sonofabitch, how did he get so close to Cynthia? Why hadn't she come to him?

"I'd like to talk to Abrán right away," Moises said.

"Why?"

"As executor I must. There's the matter of showing him the house in Santa Fé, inventorying what's there, and—"

"Have you probated the will?"

"No."

Dominic drew back. Why was Lippman waiting, unless he had something to hide. Had Cynthia listed the boy's father in the will? If so, it could ruin a lot of things. Or did Moises have a soft side? Who in the hell wouldn't fall in love with Cynthia?

"You know I'm managing the kid," Dominic said. "I have complete power of attorney," he lied. He looked casually out the large picture windows. "He's boxing for me."

"Everybody knows," Moises nodded. "It's in the papers. The kid's become a celebrity. People will be after him."

Dominic measured Moises' comment, then grinned. Hell, he thought, I don't need the kid, I've got the photos. Her Honor was ten years Abrán's senior. It was going to cost her votes.

"I'll keep an eye on him," Dominic winked. "He's just a kid. But you should see him box. Listen, just leave me a copy of the will and I'll go over it with him—"

"Can't," Moises shook his head. "I won't probate the will 'til I see the boy. I promised Cynthia."

Promised Cynthia! Where was the sonofabitch coming from? What the hell had been going on in Santa Fé? Dominic's frown changed to a smile. Okay, Moises, two can play this game, he said to himself.

"If that's how you feel, Moises. You know I only want what's best for the kid. Cynthia's kid."

Moises thought a moment. "I have to see the boy," he finally said.

Dominic grinned. "Sure, Moises, sure. I have to keep the kid under wraps because of the match, you know that. After the fight, no problem."

"I have to see him right away, Frank." Moises' voice was insistent; he was arguing with the proverbial judge that always hung at their shoulders when attorneys met and got into the nuances of a case. Push and shove, it was a natural competition bred into them at law school. He had come to Dominic expecting help, and he wasn't getting any.

"Sure, Moises, no problem. No problem. I'll give you a call," he said as he walked the attorney to the door.

"Let's get it done, Frank," Moises nodded and put on his Stetson. "Sooner the better." He walked away, whistling the tune from the latest Sherlock Holmes television series.

I need to see the will, Dominic thought. In a few minutes he was to have a meeting with his attorneys, then he was on an afternoon flight to D.C. to try to recoup the damage Walter Johnson had done there. Johnson had split the senators on the water rights issue, and now Dominic had to patch up the differences. Johnson had gotten to them early, ridiculed the river plan, swore to bring in the secretary of the interior if the city approved the plan. Even worse, he reminded the senators that the Hispanics and Indians were a large voting bloc, and if they lost their water rights, it could cost political careers.

He touched the intercom. Casimiro answered.

"Moises just left."

"Yes."

"Our friend is carrying Cynthia's will in his briefcase. I want to see it."

"Yes, sir," Casimiro answered, and he hurried to follow Moises to the lobby and into the street.

Outside, Moises paused to take his bearings. It was going to be a warm day, and by the feel in the air he knew the afternoon winds would blow. It would be ten degrees cooler in Santa Fé, and he needed to get back. He had a court appearance that afternoon, two clients to see. But it wasn't just needing to get back that disturbed him as he walked down Central, there was something about Frank Dominic that bothered him. There was one way to see if Dominic was lying, and to see Abrán: call Ben Chávez. Ben knew the city; he would know how to get hold of Abrán González.

He threw his jacket and briefcase into his car and walked into a nearby restaurant and called Ben. The writer was home, he would help. Wonderful, Moises Lippman thought, and sat long enough to enjoy a glass of iced tea. How strange it will be, he thought, to meet Cynthia's boy, someone she had never mentioned in the years he had known her. They had talked about art, the law, contracts, the impact of the newcomers who, in creating the very Hollywood-Santa Fé style, destroyed much of the old flavor of the city. But she had never mentioned Abrán. She shocked him when he wrote the will.

She had left everything in Santa Fé to Abrán. The young man would be well off, Moises thought. The house on Canyon Road was worth a quarter million; the Canyon Road area had more art galleries per square inch than New York, and the land prices were just as expensive. He knew there were enough finished paintings there to raise at least a hundred thousand. But Dominic had gotten hold of the boy, and that did not bode well. He finished his tea and walked quickly to his car.

An inner sense told him his briefcase was missing before he actually saw the empty space on the seat. He cursed himself, picked up his jacket, but no, the briefcase was gone. Had he locked the door? He should have known better. He looked around the busy street. The crowds passed by unperturbed. He turned and looked up the side of Frank Dominic's building, and he knew that up there, behind one of the dark windows, Dominic looked down at him.

What the hell did Dominic want? A look at the will? The will was going to be probated as soon as he talked to Abrán. Abraham. He liked that. There was a mystery about the boy, and it was beginning to brew in Moises' mind. Ah well, he loved a good mystery. Sherlock Holmes was his hero. Practicing law allowed very little room for mystery, it was too cut and dried. But here was a real puzzle, and it had to do with Cynthia. Cynthia was his client, and he had to protect her interests. She was more than a client, she was an artist he respected. Admired? Yes. He had felt a deep loss when he heard of her death.

He would keep his appointment with Ben Chávez and see what light the old friend could shed on finding Abrán.

13 The eastern sky was pale apricot and a sliver of a moon hung alongside a bright star in the west when Abrán stepped out of Marisa's home. The planet Venus, he guessed, and paused to breathe in the cool air of the morning. The birds sang along the river bosque, and deep in the brush a coyote cried its final call of the night's hunt. Abrán stood still to absorb the beauty and reflect. It was done, but what did the spent passion mean? He thought of Lucinda and felt uneasy. It had not only been desire he had shared with Marisa, but something deep and intimate. A refuge?

The almost violent lovemaking had been not only a satisfying comingling, but it had united them against Dominic. Now the bright sun breaking over the Sandías drew Abrán back to reality. He had slept peacefully until the call of an owl from the river awakened him. At first he didn't know where he was. The brief sleep had been deep, but once awake his thoughts were of Lucinda. Then he thought of Sara and the cryptic message of doña Tules. Tú eres tú, you are who you are. Who was he? What was he doing here?

He sighed and wondered if he would return to Marisa. She wanted him, but now it was Lucinda's image that beckoned, her whisper that tugged at him.

He looked up; the moon and Venus were disappearing into the spring day.

"Santo día," he smiled, and as he stepped onto the graveled driveway he saw a movement at his feet. He felt the adrenaline pump as he jumped back. A metallic taste filled his mouth. The bull snake that crossed his path slithered quickly under the juniper bushes lining the walk.

A shiver went down his body, and he quickly walked to his car and got in. He wanted to go to Lucinda right away, to answer the strong call he felt from her, but as he drove down Río Grande he changed his mind. She was safe, asleep in her bed. Later they were to drive north to her home. Good Friday, he thought, it's Good Friday. Today they were going to Chimayó, then up to Córdova to meet her parents.

He had deceived her. Would she know? Would she see it in his eyes? Had her dream told her he was in the arms of another woman, and had she called out to him? Was that the image he saw? He would have to tell her, and then what? Would he lose her?

The desire he had felt for Marisa was real, but it was for the moment. He did not regret the passion between them, it had united them against a formidable foe. And, her physical love had swept him into an understanding of passion: he learned that the flesh can provide insight into the soul. He had met himself in their moments of ecstasy, and he now understood a very important part of himself as a man. But still he had to find his spiritual center, something grounded in the values of Sara, something that came from the earth and the rhythms of the people, something he sensed Lucinda offered.

Sara was up when he got home. The house was warm and welcomed him with the smell of tortillas on the comal and fresh coffee brewing. She called from the kitchen, where she was making Lenten food for Good Friday: tortillas, tortas de huevo, spinach mixed with beans and a pod of red chile, and natillas for dessert.

"Hijo," she greeted him with open arms, holding out her hands so as not to get flour on him.

"Mi'jo, I'm so glad to see you. I've been worried. I prayed—" She stopped. She was about to ask where he had been and thought against it. She looked into his eyes, saw the grown man her son had become since the night of his Cynthia's death. Manhood was spiriting him away from her, and that's as it should be. He had always been a private person, a quiet boy who spent long hours to himself, now he had the right to his privacy as a man.

She knew he had been with a woman. But she had no right to inquire; he would tell her what he would. He was home safe, that was all that mattered.

"Sit down, sit and eat. I got up early this morning to pray. It was a beautiful sunrise," she said as she took the first, crisp tortilla from the stove, buttered it, and offered it to him. He broke the round bread in two and offered her half.

"Let's both eat," he smiled and kissed her.

"Only this," she said. "I want to fast today, it's Good Friday. I'll go to church this afternoon and spend the three hours of agony with our Lord, and when I return I'll eat."

She took another tortilla from the comal, and he ate them as quickly as they were put on the plate because now he was hungry, ravenous, his stomach growling as he washed down the hot buttered tortillas with fresh coffee, then wolfed the eggs, refried beans, and hash-brown potatoes liberally covered with hot, green chile. No meat on Good Friday.

He talked as he ate, telling her about the meeting with Dominic and Dominic's plan, and telling her he had met the mayor, but not telling her where he had spent the night.

He told her about Joe leaving for the pueblo and the trip he and Lucinda were taking. Then he shifted to his classes and explained he would have to take incompletes, but for her not to worry, it was only because of the training for the fight.

Finally she interrupted. "Slow down, mi'jo. Life is not lived in one day," and added, "nor in one night. If you're determined to box, then you must do what you must do. The classes can wait one semester. You have good teachers, they'll understand."

"A lot of things changing," he mused.

"Yes," Sara agreed, "but when things change, you should not forget what is at the core."

He listened. He had been thinking about "the core" when he left Marisa, thinking about his identity, his soul. What had changed so much? Why did he feel he needed a new identity to explain who he was?

"I have been thinking," Sara said, "you should go see doña Tules. She knows about people, and you are fortunate she came to you. It means something. You know, the year you were born there was a strike in the barrio against the railroad. It was a very bad thing. She helped Clemente Chávez. He was the leader of the strikers. Some say it was witchcraft, but no, she helped him to know himself. And after that he led the strikers. No one expected him, a man from the campo, a man who knew nothing about unions, to lead the strikers. It was a bad time. His wife was killed."

"What was her name?"

"Adelita. The guards fired on the people, and later they said it was a stray bullet. No, they wanted to kill Clemente and they killed his wife. Those were sad days."

"What happened to him?" Abrán asked, interested in the new pieces of the story.

"He stayed here in Barelas until his family was grown, then he returned to Guadalupe. I guess now he is an old man."

"And his family?"

"They live here. The writer you met, the one that got hurt, he is the son of Clemente Chávez."

Abrán was surprised. "I didn't know that."

"There's lots of things you don't know," she smiled.

True, he agreed. But he did know the story of the strike in Barelas and how bloody it had been. The railroad didn't give a damn about the rights of the Mexican workers. Shortly after the strike the roundhouse was moved to Flagstaff, the workers' union was broken, and the barrio dried up.

"There's another thing you should know," she said. She went on slapping the tortillas, thinking how best to tell him the strands of history that made up his past and the past of his community.

"I used to work for Mr. Johnson and his wife."

He knew, but he listened carefully.

"You know, his wife couldn't have children."

"Vera?"

"Yes, Elvira. Once I helped her, and that is part of the reason you should go and see doña Tules."

Abrán looked at Sara.

"The women who worked for Elvira knew she had tried every doctor and every remedy to have children, but nothing worked. I was only a young girl, but I knew about doña Tules. Perhaps it's because I was young and inexperienced that I mentioned to Vera that she should see the curandera. She took my advice. I was the one who took her to see doña Tules. I still remember the day, it was windy and dark, and of course doña Elvira didn't want her husband to know. But she is Mexicana, and so she knew about the work of curanderas."

"My mother was also a coyota," Abrán mused.

"Yes, Cynthia's father is Anglo, and her mother is from one of those old families from Taos. An orphan, she was raised by don Manuel Armijo and his wife. Anyway, I don't know what doña Tules told Elvira, but she came out very happy. I remember the glow on her face. Maybe she cured her, because after that Cynthia, your mother, was born. Oh, she was happy. And that sour man you see now, el señor Johnson, he was happier than anyone. He would sing and dance and show off the baby and he gave parties every weekend. To show the baby to his compadres."

Abrán sipped his coffee. "Why are you telling me this?"

"Relationships. You have to know the relationships. So you will not go and marry a woman who might be your sister, or one related to you."

She looked at her son and a sadness filled her because she realized he didn't know his father's family. He didn't know if he had sisters or brothers. He didn't know the blood of his father, and so fate could plot against him.

"Many of the families here came from the South Valley, from Los Padillas, Pajarito, Atrisco, and from La Plaza Vieja, Duranes. All the old families knew each other, there were many compadres and comadres, and so they knew each other and made the community strong and safe for their children. Your father and I, we are from the families of Atrisco. Our ancestors were from that land grant. The same one they want to sell now. Dollars don't last, only the land lasts. Remember that."

Abrán knew the history of the land grant, it had been imprinted in him by Sara's stories, and he knew the intrinsic value the land had for her and Ramiro. But now his mind returned to other matters.

"And the woman I told you I met yesterday at Mr. Dominic's office, Marisa Martínez, the mayor of the city? Where is her family from?"

"Also from the South Valley," Sara said, not missing a beat as she rolled the tortilla. So that is the woman he was with, she thought sadly.

"And after Cynthia was born?" Abrán asked, trying to redirect the conversation.

"Well, don't you see, I feel I had a hand in her birth. It was el destino. Vera had her baby, and seventeen years later, more or less, you were born to Cynthia. The same destiny was to make you mine. You see, the woman I took to doña Tules later gave her grandson to me. It is as if I had been made pregnant, and I waited all those years for you."

"A strange chain. . . ."

"Así es la vida," she nodded. "And doña Tules was the woman who cured doña Elvira. So she also, in a way, had a hand in your birth. That is why she appeared to you the night your mother died. You must go and see her."

"I will."

"And you must not be afraid. She is a woman who can see into time. She has a lot of power. She knew that Elvira could conceive, and she knew you would be born. So she is also a mother to you." She paused, turned, and looked at her son. Love shone in her eyes and on her face. "Many women will be mothers to you. Women will help you understand yourself, I can see that. But only Lucinda will give you children. Many children."

Abrán smiled. She loved to give him riddles to solve. He thought a moment and said, "Let's see. Because she is a nurse, she will deliver many children. And because she delivers them they will be like her children, and because I am her husband they will also be my children. Is that it?"

She laughed and returned to her work. "Smart kid. Mira, you've eaten enough tortillas. Go call the man who telephoned. He is very anxious to talk to you."

"Who?"

"Moises Lippman. He is from Santa Fé. His number is by the telephone."

Abrán called and Moises explained who he was and about Cynthia's will.

"I need to see you right away," he said.

"I can be there today," Abrán answered excitedly. He and Lucinda would stop in Santa Fé on the way to Córdova.

"Around one, if possible. You know, today's Good Friday," Moises reminded him and said goodbye.

"An attorney," he told Sara when he entered the kitchen. "Cynthia left a will."

"I see," Sara answered, knowing that yet a new page had been turned in her son's life, bringing, perhaps, new complications.

Abrán, hoping that maybe his father's name would appear in the will, hurried to call Lucinda, then to shower and dress.

Lucinda was ready when Abrán arrived. "I'm glad we're going," she said and hugged him. "I just talked to my mom, they're expecting us. I thought we could stop at Chimayó for the Good Friday services. A short visit."

Abrán saw the happiness on her face, but when he held her he felt he didn't deserve her. Did she sense the difference? If she did she said nothing; she wanted to know all about Moises Lippman and the will. He told her what he knew as they drove out of the city on I-25, past the Sandías and north to Santa Fé.

"I'm eager to meet Moises," Abrán said. "Maybe the will mentions my father. Maybe there are papers, letters, another diary. . . ."

"Maybe," Lucinda nodded, "maybe we'll get lucky. Just don't get your hopes too high."

"Hard not to," he smiled. "Now tell me what you've been doing."

"I cleaned my apartment. Demetria, a girl I went to school with, called and reminded me the university spring fiesta is just around the corner. She talked me into making tacos for the Chicano booth. The money is used for scholarships. I used to help when I was a student, so they still call me."

"MECHA?"

"Yes. Come with me to fiesta and meet some of the students."

"Will they accept me? I'm only half Chicano." he smiled.

"You're Chicano," she said confidently. "Blue-eyed or brown, dark or fair skin, you're Chicano."

"The fiesta's the day of the fight," he said.

"It's set? I didn't know. I'll cancel," she said instantly.

"No, don't. I have the day free. We can do both."

"Are you sure?"

"Sure."

"The paper said Frank Dominic's bringing people from all over, not just politicians, but movie actors, and Las Vegas shows."

"I wish it was over," he shrugged.

She sensed his mood; he was thinking something through. She had also sensed a distance when he kissed her.

"Joe called. He said he couldn't get hold of you last night. He called to tell us how to get to his house at the pueblo."

"We'll see him on the way back," Abrán said, thankful she didn't ask him where he had been all night.

Around them the rolling hills dotted with juniper trees wore the soft, gray-green of spring.

"The landscape reminds me of a Georgia O'Keeffe painting," Lucinda mused. "I wonder if she and Cynthia ever met."

"An interesting question," Abrán said.

"I often wonder what a man sees when he looks at O'Keeffe's arroyos and canyons. For me her work is an exploration of the woman, the allure of her body. The earth becomes the woman's body, curves of bosoms, ombligos, the stomach, thighs, the Venus mound, and flowers where pistils and pollen lie in wait. In the features of the earth she found the woman within and liberated her. She found the erotic woman."

"Cynthia's bower scene is erotic, but besides that. . ." Abrán's thoughts trailed. Did his mother ever have a lover after his father? There was no way of knowing.

"I can understand why Cynthia turned away from the body. She had loved once, and she suffered emotionally from that love. In your mother's paintings I see pure light," Lucinda continued, "the primeval light of New Mexico. You see it up in Córdova or in Taos when the sun is setting, or right after a rainstorm cleans the air. Pure light, as it must have been at the beginning of time. Cynthia painted the light emanating from within the people; she could see their auras. The people she paints are real, but they have the glow of life. In her pure light there is no deception. She was wrecked by deception, wasn't she? Made to suffer because she loved your father." She paused. "Anyway, I'm rambling on. I'm excited about the weekend."

"I like to listen to you," Abrán smiled.

As they drove on, the sun revealed sharp contrasts in the landscape. The hills and distant mesas were blue as they receded into the horizon. To the west the river valley was light green, and beyond the river rose the blue Jémez. They climbed up the red cliffs of La Bajada, then ahead of them was Santa Fé, nestled at the foot of the Sangre de Cristo mountains.

"I had a dream about you," Lucinda said.

"What?"

"I want to make love to you."

Abrán smiled. "And your papacito and mamá?"

"I'm going to take you up to the mountain where I can have you all to myself," Lucinda smiled back.

"A good dream," he said.

"Oh no, the dream was more like a nightmare. I saw you drowning, a woman was fishing for you. I could see the hook, and blood spreading in the water. When I awakened I thought the woman was la Llorona."

She reached across and touched his hand, assuring herself he was there. Nightmares were only warnings, but warnings were to be heeded.

Abrán looked at Lucinda. She knew. The images of her dream had divulged his secret.

"I—" he started to say, and she moved closer and kissed him softly and quickly.

"It was just a dream. Let's forget it. You're here and that's what matters." She leaned back into the seat and focused on the distant horizon, telling herself that the siren of the dream was only a ghost, allowing herself to be cleansed by the land.

Abrán nodded. Lucinda was intuitive. She was sensitive to things that escaped him. From what she had told him about her father, he guessed the gift came from him. Or was it a gift that came from being raised in the mountains, in a land Lucinda described as timeless? She had the ability to help people, a desire to heal the sick. Like doña Tules, she was a curandera.

Abrán looked at Lucinda. There was contentment in her eyes. She stared at the clouds beginning to form over the Jémez Mountains. Her beauty was natural, like the day. It was the beauty of spring coming alive in the llanos, mesas, and mountains of the Río Grande Valley. She is beautiful, he thought, and reached out to hold her hand.

"We're here," he said. "Santa Fé. Holy faith."

"It's become Santa Fantasy. A city which has become a museum."

She paused. "I don't want you to feel pressured when you meet my parents. Whatever you decide, I still love you."

"And I love you," he answered, and deep inside he knew he meant it. He loved her, and he wanted to share himself with her. Whoever he was, whoever he finally found within, that person wanted to share his life with Lucinda.

They found Moises' office, and he greeted them warmly. "Very glad to meet you," he told Abrán as he shook his hand. "I'm glad you came."

"I'm glad to meet you," Abrán responded and introduced Lucinda.

"Now, I want to show you the house," Moises said. "Let you get a feel for it. What do you say we walk?"

As they walked Moises wasted no time: "What's your deal with Dominic?"

"I box for him and he finds my father," Abrán answered.

"Ah," Moises said, "so he thinks the will mentions your father's name."

"Does it?" Abrán asked.

Moises stopped and looked at Abrán. A handsome kid with Cynthia's features written in his eyes. He shook his head. "No, it doesn't. I'm sorry. In all the years I knew Cynthia, she never mentioned his name. She never even mentioned you until she made the will. She wanted to provide for you. . ." His voice trailed.

Abrán let out a sigh. He had come to another dead end.

"Are there other papers?" Lucinda asked.

"She had a lot of books, but I think she corresponded very little. There might be journals. You can look around. You should leave things intact for now though; I want to inventory everything, especially the paintings."

"Why?" Lucinda asked.

"The estate needs to file tax returns," Moises smiled and shrugged his shoulders. "Suppose someone shows up and contests the will?"

"Family?" Abrán asked. What if he had other brothers and sisters?

"One never knows. Best to be safe," Moises said. "I'll do what I can to protect your interests." He took off his cowboy hat and wiped his brow, then led them up the street toward Canyon Road.

As they walked, he talked about Cynthia. He had known her as well as anyone. There was a special fondness in his voice when he talked about his client, the lonely and often misunderstood woman who lived on Canyon Road.

"She was honest," he said, "she painted an honesty into the Hispanos that's never been done before. Same faces you see on the street today, or in the villages. The gringo painters can't do that. Not a one can get the soul of the people. She did. In her paintings you look into the soul of this land."

He puffed as he continued walking and talking. "The house, and all the property therein, is yours. That means the paintings. The house is small but well furnished. Used to belong to the old Perea family. Probably worth a quarter million. It should be preserved as a historical landmark; I'm going to suggest that to the mayor, if it's all right with you. Santa Fé owes a lot to your mother, even though it didn't treat her very well when she was alive."

He talked with animation as they walked up Canyon Road, the narrow street bordered by artists' homes and galleries. Daffodils bloomed, and in warm, protected corners where the adobe walls held the warmth of the spring sun, forsythia. To the east, the blue of the Sangre de Cristo mountains had taken on a dark cast.

"It's going to get windy," Moises said.

Yes, Good Friday would turn cool and blustery, Lucinda thought with a shiver. It always did.

"Feel the light. That's what brings the artists. The quality of light." Moises paused. "That's why people come here. That's why I came. L.A. is no place to raise a family. But most of the newcomers only see the surface of things. They build million-dollar adobe homes, but they don't know anything about the people. Cynthia did. She knew the history of the people she painted. There's religion in this earth, but when you only come to rent the condo and you don't touch the mud, then you're not connected. That's the secret of the place, you have to put your hands in the mud. History's in the mud, in the earth."

He stopped in front of a small adobe. Pale earth with a flat roof and an adobe wall around it. There was a sadness about the house, a vacant feeling. Moises opened the wooden gate and they entered the garden, a small, enclosed patio.

Lucinda stopped. She felt a cool breeze on her neck, the stir of the wind as it rolled down from the mountain and rustled in the budding branches of the lilac bushes.

"Someone is buried here," she whispered. The presence was strong, a mournful, restless spirit.

"You're probably right," Moises nodded. Although he didn't believe in the visitation of the spirits, he knew some people could feel the presence of death. Death was part of the religion, and like the saints, death had a personality. It was woven into the culture.

"The records I've read suggest the Perea family was killed here during the 1680 Indian revolt. The family was never heard from again. My guess is they were buried here, and this house was built on the walls of the original home. I did the research for Cynthia; she felt the spirits too. But she made peace with them, and so she could work here."

Lucinda nodded. If Cynthia could make peace with the spirits so could she, but only for the moment. It would take a very good curandera to put to rest the souls that wandered here.

Moises opened the door and they stepped into the sala. It was dark and musty, but when he opened the curtains the light was bright and warm.

"She used to entertain here. Once in a while she'd have a few people over, to talk art and politics, and how Santa Fé was going to the dogs. Too commercial, she thought. She had to be here because her gallery was here. For her, the city had become a museum for the tourists and the rich. Nice and tidy adobes with strict building codes, and a tax rate that has driven out the natives. She hated that. The people she wanted to paint were now outcasts from the city their ancestors had established."

"They ought to tax the rich," Lucinda said, "and use the money to educate the Chicanos they drove out."

Moises led them into the studio. It was light and airy. A canvas with a rough sketch sat on the easel. The walls were hung with Navajo blankets. "She didn't keep much of her work here, but there are a few paintings in here," he pointed to an adjoining workroom.

"Look around at your leisure," he said and handed Abrán the key to the house. "Just don't move anything for now. I had new locks put on the doors, just in case." He shook hands with them. "Call me if you need anything."

"I will," Abrán nodded.

"Your mother was a great lady," he said, "She not only had talent, but she had beauty. And compassion." He cleared his throat. "There are a lot of us who miss her. I'm glad I met you. And you," he said to Lucinda. "Anything you need, call me." Then he turned and went out, whistling.

"Nice guy," Abrán said as they watched Moises amble down the street, waving to people he knew, playing to the hilt the role of the local paisano.

"He cared a lot for your mother," Lucinda said.

"Yes."

"Still does."

Abrán nodded. "Let's look around," he suggested. They spent the next few hours going through the house. They found a few completed paintings. Recent work obviously done in a dark mood with deep shadows from thunderheads and cottonwoods. Rebozos and hats were pulled over people's heads, as if they were hiding from the spectator. There was no gaiety in their eyes.

"They reflect her illness," Lucinda said.

The paintings also reflected the Mexicanos as outcasts in their own land. People in one painting were walking away from the shining city, glancing back at La Villa de la Santa Fé. In a dark alley, shadowed men drank and brawled. Expensive cars, Hollywood faces, and women in the ostentatious Santa Fé style lined the streets. The painting depicted the end of an age.

Soon Abrán and Lucinda were exhausted and hungry, and they had found no journals, diaries, or letters. "A very private woman," Lucinda said. Standing in the middle of the large sala Abrán nodded and said, "It will be best to sell this place."

Lucinda agreed. "It was her, but it's not you. Tú eres tú," she smiled, "just like doña Tules said."

"Come on, let's grab a bite and hit the road."

They bought bean burritos and Cokes from an old woman in the plaza and ate as they drove out of the city.

14 North of Santa Fé, near Española, the last of the straggling penitents were on the road, pilgrims who were walking to the Santuario de Chimayó on Good Friday. Hidden in the valley of Chimayó, the santuario was the Mecca of Catholic New Mexico, and people came from all over to pray there during Holy Week. Entire families returned to fulfill the promises they had vowed to complete, and at the same time to remind the young of the miraculous power of the small, adobe church. For these faithful believers, the earth of the valley was capable of curing the most severe illness, if one believed and did penance.

And so they came, from all the villages of northern New Mexico and from Santa Fé, Alburquerque, Belen, and as far south as Las Cruces. The walk was long for some, the body grew weary and fatigued, sores appeared on the feet, dehydration took a toll, and now the cold front pushing off the Sangre de Cristo wore them down. But they persevered.

Some would not arrive in Chimayó in time for the three holy hours at the santuario; they would not be in time to share the hours of suffering with their Cristo. Still, they sang alabados and prayed rosaries as they painfully trudged the remaining miles.

Those who were more than one day on the road would sleep outside under culverts, in bosque bowers, or huddled against the side of the road. They would eat cold sandwiches around campfires, tell stories to rival Chaucer's pilgrims', but remain serene in their exhaustion.

Others would not arrive until Good Saturday, that was fine. Next year if they made the journey again they would start a day earlier, and if friends asked as they told the story of their pilgrimage, they would remind everyone to allow for the weather, which could still turn cold at that time of the year. It was a long walk and extra water and blankets were needed, and if you carried a heavy cross as part of your penance, remember to pack first aid for the bruises and cuts.

Watch out for drunk drivers, too, they would laugh, they're dangerous. More than one penitent had been struck and killed on the road to Chimayó. And watch out for tourists, they stop you to take pictures, and the TV news is always there, blocking the road, interviewing people. Be kind, be friendly, they don't know what this is all about. Pobrecitos, they think it's a show, they don't know what it means to us.

And even though the last miles were the slowest, all the pilgrims dreamed of arriving before Easter Sunday. They wanted to get there in time to celebrate the Mass and lay their crutches, crosses, and sins at the altar of Christ or at the altar of the Santo Niño de Atocha in the small room next to the sacristy where the walls were covered with the ex-votos and milagros of prior penitents who had completed their penance and been cured.

Los santos will relieve us of our burden, the penitents on the road believed, and Cristo will absolve our sins. The saints are waiting for us; they will witness the fulfillment of the promise we made as penance for our sins, as penance for the alleviation of the illness that plagues us.

Abrán felt the faith of the straggling penitents he and Lucinda passed on the road. His mother, Sara, believed in the journey of faith and prayed daily to her santos. She had often talked of the trip she and Ramiro once took to Chimayó. It was etched clearly in her memory. Abrán promised himself to bring her next year.

They turned off the road at Española, following the narrow country road that led to Chimayó, still passing groups of penitents as they wound their way deeper into the Chimayó Valley. When they arrived at the santuario they found a large crowd gathered outside. These were the faithful who had come in time and spent the three dolorous hours, the reenactment of the suffering and death of Christ on the cross, in the small adobe church. Already there was relief on the faces of the men and women who filed from the church.

Lucinda and Abrán worked their way through the crowd. He had never been there, so she led him toward the entrance of the church. Once inside they made their way to the altar, pressed in by the warmth of the people, soothed by the whispered rosaries of the old people who knelt at the pews, engulfed by the fragrance of the burning altar candles and the earth scent of the adobe walls.

She led him to the small room to the side of the altar. The room held the statues of the various saints. On the walls hung dozens of ex-votos, the remembrances of those who had kept their promises in prior years: rosaries and scapulars, crutches, braces, scribbled notes of thanks, names of families, dates and addresses, small mementos left by those who had come to be cured. Also, faded photographs of veterans, as well as of crippled and missing children.

"Here," Lucinda whispered, "my favorite saint."

On the small altar sat the statue of the smug-faced Santo Niño de Atocha, dressed in fine lace with an array of baby shoes at his feet. He held a staff in one hand and a basket in the other. All day long people had prayed to him, and he seemed to bask in the attention.

"They say he walks the fields at night, blessing the fields, and he wears out his shoes. The women who clean the church find mud on his shoes in the morning, so they replace his shoes with baby shoes."

"Wouldn't the village dogs chase him because of that funny robe and hat he wears," Abrán teased.

"Shh. Don't be sacreligious," she said. "Come here."

She led him through a low door into an adjoining room that was only big enough for five or six people. In the center of the adobe room was a hole in the earth floor. The air was sweet with the smell of candle wax and damp earth. She whispered for him to kneel in front of the hole, and then she washed his hands and arms with the fine soil.

"With your hands you will cure people," she said, looking into his eyes. She believed in penance and in the miraculous healing power of the earth at the santuario.

"In the meantime," she winked. "I hope you knock out that guy from Las Vegas in the first round so he doesn't touch your beautiful face."

They stood and embraced, the bond of faith and earth uniting them.

"Time to go," she said and led him outside. The air was fresh and brisk, and the late afternoon sun brilliant through the blustery clouds that swept overhead.

"What do you think?" she asked as they stood by the small acequia in front of the church.

"I felt my feet were rooted in the earth," he answered. He looked at his hands and arms where the film of dust remained. "Good medicine."

"Baptism," she said and took his arm as they walked to the car. "Our love is a new life. Before there was raza here, the Indians used to come to this place. Chimayó is an Indian word; you see, they had named their universe and the sacred places. They used the earth for healing. The Mexicano who built the first chapel saw a saint standing over this spot. The earth is sacred." She paused and looked into his eyes. "If we decide to go all the way," she said, "we'll baptize our children here."

"The priest will get to know us very well," he smiled. She embraced him, felt his heart pounding, and felt satisfied.

"Now," she smiled, "let's go introduce you to Juan Oso."

They drove out of the Chimayó Valley into the hills spotted with juniper trees and yucca, and on into piñon country, taking their bearing from the blue mountain of Picurís, which was still snowcapped. They wound in and out of hills and small valleys, until they came to the valley that held the small village of Córdova. They were pilgrims from Chimayó arriving home.

Lucinda's parents, Juan Oso and his wife Esperanza, were happy to meet Abrán. Lucinda was their only daughter and this was the first time she had brought a man for them to meet. Beneath the abrazos and laughter there was a serious mood. Their daughter was now a woman and interested in taking a husband. Of course, any guest she brought would be treated with hospitality, it was part of the tradition to make the guest feel at home.

Esperanza and Lucinda disappeared into the kitchen to finish preparing the Lenten meal, and Juan Oso served Abrán a glass of wine. He took Abrán aside as they sipped their drinks and showed him the wooden saints he carved from aspen and piñon.

"Never thought I'd be a santero," he explained as he showed Abrán his work, "I was a rancher. Ran more than a hundred head of cattle up in the mountain pastures. Until the day I met the bear," he smiled and nodded toward his left arm that hung nearly useless at his side. "He chewed on that for awhile, but I was so mean and tough he had to spit me out." He laughed, slapped Abrán on the back, then filled their glasses again.

Eventually, Iraclio, the oldest son who worked for the Forest Service, came by on the way home from work. He had a drink with them and met Abrán, and so did Antonio, who taught school in Peñasco. Both were sturdy men, handsome like Juan Oso, but quiet and reserved. It would take a while for them to accept Abrán, but once they did, they would be like brothers. Tonight, though, they had their families to get to, and although their mother invited them to stay for supper they had to leave.

"La familia, Mamá, gotta get home or Vangie will divorce me. See you tomorrow," Iraclio said, and both sons kissed her. Turning to Abrán, Antonio said, "Muncho gusto en conocerte. This summer if you come up we can go fishing. Iraclio knows some good spots on the river." They shook hands and were gone, their trucks rumbling off into the New Mexican dusk that had settled over the mountain.

The cold air slipped off the snow-laden peaks into the valley, bringing a chill. The growing moon appeared again over the dark peaks. Around them the small village of Córdova settled in for the night. The cows were milked, boys took in firewood from the dwindling woodpiles in back of their houses, a lone dog barked.

"The bears are stirring," Juan Oso said, as if detecting the scent of hibernating bears awakening to the spring.

"It's cold enough for a fire," Esperanza said. "That's the way it can be up here, the spring nights are still cold."

Juan Oso brought in a load of wood and put a piñon log in the stove to warm up the room. It was a good homecoming, one that made Abrán feel at ease. When supper was served he ate second helpings of everything, and this pleased Esperanza.

"She's the best cook on this mountain," Juan Oso said when they had finished supper. "That's why I married her."

"Don't believe all his stories, Abrán," she laughed. It was clear they led a harmonious life.

After dinner Juan Oso and Abrán went into the small, front room and settled comfortably in large chairs near the stove. Juan Oso talked about his youth in the mountains, and he told Abrán about the bear that nearly killed him.

"I was about sixteen when I met a young girl who lived on the other side of the mountain. Her family was strange, they lived up there alone. Like hermits. The people from Córdova thought the mother of the girl was a witch.

"I was taking a small herd of cattle up the mountain that spring, and I met the girl on the path. She was beautiful, and I had for her the first feelings of sex for a woman. We talked a little, and she invited me to come back. And me, I was ready. Hell, I was young and those long, summer days alone on the mountain were lonely.

"I told my father about the girl when I went in for provisions, and he told me to stay clear of them. Stay away from their place, he said, but he didn't tell me why.

"What did I care. The next time I went up there I met her again, and she took me into the forest to a meadow. I had never seen the place. Right there she made a man out of me," Juan Oso whispered and looked toward the kitchen to make sure the women couldn't hear him. "All day and night I stayed with her. I lost track of time, but I felt real macho. But later I knew it wasn't right. It was sex, but I knew the girl and I were not really for each other. There wasn't any love.

"So I thought that was it, I wouldn't go back. But she would wait for me along the road when I rode by on horseback. She was hungry for me, I could tell, she wanted to get me back to that meadow. I tried to tell her no, there was no good to it.

"She kept on, showing herself to me so I would go with her, and once she told me she was pregnant, but I didn't believe her. She had a fine body and long black hair, and a smooth complexion. But something about the way we made love scared me. It was the pure and natural urge of the animal, but I knew there had to be more to it. She taught me to understand that part of myself, like every man has to learn from a woman, but I knew she wasn't for me.

"Then her father came, dark and big as a black bear, and he told me that I had gotten his daughter pregnant and if I didn't marry her he was going to kill me. I was really scared then. He was a mean man, and the story was he had killed two of his partners up on the mountain.

"I told my father the whole story, and my father went up there to talk to him, but their cabin was empty. Empty and dirty, like the den of a bear, and the smell was strong. It was not a good place. The horse he rode wouldn't go near the cabin. It reared up and pulled away, frightened.

"My father told me if I went up to that peak to be careful. Never go alone, he said. I grew up, I married, I forgot all about the girl. Iraclio was born, then Antonio then Lucinda. I was ranching, and doing pretty good. Then we had a drought, and so I thought of grazing my cattle up on that peak where the girl and her family used to live. Nobody here in Córdova ever used that area for grazing. By that time my father was dead, but some of the old men of the village warned me not to go up there. Bears, they said, bad bears.

"I didn't listen. I went anyway, ran forty head. I went alone and made camp to settle the herd down. In the night a female bear came. She spooked my horse and stampeded the cattle. I took my thirty-thirty and followed her into the forest. That was my mistake. The male bear was waiting for me. I swear it was ten feet high. I got off one shot before its paw tore into me. One blow and it broke my arm, I could hear the bone splinter. Then it locked its jaws around the arm, crushing everything, blood poured out. It grabbed me in an abrazo, hugging the life out of me. Its eyes were wild and mean. When I saw those evil eyes I knew it was the devil in the form of a bear. I knew I was going to die.

"The only thing I had left was my hunting knife. I had to reach it before I passed out. I don't know how I did it, but I pulled it and shoved it into the bear, deep as I could. I must have hit a vein, because the bear let me loose and reared back. When it hit the ground, it was a man. I swear, it was a man.

"I passed out, and in the morning when I opened my eyes there was nothing there. Did the bear drag itself away? Did the female drag it away? I don't know. Right then, I didn't care. I was dying. I had lost a lot of blood.

"But you know, life is full of miracles. That night Esperanza had a dream. She said she saw me drowning in blood, probably figured I met la Llorona up on the mountain. She got up and she hitched the wagon and by early morning she was up there. She found me. I don't know how, but her dream saved my life. She bandaged the arm to stop the bleeding, and she brought me down. My compadres took me into the hospital.

"The doctor wanted to cut the arm off, said it was poisoned. I said no, just leave it as it is. Maybe I had done something wrong, and the bear had taught me a lesson. Maybe I shouldn't have messed with the girl. Leave it, I said, I'll take my chances.

"That was just the beginning. The poison in my blood almost killed me. A long time of fever and nightmares, and the bears talking to me. During those nights of pesadilla the spirit of the bears got in me.

Maybe I became a bear in those nightmares. I talked to them. You know, when I came out of the hospital, people begin to call me Juan Oso. I had changed and they could feel it. For awhile I couldn't get near my horse, he would spook and shy away.

"I used to go up to the peak where it happened and sit and listen to the forest. Then the birds and squirrels began to get close to me. Chipmunks came up, even deer. One day a bear cub came up to me and smelled me, and I touched the small creature. He was like a child, exploring the world. And something told me the female was nearby, and it was dangerous. That's the way the female bear is, protects her cub. She was nearby, but she just took the cub away, looked at me, and together they went into the forest.

"They left me alone, but I felt good. I belonged. I had entered their world, hombre. I was one of them.

"I picked up a piece of aspen and I saw the figure of a bear in it. Holding it between my knees I begin to carve into it, just with my knife. I could see the bear in the wood, and I carved it out, made it free. Mira, I still have that first carving."

He got up and reached for an old weathered carving of a bear that sat high on top of the trastero. It was a crude piece, rough, but with a vibrancy of life.

"I carved a lot of bears at first, and then I began to see the saints in the pieces of wood I found up there in the mountain, and that's how I became a santero. That's all I do now, carve my saints. At first I wouldn't sell them, but what the hell, with only one good arm I couldn't work the ranch like I used to, and my family had to eat.

"So I made a deal with my bears and my santos; I would sell only enough to earn my living. They agreed. Now people come from all over, tourists, people from museums, and they all want to buy. I only sell so my wife and I can live here on our mountain. My kids are grown, I don't want to make money. I am happy."

Abrán listened intently to the story; he felt close to Juan Oso. This is what he had missed as he grew into manhood, a man who would tell him stories and talk about the experiences of men. Sitting with

Juan Oso made him feel complete, and he knew they would be good friends.

After cleaning the kitchen, Esperanza and Lucinda served coffee and biscochitos, and the conversation continued. They told stories and wove family histories so that Abrán would know what villages they came from and who their ancestors were.

Esperanza opened an old tin trunk, the petaca she kept by her altar, and showed them her treasures: her wedding gown, a few pieces of silver and turquoise jewelry, herbs that were used to cure her the year she got a bad flu and almost died, pictures of her family. Heirlooms. Personal family history. Her mother's rosary, her scapular.

"We came from Picurís Pueblo," she said. "See, here is my grandmother." The faded black-and-white print showed a morena in a dark, flowing dress standing next to a mustachioed Hispano. "The man is my grandfather," she said. "He came from Taos to marry my grandmother. They raised a large family. My father married a woman here in Córdova, so I was born here. But I have the blood of Picurís Pueblo in me. Part of my family is still there. I grew up here, and here is where I met Juan."

"Lucky you," Juan Oso smiled.

"You're the lucky one," she teased back. "Without me you would still be up on that mountain."

"She's right," he grinned.

"You're both lucky," Abrán said. "You have deep roots here."

He paused and they realized that what they took for granted, generations of living in the same villages of the Sangre de Cristo and roots that went deep into the soil and the spirit of the people, he did not have.

"A man can put roots wherever he finds a good woman," Juan Oso said. He looked at Abrán and then at his daughter. He liked the boy, there was a natural ease between them. He knew Lucinda would return to the mountains someday, and her children would grow up here. The soul of the mountain was in her, and doña Agapita, the old curandera who taught her so much, lived in the village. She would return, and something in his blood told him that Abrán would return with her.

Esperanza nodded. She, too, liked the boy. She could tell he was good for her daughter. What would happen, well that was up to them, but she had to let him know that he was welcome.

"It's a very simple life," she said, "but we are happy. Our children have been happy here. The people here are quiet, but once they know you, they are the best neighbors in the world."

Lucinda smiled and squeezed Abrán's hand. "I think they're giving you the Córdova Chamber of Commerce speech."

"I'm sold," Abrán said. "What about work?"

"We need a clinic," Lucinda reminded him.

"You can always find something to do," Juan Oso said. "But it's not easy up here."

"It's never been easy," Esperanza said. "My grandfather's people were cibolleros. They went from Taos to the Llano Estacado to hunt buffalo, as far as Amarillo they went. He wrote in his diary that he was going to the United States. Can you imagine that, only two generations ago and when our men went east to hunt they described it as going to the United States. Imagine the dangers they faced on those empty plains. But they survived, we know how to survive. Then the train came and the buffalo were destroyed."

"And now?" Abrán asked.

"We have a good life," Juan Oso said, "in spite of the changes. My father said our lives changed in the villages when Kearny came in with his army. Good changes, bad changes. Those who didn't learn the American way suffered. For a while most of the northern New Mexico land grants got bought up by the gringo land speculators. They used the courts, crook lawyers, taxes, any excuse to get hold of our land. The Maxwell Land Grant of the gringos swallowed up our old grants. It almost killed us. But we survived. Look, I keep this. I like to remind people of the promises the government made."

He got up and went to the trastero again and took out a piece of well-worn, faded paper. He put on a pair of reading glasses.

"This is what General Kearny told the people of Las Vegas the day he marched in. August 15, 1846. He said: 'Mr. Alcalde, and people of New Mexico, I have come amongst you by the orders of my government, to take possession of your country.'

"See what he says right there, to take possession. The sonofabitch warned us, qué no?

"'And to extend over it the laws of the United States. We consider it, and have done so for some time, a part of the territory of the United States.'

"See, they had their eyes on our land for a long time.

"'We come amongst you as friends—not as enemies; as protectors—not as conquerors.'

"Well, if we weren't conquered, por qué estamos tan chingados? Did the protection he offered stop the Maxwell thieves from taking our land grants? And has it stopped anyone since?

"'We come among you for your benefit—not for your injury.'

"Qué benefit?" he commented, peering over his reading glasses at them, as if he were lecturing in a classroom and challenging them to think about the contents of the broken treaty.

"'Henceforth I absolve you from all allegiance to the Mexican government, and from all obedience to General Armijo. He is no longer your governor. I am your governor.'"

Juan Oso looked up. "Imagine la pobre gente being absolved of their allegiance? What was going to replace it?

"'I shall not expect you to take up arms and follow me, to fight your own people who may oppose me. But I now tell you, that those who remain peaceably at home, attending to their crops and their herds, shall be protected by me, in their property, their persons, and their religion: not a pepper, not an onion, shall be disturbed or taken by my troops, without pay, or by the consent of the owner.'"

Here Juan Oso paused, took off his glasses and rubbed the bridge of his nose. "Not an onion, huh. In a few years the Maxwells and Catrons would take most of our land. And it didn't stop there. Remember that onion when you think of our history, they promised not to take it, but they stripped it away, layer by layer, until all we have left is what you see here. El corazón, the core of the onion. They can't strip the heart, it's all we have left."

He looked saddened. This part of his people's history was a history of loss. "Right after that," he said softly, "Kearny says that he will hang anyone who takes up arms against him. Well, they hung a few, and they're still hanging them."

His wife stood and went to his side. "You're tired, Juan, and the kids are tired. Let's all get some rest. We have all week to talk."

He smiled and nodded. "Bueno. Too much of this history in one dose might give bad nightmares."

Juan Oso went out to the corrals to check his animals, the few sheep and milk cows he kept, and Abrán went with him. The cold wind of the day had died down, leaving the valley in a brilliant clarity. Overhead the stars dazzled in purity.

The two men stopped to piss against the corral. The scent of pine filtered down from the mountain and mingled with the smell of their hot urine. The rumble of a nearby stream carried the cry of coyotes in the hills. A dog from the village returned the call.

"Tomorrow's going to be a warm day. You and Lucinda can take the horses and ride up the mountain. It's beautiful up there."

"Just don't meet any bears?" Abrán joked.

Juan Oso laughed. "There's a bear in every woman, just as in every man. You just got to know how to handle it, hijo," and he laughed again, slapped Abrán on the back, and with his arm around the young man's shoulder they went in.

Abrán slept in Antonio's and Iraclio's old room. He lay under the warm, thick quilts and thought of Juan Oso's story. From the hills, he heard the peaceful call of an owl. The entire valley and the mountain slept in the enduring peace of spring. That core of the onion, he thought, you can't strip that away. It will endure forever.

And him? What role would he have in it? He would marry Lucinda, of that he was sure. They would have children. So what if it took a few years to finish school, become a doctor? It was worth the wait. He had never felt so much at home as he had that day in the northern mountains with Lucinda and her family.

For the first time since Cynthia's death, he did not dream of the dark images of his father. Instead his sleep was deep and peaceful, and when he saw Juan Oso struggling with the bears in the mist of dream, it was more like a dance. Juan Oso was a bear, and the female bear was a woman. Then the images dissolved, he thought he saw the young lovers of Cynthia's bower, but when he looked closely, it was he and Lucinda who wrestled in love in the mountain meadow.

◆ ◆ ◆

15 The following morning Abrán slept late and awoke to a hearty breakfast and the picnic Lucinda had planned. Juan Oso had gone into Taos, and Esperanza was going to the church to ready it for the Easter Sunday Mass. After breakfast Abrán and Lucinda saddled the horses and set off up the mountain, following the road along the stream, then branching up a trail into the high country.

The morning was bright and warm. The bluejays and magpies called from the trees. Wildflowers sprouted among the dead pine needles, and along the trail beneath the stately ponderosa pines the grass was already poking through. Pine buds filled the fresh air with their fragrance.

Lucinda led, pointing out birds and other wildlife from time to time. She had been happy yesterday, Abrán thought. Today she was ecstatic. She was at home in the mountains.

She was dressed in Levi's for riding, an old cowboy shirt handed down from one of her brothers, and a tattered hat borrowed from her father. After a while on the trail her Levi jacket came off. The day was warm.

"We're almost there," she called, pointing. Ahead of them was an open meadow surrounded by pines and groves of white aspen. A doe and a fawn ran across the meadow and disappeared into the forest.

To the south they could see the snow-capped Truchas peak. Around them the green ridges of the mountains turned rich shades of blue as they stretched toward the horizon.

"I used to come here when I was a kid," Lucinda said as they hobbled the horses and spread a blanket beneath a pine. "Just to sit and dream. I'd look at the mountains, read books, sleep. Before I left for the real world."

"This is the real world," Abrán said and took a drink of the cool, mountain water in the canteen. It was hot; they were sweating from the ride. The smell of the horses and the saddle leather mixed with the scent of their sweat.

"Yes, this is real, and the world of Frank Dominic unreal," Lucinda agreed.

They looked south across the panorama of peaks of the Sangre de Cristo mountains.

"God's work," Abrán whispered.

Lucinda took his hand in hers. "For now, this time is ours."

"It's like dying and going to heaven," he smiled and held her close. "I've never seen anything like this."

"The mountain has everything we need. We can come up here every day."

"And your folks?"

"Will they mind? No. Life is very natural up here. They probably know what I'm feeling, but they trust me. Juan Oso wants a son-in-law, he'll probably even encourage you."

They laughed.

"And the bears?" he asked.

"They won't bother us," she said. "Juan Oso is brother of all the bears on this mountain. They know we're here, but they won't bother us. They have left their winter dens to eat." She reached across and snapped open the buttons of his shirt.

"Make love to me," she whispered. Her kiss was warm with love, its taste sweet. He pressed her to the blanket.

The wind moaned in the trees overhead; the sun warmed the lovers' sweating, glistening bodies. Around them the buzz of life awakening in the mountain was a chant, a mantra sung for the lovers. Theirs was a love so tender and natural that their soft cries became part of the song on the mountain.

When they were rested Lucinda nudged Abrán and told him to find wood to make a fire. She would fix the lunch.

Abrán went to gather wood at the edge of the meadow. As he bent to pick up old, weathered pine branches, he saw the snakes. Two mountain rattlesnakes entwined, sloughing off their winter skins, turning and twisting together, rising in the air.

"Lucinda," he whispered, but she was already by him. They watched in silence as the two snakes emerged from the thin tissue skins of winter and slid away, resplendent in the sun.

"Beautiful," Lucinda said when the snakes had disappeared into the bush.

"Beautiful?" he questioned. The snakes had aroused a primal instinct. He remembered the garden snake at Marisa's house.

"Creatures of the earth," Lucinda said as she carefully gathered the thin shells of skin the snakes had left behind. "Earth energy, mountain energy. Don't you see what it means?" She took his hand and placed it on her stomach. "You've made me pregnant."

He looked into her eyes as she held his hand on her stomach. She was serious. The mountain was the earth, her home. The snakes slept in the dark of earth, now they rose to shed their skins, to proclaim the return of the fertile season. Lucinda did not fear the snakes, they were creatures that came laden with meaning.

"My Nana will make good use of these," she said as she placed the glistening skins in her hat. "Now, the fire."

After lunch they lay in the warm sun and slept in each other's arms until a cool breeze reminded them it was time to go down from the mountain.

That evening they ate ravenously. Esperanza winked, Juan Oso looked at his daughter and was pleased. She was happy, so her happiness was his. There was little conversation that night; Abrán and Lucinda parted early with whispered good-nights. Each went to bed to sleep a deep, undisturbed sleep.

On Easter Sunday they went to church and returned to the big meal Esperanza had prepared. Abrán and Lucinda went through the motions of visiting with Lucinda's brothers and the wives and children, but when they glanced at each other they knew where they would rather be. Finally, when the meal was done, the dishes washed, and the brothers gone to visit the wives' families, Abrán and Lucinda sneaked away to the corral. The horses were already saddled.

"Juan Oso," Lucinda whispered. They mounted quickly and rode to their meadow.

Each day of their visit they escaped up the mountain, and Esperanza and Juan Oso went about their business, following their natural rhythm of life and allowing Abrán and Lucinda to have time to themselves. Luckily, it was a warm week, with little wind, one of those rare weeks after Easter when the windstorms of spring are done and summer slips in. The irascible moods of spring might yet return, but that week the gods kept the skies calm.

At the end of the week they went to their mountain bower for the last time. They sat quietly on their blanket, and Lucinda told Abrán about her recurring dream. In her sleep she saw a clay doll, the kind made by the pueblo potters, the fat earth mother with dozens of children clinging to her. The doll is a storyteller woman passing on the tales and history of the tribe.

"Last night the face of the doll was mine," Lucinda smiled. "Milk streamed from my breasts. The children around me drank and laughed and cried for more stories. Stories are like food, food for the dozens of children we will have. Now I know the meaning of the dream."

The time in Córdova had been idyllic, it had given them time to learn more about one another, to figure out their dreams. But the calm of their visit was broken on the last night by Casimiro's Cadillac lumbering toward the house in a cloud of dust. Juan Oso stepped out the front door to greet the visitors, and instantly knew that the well-dressed man getting out of the car was armed. The slight bulge under the jacket told him the man carried a pistol. A second, heavyset man waited in the car, his face hidden by the tinted window.

"What do you want?" Juan Oso asked in a stern voice. Behind him Abrán and Lucinda stepped out of the house to see who had arrived.

"Juan Oso?"

"Sí."

"I'm looking for—" he saw Abrán and smiled. "Hey, kid. You're a hard man to find."

"I wasn't hiding," Abrán said. "What's up?"

"Vacation's over, Mr. Dominic wants you back in Albuquerque. I might add he's very upset that we didn't know about this." He glanced at Lucinda.

"I'll be there tomorrow," Abrán said.

"You broke training. He wants you back right away!" Casimiro threatened. "Dominic's worried, and you've been up here. . ."

He stepped toward Abrán, but Juan Oso stepped in front of him. Both stopped to measure each other. The light from the car was enough to illuminate the resolve in their eyes.

Juan Oso could crush the man with one blow, the man could draw the pistol and fire within seconds, but neither was interested in drawing blood.

"He wants you back right away," Casimiro said and turned to the car.

"How did you find me?" Abrán asked.

Casimiro paused at the door. "We can find anyone, kid. You should know that." He laughed, then the car disappeared down the dirt road.

"We can start back tomorrow," Lucinda said.

On their way out of the village early the next morning, Lucinda and Abrán stopped to visit doña Agapita, the woman Lucinda called Nana. She was the old curandera who lived with one of her grandsons near the entrance of the small valley. They lived in a simple rock house with a faded tin roof; Nana kept goats in the corrals near the house, and in the summer she had a vegetable garden near the stream. She had practiced in the valley since she was a young girl, curing the people of the villages from Trampas to Nambé. Now, she was the last of her kind in the valley.

Her house was warm and sweet with the fragrance of herbs and roots that hung in her kitchen. She treated Lucinda like a daughter. Lucinda had spent much of her childhood around the old woman. "From the time she was seven," Esperanza had said, "Lucinda went with Nana to gather herbs. She learned to take care of the animals when they were sick. Nana is a godmother to Lucinda."

"We came to say goodbye," Lucinda said.

The old woman smiled. So, her child had grown into a woman and found a man. That was good, but there was something in the aura of the young man that disturbed her.

"Siéntense." She beckoned them into the kitchen, where it was warm and a pot of beans boiled on the stove. "Lupe," she explained, "is gone to Peñasco, so I'm alone. Siéntate. No tengas vergüenza," she said to Abrán and pulled up a chair for him.

They sat around the small, wooden table covered with a faded oilcloth and she served them coffee. Nana sensed that the young man's energy could be the power of the serpent, but something had interfered with his destiny. The boy could not see the natural path to follow, and yet he had been on that path in past lives. The father was missing, but there was something more disturbing. Another woman wanted his love.

When Lucinda gave the old woman the snakeskins they had found, the puzzle was clearer. Abrán was aligned to the energies of the earth, the snakes braved death to speak to him. His mother was an artist. His father was also an artist. That was clear.

Abrán told her about doña Tules; when he mentioned her advice to Abrán, Nana laughed and smiled.

"Sí," she said and looked at Abrán, "Tú eres tú. That is what all the world is trying to tell you, including the snakes."

It wasn't important who the boy's father was, she thought. The father and the mother were the agents to get him to earth, but the boy's soul had a much more interesting destiny to complete. He would do well in the mountains if he married Lucinda, for his aura was the color of a healer, and his hands were the hands of a healer.

"Domingo is not your friend," she told Abrán. "You will learn much from women," she said as she softly fingered the thin, crisp coat of snakeskin. "Women like us," she looked at Lucinda lovingly, "we are like the snake. We feel the energy of the earth. That intuition guides us. It must guide you," she said to Abrán.

She reached across and touched Lucinda's stomach and smiled. The girl was pregnant, the young man's seed had come to rest in her womb. Lucinda's power had drawn the spirit of Abrán into her womb.

"Do you feel well?" she asked.

"I feel wonderful," Lucinda smiled.

"Listen, child, much will come to interfere. This energy you feel is positive, but others would separate the bond that creates the energy."

"Nothing will separate us," Lucinda said and reached for Abrán's hand.

"Good. Keep strong. Cuídate," Nana said in parting.

"We'll come back," Lucinda said softly when she hugged Nana. "I promise, we'll come back."

Nana nodded, then laughed. "You better hurry, I am getting old."

16 In Santo Domingo the men were cleaning the acequias. They burned the dry brush and grass along the sides and cleared the sediment out of the ditches, digging deep into the red soil so the banks would be sturdy all summer. They patched breaks where groundhogs had burrowed, and they repaired the gates that let the water from the main ditch into the smaller ones which fed the fields.

It was back-breaking work with hoe and shovel, but because it was a communal enterprise, the joking and the stories made the time pass quickly. When the work was almost done and the acequia madre was opened, there was a sense of relief. Only then did the young men talk about going to drink cold beer in Peña Blanca.

The old men had blessed the corn and calabaza seeds for planting, as they had done from time immemorial. They would pray to the kachinas, the ancestors who brought rain, and they would pray to the santos of the Catholic church that the earth accept the seeds so the pueblo would have food. In the summer they would take the patron saint of the church, Saint Dominic, from his altar and carry him in a procession into the fields so he, too, might bless the earth and the plants.

And soon, just as soon as spring turned into summer, the kachinas would come from the Jémez Mountains. Dressed in huge billowing clouds that grew into an anvil shape, they would rise into the summer sky. The tops of the massive clouds would be white as eagle's down; beneath they would be dark and pregnant. Spring rain would come after the seeds were planted. Not much rain, but enough to slake the winter thirst. In July the fat clouds would finally let loose with summer rain, the rain of the kachinas and the santos.

Winter was done, the time of storytelling was over, now was the time of working in the fields. Amid all this timeless ceremony the old, traditional folks worried that the young people weren't guarding the culture, that too many of the young were moving into the city and forgetting the old ways.

We must stay close to our pueblo, they said, not go to the edge of our world or beyond. There you will get lost. The center is here in Santo Domingo, it is our source of life. Stay close to the pueblo and the ceremonies, dance and sing and pray for rain and good harvest. Don't start drinking booze and forget everything you were taught. Remember what your parents taught you. Stay with your family, stay with your clan. Sing and dance.

See what happened to José Calabasa? some whispered. He went away. He went to war, as did some of our boys during World War II and Korea, but they came back. José doesn't come back. He does not dance, he does not go to the medicine men. Time is different now, the world of things presses around us. The world of things pushes us out of our center, out of our pueblo. Beyond the boundary of our pueblo you lose your spirit.

These are the things Joe heard in the wind as he walked around the pueblo. He had come to the Santo Domingo mad and barged into the council meeting, demanding to know why the hell they were selling the water.

The attorneys were explaining Dominic's plan to the council. The old men listened quietly and politely as the young lawyers sketched out the benefits. They were young Indian attorneys, dressed in three-piece suits. They had degrees from law schools all over the country, they had been beyond the edge of the pueblo world, and they knew how to talk Dominic's language.

"You can't sell the water," Joe cried out, ready to fight. "Next we'll start selling pueblo land, like the Cochití sold their land. You'll have condos right here on the land of our ancestors, Americanos digging in our shrines! And soon the people with money will start telling you what to do!"

The startled pueblo policeman had rushed forward to grab Joe and haul him out, but the council president had motioned slightly. No, let him say his piece. They knew Joe; he was the son of Encarnación Calabasa, a respected man. Joe had been to a place of war, the place called Nam. Now he was reading books at the university. They knew he was troubled. He was not yet cleansed of the evil spirits of Nam.

Let him talk; every man was entitled to have his say. But the young attorneys didn't have the patience of the old men, they wanted to get on with the project, and Joe Calabasa was a washed-out vet who carried no weight.

"Since when are you an authority on our water rights, Joe?" Gilbert Trujillo challenged him. "You're not on the council, so get off your high horse. And you ain't been around the pueblo for a long time, so what gives you the right to say anything. We've been working on this plan for a long time—"

"Behind our backs!" Joe shouted, the anger he felt getting the best of him. Gilbert had stung all right. Sonofabitchin' Gilly with his highfalutin 'I'm an attorney, got a degree, and you Joe, you ain't even been here at the pueblo for years.' It stung Joe, because Gilly was right.

"Shit," Gilbert muttered beneath his breath. He grinned and looked at the council members. "It's not behind nobody's back, Joe," and a suddenly startled Joe Calabasa looked into the impenetrable faces of the old men. Their eyes gave nothing away, but because they didn't respond, Gilbert was right. Holy Coyote, they were going to sell the water!

Joe looked at his father, but Encarnación Calabasa sat so still he betrayed no emotion. His father had voted with the council, Joe thought. He felt betrayed.

His knees were weak, like a buffalo stung with the lance of a warrior; the bleeding had begun. His breath went out, and he stood looking at the council members for a long time. A fly droned against a windowpane. Joe felt his heart pounding. The deal was already done, they were going to sell the water. The old men had no power. The young kids like Gilbert were running the show. Joe shook his head sadly and walked out.

There was nothing to say; he had no power of persuasion. He hadn't been home for years, so he was like a stranger in the pueblo. He had not yet cleansed himself of the war; he had not yet danced. Yes, he was helping with the acequia, which was a beginning because he was working with the men, but it would take time before he reentered the circle of the pueblo.

He needed a drink, his mouth was so dry. Around him the wind whipped up the dirt of the street, a skirt of dust, exposing the dry bone of earth beneath.

The day was warm and the pueblo seemed deserted. Joe picked up his shovel and headed for the acequia where the crew was already at work. Once there he tackled the job with an awesome, angry energy.

The rest of the men stayed out of his way. He was a mad buffalo outdistancing the best of the workers, a machine plowing through the earth. He mumbled to himself, thinking of the water that came from the Río Grande down the main ditch. He thought of his visions.

Three nights in a row since coming to the pueblo, he dreamed he was pinned to the ground, and around him squatted Viet Cong. They had tied his arms and legs in four directions and stripped him naked. Overhead a vulture circled and then dropped to perch on him. The giant bird ripped his body open and ate at his heart and liver.

The pain was real, so real he awoke screaming, clutching his chest. Each night he had crept out of the house to the acequia to wash his face and arms, and always behind him he felt the presence of his father, saying nothing but watching over him, waiting for his son to return.

By noon Joe was exhausted from digging. He had done the work of three men and blisters bled on his palms, his muscles throbbed. As Joe sat, the women brought food for the men: chile stew with meat, beans, and Indian bread baked in the hornos.

His mother served his father and then Joe. "How do you feel, mi'jo?" she asked. She placed the food in front of him where he sat alone. The other men sat in a group under the huge cottonwood tree on the cool acequia bank, but Joe sat under the hot sun. Why was he punishing himself? she wondered.

"Okay, Mom," he nodded. He looked at her. Flor de Calabasa, his mother, a woman who took the pollen of his father. Spanish blood and Indian blood mixed in Joe, as it had in people for hundreds of years along the Río Grande. He was a Santo Domingo man, but in him ran the blood of the conquistadores, the old Spanish blood of the conquerors of his people, the blood of Coronado who marched up the Río Grande in 1540. Men of iron, the old people of the pueblo called them. They took our food and women. The hermanos Franciscos destroyed our kivas and our sacred objects, and they left pestilence in their wake.

But what the hell, isn't that what all conquerors do? Joe thought. Didn't we take the women of our Nam brothers? In the hootches of the villages or in Saigon flophouses, we took the women and gave birth to a new generation of mestizos. Nam babies running around with blond hair, kinky hair, Indian and Chicano color in their skin. It would not be an easy life for them, either.

"Don't work so hard," his mother said, and turned to look at his father, who didn't look up from his meal. She wanted to reach out and touch her son, hold him as she had when he was a child, but that was not permitted. Things were hard enough for her son. Her son who had been wounded in the war nobody won; her son who preferred to live in the city and read books. Was it too late for him to return home?

She turned and walked with the other women back to the pueblo.

Joe watched her walk away. Did he blame her? Or did he blame his father? No, their love had been good all these years. But why did it matter that he had Spanish blood in him? When he started school in

Peña Blanca, the Mexican kids used to tease him and he would fight. When he came home bloodied, his mother would clean him up and say, "Don't fight. Remember, they are your cousins."

Joe glanced at his father. He had been a farmer all his life, preferring the life and rhythms of the pueblo to the better-paying jobs in Santa Fé or Alburkirk. A farmer like the farmers in the Nam villages, like his father before him. He planted seeds in the soil, praying for the rain as he prayed for his son to return, hoeing and mixing his sweat into the earth.

Joe thought of Bea. How simple and good to have a woman who would have your children. Children raised like corn and squash.

"If you had been a girl we would have called you Squash Blossom," his father liked to kid him. "Flor de Calabasa, just like your mother. But it was San José fiesta day, and the old priest got hold of you and dunked you in the acequia. Baptized you José."

Joe's cousin, Charlie, called him Mad Buffalo, Warrior Who Destroys. I scattered seeds from my M-16, seeds of hate, Joe thought.

You, too, can be an All-American Indian, the recruiting sergeant said. We'll make a Marine out of you! All-American Indian Jerk is what they should have said.

"Yeah, a jerk," Joe said aloud, and the men glanced at him. He was speaking his thoughts again.

The men had finished eating. The older men smoked, the younger men joked. They were talking about the good food they had eaten, when cousin Johnny began teasing Rollie about eating too much white bread because he was living with an Anglo girl from Bernalillo. Rollie and his girl had an apartment in the city; Rollie was taking classes at the tech school.

"You eat white bread and pretty soon you start getting white," Johnny said.

The story was that the girl only fixed Rollie white bread and boiled egg sandwiches. He came home so sick his mother had to give him a strong laxative. They said his stools came out wrapped in Rainbo Bread plastic wrap.

"Yeah," cousin Rabbit said, "watch out." Rabbit was a good-looking young man who made the rounds of Santa Fé bars picking up lonely tourist women.

"What are you talking about?" the others booed Rabbit.

"You been making it in Santa Fé!"

"One of those Mexican boys is goin' run you over in his lowrider car," they laughed.

"Dead rabbit."

"No more humpin'."

"Ah, white women treat me good," Rabbit smiled. "I got what it takes. You guys can't even make it with Cochití girls."

Somebody filled a bucket of water and splashed it over him, then they ganged up on him and threw him into the acequia, and a bunch of them jumped in and started dunking each other.

Then one of the old men called; it was time to get back to work. The young men climbed of the ditch, soaking wet, laughing, feeling good. Joe had watched, but he had not joined in. He felt too old to play with the young men, too young to sit with the elders. He was outside the circle.

He looked up to see a trail of dust coming toward them. It was Abrán's car.

"My friend," he said, and smiled.

A slight nod from his father said, go, you've done enough work for one day. Joe shouldered his shovel and walked to the road.

"Where have you two been?" he asked. They shook hands softly, good friends meeting.

At the house Flor was glad to meet Abrán and Lucinda, and happy for her son. Friends were good for him. Later, when Encarnación came home, she served a big dinner, all of Joe's favorite dishes. Afterwards they sat in the front room, drank coffee, and talked. The pueblo was in a festive mood now that the acequias were clean. Neighbors dropped by to say hello and to see who the visitors were. It was Saturday night and there was a big dance in Algodones.

Bea and her mother came by the house. Joe didn't know if they had just dropped by or if his mother had invited them. He knew the two mothers plotted to get them together. Tonight he didn't mind, he was home with family and friends, and Bea looked beautiful in her velvet dress and turquoise jewelry. She had braided her dark, shiny hair so that it fell around her right shoulder. Joe had never seen her look as lovely.

"You look like you're goin' dancin'," Joe's father said. Bea's mother shook her head.

"Not dancin', we just came by to say hello."

Joe introduced Bea and her mother to Lucinda and Abrán.

"We should go dancing," he said. "Look at us, all dressed up. Everybody's going."

"No," Bea's mother said. "Too much drinking."

"The boys worked hard all week," Encarnación said, "they deserve a break."

"It would be good for them," Flor agreed. She looked at her son. He had combed his hair in a chongo and tied it with a ribbon borrowed from his father. The cowboy shirt was also borrowed from his father. He was a handsome man, and she was proud of him.

"I want to go dancing," Joe said. He looked at Bea.

"I'm for it," Lucinda nodded.

"Hey, I usually dance with a jumprope, but this sounds good," Abrán smiled at her.

The gay mood in the air was infectious, except for Bea's mother. She shook her head. "Too much drinkin', too many accidents."

"We would be careful," Bea said softly.

"I promise not to touch a drop," Joe swore.

"Come on, Hazel," Encarnación prodded Bea's mother, "let her go. The kids got to have some fun. I remember when you were young, you liked to go to those dances in Peña Blanca."

Bea's mother blushed. "That was different, there was no drinkin' then."

"There's always been drinkin'," Encarnación shrugged. "Joe told you he ain't goin' drink."

"Ma, you used to dance?" Bea asked.

"Sure," Encarnación nodded, "she never missed a dance. The Spanish boys at Peña Blanca were always after her."

Bea's mother blushed. "All right," she consented, "you can go. Or Carney will make up stories about me. But you got to be home early."

Bea hugged her. "Thanks, Mom."

"All right," Joe shouted. "We're goin' 49er! Stompin' mad! Come on," he grabbed Bea's hand and led Abrán and Lucinda outside. "Let's go!"

"Be home early!" Bea's mom called.

"Be careful," Flor said as they waved goodbye.

They packed into Abrán's car and headed for Algodones, where the little bar was packed with natives from the surrounding villages. Even couples from Alburquerque came to the old cantina. A small band played rock and roll, a few country-western, a few oldies. Like any other Saturday night in a small town, old acquaintances were renewed and new ones made. Young men met young women, and one or two of the liaisons would lead to one-night stands. Some would lead to marriage.

If Joe had a woman, Flor had said, he would settle down, raise a family. They liked Bea, and before Nam came, everyone thought they would get married. Then Joe joined the service, and when he came back, he was a changed man. Not even Bea's patient love could draw him back to the pueblo.

When the music finally stopped, Abrán and Lucinda said goodbye to their friends with promises to meet soon. Joe and Bea would catch a ride back to the pueblo with his cousin, and Joe swore he would be in Alburquerque for Abrán's fight.

"Call my folks' place. I'll be here," he smiled. The anger he felt at the council had dissipated, but for how long?

They shook hands, said goodbye, and in the cool of the spring night, Abrán and Lucinda roared out of the glass-littered parking lot toward the city.

Overhead the glitter of the stars was dimmed by the lights of

Alburquerque, and the beauty and mystery of the northern mountains was suddenly gone. Reality now was the high, semi-arid plateau and its city that straddled the Río Grande. Yesterday's breeze had cleaned out the valley, but now, even in the calm of the night, a thin cloud of pollution hung over the city.

"Not like Córdova," Abrán said.

"Sometimes I wonder why I come back," Lucinda nodded.

"Why do you?"

"Work."

"You know, I like the idea of the clinic," he said. "Is it being too idealistic?"

"Maybe," she smiled, "but somebody has to believe."

Again he asked her, "Do you really think you're pregnant?" He had asked a dozen times already.

"I'm sure," she answered. "Scared?"

"Maybe a little," he answered.

"Want to change your mind?"

"No way. I want you, I want whatever comes with you. It's just something I have to get used to. Joe and I used to talk about marriage. He wants to marry Bea. He knows he needs her, but now it looks like I beat him. They can be our padrinos."

Lucinda nodded and held his hand. Her thoughts were focused on the growing life she felt within. Of course it was too soon for her body's imperceptible changes to tell her anything, but she knew—deep in her soul she knew she had conceived, and Nana had confirmed her intuition.

A few weeks ago, Abrán thought, becoming a father was only an abstract thought. Now it was real, and the more he thought about it, the more he liked the feeling. He knew Sara would be happy.

The house and paintings Cynthia had left him would help. A medical career was more of a reality now. He *could* help people, and he and Lucinda could eventually work together. Devoting his life to the clinic she envisioned in the northern villages was something he wanted to share. Now he knew its importance to the people. And now he had the resources to help make the dream a reality.

He sighed. There were others like him, Chicanos who had one parent who was Anglo or Black or Asian. The new mestizos. They would have to find their identity, as he was trying to find his. At first he had been full of anger; he didn't want to understand doña Tules' message. But now he felt strong. He had found Lucinda's love, the love of her parents, and the trust of Juan Oso. He had reaffirmed his commitment to Sara, and he was happy. He would accept his dead mother, make peace with her even though he had never known her, and he would find his father.

He thought about his child. He would be a good father, the best possible. If he could just be done with Dominic.

"Dominic's going to be pissed," he thought aloud.

"Who cares," Lucinda whispered, and snuggled at his side. "Maybe you should just drop everything."

"I can't, I gave my word."

"You men. Your word, your honor."

"It's got to be worth something," he said.

"It is, but you know he's not good."

"I'll be done soon. I want to see doña Tules. Been thinking a lot of that old woman."

"And your mom."

"I'll have to take her up to Santa Fé to see the house."

"And to Córdova to meet my parents."

"All these responsibilities," he smiled.

He dropped Lucinda at her house, promised to take her to dinner the following night, then drove home. He slept peacefully until Sara's coffee and breakfast aroma roused him the next morning. He told her everything. She was pleased, but her mood was subdued.

"How strange is destiny," she said. "The mother who could not care for you when she was alive has come back from the grave to help you. She did love you, but. . ." She paused, glanced out the window. He waited. "You have to make very wise decisions. Don't give up who you are. . ."

"I won't," he said, and leaned to kiss her forehead. He thought she meant not to forget about her, but she really meant that he had within him the knowledge of his identity. Not even a change in fortune should alter that.

"The ways of the world can distract you," she said, then, realizing how ominous her thoughts were, she changed the subject. "There were many phone calls. Everybody wants to talk to you. And your picture's in the papers. I go to the store and everybody wants to know about you." She paused and grew silent again.

"What's the matter, Mamá?" he coaxed her.

"Be careful," she said. "Don't change too much. I don't want to lose the son I have."

"You won't. This is going to work out fine. Lucinda and I want to take you up north to meet her parents. You're going to like them, and you'll like the mountains. Who knows, you might like to retire up there. ¿Qué dices?" he laughed to cheer her.

"Who knows," she shrugged, "but I think I'll probably stay right here. The memory of your father is here, my friends are here."

"What makes you happy is what I want. Besides, I can come for you when you feel like seeing your grandkids."

"Grandkids?" her eyebrow arched. He nodded, and she flung her arms around his neck and cried for joy, her tears staining his shirt. "Imagine, grandchildren. I'm happy, mi'jo. I'm happy for you."

After breakfast he put on his workout pants and sweatshirt and jogged to the gym. He worked out the rest of the morning, then returned in time to help Sara clean her rose garden. They dug around the bushes and he cut away the old stems. She told stories as they worked, about people she had known. After a late lunch Abrán relaxed and flipped through the newspaper.

"The shit has hit the fan," he whistled softly.

The papers were blowing up the mayoral race, pitting Dominic against Johnson. In typical fashion Martínez was already discounted as far as the editorials were concerned. A series of stories on the sports page probed into Abrán's life. He was a mystery man nobody could find that week. Dominic was accused of hiding him. The fight itself had suddenly become the hot news item, moving from the sports page to the front page. "Abrán González Returns to the Ring," the headlines announced. Was the former Golden Gloves champ ready for a pro fight? Too much, Abrán thought as he put the paper down and stood to read through the phone notes Sara had taken. There was Marisa's number. I can't, he thought, not now.

Late in the afternoon he drove to Dominic's, rode the elevator up and announced himself. The secretary buzzed Casimiro, and he escorted Abrán into Dominic's office, offering another warning. "You fucked up, kid."

The cool poise Dominic always affected disappeared when he saw Abrán. He was livid. "Where in the hell have you been?" he shouted.

"I went up north—"

"Who in the hell gave you permission to go up north!" Dominic roared back. "You broke training. One fucking week! The most important time! You knew the fight date was set!"

"I'm okay—"

"The hell you're okay. You've been fucking around. First fucking the mayor, then that little bitch you run around with!"

Abrán's response surprised even Dominic. He reached out, grabbed Dominic by the lapels, and jerked him off his feet.

"You never call Lucinda a bitch!" he shouted in Dominic's face, fighting the impulse to hit him as he shoved him back. In the same split second the two dobermans attacked. They had followed Dominic into the room. When the stranger grabbed their master, they both jumped at once, fangs slashing, killer growls in their throats. The big one knocked Abrán sideways, the smaller dog grabbed his leg and clamped its teeth. Blood appeared instantly.

"Down! Down!" the startled Dominic shouted. "Back down!" He had to pull away the dog that had grabbed Abrán's leg. "Back, Diablo! Back, Ali!" Casimiro ran in to help.

"Shit!" Dominic cursed as the dogs backed down, whined, and allowed Casimiro to lead them out onto the terrace. "Don't ever pull that again, kid. Next time I'll let them kill you." He straightened his collar and looked at Abrán. "Let's see that." He pulled up the pantleg, revealing the bleeding shin. "Holy fuck! That's all we need! Cass! Get him to a doctor."

"Can you walk?" Casimiro asked.

"I'm okay, it's just a cut," he pushed Casimiro away. There was pain, but it was deadened by his anger. He wasn't done with Dominic.

"I don't care how much you know, Frank, just don't you ever bad-mouth Lucinda again. You do and you won't have enough dogs to keep me back!"

They glared at each other, Dominic gritted his teeth in anger. The little sonofabitch needed to be put in his place. Okay, two could play the game. He smiled.

"Take it easy, kid. Get the cut bandaged. You got a fight this week. I just hope to hell you can still fight."

"I'll be at that fight!" Abrán shot back. "You just make sure you're there! And with the information you promised!"

Casimiro stepped in between the two. He had never seen his boss so angry. "Take it easy," he said and pulled Abrán away.

On the terrace the dogs clawed madly at the glass window and growled to get in.

"Get him outta here!" Dominic shouted, the veins along his temple pulsing, his body trembling with rage. The kid was going to cost him. He was too goddamn independent.

Maybe I made a mistake, Dominic thought as Abrán and Casimiro walked out of the office. The cocky sonofabitch is feeling his oats. He had fucked the mayor, the papers make him a hero, so he thinks he has the world by the balls.

"I'll show him," Dominic cursed, "I'll show him."

17 The doctor sutured the cut. "Sharp and deep," he said. "Stay off your feet, rest the leg for a couple of days," he ordered. "I'll talk to your trainer, make sure he knows what to do. It should heal by fight time," he said and crossed his fingers. "Use the crutches, just to keep the weight off."

Abrán went home to rest, but he couldn't. Sara was visiting her comadre and that meant they would drink beer and play cards all afternoon, then spend the evening making enchiladas. She wouldn't return until late. He tried Lucinda and there was no answer. He begin to worry.

He pulled the shades and tried to sleep, but something was nagging at him. Dominic? The man was crazy, but even the thought of backing out of the deal was out of the question. Abrán had given his word.

The phone interrupted his thoughts. "I've been trying to reach you all week," Marisa greeted him. "I want to see you. I'm throwing a little party. Just a few people. Can you come?"

Abrán hesitated. No, he knew he couldn't see her.

"I'm sorry," he answered.

"I want to see you," she said. Her voice trembled.

"It won't work," he said.

"It can," she answered, her voice hesitant. "It was too good the first time not to try."

"I have a girl."

"The nurse," she said.

"How did you know?"

"I talked to your mother. I don't want to sound like I'm meddling, your time is yours, but I really want to see you. I can cancel the party if you will just come over. We can swim."

"I don't think it would be fair." He paused.

There was a long silence, then a sigh. "You have my phone number. Call me anytime. I really want to see you." She hung up.

He got up slowly and went into the kitchen. Sara had left a snack in the refrigerator, but he wasn't hungry. He glanced out the kitchen window into the soft, spring dusk. Kids played in the street, a couple of Mexican workers walked by.

Lucinda, he thought, where in the hell are you. I want you here with me. He tried her number again, and still there was no answer.

Tú eres tú, the words sounded in the whisper of the trees as a gust of wind moved through the barrio elms. You can only be who you are, inside, but that person was strangely connected to a past that kept revealing itself in unusual twists. Who knew the past? He thought of doña Tules, and grabbed his jacket. Outside, the warm spring evening greeted him, as did the friendly sounds of the barrio. Without hesitating he headed down the street toward the home of the curandera.

The people in the barrio treated doña Tules with respect and distance. She walked the back streets and alleys of the neighborhood at night, and she was used as an excuse by the mothers of the barrio to get their children home on time: "Doña Tules is going to get you," they would say. But doña Tules never really got anyone, and she really wasn't la Llorona, the weeping woman of the folktales.

Sara had told Abrán the story of this old woman who lived in a small house under the cottonwood trees by the river's edge. She had been a lovely young girl. Her mistake was to fall in love with a traveling salesman, a man who sold women's shoes and finery. He had lured her to the river with false promises, gotten her pregnant, and then discarded her. Her father, an old, wealthy merchant from the barrio, cast her out of the family for the shame she had brought his good name. His honor dictated that he disown her. No one really knew if she ever had her baby or if it died at childbirth, but a child was never seen. Did she, like the Llorona of legend, drown the infant in the river?

After the scandal died down, the young doña Tules appeared on the streets of the barrio, dressed in the tattered white dress given to her by the salesman. She wore lace gloves and black patent-leather shoes, shiny at first but then, over the years, covered with mud and dust and worn down to the crust of leather. Her family had long since moved away, and she lived alone. The barrio got used to her, and as she grew older she kept more to herself and grew more into the mythic woman of stories told in the barrio.

Generations came, moved away, or disappeared into the flow of history. The seasons, reflected in the towering cottonwoods of the bosque, changed along the river valley, but doña Tules remained. She got older and left her home only at night, followed by her dogs. The people who needed her advice found her in the dark of night. Lovers who wanted love or revenge sought her out.

The old woman who had had little love in her life became an expert in the affairs of the heart. People said she could help those who wished to possess a beloved; she could give advice on how to bring a lover to his knees. Likewise, she could prepare remedies that would bring harm to the unfaithful. None of this was true according to Sara. To her, doña Tules was a curandera who knew how to cure people. But the rumors persisted.

Doña Tules warned those who came to her that the power was not in her remedies, the power was in the emotion they carried in their hearts. El mal ojo, the evil eye, was a stare of excessive love, and it was far more dangerous than any remedy she could brew. Revenge in the heart, fed by passion, was more destructive than the simple amulets and powders she dispensed. Only the desperate sought her help, because the desperate were already swept up by the fire of passion or revenge.

Rumors, Abrán thought as he approached her small house, a hut hidden in the shadows of the trees. Her old dogs growled, but perhaps smelling the lingering scent of the dobermans, they did not challenge him. Why had the old woman appeared to him the night his mother died? Did she know death was in the air that night? And because she had been in the barrio for so long, could she possibly know something of his father? This is what he hoped as he knocked on her door.

The old woman opened the door slightly. Her piercing eyes looked at him, then she smiled. "Abrán," she said, and led him into the small room that served as both kitchen and bedroom. The air was thick with incense, the sweet fragrance of herbs almost stifling. She motioned to a chair at the small table, and he sat.

"I will fix you some coffee," she said.

"No, gracias," he thanked her. "I came because—"

"Oh, I know why you have come," she said as she turned to her altar to light a candle. "I have known you since Sara and Ramiro brought you to the barrio. Ramiro was a good man. And your mother, a good woman." She sat and looked at Abrán. The candlelight danced in the small room. A thin line of incense and candle smoke rose past the plaster saints that adorned her altar.

Abrán smiled. The woman accused of being la Llorona of the barrio and who had leaped across his path the night he drove to the hospital was no terror, she was simply an old woman. She lived alone. Is that why the people mistrusted her? Had the years spent alone brought a special gift that allowed her to peer into the souls of those needing help?

Abrán cleared his throat. "Ramiro wasn't my father," he said, and felt guilty for denouncing the old man.

She looked at him. "No, he was not your blood father, but he raised you. He took care of you and Sara. That is all a son should ask."

"Yes, I know Ramiro was good, but I also have to know my real father."

The old woman shook her head. "I have told you all you need to know. . . ."

"Tú eres tú," he said.

She smiled. "Men are blind."

"What does it mean?"

She sighed. "The person within is all you have to know. You are your own father. Each man is your father, each woman is your mother. It takes time to understand this, but when you do, your soul will be at peace."

She turned and stared at the candles. Abrán shifted in his chair. Yes, each man was his father, he was connected to that brotherhood. There was a pool of experiences and insights that they shared: a stirring in the blood at the core of their manhood, the sex between their legs that defined their sexuality. He had felt that shock of recognition when he met Juan Oso. Lucinda's father could be his father—that is, they could have a fulfilling father-and-son relationship.

But there was also the father whose sperm was planted in Cynthia's womb, a man whose blood was his. Who was this man? Where? The old woman dealt in cryptic phrases, but he wanted real answers.

"What do you know?" he asked, disturbed by her quietness. "Tell me and I'll pay you."

She laughed a deep, hoarse laugh that irritated him.

"Pay," she said and rose. "Pay an old lady? What do I need? Will you buy me a pair of dancing shoes, red ones with high heels? Yes, red with gold straps. And when I dance, the men will turn to look at my ankles—" She laughed so loud it echoed in the small room. "That's what I was promised when I was young, but the promises of youth are never kept. You have not kept your promise," she said and stared at him.

Her look sent a chill through him. "What if now you have fathered a child in two women? Will you claim both? I told you who you are so you would be at peace with yourself," her voice rose, "but you have not listened!"

"Why me?" Abrán cried out.

"Because of Ramiro," she said. "Years ago he helped me, he and Sara. When I had nothing to eat and no place to sleep, they took me in. Kind people, they asked nothing in return. I promised then that if I could ever help them, I would do so. And so the night I had a vision of your gringa mother dying, I went to you. Your world was about to change, and I knew the change would be painful."

"How did you know Cynthia was my mother?"

Doña Tules laughed. "All the old people of the barrio knew. You can't hide a thing like that. We said nothing because we did not wish to trouble Sara. She is a good woman, and it pleased her to have a son. Why should we take that happiness from her?"

"Then you must know about my father!" Abrán stood.

"The boy from the barrio?"

"Yes."

She shook her head. "I had dreams during that time. Many people came to me for help, it was a time of turmoil. The people of the barrio were suffering. I told them my dreams, I helped them understand their own dreams, that is all I could do. One man I remember, because he had an aura like yours. A very strong man."

"Who?" Abrán whispered and held his breath.

"Clemente Chávez. Yes, that was the man's name, and I still remember his dream. He thought he could change the course of history." She gurgled a laugh. "A common affliction of man," she smiled.

Abrán felt himself shiver. He recognized the name. Sara had told him Clemente was the man who led the strike against the railroad.

"Look at your hands," she said. "You have a gift in your hands, you can cure people. You should be my assistant, then we could really make some money," she sputtered and broke into laughter. She laughed uproariously, rocking back and forth, her rheumy eyes filling with tears. The tears streamed down her wrinkled cheeks and she wiped at them with her small, weathered hands.

"A curandero following doña Tules down the streets," and her mumbled images sent her into new outbursts of laughter. "But you have to stop playing with the girls," she said, "because it takes all your energy, and if you have no energy you cannot have good visions!"

She laughed anew, and Abrán stood and stepped back. The old woman was crazy. Her laughter irritated him because he felt he was the object of her fun. He fumbled with the door and stepped out. The low growl of the dogs reminded him of their presence.

He walked into the dark. "Don't forget the red shoes!" doña Tules called from inside, and a new peal of laughter echoed in the dark.

Abrán limped home, the pain of his wound intensifying with every step. He cursed himself for not driving, and for not bringing Lucinda with him. Then again, doña Tules had blurted out that thing about the two women, two sons. Damn her. What else did she know? Witch. Crystal-ball gazer. He shook his head. Why was he taking out his anger on her? She had only told him what was true.

Doña Tules said the old people of the barrio knew he was not Ramiro and Sara's son. He was part Anglo. A coyote, the people said. They had kept quiet because of Sara. He didn't blame Sara, though. She had tried to protect him. He realized how little he knew about the world of women, and how quickly it was opening up to him. What he had known came from Sara in her role as a protective mother. Lucinda's curandera said that he was to learn from women.

He was sweating by the time he got home, and his leg was throbbing with pain. Doña Tules knew about Lucinda and Marisa. What if both were pregnant, she asked. The thought frightened him.

The house was dark; Sara was still out. He had to see Lucinda. She would know what to do. She would wash the wound with osha and dress it with fresh bandages. She was the only curandera he needed, he thought, as he got into his car and drove out of the barrio. Tú eres tú, the cry of doña Tules echoed in the shadows of the elm trees. Confounded by the old woman's meaning, he yearned for Lucinda's touch.

He drove quickly to Martíneztown and parked in front of her apartment. The bright light shining in the window welcomed him; he breathed a sigh of relief. She was home, she would care for him, and when he told her about doña Tules and the red shoes, they would laugh together.

Limping, he made his way to the door and knocked. A shadow moved at the window. He knocked again, and still no answer. He called her name, "Lucinda! It's me, Abrán!" This time he knocked forcefully. The same ill feeling that had plagued him all day returned with a numbing weight. Something was wrong. He was about to throw himself against the door when it opened only a crack.

Why did she have the chain on? Lucinda had been crying, her eyes were red and puffed, full of tears.

"Let me in," he said, but she didn't move. "What's the matter? What's wrong?"

"Oh, Abrán," she cried, the tears shining in her eyes. "How could you, how could you?"

"What? What's happened?" The feeling he had lived with all day suddenly became a lump in his throat. She knew about Marisa, someone had told her.

"Say it isn't true. Please say it isn't true, and I'll believe you," she sobbed softly. She looked into his eyes.

He shook his head; his stomach churned and made him sick.

"You were with her that night," she cried, "then you spent all week with me." He could feel her emptiness.

"I was going to tell you, I swear I was going to tell you!"

She shook her head in disbelief. "You made love to her, then came to me."

"It wasn't love!" He struggled desperately to find the words to explain, but there were none. The hurt was too deep. He had been unfaithful to her, and it had devastated her. The light that had been there from the moment they met was gone.

"It just happened," he said softly and shook his head. His body trembled, he felt weak. What was there to say? Nothing. She knew.

"It's true?" she said.

"Yes."

"And this past week—oh God, Abrán, how could you? How could you?"

"What happened. . ." He couldn't find the words to explain. "It meant nothing. It won't happen again. You're all I care for. Forgive me, forgive me this one time and. . ." He couldn't finish. He knew he had wronged her.

She leaned her head against the door and was silent. Then she whispered, "Someone called. I didn't want to believe it."

"Let me come in, let me try to explain."

She looked at him and shook her head. "There's nothing to explain. I wouldn't have minded if you had had other women before. But this past week. I can't forgive. I trusted you."

She pushed the door, but he held it.

"You've got to understand!" he shouted.

"I don't want to see you again," she answered in anger, her voice rising with the hurt she felt. "Don't come here anymore!" She slammed the door shut.

"Lucinda!" he shouted, "Lucinda! Let me talk to you!" He banged on the door, but there was no answer. Across the street a neighbor's porch light came on, a dog barked. If he persisted, the police would come, and that would only make things worse.

He slumped down on the steps. The tears flowed and he felt the sobs of pain and loss take over his body.

He had not cried like this since he was a child. A wound opened in his soul, and he realized how much he loved Lucinda. He didn't want to live without her.

"Lucinda, Lucinda," he cried and lashed out at the porch post.

There was no answer. She had turned the lights off, for she, too, was emptying herself of the deceit she felt. Cradled in her bed she cried until there were no more tears. Why? she asked, why? But there was no answer. He had deceived her; that was the reality.

Abrán stumbled toward his car, got in, and drove down the street. The barrio was deserted; only an occasional car moved in the streets. He turned into the neighborhood park where he and Lucinda had walked one day after work. The headlights of his car flooded the sculpture at the edge of the park. The bright statue showed a tall Aztec warrior, a cry of anguish visible on his face, a dead woman in his arms. Only death would reunite these Aztec lovers.

In the lights of Abrán's car the colors of the sculpture looked garish, the warrior's grief intensified by the shadows. Abrán remembered the afternoon Lucinda and he had stood hand-in-hand in front of the statue. The day was bright and calm, the sparrows chased each other in the trees. They were happy then, and Abrán had told Lucinda he would be her Aztec warrior. Always. Their love was for always. They had laughed in the light of day, but now in the dark of night his promise rang empty. He cursed himself.

Who had called Lucinda? he wondered as he looked at the statue looming over him. These two lovers also had an enemy—the father of the girl had refused to let them be together, and so the girl was sacrificed. Only death could unite them. What would Juan Oso say when he knew Abrán had deceived Lucinda? Would he, too, forbid Abrán to see his daughter? Would Lucinda die of the same despair Abrán felt in his heart?

Dominic! he thought. Dominic called Lucinda! Abrán gritted his teeth and his hands clenched the steering wheel until his knuckles turned white. "Damn you, Dominic!" his cry echoed in the dark.

But when his wave of anger subsided he knew there was no one to blame but himself. He should have come clean right away, confessed everything. But what difference would that have made? None.

He started the car and drove down Edith toward Central. The bright lights beckoned, night people walked the streets. On the corner stood a young prostitute, one of the East Central girls who offered a quick trick for a few bucks. Homeless people wandered up and down the street, looking for shelter for the night, looking for the safety of the underpass, where they could huddle in their cardboard boxes. They crept into alleys to sleep, to wait. Even the deserted Albuquerque High School building became a haven for the night.

So many night people, homeless people I haven't seen before, Abrán thought. Why? Were they waiting for Dominic to offer his pie-in-the-sky plan, the big project that would transform the city? Would the homeless women be the croupiers he needed in his casinos and the men the gondoliers on the boats? It was crazy. Dominic didn't give a damn about these people. Nobody did. They were, like Abrán, shadows without hope.

The people on the street had lost in love, lost jobs, lost their health, lost respect. They were shadows you didn't see, until you felt loss. Now Abrán was like them, a man without hope.

Tú eres tú, doña Tules had said, and for a while that had started to make sense. But now he had even lost the woman in whose eyes he saw his reflection. He had not been alone, he had been connected to her.

He pulled into Jack's parking lot and, dragging his throbbing leg, made his way into the bar. Drink, that's what he wanted. Something to kill the pain and the loss.

"Whiskey," he said, and the waitress, Angel, looked at him strangely. She served him a shot of bourbon, and he drank it down in one gulp. The whiskey burned his stomach. "Another," he nodded, and she obliged. He was going to get drunk, and after that, well, nothing much mattered after that, he thought as he tossed down the second shot.

◆ ◆ ◆

18 The effect of the bourbon was immediate, a warm numbness seeped through Abrán's body. It's not going to take much to get drunk, he thought. He was looking into his fourth glass of bourbon when he felt a hand grip his arm. He turned to see Ben Chávez.

"Not good for boxers in training," he winked.

Abrán pulled his arm free, spilling some of the bourbon on the bar. "Mind your own fucking business," he slurred and drank what was left in the glass. He signaled Angel for another shot.

"Hijo, you are my business," the writer said calmly. "When a man drinks alone, it's no good."

"I said—"

"I know," Ben shrugged, "you said mind my own fucking business. But everybody in this bar is my fucking business. My characters," he smiled and waved in the direction of the dark, smoke-filled bar. The denizens of the night turned and nodded, some called for him to return to the table and read the poem he had promised.

Abrán looked into the writer's eyes. This man, too, had been drinking. Who the hell was he to talk? His eyes were glazed, his smile lopsided. Why was he drinking? What was his pain?

"Sorry," Abrán said. He could feel the words getting thicker in his mouth. "I thought Dominic was your business."

Ben nodded. "Ah, señor Dominic. So he's on your mind. Forget him, tonight we're partying," he motioned in the direction of the table where his friends sat. Poets, writers, lovely women.

At the edge of the table, huddled together like a couple of wet cats in the rain, were two penitentes from Española—gaunt homeboys with red-rimmed eyes from too much marijuana and beer. Abrán thought he had seen the two on the road to Chimayó a week ago. Left over from Lent, the penitentes still wore their battered crowns of thorns.

Abrán pressed the bridge of his nose, rubbed his eyes. The homeboys were bleeding where their crowns cut into their foreheads. Or was it the light from the flickering Bud sign?

"Are those guys bleeding?" he asked.

"We're all bleeding, in one way or another," Ben answered. "Doing penance. Once a year when the bad blood of spring draws me into depression and I cannot stand the pain, I get in this mood. I drink, I cry, I hug the trees, and play sad mariachi music. Listen!" Through the smoke-filled air came the wail of Cucu Sánchez, mourning his lost love. "I also read poetry," Ben Chávez continued, "to express my joy for spring. Spring sadness."

"Spring madness?" Abrán repeated.

Ben nodded. Is this what Abrán was feeling? Is this why he was drinking? The papers said the kid had disappeared for a week, but Ben knew he had been up north with Lucinda. He wanted to reach out and comfort the boy, but he couldn't.

"Join us," Ben said gently. "Otherwise my friend doña Loneliness will pick you up." He motioned toward the jukebox.

Abrán looked, but saw nothing.

"The lady in red, the whore of lonely hearts," Ben smiled. "She's dressed to kill tonight. A beautiful woman, but if she gets under your skin, she's deadly. Come on, join us. Don't drink alone."

Abrán looked again. He couldn't see the woman, but apparently

Ben did. The air was thick with smoke, a haze, tinged with the sweet scent of marijuana and the yeasty smell of beer. Eyes were glazed; evidently the party had been going on all night. He allowed himself to be pulled toward the circle at the table.

A few of the barflies recognized Abrán and swarmed around him. "Hey, kid, wanna drink? Have a drink on us. How's the training goin'? Gonna whip Bo Decker? Come on, Anthony, set 'em up!"

Ben Chávez pushed them away. "Give the kid a break." He pulled Abrán toward the table where his friends waited. "And," he winked at Angel, "give him ginger ale."

He introduced Abrán all around, but the names were only buzzes; the bourbon had made Abrán's head swim. He never drank whiskey, so the shots had hit him hard. He looked at the two penitentes who sat across from him, sadly sipping their beer, and wondered if they were real or shadows of the booze.

Around him a heated argument was being led by a Marxist critic who taught at the university. He insisted that only a class struggle was going to help Chicanos, and he sure as hell wasn't going to stick around to hear poetry, which he called "fantasy fluff."

The two penitentes gulped down the beers, their faces sad, their eyes as full of pain as Goya's suffering penitents looking at Cristo on the cross.

"Someone forgot to tell them Lent is over," Ben Chávez whispered. "They just wandered in. Being from Española, they never turn down free beer."

At the jukebox the shadow of Julio Iglesias crooned a love song with all the 'th's' in perfect place. Someone knocked over a glass, washing cigarette butts and pizza crumbs from the tables onto the floor that already reeked of beer. As Abrán watched, the beer mixed with the blood of the penitentes and the rest of the trash on the floor and flowed out the door and down the street. Central Avenue would be awash in blood and beer, he thought. Dominic's canals would be filled with the debris and blood of the city.

"I'm drunk," Abrán slurred. The entire room was swirling; a sour taste burned his throat.

"You're okay," Ben said at his side. "Want you to meet two of my favorite characters, mis hijos," he said. "Juan and Al." The faces of the two young men appeared out of the dark.

Homeboys, Abrán thought. They looked familiar. Maybe he had seen the two in the barrio. He squinted. Cholos through and through, slightly reminiscent of the '40s pachuco style. But no, he didn't recognize them. Plain barrio homeboys.

"They're like sons to me," Ben said, his voice trembling as he spoke. He could call his characters his sons, but not Abrán, his own flesh and blood.

"Hey, bro, good to meet you, ese," Al smiled and gave Abrán the old Chicano handshake.

"Pleased to meet you, Mr. Abrán," Juan said politely.

Their shining faces beamed with good faith. Abrán had to smile. Characters like these existed only in novels. He looked at Ben Chávez. His sons, he had said, figments of his imagination.

"We're going to be there for your fight," Juan said.

"Orale," Al agreed.

"These guys for real?" Abrán mumbled.

"As real as their story," Ben said above the noise of the arguments and calls for beer. The Marxist critic took one parting shot, berating the fate of Chicanos, then stomped off because nobody was listening to him.

"Read the poem," a woman shouted. The others took up the chant, beating their glasses on the table.

I'm drunk, Abrán thought, I'm really drunk. What the hell, that's what he wanted. He raised the glass in his hand and drank. He winced—ginger ale. The table spun around him. Someone pulled the plug on Julio Iglesias and the bar grew quiet. Even the bartenders turned to listen as Ben Chávez gathered up the papers from the table, the poem sopping wet with beer.

"Gimme a cigarette," Ben said, and someone handed him one.

"Arms of the women, I sing!" he began in a loud, sonorous voice. The men around him beat the table with their glasses, shouting "¡Ajúa! ¡Qué vivan las viejas!"

"Arms of the women, I sing," he repeated,
"arms of the women I have known,
women I have left behind
as I, a proud Chicano boy, set out
to find Aztlán. "

With this, he launched into his epic poem of Juan and Al, two Chicano homeboys in search of the mythic Aztlán. He told how Juan and Al flew with the goddess María Juana into the dark and ancient time of the Aztecs. There the two set out on a trip with forty of Moctezuma's shamans to the original homeland of all Chicanos, Aztlán. In Aztlán they met the mother of all the Aztec gods, Coatlicue, and it was she who warned them that the Spaniards were coming to destroy Tenochtitlán, the sacred city of the Mexicanos.

Up and up the writer climbed into ethereal realms on the power of his poem, not noticing those who got up and left, or those who went to play pool in the back room. He was on a roll, deep into the story, and in his heart he dedicated the poem to Abrán. In the beginning was the word, then flesh followed. Each man could create himself in his own image. Abrán could find himself in the brotherhood of all men. Juan and Al were his brothers, all cholos were brothers, and finally Abrán could know him, the writer, as the father.

Abrán, born of the Mexican father and gringa mother, was the new Chicano, and he could create his own image, drawing the two worlds together, not letting them tear him apart. Abrán, the new mestizo.

Into the late hours Ben recited the story of Juan Chicaspatas and Al Penco. He told how they were given the sword of life by the goddess, the sword of life that became the tree of life. And how they were given the commandment to return to the barrios of Aztlán to help the poor and the outcast. They were to help their people by becoming troubadours, wandering minstrels, like the old cuentistas who went from village to village to tell the Chicanos their history and legends.

For Abrán, the dark, smokey cantina became the jungle where the shamans of Moctezuma traveled long ago. I am who I create, the writer was saying, and Abrán could feel Ben's eyes on him as he read.

The few who stayed to hear the story to its end felt the deep emotion of the writer. They had never heard him read with such passion. His words carried them into the history and reality of Aztlán, and the myth in the poem became real. Juan and Al became real. Abrán felt the bond—Juan and Al were his brothers, his carnales. He raised his hands and wiped the tears from his eyes. Poetry was as strong as love.

Ben Chávez finished and looked at Abrán. He reached out and touched his hands, held them in his. Around them there was silence. Customers had come and gone, those at the table had wandered off, home to sleep, to play pool in the back room, or to make love. Poetry did not move the fate of the world, it only moved one soul at a time.

"Beautiful," Abrán nodded. The fog of the bourbon had lifted.

"Powerful," Juan and Al agreed.

Abrán thought of Lucinda. He needed her; he would go to her. He tried to stand and felt the pain in his leg.

"Cuidao," Ben said, "you better not drive."

"I can drive," Abrán said, "I'm okay. Thanks for reading your poem."

Ben looked at Abrán. "When we met, you drove me home, now I return the favor. Juan, you and Al drive our friend home."

Juan jumped forward. "Sí, capitán," he saluted.

"Juan, don't call me capitán. I'm just a writer, a plain man who plays with words, a creator of souls. . ."

Juan winked. "Whatever you say, maestro. Come on, Al." Each put an arm under Abrán's arms and lifted him.

"Buenas noches," the writer said.

"Buenas noches," Abrán mumbled. He was beat, so tired he could hardly keep his eyes open.

"Buenas nalgas," the old man who was sweeping the floor added, his laughter echoing in the dark and dreary midnight bar.

"Menudo in the morning!" Ben called. "You're in good hands." The three brothers were already out the door into the Alburquerque spring night, a night laced with the thick aroma of beer and the perfume of the first lilac blossoms.

Abrán would be delivered home, safe to his bed. That's what folk heroes were for, to help those in need.

"Cantinero!" Ben Chávez turned to the bartender, "a drink for me and my lady friend. ¡Tequila!"

"There are no ladies here," the bartender answered gruffly.

"What does he know," the phantom doña Loneliness said as she sauntered across the empty bar to sit beside Ben. She winked a heavily mascaraed eyelash. The shoulder strap of her red dress slipped, accentuating her thin shoulder, then she popped her bubble gum and smiled at Ben.

"Bar's closed," the bartender growled. Poetry readings in bars never worked, he should know that by now. Counting through the receipts at the cash register, he saw he was fifty bucks below the normal take. Poets kept the paying customers away. Nobody wants to face the truth when they're having a good time.

The writer felt the tension in his shoulders; it had been a long night. "One for the road," he called, and the bartender responded, "Go home."

Doña Loneliness primped her hair, a bright wig of glossy red that sat high on her head like a halo. She swung her leg and whispered, "Let's go to my place."

"Coffee time!" the bartender said, serving a steaming cup of hot, dark liquid that had been brewing all day. Ben drank.

"It's time to be alone," doña Loneliness whispered. "The poem is done and the crowd gone home."

She recrossed her legs, her dress drawing up and exposing a thin thigh. Ben reached into his pocket and took out a few crumpled bills that, with a flourish, he dropped on the table.

"Okay, time to go home. When you have no money they treat you like a common attorney," he laughed and took her hand. "My kind of woman," he smiled and kissed her hand.

"My kind of man," doña Loneliness smiled back through chipped teeth.

He rose and stumbled in the dark, knocking over a chair. She put an arm around him, steadying him, and together they walked out of the stagnant air of the bar into the cool night. A street cleaner rumbled by and swept away the beer, blood, and trash of the night's revelry. Overhead the universe swirled around Alburquerque. Ben Chávez looked into the heavens, recognizing old stars. "We are nothing in the face of the creation," he said. "Nada. We write stories and poems to the gods. Who are we? Nada. Why are we here? Nada."

He held out his arms spun around, slowly at first, then faster and faster, a lone figure in the asphalt parking lot, singing, "¡La vida no vale nada. . .la vida no vale nada! Comienza siempre llorando, y así llorando se acaba. . ." A Zorba the Greek of the parking lot, an urban man saddened by spring.

"We are nada, and even love dies," he whispered when his dance was done.

He stood alone in the parking lot. He knew why he was sad. Cynthia had died and their bond was broken, yet their promise kept him from reaching out to Abrán. That is why his old companion of the heart had come to him.

Doña Loneliness sat on the hood of his car, freshening her lipstick, coyly waiting for him.

It's always been like this, he thought. The garbage piles up, the blood of our cholos is spilled in the streets, poets read for money and starve. Somos un puño de tierra. Todo se acaba. Nada queda. Perhaps, just perhaps, Cynthia's story would survive. And Abrán. . . .

It was time to go home. As he turned to leave, he sang the words of a sad song. "Cu, cu, rru, cu, cu, paloma. . ."

Doña Loneliness pulled him toward his car. "You are too sensitive," she said sweetly, her breath smelling of stale beer and bubble gum.

"Ah, yes, the sensitive man exposed," Ben nodded. "My Abrán exposed. Why did we ever create such a complex life, Cynthia? Why?"

"I will comfort you," doña Loneliness whispered. She nibbled softly at his ear and crept into his heart.

Ben started the car and drove into the dark. Above him the towering elms of Clyde Tingley created a bower of darkness. Every city needs a good mayor, Ben thought. A person of vision, a first-class político. A man who can plant trees is a man of vision, even if years later the trees are beetle-ridden and soil cars with their sap. What will Dominic accomplish with his vision?

Everyone knows Marisa will do best for the city, but she ain't going to win. That's politics. Dominic will get something nasty on her.

He drove west, across the deserted downtown area into the Country Club area, then over the narrow Tingley Drive. He drove this route often, to feel the mood of the water of the large pond.

Tonight the water was calm, reflecting a sliver of a moon, the old horned moon of childhood. A lone lantern dotted the southern shore.

"Some sonofabitch fishing," Ben said. It never failed. He had driven the road of the small lake in all seasons—in the coldest and thickest snowstorm of winter, dark spring nights, and always there was at least one fisherman sitting on the lonely shore. Now it was early morning and the fisherman sat by his campfire, dozing and dreaming of catching the last trout of the season before the summer heat turned the lake into a stagnant quagmire.

The elm trees clung to the sandy bank, the water was thick with winter moss and algae, and still the persistent fisherman fished. Liver bait. Heart bait.

Hope springs eternal in the fisherman's breast, Ben thought. Hope springs eternal in la raza, even though we're the más chingados hijos de Dios. We keep hope alive. We come to Tingley Beach to fish, to relax, drink beer, enjoy the day. Pobres y chingados, we still bring our familias to the edge of the lake to rest. To tell stories. Dominic will put one of his casinos here, push the raza farther into the bosque of the river where the homeless sleep.

"You're really moody," doña Loneliness whispered. "Go ahead, let it get you, let it seep into your heart. Be moody, be blue, think of the poverty of your raza, think of them forced out of their own barrios. Gets to you, doesn't it?"

She touched the radio and the dark interior of the car echoed with blues.

Slowly he drove across the river, El Río Grande del Norte, river of dreams, river of cruel history, river of borders, river that was home.

Doña Loneliness whispered: "This is the hour of la bruja, la Llorona de Río Grande. This is the hour of lonely hearts."

West Central was closed down, quiet, deserted. The lowriders had gone home, and even Coors Boulevard was empty. A cop car sat outside the all-night convenience store. Inside the boys in blue drank coffee, ate donuts, and waited for violence to strike. Violence and loneliness stalked the streets of Alburquerque.

At home a warm bed waited for Ben. He knew he could destroy the mood of loneliness in the arms of his wife.

"Don't think of her, honey," doña Loneliness said, putting her arm around him. "Gonna take more than a drink to kill the blues," she hissed as he drove into his driveway.

"Go find another sucker," Ben responded. "I build my rooms round so loneliness can't crawl into corners. Vete a la chingada."

"Ingrato," she said. "I come to you when you're lonely, but the minute you get to momma, it's good-bye." She was mad. The hearts of poets and writers were her favorite haunts. Ah, but the Alburquerque night was young, and Loneliness knew her way around the city.

"Adiós," she said, "buenas nalgas."

He smelled his wife's perfume in the dark. "Elena," he whispered.

"It's late," his wife said.

"Yeah, sorry. Some of the old gang talked me into reading the Juan and Al poem," he explained without turning on the lights. He sat on the edge of the bed in the dark room and began to undress.

"How did it go?"

"You know, nobody cares about the homeland anymore. . ."

"Dominic called."

"What did he want?"

"Says he has some pictures he wants you to see."

"One of his tricks, I bet."

"Moises Lippman called, too."

"What did he want?"

"He wants to know if you have the Matanza painting."

"So that sonofabitch is interested? He has a nose for digging out stuff. Should have been a detective."

"It gets very complicated, doesn't it?" his wife muttered in her sleep. She turned onto her side, she was already asleep again.

"Yeah, it does." He went into the bathroom, brushed his teeth, then crawled into the warm bed.

"Buenas noches," he prayed for those he loved. "Virgen de Guadalupe, guarda nuestra gente. Cover us with your manta, aunque estamos chingados."

19 Walter Johnson stood in front of the full-length mirror in his bedroom and methodically tied his tie. He wore a look of self-confidence, a sprightly air as he hummed an old tune. Today was an important day. He had invited some of the leading businessmen and politicians to an afternoon cocktail party. Today he would announce publicly; he would accept their endorsement and run for mayor. He had spent the last month courting the businessmen in town and the Washington delegation. What he found made him smile. There was a groundswell of businessmen who didn't want Frank Dominic as mayor, and they sure as hell didn't want him as governor four years down the line.

Confidentially they whispered to him that they were afraid of Dominic's plan. The Rio Grande project he envisioned was doomed to failure; the rumblings of lawsuits were already in the air. The editor of the local paper, who had once lauded the plan as a vision of the future for the city, had changed his mind and had run a story comparing Dominic's plan to the canals on Mars. Impressive, but full of dust. A Martian Nightmare, the paper called the proposal. That made Walter Johnson smile.

Dominic had continued to bring in engineers, and their arguments before the City Planning Commission were persuasive. It didn't take that much water to fill the canal system, small pleasure boats could float on two or three feet of water, and small electric motors created no pollution. The Planning Commission was split, and so the City Council would be split. Marisa Martínez might have the final vote, but the split could create a vacuum, and Walter Johnson was ready to step in.

On an issue like this, people didn't look at facts and figures, he thought. Not when their emotions are involved. Frank Dominic wants to tear up the city and create a Martian Nightmare, that was the issue to keep attacking him on. The environmentalists were already against it, too much of the river bosque would have to be sacrificed.

Walter Johnson looked at himself in the mirror and the smile spread wider across his face. The Department of the Interior was already considering a lawsuit, as was the BIA on behalf of the pueblos. On and on the rumor list went. There were just too many parties to the water rights for Dominic's corporation to work. The senators and representatives in Washington were not happy either. Dominic had gone around them, created the plan without them. His first political mistake. Exactly what I need, Johnson thought. In Washington the question was not if Dominic's plan would fail, but when. He was going to drag the entire state into one more business fiasco.

"Missing the opportunities," Johnson muttered. "We're the last of the fifty states that anyone remembers. I can change that. My friends know that."

His friends were the power elite of the state and city. The senators and congressmen would be there today, as would representatives from the utilities and the big Albuquerque firms. Old friends he had worked with, the same ones who drafted him to run for mayor.

Damn, that's what pleased him, their trust in him and the fact they felt he still had the vigor to run the race. Only he could beat Dominic. Marisa Martínez had bungled the economy, and the Japanese plant she envisioned was still on the drawing board.

Outside in the garden he heard the Spanish voices of the waiters finishing the arrangements for the reception. With one last confidant look in the mirror, he walked across the room to his desk. He sat down to make an entry in the notebook he kept, an entry he thought he should have written long ago:

The day I decided to enter the public world and run for mayor of the city was the most important in my life. I now have a purpose, and the feeling is exhilarating. This city has been good to me, I have prospered here, and I have helped build it. Frank Dominic would change the entire character of the city, change it for his own profit. I cannot allow the rape of this city, the despoliation of the river and its bosque, and so I enter the battle to preserve that which I love: this grand city, Albuquerque.

He lay the pen down and thoughtfully looked out onto the patio. Waiters in black moved around the linen-covered tables, placing arrangements of flowers. Women in serving uniforms calculated the number of the guests and how best to serve each one. Vera had orchestrated the party. It was a talent she had. They used to entertain a lot, when they were young, on their way up. Those were good times, the power structure in the city was small and the business associations clear. Perhaps too clear; it had been rough going.

It was Vera who had provided his center of strength from the beginning. Vera had an instinct for survival. He looked out the window at the green trees and bushes of the garden and remembered don Manuel's words. "She's Judía, Walter. Jew. A Spanish Jew from those old families who came with Oñate. Los marranos, the Catholics used to call them. Sure they became Catholics—they wanted to stay alive, didn't they? But they're Jews. They have Jewish blood."

The crypto Jews of New Mexico, Johnson thought. They converted at the point of the Spanish Inquisition's sword and lived within the embrace of the New Mexican Catholic world for centuries. But what is in the blood is not forgotten, nor forgiven. It was Vera who had named the boy Abrán. She goes to church at Old Town with her Spanish friends, but she dreams of Jerusalem.

"No importa, don Manuel," he had told the old man. She had saved his life, and she had a business sense, that's what mattered.

She had washed his lifeless body with vinegar and cold water until she killed his fever. She covered his eyes with slices of potatoes to save his eyesight. Every night she massaged him with alcohol, kneaded deep into his muscles to bring back the circulation. When he could sit up she fed him. "You have to eat," she commanded.

Beans, potatoes, mutton, tortillas, goat cheese from Isleta, squash and corn, and all smothered in hot chile. Green in summer and red in winter, the chile was always there, burning its way down his gullet into his stomach. It cleaned him out, burned away the TB. Born again on New Mexican chile—it's something these newcomers can't understand, he thought. I can't eat a meal if I don't have a bowl of chile on the side. Comida sin chile no es comida, as the Mexicans say.

"We put enough chile in him to flush out everything!" don Manuel used to say.

That old patrón had made the careers of a lot of the state politicians, and he had a story to tell about each one, mused Johnson.

"Order us a bowl of green chile stew," don Manuel says when we have lunch at the Petroleum Club, slapping me on the back and roaring with laughter. He knows we don't get any chile there or at the Rotary lunches or at most of the dinners I have to attend in this town. But on days when we need our chile fix we go down to Barelas or the South Valley or Baca's and sit and eat two or three bowlsful of the hottest stuff we can get. Then we remember the old days.

Don Manuel knew the Hazeldines and Stovers, he was a kid when those Anglo merchants built New Town. Don Manuel knows the history of every man and building in this city, he knows all the old families. He's a patrón and he has political power because he's done a favor for each one, and when it's time to call in the favor, he does. That's what we mean when we talk about the old patrón system of politics, men who did a favor for every single family in the community, and come election time they ask for the favor to be returned. Hell, things have been done like that in this valley since the Spaniards came.

Maybe that's what I'm doing now. All those years I was making loans and taking chances on people, doing favors to make the city grow. Now it's time to call my favors in, he smiled contentedly. Of course he thought of himself as a patrón; he was a man of power.

"You ain't nothing but poor white trash," don Manuel often told him when he had a brandy too many. "When you got here you didn't have a penny to your name, Walter. Don't forget, I lent you your first twenty pesos!"

The old sonofabitch was right. But it was Vera's idea to buy the land. "The Mexicanos and Indians are going to stay in the valley," she said. "They do not leave the land they cultivate. But this city is going to grow. Look!"

She pointed east in the direction of the Sandía Mountains. I looked and saw nothing but sand and sage from the railroad to the mountain. The university sat up on the hill, and a few houses here and there dotted Highway 66 as it entered Tijeras Canyon, and farther east the government had put in Kirtland Air Force Base during the war. But the area around the base was growing; soldiers returning from the war were looking for cheap housing. The war had spawned the government complexes, and the people who worked in those labs and at Kirtland and Sandia bases needed homes to live in.

Before Kirtland there were only the sand hills as far as the foot of the mountains. Coyotes, jackrabbits, tarantulas, and vultures. A few sheep were grazed up there, but it was pretty sorry country.

I remember the day Vera and I walked up there. It was a quiet afternoon, the heat of day had waned.

"Fill your lungs with this dry, clean air," she said, and I did as she commanded. "Así," she coaxed in Spanish, and taught me to breathe. That high desert air and the chile were killing the TB in me.

"Otero has this land for sale," she said that afternoon as we walked up past the university.

"Yeah," I said, "a hundred acres, but it's worthless."

"Buy it," she said, standing firmly as if she were carved out of that sandy soil. She looked down at the small city that huddled along the river.

"It ain't worth the few bucks he's asking," I insisted.

"Don't be a pendejo," she said and pointed down at the city. "The city has to grow. The government keeps adding to the base, the banks have good accounts, the air base people are begging for places to live. The people of the valley aren't going to give up their farms. But the city has to grow. It's going to grow up here."

I shook my head. No way was that town ever going to come up this far. There was sand from where we stood clear to the foothills of the mountain.

"The soldiers need homes," she repeated.

"I ain't got two cents," I protested.

"Borrow," she answered. "We will work and pay the loan. I am strong, I will work hard."

I looked in her eyes. She meant business; there was the same determination that I had seen when she nursed me. Once she set her mind to it, she would get the job done. Yes, the base was growing, and the soldiers coming back from the war weren't returning to their small New Mexican hometowns—they were moving into Albuquerque in search of jobs. The whole state was changing, the businessmen who huddled over bowls of beans and chile and Italian pasta for lunch at the bars and cafes downtown were convinced. A boom was coming. It was in the air.

Vera believed it was going to grow to the east. "There will be homes, schools, shopping centers like you've never seen. Clear to the mountain!" she exclaimed. Her new Jerusalem was right beneath her feet, and she wanted to be part of it.

"Tú sabes," I said incredulously, because I suddenly understood what she meant. She wasn't just dreaming aloud, she was serious.

"Sí," she answered forcefully, "Sí. Yo sé."

Then her dream became my dream, and I could see the city growing on the mesa all the way to the mountain. Whoever owned the land owned the future. I grabbed her hands and waltzed her round and round on the sand, then we hurried back to don Manuel's cantina. Laughing and running all the way, we were like kids who had just been handed a bagful of candy. I was gasping for breath and coughing when we burst into the bar. Vera, the orphan-girl barmaid, held me up and coaxed me on: "Ask him."

"I wanna borrow a hundred dollars," I said to don Manuel.

He looked from me to Vera then up toward the East Mesa where the sun was setting purple on the Sandías. He knew we'd been walking up on the mesa.

"So you've been bitten," he said and laughed softly. "You think there's gold in the sand. Just like the old conquistadores who saw this river valley. They saw the reflection of sand in the Indian pueblo mud bricks and thought it was gold."

"There's gold there," I said and Vera nodded. "Gold in the sand, all right. Lend me a hundred bucks and I'll prove it."

Don Manuel nodded. Maybe he thought it was a way to get a barboy, because nobody wanted to do the dirty work, or maybe he really wanted to help me and Vera. The point is, he emptied the cash register drawer on the bar and counted out a hundred dollars in dimes, nickels, quarters, and crumpled dollar bills.

The next day I bought Otero's hundred acres, and I continued to buy any piece of land I could get in the area. Vera and I bought whatever came on the market, and we worked our flesh to the bone for every penny. We cooked, served tables, bartended and ran errands by day, and at night we washed the dishes and dirty floors of the cantina, scrubbing by hand the spit and beer off the floor. I became the butt of jokes for the businessmen who gathered there to eat at noon. The word had gotten out that I was buying the worthless land on the mesa and I had more offers than I could handle.

Around me the men laughed. "Nothing out there but sand and coyotes!"

"And locoweed."

"Maybe Walter ate some of that locoweed," they laughed.

"Land's so worthless you can't even run sheep on it."

They dropped their nickel tips at my feet and went out laughing. Vera bent to pick them up. "Paciencia," she whispered. "It will take time, but we will have the last laugh."

I gritted my teeth and worked as don Manuel's slave late into the night. At night Vera and I lay together, too exhausted to talk. She would hold me before I went asleep, and her whisper was always, "paciencia."

Patience and sheer hard work. It paid off. In a year I sold a piece of the land I had bought near the base, tripled my money, and bought a corner bar on Central, just down from don Manuel's. He never forgave me for that, because I could pay his debt, and I gave him good competition. Years later I built my first bank on that same corner, a bank built from the nickel beer I sold and Vera's taco and enchilada lunches.

A few years later I made my move to build a home in the Country Club area. The businessmen who lived here in those years ran the city. A few were buying in the North Valley and up toward Ridgecrest, but the real core of social life revolved around the Country Club. Vera and I thought we had paid our dues, worked hard, prospered, built a network of business acquaintances. But when they learned we were going to build a home the deal went sour.

I couldn't believe it. In my naiveté, I had banked with the best of them, made them loans, gone to lunches with them, served on a few city committees, on the hospital fund-raising board. But the minute I wanted to live in their neighborhood, they turned on me. The reason came back in whispers: Vera is Jewish. The old prejudice was a kick in the face. Vera took it hard, she blamed herself, but she knew if we fought them our bank wouldn't survive. It was a lesson I never forgot.

"I warned you," don Manuel said the day I turned up at his place in a fighting mood.

"The first mayor of this city was a Jew!" I banged my fist on the bar. I didn't care who heard. "Now the sonsofbitches won't let me build because my wife has Jewish blood!"

"Take it easy," don Manuel quieted me down. "Sure the first mayor was a Jew, and a lot of the first businessmen in this territory were Jews. They were merchants who came in and traded with the Mexicanos. A lot of them became millionaires, but these New Town Anglos don't like Jews, and they sure as hell don't like Mexicans. You can do business with them, and they'll borrow your money, but just don't try to move into the neighborhood. You should have known that, pendejo."

God, the beer tasted bitter. It hurt because I had promised Vera the house, promised she'd never have to work another day in her life. I owed her.

"What can I do?" I asked don Manuel.

He smiled. "Genealogy," he said.

"Genealogy?"

"All you have do is get Vera a new bloodline. Make her Catholic instead of Jewish. They don't like that much either, but they accept the Italian businessmen now, and they're Catholic. It's a step up."

"How in the hell do I make her Catholic?"

"Papers."

"Buy papers?"

"A good attorney can get you the papers you need. That's all they want, Walter, a few papers that erase the Jew part, and then you can build. Believe me, I know these people. And while you're at it, throw in a little aristocracy. Spanish royalty. Make Vera a cousin of a distant duke. That will put the stamp of approval on it."

Don Manuel knew what he was talking about, and he knew the fragile relationships of the ethnic groups in the city. Each one had its prejudices, but there were ways to work around the bigotry. He sent me to an attorney in Old Town. Eduardo Ortiz de Aragón Delgado, a man who could fix anybody's family history. He wrote to Mexico and in a few months a letter came back, with a certificate of baptism and a letter of genealogy. Vera was now connected to a duke who took part in the conquest of Mexico.

Delgado discreetly sent a copy of the paper to the social editor at the newspaper, a small article appeared, lauding the aristocratic origins of Vera Johnson, and in a week I received my permit to build. We were invited to join the Country Club, and welcomed with open arms into the brahmin class of the city. All the time we were building our house the papers carried articles on the progress. It was the biggest and most fashionable house ever built in the area, and I was welcomed as a city father and one of the richest men in the ruling class. A few papers that established a bloodline had done the trick.

I then branched out into the construction business, made loans, and captured the house market that was booming on the East Mesa. I built almost everything between the university and the base. I financed the subcontractors, helped the Mexican boys coming back from the war set up construction businesses. Best workers I ever knew; I needed those boys. Nothing can be built without the subs, and I had loyal subs who wanted a slice of the pie, a share of the free enterprise system that had finally come to this barren land.

"Pour water on the desert and it will bloom," Vera used to say. I poured water, and cement, from downtown to the mountains, and the city blossomed. We made Clyde Tingley run interference, made him the bulldog to deal with the politicians. I learned a person doesn't have to be in the mayor's seat to run City Hall.

Only one thing was missing: children. Vera was barren. She couldn't conceive. Everything I touched turned into money, but Vera couldn't get pregnant. In banking you need family; banking is a family business. I was building an empire, but there was no one to pass it on to. We tried every doctor and remedy under the sun, and we had almost given up hope when Cynthia was born. God had answered our prayers, the years of waiting were done with. Then we were to begin the truly happy years of our life together.

Walter Johnson heard someone behind him. He turned to see Vera standing by the door.

He closed his journal and rose. "My, you looked elegant," he smiled. She wore a pastel cocktail dress that highlighted her natural beauty.

"I didn't want to disturb you. You looked so deep in thought." She stepped toward the desk, smiled. "And, if I may say so, you look handsome, Mr. Johnson."

"I was thinking about the past, Vera," he said and took her hand. "How hard we worked, the year we built here."

"Difficult times. . ."

"But behind us. I've put everything behind us. This getting involved in politics is the best thing I ever did, Vera. Hell, a year ago I was thinking about retirement, spending time on the golf course. But now I feel invigorated! We're not going to let Frank Dominic ruin this city, not if I can help it."

He spoke enthusiastically, his eyes glowing with the spirit of the upcoming campaign, his voice quivering with a resolve she had not heard in years. The race for mayor was more than to beat Dominic, she thought, it was a way of proving himself. All of his officers in the bank and in the construction company were younger men, men with new ideas and new ways. They encouraged Walter to take a back seat, to play golf, and to serve on charity and education boards. But the more he did that, the more his spirit withered. Now the mayor's race had rekindled all his old instincts, and he was looking younger and more vigorous than he had in years.

"Our guests are arriving," she looked toward the window. The first of the guests were on the patio, women in spring cocktail dresses and men in dark suits. Greetings and laughter filled the air.

"Let them wait," he said impatiently. "Listen to what I'm trying to tell you, Vera. I know things haven't been right for a long time. But what's happened is done with. We've led our separate lives, like strangers, for too long. Now I have a chance to get involved, to make a difference. I need your help. Just like old times, the two of us together. What do you say?"

"You know I've always been at your side."

"Yes, you have. Now we can give this mayor's race a real go! But I'm going to need your help."

"Forget the past."

"That's what I've always said. I gave up my past when I came here.

The past died for me. I gave myself a new name. And you, you had to give up your Jewish past, too. So we could get where we are."

She looked into her husband's eyes. They were cold and determined as always, but with a hint of warmth as he talked about moving ahead.

"We had to give up a lot," he said. "I was a man destined not to have children."

What did he mean? Did he know the secret she carried in her heart? For a moment she felt pity for him, and she hated herself for the complications she had brought into his life.

"So be it," he turned and smiled. "It's been a good life, all in all."

"Yes," she lied. It had not been a good life. What good was life without a real family? Perhaps it wasn't too late to bring her daughter's son back into the circle of the family, perhaps that would rescue the gray years she saw ahead of her.

"We have to take the boy in," she whispered. "Why make him suffer for the split between you and Cynthia?"

"This isn't the time to be discussing that," he frowned. "The boy's a grown man. What am I supposed to be now, a grandfather? No, it won't work. He's working for Dominic. For God's sake, even if I felt something for him I couldn't go begging Dominic. Give him money if that's what he needs, but I can't lie and say there's any love between us. I didn't see or speak to Cynthia the last twenty years of her life! Why should I feel anything for the boy?"

He shook his head. "It's best to let it die, Vera. Help me with the race, I am asking that. It means a lot to me."

She saw tears in his blue eyes, the passion she had seen long ago whenever he undertook a new challenge. She hesitated for a moment, then nodded. He was her husband, they had been together too long and through too much for her to say no.

"I knew I could count on you," he beamed and embraced her. "Now let's go out and greet our guests. Both senators will be here, and the congressmen. We haven't had a gathering like this in a long time." He felt her hesitate.

"Let me sit a moment."

"Is something wrong?" he asked apprehensively. She was pale. "I saw Doc Mills out there, can I get him?"

"No, no. Let me sit. You go, don't keep them waiting. I'll be out in just a moment. . . ."

"The excitement," he smiled and let go of her hand. "Okay, catch your breath, but don't keep us waiting. Lot of people you haven't seen in years out here." He kissed her cheek and walked purposefully out the door.

Vera sat in an armchair next to the desk. She watched her husband stride out, as ebullient as ever. It was the challenge, and the hate he bore Frank Dominic, that revived him. The guests turned to greet him, all with shining smiles, for the man they knew would carry their values and battle cry into the mayoral race.

Vera looked at the desk where her husband kept a small photo of their wedding. Elvira Aguirre Armijo, the orphan girl, marrying Walter Johnson, a man just recovered from TB. Married in San Felipe de Neri in Old Town, because she had always wanted a church wedding, a wedding that would make her respectable.

Don Manuel and his wife, doña Eufemia, were their padrinos. They held the wedding dance in don Manuel's cantina. Vera remembered the wedding march, the loud polkas, and romantic waltzes of the músicos they had hired. The dance had overflowed out into the street, the wine was free, courtesy of don Manuel, and half of Old Town had gathered in the cantina to dance the night away.

They were happy. But Walter grew restless. "I don't want to spend the rest of my life working for a Mexican," he said. "I want to be my own boss. Why should I be a slave for don Manuel?" That's when she told him about her vision. In a dream, she had seen the city spreading east toward the mountains. In a few years those mesas of sand would be covered with homes.

She, too, wanted to flee the drudgery she had known all her life, and Walter's offer of marriage was the first she received. She was tired of the long hours of work at don Manuel's cantina, without hope, without a future. With Walter she could share the work and dream of something better, and raise a family.

Walter listened to her, and slowly she told him of her past. She told him of the nightmare that haunted her. In it she saw the figures of her father and mother in the roaring fire that had killed them. She was two when the fire engulfed her father's business and the upstairs room in which they lived. Vera had been saved because her father wrapped her in a blanket and threw her out the window.

She remembered her mother, a dark-haired woman with a light, creamy complexion who sang lullabies in Spanish. When Vera had Cynthia, the memories came back, and she sang her daughter the same lullabies. Her father, Adán Matías Aguirre belonged to an old family from the Taos area. Shortly after marriage Adán Matías had moved to Alburquerque, where he became a wagon merchant who rented out mules and wagons. He had quickly captured the trade. After his death Vera remembered that don Manuel had once told her the deadly fire was set by a business competitor.

"Judía," the kids who played in the street outside the cantina called her. The kids were vicious, and so her world became one of work in the cantina. When she ran errands she was subjected to their taunts: "¡Judía, Judía, que mató a Cristo!" But she followed the Armijos to church, learned to pray to Christ. How could the children accuse her of killing the Lord? She didn't understand, but she came to realize she was different. The Catholic kids made sure of that. Finally she asked doña Eufemia and was told that Judía meant Jew. And so she learned to keep to herself; she grew up without friends.

Perhaps it was the lonely years spent as a child that made Vera yearn so desperately for a child. She *had* given Cynthia love, and she secretly resented her husband because he had so little love in him. Even now, after all those years, he still could not accept Abrán. Abrán was innocent, as all children were innocent. It was not fair that the sins of the parents be visited on the child.

"Not fair," she whispered bitterly. Did Walter know her sin? she wondered. Had he sensed it? Why had he mentioned just now that he had been destined not to have children? Had he known all along that Cynthia was not his daughter? Had Cynthia sensed it and flung it at him when she was fighting to keep her child?

I wove a complex web, she thought, as she glanced out the patio door at the guests. More had arrived; soon she would have to join them. But for the moment she had no strength to rise. For the moment, the poignant and bittersweet memories tugged at her.

Obsession, that's what life was all about. Walter became obsessed with his desire to make money, to be someone, and she became obsessed with the desire to have children, despite the doctors' claims that she was barren.

Her obsession became a fear. She searched desperately. She saw all the doctors in Alburquerque, she tried spas and different mineral waters and remedies. She visited the hot springs in the Jémez Valley, up north in Ojo Caliente, and near Las Cruces at Radium Springs, but to no avail. Her fear grew and she turned to religion, visiting Old Town church every day, spending long hours on her knees praying to the saints.

In the end, it was Sara, her maid, also without child, who told her about the curandera in the barrio. Vera remembered when they crossed the shaky wooden bridge over the irrigation ditch. It was spring and a dust storm had come out of the west. The strong wind clawed at her coat. As she and Sara crossed she saw herself reflected in the muddy canal water. Then she heard a long, mournful cry. What if she were too late? What if she were too old to have a child? Was this cry a warning?

"La Llorona," Sara whispered and pulled her away. "Venga señora, we will not be frightened by stories of the woman who cries by the river."

Sara resolutely led her through the dark, wind-swept bosque toward the house of doña Tules. Around them stretched the barrio, the frail wooden homes and tin shacks straining in the cruel wind. Loose tar paper and pieces of tin flapped on roofs.

In a dark bower of cottonwoods they found doña Tules' hut. It was strangely quiet beneath the giant trees; the wind seemed to whip overhead and leave in peace the older woman's home. Sara knocked, and after a pause, doña Tules appeared and let them in. She was expecting them.

Vera remembered the room as warm and pleasant. An herbal fragrance enveloped the room and a strangely peaceful and safe feeling settled over her. Doña Tules spoke only Spanish: "Yes, you're the muchacha that don Manuel and his wife raised," she nodded. "I remember you when you were a child." She went on talking, her voice soft and confident. She moved easily into the examination and asked Vera to pee in a basin so she could look at her urine. She also gave her a soothing tea to drink. Vera was then told to take her clothes off and lie down, and with her supple fingers doña Tules probed gently, pressing softly into the area around her small intestines and uterus. All the while she asked Vera questions about her periods, and then about her husband.

When she was finished she told Vera to dress and went to her altar to light a candle to la Virgen Guadalupana. She prayed, and when she was done she sat by Vera and held her hand. She said the words Vera had yearned to hear all those years.

"You are not barren, my child, but your time to have a child is quickly passing."

Vera felt numb at first, then the tears filled her eyes and the sobs came. She hugged the curandera. Doña Tules had answered her prayers—she could conceive!

"Gracias, gracias," she said over and over.

"Do not thank me," the older woman shrugged. "Any doctor could have told you the same, except in cases like this they tend to protect the husband. Men do not want to believe that the problem may be with them. Listen," the curandera whispered, "I have prayed, and a vision came. You can have a child, but not by your husband."

What she had said about Walter would not sink in until later. At that moment Vera was too overjoyed with her new knowledge, and she rushed home unaware of the wind that hours ago had torn at her.

It was only when she burst into their house that she realized she couldn't share the news with her husband. He wouldn't understand, he would deny it, and possibly be hurt by the curandera's news. What good was the knowledge if there was nothing she could do about it?

The depression returned, and Vera fell into her old routine. She consulted more doctors. She spent a week at Hot Springs. She walked in the desert and ate a healthy diet. A strange resolve grew in her, and in her dreams she saw the child that she knew would inhabit her womb.

Then one day a friend mentioned a new gynecologist who had just opened an office at Lovelace Clinic. "He studied in New England," her friend said, "and he is handsome. He has the most beautiful blue eyes you've ever seen. The women are crazy about him, and he has a social event to attend every night. He's engaged, but not yet married," she whispered.

Vera didn't care what he looked like, but she would try anything. She called for an appointment and when they met, she liked his manner at once. Yes, he was handsome, but more importantly, he was warm and caring. When he was done with the examination, they talked in his office. His findings were the same as doña Tules's. She could have children; it was not too late. It was the first time a doctor had been so positive, and again Vera was overjoyed.

He sensed her joy and understood that the woman was at a very vulnerable period in her life. He learned that the woman was obsessed with having a child. She had never been able to talk to Walter, and now the suppressed need and her dreams came pouring out. The doctor listened patiently, with understanding.

The talk drifted from his explanations of the medical data to their lives. The natural attraction they felt for each other went quickly beyond the relationship of doctor and patient. When they parted he prescribed a light sedative; he wanted her to rest, and he insisted that she come to see him the next day.

The following day she told him more about her past, and he talked about his life. He had grown up in the East. The son of working-class parents, he had worked hard to get through medical school. He was committed to the new medical techniques available to women. He was in the vanguard of a new generation of doctors who listened to women patients.

She was impressed by his sensitivity, and she realized he was lonely. They were both lonely, and they talked late into the afternoon.

When he took her in his arms it was a natural consummation of the desire each felt. It was a quick and passionate affair, the only one for her.

A few weeks later she discovered she was pregnant, and she immediately became consumed with the long-awaited event. The handsome doctor from the East had moved on to other affairs, the gossip said, even though a month later he had married. Vera didn't listen to the gossip; she had no interest in the doctor's life, and eventually Cynthia was born without a problem. She did occasionally wonder if the doctor knew, given that they belonged to the same small social circle and that from time to time they saw each other at social events. But they respected each other's formal distance. There was no need to have further communication. The brief affair had served its purpose for both, although in far different ways.

"Señora," a voice roused her from her reverie. A maid stood at the door. "I do not wish to disturb you, señora, but the señor asks for you to come."

"Thank you, Graciela," Vera smiled. She stood and walked to the door that led onto the patio. Adultery. She had committed adultery. The thought haunted her all those years. She was a woman of deep faith and values, but she had sinned. She had been driven by the obsession to have a child. Her desire had been stronger than all the rules she held dear. Had it been worth it?

Of course it was worth it! The vows of marriage paled when she thought of the fulfillment she had found when she was pregnant. It was something deep in her that she had always wanted. She came to understand it as God's will.

She looked out the window into the bright, warm sunlight that filled the patio. Walter stood in the middle of a group of men, holding forth on the mayoral race. She wondered if he had ever had an affair. It was possible, he was a handsome man, and a man of wealth and influence.

As she stepped out into the garden she realized the gaiety of the party and old friends could not lift her spirit. Deep inside she hated the political arena. Now Walter was caught up in the fervor, and she had been called upon to be the dutiful wife.

She moved slowly across the flagstone patio, greeting the guests as she went. The tinkle of cocktail glasses filled the air. The powerful men of the city had come to lend their support to Walter.

Here in this garden, secluded by high, ivied walls and lilac bushes, they could feel at home, exchange confidential information. Purple petunias grew luxuriant and flowered brightly in the clay pots, while overhead the old cottonwood trees shimmered with foliage.

"Vera," Walter smiled when he saw her, "here comes my better half."

"You're looking well," Senator Culson greeted her. Then to both of them. "You both look great."

"Never felt better," Johnson boasted. "I'm ready for the battle."

Vera smiled and greeted the men in the group. She knew most of them as friends, but there were some young men she didn't recognize. These were the newcomers who were just beginning to make their mark in the city, Anglo businessmen who supported Walter Johnson.

"Vera's volunteered to be my campaign manager," Johnson joked and put his arm around her. The men laughed politely.

"You're going to need a good one," old don Manuel said. Now old and fat, his gray skin hanging in jowls and his feet so swollen he could barely walk, he still represented a formidable presence in city politics.

Don Manuel clutched a cane in one hand and a glass of bourbon in the other. Beside him stood his wife, doña Eufemia, Vera's adopted mother. Vera greeted her and kissed her lightly on the cheek, politely braving the old woman's thickly powdered skin and cheap perfume. Dressed in an old-fashioned black satin gown with a lace collar, a silver filigree brooch at her throat and her dyed, jet-black hair held in a chignon, doña Eufemia was a study of the old Mexican matriarch. She never left don Manuel's side and listened closely to everything that was said. Later, in the privacy of their home, she rendered her opinion. Then it was don Manuel who listened.

Vera could never meet doña Eufemia and don Manuel without remembering how hard the couple had made her work as a child. Now, crippled with old age, the two still held fast to their position of power—don Manuel could still deliver much of the South Valley vote. And the two clung to their dignity, a pride in being heirs of the Spanish past. Vera looked at them and pitied them. They had to pretend to be Spanish and not Mexican in order to be accepted into Walter's circle.

"Frank Dominic's no pushover," don Manuel muttered.

"I don't expect him to be," Walter Johnson answered sarcastically, "but the man's a fool if he thinks we're going to accept his wild plan."

The men around him chuckled. "Interior's going to shoot it down," Senator Culson smiled.

"I think you're missing the point," don Manuel coughed.

"What is the point, don Manuel?" Vera asked.

"The point is the people like what Dominic's telling them. They like the excitement of gambling, casinos, the Cowboys playing football here, the dog tracks." He paused. "Come to think of it, I like the plan."

The men laughed nervously.

Don Manuel sipped his bourbon and grinned. "People like a good time, eh? And that's what he's promising. You're going to see thousands of my people at his party." He clutched his cane and handed his glass to his wife. He needed another drink. The men nodded; he did have a point.

20 When Dominic found out Abrán hadn't been at the gym the past four days, he exploded. He shouted for Casimiro to get hold of the trainer and meet him at Abrán's. His office reverberated with his foul mood as he marched out shouting orders right and left, leaving secretaries scurrying in his wake. A few minutes later he pulled up to the curb in front of Abrán's house and stormed toward the front door. Right behind him were Casimiro and Sánchez.

"Where in the hell have you been, kid! A deal's a deal!" Dominic shouted when Abrán opened the door. "Either you keep your word or you don't! The fight's scheduled for tomorrow, and you haven't been at the gym! What the hell kind of show do you think I'm running! If you can't fight and I forfeit, it's not going to look good, kid! And I don't like to look bad!"

"I'll keep my word!" Abrán responded, "you keep yours!"

"I have a lot riding on this," Dominic gritted his teeth, "and you're not going to blow it!"

Sánchez diplomatically stepped in. "Listen, kid, we have to check you out. We can still save this, if the leg is good, and if you want to give it a shot."

Abrán looked at his old coach. How many times had he drilled into the kids at the gym the importance of discipline, training, the commitment and focus of energy needed to step into the ring.

Abrán nodded, "I'm okay, I feel fine." But inside he knew he wasn't hungry to win the fight. Everything was on the back burner; only Lucinda mattered.

"Okay," Dominic nodded. "Okay, that's the spirit. Damn show's coming up, I don't want any problems." He smiled at Sara, who was standing behind Abrán. "Gracias, señora, gracias." Then he turned smartly and walked back to his car.

Sánchez wiped the sweat from his forehead. "First thing we gotta do is check the leg."

"Leg's fine," Abrán shrugged.

"The cut is healing," Sara said, "I cleaned it and put fresh bandages on it. But he shouldn't fight."

She knew her son, and she knew the misunderstanding between him and Lucinda had drained his spirit. In the ring he would be thinking of her, and that was no good. If Sánchez, who had trained her son for many years in the Golden Gloves, could not see that, then her son might get hurt.

"Doc's gotta check it," Sánchez said. "And I have to put you under wraps. We have to know if you're ready, kid." He was serious. Dominic's orders aside, he had his own professional standards to uphold. The ring could be an arena without mercy; he didn't want Abrán hurt.

The young man nodded. He trusted Sánchez, and he knew in a few days all this would be over. He wanted to set things right with Lucinda, but now there was no time.

"I'll get my bag," he said.

"Don't be long, kid, we got a lot to do."

Sara followed him into the bedroom and stood at the door while he packed his gym clothes. "Are you sure you feel well?" she asked.

"I feel good, jefita," he smiled. "You going to come?"

She shook her head. "I told you when Junior died, give up the gloves, go to school. I am afraid when I see you get hit."

He hugged her. "The absolute last fight, Madre. Listen, if Lucinda calls. . ."

"I'll explain. You want her there."

"Sí," he smiled, but she saw through his smile. "Hey, no tears. I'll be back," he kissed her.

"When?"

"As soon as the fight's over."

"It will seem like a long time."

"No longer than when I took Golden Gloves trips."

"Yes, and you don't know how many rosaries I prayed for you."

"Pray one more," he kissed her. "Don't stay home worrying, go visit your comadres. Promise." She nodded. "That's better," he embraced her. "I'll be back."

He joined Sánchez and they quickly walked out. At the curb he turned and waved. "If Lucinda calls, tell her I'm saving a front-row seat." Then they were gone.

Sara watched the car and stood staring long after it had turned the corner. Had she done the right thing by letting him go? Could she have stopped him? No, he had to choose for himself. He had an obligation he felt he had to honor. Once she had sheltered him as a mother, but she could not do that forever.

She thought of calling Lucinda, but that would be interfering. She did not want to be the busybody, Mexican mother. She had to let him go. His pain was hers, but she would suffer alone. She would unload her worry at the altar of her saints; they would listen to her prayers. She would pray to San Martín de Porras, the black saint who was Ramiro's favorite, then she would turn all the statues to face the wall until Abrán returned safe.

The phone rang as she walked back into the house. It was Moises Lippman. His voice was urgent.

"I need to talk to Abrán," he said, and she explained he had just left for the gym. He could only be reached through Mr. Dominic. There was a pause.

"Tell him he has to find a painting called 'La Matanza.' Can you remember that?"

"Of course I can remember," she snapped back. "But how can he find a painting when he's at the gym?"

"Abrán told me Cynthia describes a matanza in her diary."

"Yes, he read the description to us."

Moises groaned. "It's just a hunch, but I've been mulling it over, and I remember once Cynthia told me about a painting in which she painted a young man she loved. It might be Abrán's father. I think Abrán should look at it."

"Santo Niño," Sara said softly. That would be a revelation. "But he's gone."

"It's just a hunch," Moises Lippman said. "I'll try and reach him through Dominic. But even if the painting shows Abrán's father, this might not do us any good. I can't find the painting in a single catalogue. Thank you, Mrs. González. Gracias."

He hung up and Sara turned to her altar. Abrán had told her about Moises. The man was trying to help, but what good was the idea if no one knew who had the painting?

She sighed. Yesterday my son was a young man, living with me, our life was simple, she thought. Now all these people want something from him. She felt unsettled, the concentration for prayer would not come. Finally she said, "Excuse me, San Martín, I must do something before I pray. I must call José. He will know what to do."

She called Joe but he wasn't home. His mother sounded worried.

"Joe said he wouldn't miss the fight, he planned to go. But something happened. Two days ago he spoke to the pueblo council again, but they wouldn't listen. They sat there like old mules, and the attorneys made fun of Joe. He was angry, and he knocked the table over. They called the tribal police and almost put him in jail. They're gonna sell the water anyway, they said, and there's nothing Joe can do. . . . Joe started drinking."

Sara felt the woman's anguish. The two of them were alike, both suffering the tribulations of their sons. She thanked Joe's mother, and reminded her if Joe came home he must call. Maybe he could help Abrán.

Sara returned to her altar, but there was little solace in prayer. The disquietude grew. Sons leave their mothers, she thought, and we cannot help them. She prayed through the night for Abrán, and she prayed for Joe Calabasa to help him.

Sara's prayers found Joe asleep the next morning under an old cottonwood behind the bar in Peña Blanca. After the fracas at the council he had gone on a binge, drinking all day, then late into the night. Now he was awakened from his drunken sleep to find himself slumped against a tree. The sun was already overhead.

"Where the hell am I?" he asked, wiping dust and weeds from his clothes. Someone had called his name; he looked around. He mistook the buzz for the old Agent Orange headaches he used to get. God, I tied one on, he thought. His tongue was dry as weathered cowhide. He needed a drink.

His impetuous anger at the council meeting had frightened him. He knew he had gone crazy, and he was afraid he might have hurt someone. It took three cops to haul him out, and they had all wound up in the dust of the street. Only the governor's intercession had kept him out of jail.

That's why he hit the bottle, to assuage the anger. But going on the booze again just awakened the old Nam nightmares. He needed a cure, and so he shook himself and walked to the cantina to buy a six-pack. The first beer cleared his head, the second one stopped the trembling.

"Hey!" he called to a kid who passed by on a bike. "What day is it?"

"Friday," the kid called back.

Friday? He had been drinking for two days, not one. And Friday was important. Why? Ah damn! he remembered—Abrán's fight! He had to get there. He looked at himself in the dusty bar window. He was a mess, and he couldn't face his mother. He went into the bar and made some phone calls, first to Abrán, but there was no answer. Sara was asleep at her altar.

He called Lucinda, but there was no answer there, either. Joe thought hard. The kid was probably at the gym, and, he remembered, Lucinda was going to sell food at the UNM fiesta. The two events, the annual university spring fiesta and Dominic's big party were happening on the same day. He had to find Lucinda; he could clean up there and she could get him to the fight.

Joe started up the road to the pueblo. A truck passed him, old men going to the fields, but no one going toward the interstate.

He sipped on a beer, and that helped ease the soreness. The tribal cops hadn't been easy on him, but he could bear the bruises. What he couldn't stand was that he had screwed everything up. The pueblo was going to make a deal with Dominic and there wasn't a damn thing Joe could do about it. And worse, he had shamed his father in front of the elders. Joe felt useless, broke, and he didn't even have a car to get to the city. No wonder the old men of the pueblo who passed by in the truck shook their heads when they saw it was José Calabasa. Poco loco en la cabeza, they thought sadly.

Bea, so much depended on Bea. She knew he wanted to stay in the pueblo; he had told her he wanted to dance in August, and she had encouraged him. But how long would she wait?

I want to be big and fat and strong to dance, he thought as he walked. In his mind he saw the two long lines of dancers in the main plaza. One line the male dancers, the other female, both dancing softly on the belly of mother earth. They would dance and clouds full of rain would rise over the Jémez.

He could hear the drum, the song of the singers, the chorus of men. He could hear the bells jingling on the dancers' ankles, the gourds rattling like dry grass in the wind before the storm, and the turtle-shell rattles around the dancer's waists making the sound of falling summer rain. And he could see the rain, impregnating the earth until all was dark, wet, and clean.

Bea would dance with the women, barefoot, the tablita on her head painted as blue as the New Mexican sky, the tuft of feathers on top replicating the white clouds of summer. Her arms would be adorned with silver and turquoise bracelets, and as the people danced, the earth would vibrate with life.

I want to dance with Bea and make her fat with my children, Joe thought as he approached the pueblo. I will offer Saint Dominic cornmeal. I will go to him where he sits in the choza, the bower made of evergreens, the altar the Catholic men and women prepare for him. Cornmeal for the blond-bearded santo who speaks to the kachinas.

I want to be dancing by summer, he thought, I don't want to be alone. He knew his mother had stored his fox skins, his bells, and his dry deer hooves. Everything was in a cedar box waiting for him. His father had asked, "You gonna dance?" And now he knew he would say yes. He saw himself painted ochre, the mud color of the earth. Pounding the earth he would dance.

He had finished three beers and had three warm ones left when he entered the pueblo. He hoped he didn't have to see his mother or father. The important thing was to get to Alburkirk. He spotted his cousin Sonny's truck.

"Come on, Coyote, help me now," he prayed, and the old trickster appeared beside him, dressed in purple pants with a gold chain draped on one leg, a bright green velvet shirt, bright red suspenders, sunglasses, a wide-brimmed straw hat, and new Indian tewas on his feet. He looked like a pachuco from the '40s. "Key's under the floor mat, bro," the crafty Coyote spirit said. "You got no choice."

"You're right, brother," Joe nodded. "You know best." He threw his three beers inside and jumped in. In a few seconds the engine roared.

"I'll thank Sonny later," he smiled and peeled out of the pueblo, leaving a thick trail of dust in his wake. Sitting next to him, Coyote flipped open a beer and passed it to Joe as they headed south on I-25.

"Stay cool," Coyote said as he fiddled with the radio dial. Every station crackled with the big news, the Frank Dominic announcement for mayor was only hours away, celebrities were arriving from all over the country.

The National Guard had been called out by the governor to patrol the highways and keep order; the airport was packed. The sports announcements focused on the fight. Abrán's opponent, Bo Decker, it was revealed, was owned by a Vegas group, and they were pouring money into the fight. Vegas and Atlantic City bookmakers had the purse at over a million. And there was a rumor that Abrán had injured himself, that he wouldn't be ready for the fight.

"Doesn't sound good," Joe said, as he finished his last beer. He got off the interstate at the Central Avenue exit and headed for Jack's. "Nothing sounds good," he muttered. The parking lot was empty, and in the west a strange configuration of cirrus clouds was forming. A big wind's gonna blow, Joe thought as he walked into the bar.

Inside, Jack's was a tomb.

"Everybody's at the university fiesta," Angel shrugged.

Joe phoned Lucinda again, but no answer. He bought a couple of six-packs, thanked Angel, and got in the truck and headed toward the university. The campus was packed with students, the streets were blocked. There was no parking. Lucinda would be at the Chicano Studies booth in the central mall, and the only way in was to gun it up Yale. The university cops had closed off the street, but Joe barreled past the barricade. He jerked the wheel left and the truck took off across the lawn, over a small knoll, spreading sunbathers in its wake as it hydroplaned into the duck pond. The splash sent ducks squawking and sprayed goldfish high into the air.

The truck coughed, sputtered, and settled into the water. Joe pushed open the door and the water rushed in, carrying two frightened, quacking ducks. A dozen jocks jumped into the pond and surrounded the truck.

"What the fuck you think you're doing?" someone who looked like a Lobo fullback growled. He peered in, saw Joe's size and changed his tone. "You hurt?"

"Nah, gotta get out of here."

"You can't drive this thing on campus," another jock said.

"Come on, let's get him outta here!" the fullback shouted, and they got behind the truck. Joe gunned it and it chugged out of the thick mud onto the grass.

"Thanks!" Joe called.

He turned the truck around and cut across the lawn, trailing water and moss. He burst through a wooden fence and wound up under the pine trees near the back of the library.

"Perfect!" he grinned at Coyote and gave him a high five. He grabbed a six-pack and a pair of binoculars cousin Sonny kept in the truck and headed toward a door. The library was the tallest building on campus, and he knew the best place to spot Lucinda was from the top. No sense in fighting the crowd. He opened the door and slipped in.

The stairs took him up five floors of stacks to where he went through a trapdoor onto the roof. "Muy bueno," he thought. Crows wheeled and cawed around him. "Quiet, brother crows," Joe said. "I don't want the cops to see me."

He scooted to the edge of the roof and peered over. The mall was packed tight with students; the warm day had touched the hearts of the sun worshippers and the majority of them ran around exposing every bit of skin that was morally possible. Joe opened a beer and swept the mall with the binoculars. The coeds from the northern climes had disrobed in the warm sun. "Thank you, grandfather sun," Joe grinned, as the beauty of the young women came into focus—luscious corn-fed curves from the midwest.

He swept the binoculars toward the pond where moments ago his truck had landed. Its banks were swarming with sun worshippers: sorority girls chased by beer-guzzling frat boys, a family of hippies left over from the '60s selling brownies laced with marijuana, and rings of freaked-out students bobbing, weaving, and soaking up beer.

Music blared from various spots around the campus. On one stand mariachis trumpeted loudly, at another a country-western band gathered cowboys and cowgirls to stomp dance, and near the pond a raggedy cajun-zydeco group nasaled its love songs. It was cultural diversity at its best—everybody enjoying everybody else's music, food, and sex.

A sputtering, buzzing sound overhead temporarily drowned out the music. Joe looked up and saw a helicopter cut across the sky, heading downtown. Frank Dominic's guests continued to arrive.

He had to find Lucinda, but he couldn't spot her in the mad, twisting frenzy below. Bellies rubbed, more layers of clothing came off, dancers grabbed heartily and lustfully at each other. The duende spirit of the fiesta ruled as the beer flowed and the air grew mellow with marijuana smoke. Shouts of "¡Viva la fiesta!" exploded out of the undulating sea of people. A Jesus freak who preached gallantly on a Coca-Cola box disappeared under a mass of sorority flesh.

"What a way to go," Joe smiled. He sat and hung his feet over the edge of the library roof. He felt calm. The kids were having fun, and why not. Tomorrow they had to live and work in Dominic's world.

He swept the binoculars across the food booths. Tacos, enchiladas, souvlaki, tofu, hamburgers, gyros, lox and bagels, Navajo tacos, carne adovada with beans, vegetarian plates—every conceivable food served up with green chile and beer, but no Lucinda. Had she given up? Was she with Abrán?

He swept the area around the pond again, zooming in on the hippie momma selling brownies. A little girl at the mother's side looked up and saw Joe. She tugged her momma's skirt and pointed to what looked like and Indian sitting on top of the library. The momma shaded her red eyes and looked up. "Oh, wow, for sure," she smiled and waved. "Far out," she said and went back to selling her high-powered cakes.

Joe stood up, a terrible pressure filled his groin. "When's the last time you pissed, Coyote?" he asked as he took his first leak of the already long day. The hot, steaming yellow liquid foamed as it hit the roof. It was a torrent that flowed across the tar and gravel flat roof, finding its cracks and crevices. The huge splash washed into the stacks, ran down the spines of books, soaked reference tomes and microfilm. Even the classics were not spared.

"You piss on white man's words," Coyote laughed.

"About time," Joe grunted as the hot stream flowed. On Monday morning the librarians would find the books slightly damp and say, tongue in cheek, "Smells like pee."

"Sweet revenge," Coyote laughed and joined Joe. "Coyote Who Pisses On Broken Treaties," he whooped. The size of his organ, the subject of many stories, cast a long shadow. The brownie momma glanced up again, smiled, and said, "Far out."

Joe zipped his pants and shivered. It was going to get dark and he was wasting time. Where in the hell was Lucinda? How could he get into the fight? He didn't have a ticket. He didn't have anything but a growing feeling that he had to do something. Abrán's mom, he thought. My last try.

Joe slipped through the trapdoor and slid down the stairs. The truck was waiting for him, as was a man dressed only in bermuda shorts and cowboy boots. "Halt. I'm the president," he said. Two university cops stood at his side.

"You can't park here!" the president growled.

"Sure I can," Joe answered, edging toward the truck slowly. "This is an old burial ground; I came to visit my ancestors."

"Since when?" the president puzzled, looking at the cops, who shrugged.

"Since long before the white man came," Joe said, jumping into the truck. "Do your stuff, Coyote!" he prayed, turned the ignition, and the engine started. "Hallelujah!" he shouted and shot away.

A traffic jam awaited him on Central, but once in the barrio, the streets were empty. Sara greeted him at her front door.

"Joe, I prayed you would come," she embraced him.

"Where's Abrán?"

"At the gym."

"And Lucinda?"

"I think they had a fight. There's no answer when I call. I'm worried, Joe," Sara shook her head.

"Nothing to worry about," Joe tried to calm her, but he knew he couldn't help. They wouldn't let him into the fight.

"A man called, the attorney from Santa Fé. Moises somebody. He sounded worried."

"What did he say?"

"He wanted to tell Abrán about a painting. 'La Matanza.' A scene Cynthia describes in her diary. No one knows where the painting is. He thinks Abrán's father may be in the painting."

Then it hit Joe—the painting was in the writer's study! He saw it the night after the scuffle at Jack's.

"Damn!" he cursed himself.

"What is it?" Sara asked.

"The answer! It's been right there in front of me!" Joe smacked his forehead and started for the truck. "Gotta go!"

"Where?"

"See Ben Chávez!" he called back. "Don't have time to explain. If Abrán or Lucinda calls, tell them I know!" he shouted.

"Know what?" Sara called, but his answer was lost in the rumble of the truck as he took off down the street. Joe sped across Tingley Beach and up toward the West Mesa. This is how it began, he thought, weeks ago, when they drove the writer home.

Joe remembered the day clearly. In the writer's study Joe had been looking through the bookshelves when he came upon the large painting hanging on the wall. "La Matanza," that was it. There in the painting was Abrán looking out at him, and he remembered smiling and thinking how all cholos looked alike. He had thought of teasing Abrán because the kid in the painting looked just like him. Now he knew the boy in the painting was Abrán's father, the same face as Abrán.

"¡Baboso!" he cursed as he stepped on the gas. "It was right in front of me and I missed it!"

Moises had put the puzzle together. Did Ben Chávez know all along? And why didn't he come out and admit it? What did he have to hide? If he's not there I'll bust the door down, Joe cursed and gunned the truck up the hill.

The sun was setting over the volcanoes as the truck skidded into

Ben Chávez's driveway. The wind was kicking up. Hope it cleans the land of Dominic's fantasy, Joe thought. No more deals with the devil.

Joe opened the truck door and the two ducks from the university pond waddled away; the goldfish sloshed on the floor.

"You stay here," Joe said to Coyote. "I'll take care of this."

The Chávez home was quiet and somber in the dusk. The adobe walls glowed with the last light of the sun; the front patio was green with grass and bushes. A peaceful place, Joe thought. Why had Ben Chávez kept quiet all these years? Did Walter Johnson buy him out?

Ben Chávez met him at the door. "I've been expecting you, Joe," he smiled, and led him into the cool, dimly lighted house.

Joe followed him to the terrace. "Sit," Ben offered a chair.

The panorama of the valley and the city spread out before them. The river bosque cottonwoods were brushed by the lime green of tender spring leaves. On the other side of the river the city was bathed in light as the last rays of the spring equinox sun shone like burnished gold on the glass windows of the Northeast Heights. The light reflecting on the windows made the city appear on fire, the fire of El Dorado, the flaming fantasy of the Seven Cities of Cibola.

Helicopters buzzed in from the airport toward downtown. Sirens filled the air. Hot-air balloons anchored to the ground began to light up like giant jack-o-lanterns. A few daring ones had lifted, but the restless wind pushing in from the west was going to ground them.

Suddenly a burst of fireworks lit up the sky around the sports stadium. "The Dallas Cowboys have just arrived," Ben Chávez smiled, "just like Dominic promised."

"Coffee?" he asked. "Juan, bring our guest a cup of coffee. Sit down, Joe, enjoy the sight."

Juan Chicaspatas and Al appeared with a cup of coffee. "¿Cómo 'stás, Joe," they said. "You going to the big party?"

Joe took the coffee with trembling hand. "Damn right I'm going!"

"Bueno, patrón, con su permiso," Juan said. "we're going to the fiesta."

Al smiled and sleeked his hair back. "I promised a fat lady from

Old Town a dance—how can I deny her the pleasure? It's part of being a folk hero."

Ben chuckled. "You have to treat the ladies right when you're a folk hero."

"¡Ajúa!" Al shouted.

"Vayan con Dios," Ben gave them his bendición.

Juan hesitated. "Tomorrow we'll be going on to Denver," he said.

Ben Chávez understood. He knew his characters should be out in the world doing good. It was sad, but that was the reason for their being.

"There's a big United Farmworkers meeting up there, so we thought we'd check it out."

"Our raza in Denver need a lot of help," Ben nodded.

"Sí, patrón," Juan agreed as they shook hands.

"If you come back this way, aquí tienen su casa," Ben said. Joe heard the sadness in his voice.

"We'll be back," Juan assured him. "Adiós." The two turned and walked toward Coors, where they planned to catch a ride.

Joe looked at the writer. Dressed in a tux, he looked dignified and handsome. The sonofabitch was going to Dominic's party.

Upstairs Joe heard a woman humming. "Who are you talking to?" she called.

"José Calabasa," he called back.

"I thought maybe one of your characters," she laughed.

"She says I talk to my characters," Ben turned and whispered conspiratorially to Joe.

Joe felt uneasy. Around him vague shadows moved, shadows that became more pronounced as it got darker. Joe felt spirits, the writer's family of characters.

Elena appeared on the balcony of the bedroom. Her eyes shone in the dark. She waved at Juan and Al as they disappeared into the dusk, then leaned over the balcony railing and said, "It's sad to see them go, but they'll be back."

Ben Chávez nodded. "Yes, once you deliver a soul into the world it enters the cycle of creation."

A curandera, Joe thought, as he looked at the writer's wife. A shaman. Owl eyes shining in the dark. Midwife to the writer who gives birth to his characters. Does she know about Abrán?

She smiled at Joe, her eyes reflecting the lights and fireworks exploding downtown. "How are you, Joe."

"Fine," he responded distractedly

She then looked up across the valley and shook her head. "Looks like Frank is sacking Troy."

"You look lovely, Elena of the divining cards. Come with me," Ben Chávez implored.

"You know I can't stand that man. Besides, La Compañía is presenting a play I want to see. García Lorca set in Belen. I'll be happier there. But enjoy yourself. Adiós, Joe."

Joe mumbled a good-bye as she disappeared back into the room.

Ben smiled and again leaned close to Joe. "She knows my characters are my children," he said. "Each one goes out into the world and fulfills his destiny. Some die, but all remain with me in spirit. They live with me."

Joe shook his head. I don't have time to listen to all this shit, he thought. In a few hours Abrán steps into the ring. I have to know what the man knows.

"I came to see the painting," Joe blurted, 'La Matanza.'

"Ah," Ben smiled, "so you and the trickster have sniffed something out."

"Someone named Moises called Abrán's mom."

"Moises Lippman, my old friend. I should have known Sherlock would sooner or later trace the painting."

"He told her about the painting. Sara told me, and that's when it hit me. You have it. I saw it the afternoon we brought you home."

"And now?"

"I just want to help Abrán, and I don't have much time."

"No, you don't," Ben agreed. "I've been writing all day, wondering how Dominic's big party is going to turn out."

"I don't give a shit about Dominic, what about Abrán?"

Ben shrugged. "I don't know. Life is more than the painting one creates from it. In a painting you can more or less resolve the interaction of light, create relationships with colors that please, then put a frame around the canvas and move on to another painting. But in a story, there is no frame. It spills over the edges—"

"I didn't come for a lesson," Joe said impatiently, "I want to see the painting."

Ben smiled. "That's fair. You figured the puzzle, you get to see the painting."

He stood and Joe followed him into his study. On the desk sat the computer, the monitor glowing with the last few scenes of the novel he was ending.

Ben flipped a light switch. He had moved the painting so it hung directly over the computer.

For a moment Joe was stunned. The faces and colors jumped out at him, and there peering at them was the young face of the writer, Abrán's father.

"Why didn't you tell Abrán?" Joe asked.

Ben Chávez stared vacantly at the painting. "I promised Cynthia. She's the one who suffered. She's the one who was alone when Abrán was born and taken from her."

"You owed him!" Joe snapped and turned on the writer.

"Owed him what? Life? The life I gave him? No, Cynthia gave him life. I died, or I was the same as dead. I couldn't help her! I couldn't help myself! I was laid up in the hospital. When I got out I went to see her, but she wasn't the Cynthia I knew. Walter Johnson had broken her! Giving up the baby killed her spirit. There was nothing we could put back together. Maybe it was destined to be, she said, maybe it's best for the child to have parents who can bring him up in an atmosphere where there's love. There is no love left in me, she said. He killed her by taking her baby."

Ben paused. The memory was bitter, etched into his soul.

"She made me promise never to see the child. You see how things shattered? Abrán was not to know either one of us. I died too," he added morosely.

"When did you find out it was Abrán?" Joe asked.

"Maybe I've always known," Ben said. "That's been my penance. Maybe it was a few weeks ago when Dominic told me. Either way, I can't tell Abrán. Don't you see, I'm afraid to tell him."

"Why?" Joe pleaded.

"Because I'm afraid to look in his eyes and tell him I let him down," Ben whispered.

Joe looked into the writer's eyes. The man gropes for the truth, he writes novels, and the world thinks the truth is in the story. But it isn't. The realization made Joe feel closer to Ben Chávez. He was a man, like any other man. Whatever the truth or answer to Abrán's story was, it was lost in the time of youth. The torment Joe saw in the writer's eyes told him the man had suffered enough.

"You were the kid from the barrio."

"Benjie. That's what the gang used to call me. Now it's the writer, Benjamín Chávez, struggling to find himself in his stories."

"Let's help Abrán," Joe said. "We can still get there in time. He doesn't have to fight for Dominic. You can tell him the truth!"

"I can't, Joe, I can't. If Cynthia couldn't have him, why should I! Revealing who I am is not going to do Abrán any good!"

"Then I'll go, I'll tell him," Joe said.

Ben shrugged. "What you should be doing is saving yourself, Joe. Go back to the pueblo, save yourself."

"I will," Joe answered. "As soon as I take care of this I'm going back to the pueblo and I'm never coming out. The animals here can have the whole enchilada, but I gotta help Abrán."

Joe turned, found his way through the dark and past the spirits of the house to the door. He stepped out into the garden. It was cool and moist. The green fragrance of spring filled the air.

"I have to tell Abrán," Joe said as got into the truck. "He has to know. They gave him up because they loved him. They wanted him to live!"

He thought he was speaking to Coyote, but when he climbed behind the wheel he realized the cab was empty. There was a note stuck to the steering wheel.

Hey, bro, now you got the answer, you can do the rest. I ran into these cholos who are going up to Denver. There's a woman up there who thinks I'm numero uno, so I'm going with them. Alburkirk is getting to be a dull town. All the old warriors are dead or in jail. But keep some ears of corn warm in case I come by Santo Domingo this summer. Take care of yourself.

Ciao, Coyote.

Joe laughed, started the truck, laid a strip of rubber all the way to Coors, and headed for the Convention Center.

21 As Joe zig-zagged through crowded streets and back alleys to get downtown, Lucinda drove from her apartment toward the Convention Center. Usually the Martíneztown streets were empty at dusk, but today the university crowd, having exhausted their booze and food, spilled down the hill. They were joined by a procession of lowriders who had found Central closed to cruising. The crowd, riotous and boisterous, danced in the street as it inched, en masse, down the hill to join Dominic's big party. The word had spread that he was handing out free hotdogs, beer, and Duke City Tacos spiced with his authentic salsa. He had set up giant screens around the mall, where the crowd could watch the boxing match. Some Chicano fight fans had camped overnight to get good seats in front of the screens. La raza was betting everything on the kid from Barelas.

Around Lucinda the students moved in waves, dancing to the booming beat of ghetto-blasters and car speakers. As her car crawled up the Grand overpass, kids jumped on her hood and trunk. Others banged at her windows and laughed. It was a madness that frightened Lucinda. The mood of the fiesta had turned ugly, the fun of the afternoon had taken on a mask of darkness. It wasn't just beer and booze anymore, the easy drugs of the city were in the pipeline, oozing down each side street and readily available to anyone who wanted a hit. The city was on a high, a springtime orgy to rival any Mardi Gras.

Lucinda shivered. These were the good times Frank Dominic promised. Abrán wasn't safe as long as Dominic had something he wanted.

She flipped on the radio. Every station carried news of Dominic's party. In Santa Fé, one announcer shouted above the roar of whining engines. The governor had called out the National Guard, and taking advantage of the press opportunity, he was commanding an old battalion of five World War II tanks down I-25 toward Albuquerque. He was dressed in an army uniform, goggles strapped over his eyes, a white silk scarf flying in the wind as the lead tank came rumbling down La Bajada.

Lucinda laughed. It was ludicrous! The whole thing was a nightmare. She switched stations. Spanish or English, all were reporting the party. The roads were clogged. The city mall was packed. Hordes of people were carousing on every corner. Bonfires had been lighted. The crazy frenzy gripped the city.

"Dios mío," Lucinda prayed. She didn't know whether to laugh or cry at the madness around her, but she did know she had to get to Abrán.

Her car finally edged to the top of the overpass. From there she had a clear view of the city. On the western horizon a billowing cloud of rust-orange dust stood poised to sweep down over the city. She had felt the storm coming all day.

Below her the Convention Center was aglow. The strobes of the giant searchlights sliced through the night. All around the mall, vendors had set up stands. Everybody was trying to make a few bucks at the fiesta. The city had become a giant flea market, everything and anything was for sale.

From the center of the glowing downtown area rose Dominic's tower, ablaze with light.

Lucinda imagined Dominic standing on the terrace of his office, looking over the city. He would pull his cape over his shoulders as the cool wind from the west blew in ahead of the storm. Then he would descend with his wife and retinue, walk through the tunnel that connected his building to the Convention Center, and make his entrance. He would make his grand announcement speech and cut the ribbon to unveil his plan. Lucinda pictured him gloating as he shouted, "Let the games begin!"

Then Abrán would step into the ring, and it would be too late.

Lucinda lowered her window, pressed on her horn, and shouted at the crowd. "Get out of my way, pendejos! ¡Hijos de su chingada!" Those pressed around her car and riding on the hood laughed and raised their beers. "Go for it, lady! Go for it!"

Overhead, drowning out the cheers, a helicopter buzzed low and barely missed the top of the overpass as it dropped toward the landing space on the mall. Lucinda cursed the pilot as loud as she could. Searchlights illuminated the copter for a few seconds, then the bug settled to a landing and was lost from sight. Her car edged forward but came to another stop. Patience, Lord, give me patience, she prayed. I must get to Abrán. She leaned her head on the steering wheel and thought about the visit she had paid Marisa Martínez the day before.

She had trembled as she walked into Marisa's office, and felt even smaller when the woman came from behind the desk to greet her. She was tall, assured, beautifully tailored. Gorgeous. Her clear eyes cut right through Lucinda.

The secretary who had let Lucinda in stared briefly at the two women as they sized each other up, then turned and closed the door behind her.

Marisa said hello and offered a chair. Lucinda sat and looked at the woman, so secure and fresh in her navy-blue spring suit. One bottle of the mayor's perfume would cost a nurse a week's pay.

"I'm Lucinda," she said.

"I suppose we had to meet," Marisa said softly as she studied the young woman.

Lucinda took a deep breath.

"Was it you who called me, and told me about you and Abrán?" Lucinda asked.

Marisa Martínez shook her head. So Dominic not only had the pictures taken, the sonofabitch was playing games with the girl. Why? To keep Abrán in his place, use him until the elections were over? Marisa had copies of the nude pictures in her desk, sent, no doubt, by Dominic. The note that came with them suggested she drop out of the race—if not, the pictures hit the morning paper.

She gritted her teeth, then tried to smile. No use making Lucinda suffer, Abrán's choice was clear.

"No, it wasn't me. And I'm sorry if that's the way you found out. If you had to find out. Look, Abrán and I met once, and I haven't seen him again. I'm not going to lie to you. If I thought there was a chance. . ." Her voice trailed off, her gaze turned toward the window.

"Do you love him?" Lucinda asked.

"Yes," Marisa answered.

"I'm sorry, I have no right to ask you that," Lucinda apologized and stood to leave. "I'm sorry I came."

"No, wait," Marisa went to Lucinda. "I know this is awkward. It's not as if we were enemies. We didn't start out to be enemies. In fact, we could be friends. It's Abrán who decides about his life."

Lucinda nodded. "Yes. He has to decide. And no, we don't have to be enemies."

Marisa smiled. "I've always had my life together, I've always known what I wanted, and I've always gotten what I set out to get. But now," she looked wistfully at Lucinda. "Sit down, there's something you should know."

Lucinda sat and Marisa pulled up a chair in front of her. "It's going to sound sordid, but it really wasn't. The ugliness is in the minds of those who do things like this."

"What?" Lucinda asked.

"Abrán and I. . .made love at my home. We swam, it was a warm evening. I should have known better, but that's all water under the

Río Grande bridge. The point is someone took pictures, pictures that are going to be used against me in the campaign."

"Pictures of you and Abrán?" Lucinda said.

"Yes," Marisa nodded. "They're going to try to make me into a whore, a woman without morals. You know, it was the first—" She stopped.

"What are you going to do?" Lucinda asked.

"What would you do?" Marisa shot back.

"Look, I came to see you to tell you to leave Abrán alone," Lucinda said, her temper rising with Marisa's. "I thought there was going to be a fight, and I am prepared for one."

"So that's how you settle things, with a good fight?" Marisa asked, almost mockingly.

"Yes, when I believe in something enough," Lucinda answered.

Marisa nodded with a sigh. "So I have to fight Dominic and Johnson."

"You have no choice. You know what kind of men they are. They don't really care about the people, they care about power."

"And if the pictures are released to the paper?"

Lucinda turned and looked out the window. Abrán and the mayor for all the world to see. Images of what the pictures might look like flashed through her mind.

"It's not right for them to do that, but if they do, then you have to take the consequence. What you do in your backyard is your business."

"Yes, it is *my* business," Marisa agreed, and Lucinda realized that what the mayor said was true.

"Yes," Lucinda agreed, swallowing the lump in her throat.

"And Abrán?"

"I can't answer for him," Lucinda replied and stood. "All I can do is try to help him."

"I'm glad you came," Marisa said and held out her hand.

Lucinda paused, looked into the eyes of the woman she thought only hours ago she was going to hate. She knew Marisa had the most important decision of her life to make. Choose to fight and the city papers would brand her a bad woman. Pictures in the nude did not get politicians' votes.

She reached across and shook her hand.

Marisa walked Lucinda to the door, where they paused and looked at each other again.

"Buena suerte," Lucinda said.

"Good luck to you," Marisa returned the smile.

22 Lucinda was jolted from her thoughts by a policeman tapping on her car window. "You can't park here, lady. Keep moving." No, she shook her head and jumped out of the car. Abrán's in there.

She ran down the hill and fought her way through the crowd to the police barricade. How do I get in? she thought as the invited guests promenaded past the police and ropes that kept the crowd in check.

"Step back, lady," a policeman said sharply as Lucinda tried to push forward.

Well-groomed men in tuxedos and women in evening gowns alighted from shiny, black limousines and strutted up the red carpet into the main hall of the Convention Center. The glitter of diamonds and smiles lit up the night.

Strobes flashed, and the cable television crew filming the event closed in for tight shots of the Hollywood celebrities. The crowd ohhed and ahhed as the wealthy and powerful emerged from cars and waved at spectators.

Lucinda looked down at her own dress and realized she was a mess. She searched the crowd for a face she knew, but there was no one.

"Pendeja," she blamed herself. She had come all this way only to be stopped at the door.

"The police chief!" someone shouted as his car drove up, its bright lights flashing, the siren wailing, with a half-dozen motorcycle cops as escorts.

"The chief!" the director of the television crew shouted. "The mayor's with him!" He pressed his crew forward.

The chief jumped out and turned to assist Her Honor. The crowd cheered as Marisa Martínez emerged from the car. She was their darling, and she always drew applause. In her low-cut, white-sequined gown she was as beautiful as any of the Hollywood stars. More beautiful as she smiled and waved to the crowd.

The press closed in, shouting questions and pushing to get a good shot of the stunning figure that always made good front-page coverage. Marisa paused to answer questions.

"Didn't expect you here tonight, Your Honor!" one reporter shouted.

"I'm thinking of hiring Frank Dominic to run the Convention Center when I get elected!" she shouted back. The crowd laughed.

"You're trailing in the polls! Any comment?"

"It's not over 'til the fat lady sings!" Marisa shouted back. "You're all going to vote for me, aren't you?" she addressed the crowd and the people shouted a roaring yes mixed with applause.

"Believe me, I'll invite you to my party," she joked, and the crowd roared again. At that moment she spotted Lucinda.

"You belong in there" she said.

"No ticket," Lucinda responded.

"Let's get this lady a front-row seat," she smiled, and the crowd shouted its approval. The chief nodded and the rope was lifted for Lucinda.

The camera crew pressed forward as Marisa linked her arm in Lucinda's and smartly walked into the center.

A voice boomed, "Just arriving, the mayor and her escort, the chief of police. . . ."

"You owe me one," Marisa said as they regally entered the lobby. Friends instantly surrounded the mayor, but Marisa held on to Lucinda. "Keep close," she cautioned.

The Convention Center was charged with excitement. The television lights bathed the scale model of Dominic's plan, which was covered with a large, shiny veil emblazoned with the crest of the Duke of Alburquerque. In the lobby, sipping champagne, the guests mingled, gossiped, laughed. Those who had doubted Frank Dominic were impressed. Not even the old politicians had ever seen anything like this. Dominic's camp, meanwhile, was exuberant. Their man was riding the crest of a wave, and when he unveiled the scale model of the new Alburquerque, there was nothing that could keep him from becoming the next mayor.

"There are Democrats and Republicans in this state, that's the way it's always been. Rednecks, cowboys, good ole boys, and the Mexicans," an old político nodded as he chewed on a Duke Taco and enjoyed the free champagne. "But the Dominic coalition is going to bring them all together. By God, it's a new era of politics."

"Good for the city," his friend answered.

"Hell, he's gonna put Albuquerkee on the map! We can do better than Dallas!"

"And Denver!" a man roared.

The excitement was infectious, but Lucinda only wanted to find Abrán. She tugged at Marisa. "I have to see Abrán."

"Wait until the fight," Marisa said and turned to smile at the cameras that continued to follow her.

But I have to see him now, Lucinda thought, or it might be too late.

At that moment someone called her name and she turned in time to see Joe plow through a line of security guards near the door. Two grabbed him, but he dragged them along.

"Lucinda!" he called again.

"Joe!" she cried and pushed to get to him.

"Get a shot of that!" the director shouted at his cameraman. "Looks like a real Indian!" And the camera turned to zoom in on Joe as he fought his way forward.

"I found Abrán's father! The writer!" Joe shouted. "Over there!" He pointed and Lucinda turned to see Ben Chávez standing at the foot of the escalator. He had been there all along, watching the antics.

"He knows!" Joe shouted as batons swung into view. The first blow caught Joe on the forehead and staggered him. Another sent him sprawling to the floor, blood running from his forehead.

"Is that real blood?" The director of the camera crew shouted, bringing his men in for a close-up.

"Nah, just part of the show," a policeman smiled. Three other cops had jumped on Joe and pinned him to the floor. They didn't need any more force, Joe's mad rush was over, the blows had laid him out.

Lucinda struggled forward and knelt at his side. Joe's eyes fluttered open. Above him he saw Lucinda's face, around her the ugly faces of a dozen policemen, and beyond that a bright light he thought was the sun shining on the Valle Grande of the Jémez Mountains.

"Joe?" Lucinda felt his pulse. It had dropped. "Doctor! We need a doctor!" she shouted.

"I found the painting," he mumbled. A team of paramedics appeared around Joe. One of them slipped a collar around Joe's neck while his partner opened a stretcher. "It's all right, lady, we'll take it from here. Just a little accident."

"Which painting?" Lucinda asked.

"Don't lose that shot!" the director shouted as they lifted Joe onto the stretcher. All along the spectacle had been beamed outside, where the anxious crowd surged toward the screens at the sight of blood. "Fight! Fight! Fight!" the chant went up.

"Ben Chávez is Abrán's father," Joe muttered. "I found the painting—"

"The writer?" Lucinda repeated. Joe's pulse was dropping, he was going into shock. She felt someone beside her and turned to see Ben Chávez kneeling next to them.

"Tell her," Joe said as the paramedics secured him to the stretcher.

"How is he?" Ben asked.

"Weak pulse, he may have a concussion. We gotta get him outta here," the paramedic yelled.

"He needs to get to a hospital," Lucinda snapped.

"We know, lady. We've got a clinic set up downstairs, lots of doctors on call. He'll be all right," the medic in charge responded as they lifted the stretcher.

"Tell her!" Joe grabbed Ben's arm.

The crowd pressed forward, thinking the whole thing was part of a Wild West show staged for the television cameras.

"Move back, folks, make room," a policeman ordered.

Lucinda looked at Ben Chávez. Abrán, she thought, it was Abrán. Joe had found Abrán's father. "Why?" she whispered. "Why didn't you tell us?" Ben could only look away.

"Find Abrán," Joe whispered, as he let go of Ben.

"I'm going with him," Lucinda said.

"Is there anything I can do?" Marisa asked, approaching Ben. Ben Chávez shook his head. There was nothing anybody could do, he thought as he watched Lucinda and the paramedics disappear into the thick crowd, the same crowd that instantly forgot the violence when a booming loudspeaker heralded Frank Dominic's entrance.

Ben looked at Marisa, and both turned toward the second-story terrace where television lights and cameras illuminated the Dominic entourage.

"Ladies and gentleman," the voice of the announcer said, "it gives me great pleasure to introduce the man who needs no introduction, the man who not only has a vision for our city, but a man who can actually make that vision a reality! Señores y señoras, el hombre que va a ser el alcalde mayor de Alburquerque, esta gran ciudad del Duque, Mr. Frank Dominic!"

The crowd roared as Dominic, a cape swung over his shoulders, raised his arms and gave the victory sign. Just behind him stood his wife, around him advisors and friends. The cameras zoomed in on Frank Dominic, and his image and the sound of thunderous applause were beamed to the giant screens around the city. The moment of glory Frank Dominic had dreamed about was finally here.

"Ladies and gentlemen!" Dominic's voice boomed over the loudspeakers, "¡Caballeros y señoras de Alburquerque! This is an historic day for our city, la ciudad del Duque! This city named after the royal family of the Duke of Alburquerque will once again regain its rightful heritage. As a descendent of that royal family. . ."

Ben Chávez winced. The myth of Spanish blood had come full circle, and Frank Dominic now believed he was related to the old Duke. He looked at Marisa and she, too, shook her head.

"Tonight I stand here before you to revive a tradition of Spanish royalty in our beautiful city. Tonight we celebrate the first fiesta del Duque de Alburquerque! And tonight I humbly offer my name as candidate to be the next alcalde mayor de la Ciudad del Duque, the next mayor of the Duke City!"

A new explosion of applause interrupted Dominic's speech. Marisa looked around confounded. The crowd had no problem with Dominic's claim to Spanish royalty—on the contrary, they loved it! He had become part of the myth of the Spanish conquistadores! Who cared if he didn't have a trace of Spanish blood in him? He wore the cloak of the Duke, he was reviving the fiesta, and he would be the next mayor of the city.

"¡Viva Frank Dominic!" the crowd shouted. "¡Viva Dominic! ¡Viva Dominic!"

"Alburquerque is one of the Seven Cities of Antilla which the Spanish conquistadores searched for," Dominic continued. "Now we know they were right. Coronado and later Oñate, the first Spanish conquistador to set foot in New Mexico, looked for Cibola, and tonight I am here to proclaim this city we love as the new Cibola! Our new Camelot!"

The crowd roared its approval. Cibola! Camelot! The words rang with history.

As the applause rumbled through the building, Ben Chávez glanced at Marisa Martínez. She had turned pale.

"Tonight I am unveiling the plan all of you have waited so long to see. The plan to revitalize downtown Alburquerque, the plan to create a new city, a new economy!" He paused and looked down at Marisa

Martínez. Now was the time to deliver the final blow, he thought. No matter how beautiful and vulnerable she was, standing there, no matter how much he'd give to have one night in bed with her, politics were a matter of survival, not love.

"My opponent, Her Honor, is here tonight," he pointed and a hush fell over the audience as everybody turned to follow the television lights. Marisa forced an unperturbed smile and waved as the light shone on her for a few seconds.

"My opponent will tell you we have to depend on the Japanese to develop our economy, depend on the Japanese to get jobs, depend on them to bring in this new plant. Well I am here to tell you that we don't have to depend on the Japanese! We have to depend on ourselves!"

There was silence, then thunderous applause. He had given them the message they wanted to hear: the hell with outsiders, Frank Dominic could get the job done! They clapped and cheered and stomped their feet on the floor. The Dominic workers began passing out party hats, whistles, confetti.

Dominic looked at Marisa and smiled. Your time's over, baby, his grin said. He looked at Ben Chávez standing next to the mayor. I told you, Benjie.

His gaze then swept the crowd and he raised his arms. "I promised you I could do it, and I will do it!" he shouted.

The crescendo of applause and cheering rocked the center to its foundation.

"I am going to bring tourism, our cleanest industry, to Alburquerque, and make ours the richest city in the Southwest. You've heard about the city I want to build, and now I invite you to see for yourself what we can make of our great Alburquerque!"

He glanced at Casimiro, who pushed a button, and the silk veil lifted slowly from the model. The crowd pressed forward and a gasp filled the lobby. In front of them, modeled to scale, in living color and with exact details, the citizens of the city saw for the first time the new Venice of the Southwest.

Casinos lined the downtown canals, which all emptied into a moat around Dominic's Duke City Plaza. There were parkways, a new sports stadium, Duke Kiddieland, horse-racing tracks, helicopter pads, high-rise hotels. So exact was the model that the names on the buildings were bright enough to read.

For a moment there was silence, then whispers as the guests excitedly pointed things out to one another. The overhead camera beamed the picture to the screens out on the mall, and there, too, the rowdy crowd grew still for a moment. What was there to say? It was a fantasy, and if Dominic could make it happen, then he should be mayor!

"A lifetime of work," Dominic said, a man humbled by his own ingenuity and accomplishment. "And I have done it for this city I love. . . ." His voice was hoarse with emotion.

"Sonofabitch is really hamming it," Ben whispered.

"But they believe him," Marisa whispered back.

"Trust the people," Ben whispered. "New Mexicans love a fiesta, especially if there's free tacos and booze, but in the morning, they're pragmatists."

"In the morning they get the second part of Dominic's treat," Marisa said, trying to sound upbeat. But then, as Dominic droned on, she thought she felt a subtle change in the crowd.

"We are here tonight to celebrate the spirit of those first Spaniards, the conquistadores who came up the Río Grande in 1540 in search of El Dorado. They had a dream that the villas they founded could be cities of the future, cities of gold, cities that prospered in the desert. What courage, what pride, what vision those explorers had! Tonight we tell those brave men and women that we have kept their dream, we will build the El Dorado of the Río Grande!"

Scattered bursts of applause interrupted Dominic, but not nearly as thunderous as before. The announcement was wearing thin, and the onlookers began to glance at each other and whisper.

"El Dorado?"

"A bit schmaltzy, isn't he? Wearing that cape."

"You notice the casinos are all lined up on real estate Dominic owns."

"Yeah, and where's he gonna get the water?" someone asked, the question gathering momentum as it rippled across the crowd.

A few of the conservative ranchers who had come up from the southeastern part of the state scrunched their cowboy hats over their weathered brows and looked worried. They didn't like the legalized gambling effort afoot in Santa Fé, nor did they like the idea of converting Albuquerque into another Las Vegas. There was nothing in Dominic's plan for them. As far as they were concerned it was one more big project for Albah-kirk with nothing in it for the small towns of the state.

"Who does he think he is?" scoffed María de Los Reyes de Córdova Sánchez Ortiz y García, the grand dame of New Mexico's Spanish past. She held her nose in the air, adjusted her chignon, and said loud enough for those around her to hear: "Dominic a descendant of the Duke's family? He's got about as much Spanish blood as my Chihuahua dog."

From his perch above the crowd, Dominic sensed the unrest. There were always the skeptics, the same people who said man would never fly. They had to be won over, or trampled beneath the march of time. Join me and you profit, he thought, oppose me and you're the detritus of history.

Then someone in the crowd dared to shout: "Where you gonna get the water, Frank?" There was a hush.

"We are here to celebrate!" Dominic finally shouted, unmasterfully ducking the question. The last thing he wanted was to turn his party into what surely would be a heated public debate.

Marisa turned to Ben. "Looks like the cracks in the dam are appearing."

Ben smiled. "I told you, trust the people."

"We have a lot of shows lined up for you folks," Dominic continued, "so enjoy yourselves. Tomorrow I will call on you to help my campaign. We can build a new city together, but I need your help. Let your legislator know where you stand! This summer I'm going to count on your vote. There's a lot of work ahead of us, there is greatness ahead of us! But tonight we enjoy ourselves! We have some of the best shows from Las Vegas waiting for you. Sit back and let Frank Dominic entertain you in royal style. ¡Qué viva la fiesta!" he shouted, and hurried off the terrace.

"¡Qué viva la fiesta!" a few sections of the crowd shouted back. The applause was scattered, except for the Dominic supporters who roared with approval. On cue they cut loose with the party whistles and confetti. Colorful paper streamers filled the air, and a mariachi band led a line of enthusiasts around the lobby to the tune of "For He's A Jolly Good Fellow." To the Dominic backers, their man was as good as in office, and they still had all summer to play politics.

Other people drifted off to the different shows, or to munch at the plates laden with guacamole dip and taquitos, and to fill their glasses with champagne. But the champagne had been replaced by warm beer and the tacos by corn chips.

"Quite a show," Ben laughed.

"A sham," Marisa said. "If the people of Alburquerque fall for this they don't deserve me." Her spirits had returned. One show would not the election make, and she was determined more than ever to fight Dominic all the way.

"They deserve you," Ben said.

"Thanks. See you at the fight," she said and kissed him lightly on the cheek. The police chief, who had waited nearby, took her arm and together they walked away.

Dominic's speech, Ben thought, pure theatrics and pablum for the masses, those who like to dress in funny hats, snake around the floor, and pretend every rally is a New Year's party.

Ben looked around and found himself alone again. He made his way toward the arena, where the fight was about to start.

Dominic had made sure Ben Chávez got a ticket. You're one of us, the invitation said. Get on the bandwagon. Remember the vow we made in high school? To stick together. We were the chosen few. Remember we said that when one of us made a big play, the ranks would close in and support? Dominic was plotting his career while still in student council, Ben thought.

What would Cynthia think? Would she say, go and tell Abrán you're his father? It is time. The secret is no longer a secret, maybe it never should have been.

He paused and thought he smelled a fragrance, the fragrance of their love. After all these years he sometimes sensed that her spirit was with him. He looked around. Was she here? Speaking to him? No, she, the breath of love and beauty in his turbulent youth, was not there. She was gone, she had been gone for a long time.

Had he wasted his life writing books? Is that why he wrote? So he could finally write the one story that would help heal the secret ache in his soul? The sense of loss that overwhelmed him? Lost youth. Lost love. He knew that sooner or later all relationships ended. Knew that love ended. Memory survived for awhile, and then it, too, was gone. Would the story last? he wondered. He shook his head. He knew better.

Ben entered the auditorium. The ceremonies had already begun and the fighters stood facing each other under the bright light of the ring. He walked down the steps, agonizing over the decision he had to make. Behind him the doors closed, casting the auditorium into darkness. The writer continued slowly toward the ring, mesmerized by the figures of the boxers swimming in the light.

The voice of the announcer thundered in the dark, silencing the crowd. Ben counted the steps: thirteen, and he was ringside. He vaguely heard the voice introduce Abrán, the Duke City Kid, and then Bo Decker, the young man from Vegas. Both were superb young men, athletic, gifted. Their muscles glistened as they faced each other, ready to fight.

Could he tell Abrán the truth? Ben wondered, or were all the years of silence too much to bridge?

"Abrán," he whispered and looked up at the ring.

"Abrán!" he called, and Abrán turned. "Hijo," he said as he put his hand on the edge of the mat. Suddenly Ben felt a strong grip on his shoulder.

"Benjie, I'm glad you came. You're just in time," Dominic smiled, motioning to Casimiro to release Ben.

"You feeling okay, Ben? Here, sit here. Ringside, Benjie, by me, right where I want you. Just like old times, huh?" Dominic slapped him on the back and pushed him toward the seat.

Ben Chávez looked into the face of a beaming Frank Dominic. A few seats away he saw Marisa Martínez, and the smiling police chief. They were all here now, at Dominic's command performance.

"The kid looks great!" Dominic whispered in Ben's ear. The bell at ringside sounded and Ben looked up and to see the boxers meet in a flurry of punches.

The Vegas fighter was thick across the shoulders. He came straight in, flatfooted, took the punches, then rolled to the side and struck from there. His hands were quick. After he landed his punches he pulled back and came in again, a tactic that meant he was determined to go the ten rounds and wear Abrán down with solid body punches.

Abrán could dance, and his combinations cut through to the opponent's face, but the face was a mass of petrified volcanic lava, dark and solid. Round One ended, Two began, and Ben Chávez sat frozen, unable to move. He looked at Abrán and saw the wound in his leg was bleeding. Why had they let him fight? He looked at Dominic and Casimiro. Their confident expressions were the answer—Dominic was going to sacrifice Abrán.

In the sixth round Abrán went down. When he got back up he was limping.

Ben Chávez finally turned and grabbed Dominic. "You have to stop it!"

"He's all right, Benjie, sit down," Dominic insisted. From behind, Casimiro gripped Ben's shoulder.

"He's bleeding! You want to kill him!"

"The doc says he's okay," Casimiro said.

"It's okay, Benjie. Look at the crowd. It's blood they want, and they're getting it. I can't stop the fight—"

"Then I will!" Ben screamed.

Dominic held him. "Look, Ben, the kid's okay. People have a lot of money riding on this fight. Look around, Ben!"

Ben looked down the row of men who had come to see the fight. Men in expensive suits, their chubby fingers studded with diamond rings; men who had come from Las Vegas because the battle in the ring was not only fun, it was their livelihood.

"Too much money riding on it, Benjie. Relax."

Ben slumped back down. There was nothing he could do. He couldn't stop the fight, he couldn't help Abrán. Dominic was in charge, and the sonofabitch had doublecrossed his own fighter. He was betting against Abrán. Between rounds the doctor changed bandages on the wound, and Abrán came out for the seventh and the eighth, but again the blood seeped through.

He was weak. There was little power left in his combinations, and he danced flatly to keep away from the punches that kept raining down. Still the crowd cheered for him, their favorite, the Duke City Kid, the underdog.

In the ninth round, Decker scored a solid combination that staggered Abrán. He backed Abrán to the ropes and punched at will. A cut opened above Abrán's left eye. He struggled to protect himself, but Decker's blows landed with fury. Abrán had never been knocked down, his instinct kept him on his feet, but he knew he couldn't last. The crowd called for him to rally, but Sánchez picked up a towel. He looked at Dominic, pleading they call it quits.

"Let 'em fight!" Dominic yelled, and Casimiro moved quickly to Sánchez's side to make sure the command was obeyed.

"He's hurt!" Sánchez pleaded.

"You heard! Let 'em fight!" Casimiro repeated Dominic's words. He jerked the towel from the trainer's hand.

Dominic's guests nodded and smiled. Sure, let them fight. We came to see a good fight, and we have a lot of money riding on it. Show us what you got, kid.

At the end of the round, Abrán slipped and hit the canvas. Only the bell saved him. Sánchez and the doctor struggled to get him to his corner, where they worked to revive him. The crowd was on its feet, shouting for Abrán to finish the fight. "¡Uno más! ¡Uno más!" One more round!

Lucinda, who had made sure Joe was okay, made her way into the auditorium. As she entered she saw the bleeding Abrán stagger to his corner. She screamed and ran to ringside.

"Abrán!" she cried.

He looked at her through puffy eyes and smiled. "Lucinda."

"Stop the fight!" she shouted at Sánchez, but all he could do was shrug and look at Dominic.

"Get her outta here!" Casimiro shouted, but Ben grabbed him by the collar and sent him crashing to the floor.

"Leave her alone!" Ben shouted, his anger boiling, the weakness departing. He was ashamed of himself. Lucinda had the courage he lacked to defend Abrán.

The audience craned their necks to get a look at the theatrics at ringside.

"Joe found the painting that shows your father's face," Lucinda shouted at Abrán. "Do you understand? Joe found 'La Matanza'!"

"Where?" Abrán nodded.

"Abrán, it's him," she said and turned to look at Ben Chávez. "He's the young man in Cynthia's painting!"

Their eyes met. "You," Abrán whispered.

Ben Chávez nodded. He raised his arms and touched Abrán's bloodied gloves. Father and son meeting for the first time.

"It's over, Abrán!" Lucinda said. "You don't have to fight! Dominic has nothing for you!" She looked at Dominic. He seemed as surprised as Abrán by the revelation, and stared at Ben.

"It was you," Dominic whispered. Maybe he had known all along, and he had never wanted to admit it. Cynthia had loved Ben. Abrán belonged to him, just as Cynthia had belonged to Ben.

"Frank?" Casimiro touched him. Policemen swarmed around them.

"You okay, Frank?" the police chief asked.

The bell rang for the tenth and final round. Both boxers stood.

"You don't have to!" Lucinda cried.

Abrán looked at her then at Ben Chávez. "I have to," he said. "For me."

Abrán looked at Ben, and the two acknowledged each other with a faint smile. Then Abrán turned and danced into the middle of the ring. The search is over! he thought.

"You don't have to fight!" Lucinda cried, but her plea was drowned out by the roar of the crowd.

This is for me, Abrán thought, and he plowed in with a series of combinations that staggered the surprised Decker.

No one was more surprised than Dominic. He looked at Casimiro. They had known the kid couldn't last, not with the cut in the leg as bad as it was. That's why they had put their money on Decker.

"Get him outta there!" Dominic shouted and Casimiro moved forward, but Sánchez and Ben Chávez stood in the way. "You wanted a fight. You got one!" the coach smiled.

"Yeah! Let him fight!" Dominic's guests shouted.

The crowd roared. "Get him, kid! Get him!"

Ben and Lucinda stood side by side, cheering for Abrán. The tide of battle had turned, and now Abrán stood toe to toe with Decker and slugged it out.

Dominic shook his head. He turned and looked down the front row. Even Marisa Martínez was on her feet.

"Stay in there, Abrán! Stay in there!" Marisa yelled.

Both fighters were exhausted. Abrán's left eye was almost closed, but he felt revived. He knew his father! The revelation flowed through him like raw energy. He stalked his opponent and cut him down with an exhibition of punches that electrified the crowd.

Now I know! he kept repeating. I'm free! He should have listened to doña Tules and his mother, listened to Joe and Lucinda—they had told him all along that he was who he was. Tú eres tú, a free spirit come to create his destiny in the world. He was still punching when Bo Decker hit the canvas and the bell ended the fight. Sweating, bloodied, and exhausted, he turned and raised his arms in victory. He had won the right to know his father and he hadn't done it for Dominic. He had done it for himself!

The trainers swarmed around him and lifted him onto their shoulders just before his knees buckled. They carried him triumphantly around the ring, then to his corner where Lucinda waited to embrace him.

"I love you!" she said over and over, "I love you!"

The auditorium shook with the thunder of applause and cheers. Outside in the mall, those watching the screens also went wild with joy. A hero had been born, a kid out of the barrio had beaten a fighter with a reputation. That's what the people wanted, a hero. Someone who came out of their own background to make something of himself. The Barelas Kid, the Duke City Kid, a kid they had seen grow up in the barrio. El güerito, the kid who had the gringa mother. He was all right. He was one of them.

The mob danced in one wild embrace. Forget Dominic's plan; tonight they had someone who brought joy to their hearts. They didn't care about the wind that had whipped up, the gusts that would bring the last windstorm of spring and create havoc with Dominic's giant screens and helicopter rides. Later the crowd would scurry home, but for the moment, an unbridled, palpable joy filled the air.

23 The following morning Abrán awakened to the feel of clean, starched sheets. A hospital bed, he smiled. I'm alive. He felt bruised and battered, but he knew he was going to be all right. He turned his head and saw Lucinda dozing in the chair by his bed.

He smiled. His left eye was closed, his nose was raw and swollen, his leg ached, but he felt strong and renewed. The fight had been good, he had made amends, he thought as he looked out the window. The valley had been blown clean, a near-summer day shone with brilliance. Sparrows twittered and chased each other in the juniper trees outside.

He began to sing. "Estas son las mañanitas, que cantaba el Rey David, a las muchachas bonitas, se les cantaba así. . ."

"Abrán," Lucinda opened her eyes. She stood up and felt his forehead. "How do you feel?"

"Sore, but okay."

She kissed him softly. "The doctor said you were going to feel like a truck had run over you."

"Joe? How about Joe?"

"He has a slight concussion, but he'll be fine."

"Can I see him?"

"In a while. He's fine. He'll probably be released today. Are you hungry?" She asked and opened the window. The air was fresh and clean.

"I'm starved. What time is it?"

"Nearly noon," she said and pressed the nurse's call button. "I made a deal with the head nurse," she smiled. "Half an hour after I call, you are going to get the thickest steak you ever saw. Con chile verde, potatoes, and hot tortillas."

"Half an hour?"

"First your bath," she smiled as she filled a basin with warm water and soap. Then she pulled back his sheet.

"Hey," he protested weakly.

She smiled, kissed him softly, and begin to scrub. The warm water was soothing, and his bruised body tingled pleasantly as she washed him.

"Feels good," he said and closed his eyes. The sweat and grime of the fight was washed away and replaced by the sweet aroma of the lemon soap mixed with Lucinda's perfume. He felt the tension releasing as she scrubbed his body. He remembered the snakes on the mountain shedding their skins. He moaned; Lucinda laughed.

"You're good," he said.

"Trained by the best curanderas in the northern mountains," she answered.

"They didn't teach you this," he smiled, trying to pull her onto the bed.

"Some things come naturally," she teased. "Behave. There's time for that. Right now it's your health we have to take care of."

"Nothing wrong with my health," he grinned.

"All parts intact," she smiled. He closed his eyes and let himself be massaged.

"Good," he whispered, and a light, peaceful sleep came over him.

He dreamed of the northern New Mexican mountains, and the meadow where they had made love. He also dreamed of the streets of Alburquerque, but instead of the manswarm of his old dreams he saw the face of the writer. They met, shook hands, and embraced. When he opened his eyes, he saw Lucinda at his side. She was wheeling in a food tray.

"I fell asleep?"

"You sure did," she smiled and raised the bed so he could eat.

"Felt great."

"Now it's time to eat." She lifted the lid from the plate, revealing a rare steak and fried potatoes, two eggs smothered in green chile, and hot tortillas. "I know the chef," she winked.

He tore into the meal with a hunger he had never known before.

"I saw the doctor in the hall. He'll be in to check you later, but he's sure you can go home this afternoon. He wanted you in for observation, x-rays. No broken bones. You're a free man, Abrán."

"And us?" Abrán asked.

"Same as before," Lucinda smiled. "Last night I had to see you. I love you and I knew I had to be by you."

"I want you," he said without hesitating.

She looked into his eyes and touched his cheek tenderly. "It hasn't been that long, has it? Only a few weeks in spring. We met here, the night Cynthia died. Now we're together again, and that's what matters." She kissed him lightly.

"I think I'll let Moises take care of everything: the house, the paintings. Why don't we just spend the summer roaming your northern mountains."

"And your father?"

"I saw him in a dream just now. I found what I was looking for, but I don't want to push him. You and I can find a house in Córdova, rent it for the summer, have him come up. See how things work out."

Lucinda nodded.

"The past few weeks have knocked a little sense into me," he said. "Last night, when you came ringside, I knew I had wanted too much. I lost touch with what I already had."

Lucinda understood. It had been a difficult journey for Abrán.

"And I lost touch with you," he added.

"Us." She took his hands and placed them on her stomach.

A knock at the door interrupted them. Ben Chávez peeked inside. "Okay to come in?"

"Yes, yes, come on in."

"I brought your mom with me," he said as he entered.

"Mi'jito!" Sara cried and ran to embrace Abrán. "Your eyes. Ay, Dios mío. How are you? And your face? You never got this in Golden Gloves. Ah, it's so good to see you. And you, Lucinda," she hugged Lucinda.

"I'm fine, Mamá. Be home this afternoon. It's nothing, de veras. I can see through it, it just looks shut. Mira." He opened the puffed, red eye.

"Ay, it looks better shut," she teased.

"You should see the other guy," Abrán joked.

For a moment she was caught off guard, then she laughed. "Malcriado. I'm glad you're well. But no—"

"I know, no more fights. Don't worry, I'm cured."

She hugged him and turned to look at Ben Chávez. She went to him and took his hands. "Now you have found your family. . . ."

She remembered him when he was a young man of the barrio, the son of Clemente, the man who led the strike twenty-one years ago. Time was a cycle, it came back to reveal things. The memory of the people would not die. In the face of the writer she saw Abrán revealed.

She turned to Abrán. "Doña Tules came before sunrise, and she had breakfast with me. She told me you were all right. Lucinda had called, but when doña Tules told me that, I could rest."

Abrán could see the lines of worry etched in her face. It had been a hard night for her.

"I'm going to see José. Ay, what a night. I'll wait for you outside, Mr. Ben Chávez," she said. "Tonight I'm cooking a big meal. You come, and bring your esposa. We can have a fiesta, get to know each other."

Ben nodded and Sara went out of the room.

"Great woman," Ben said, "We had a good talk on the way here. I think she's going to adopt me, too."

"Yes, she is a good woman," Abrán nodded.

For a moment there was silence. Ben Chávez cleared his throat. "A great tenth round," he smiled and looked at Abrán, and Abrán laughed softly.

"Yeah, a great tenth round," he repeated.

Ben wanted to hug Abrán, to laugh and cry with him, and he wanted to ask forgiveness.

"I need to explain," the writer said.

"Wait," Abrán said. "There will be time to talk later."

Both knew there were too many questions to be answered at once. Too many lost connections that had to be set right. One meeting could not capture the past or the emotions of those twenty-one years. They would have to learn about each other through time and patience.

"I guess I should say hello to Joe," Ben said. "By the way. the front page is all about Dominic's party. There's a picture of one of the television screens that the wind knocked over. The headline says 'Dominic's Bid Blows in Wind.' The editorial really hurts his chances for becoming mayor."

"Good," Lucinda said, "He's just like every other developer who ever wanted to make a quick buck."

"The State Water Engineer's Office has filed suit against Dominic's corporation. Looks like it's beginning to unravel. Nobody ever thought he could buy that much water without a pile of lawsuits. Not in New Mexico. Some people haven't forgotten that a few years ago when the winter inversions choked the valley with smog, it was Frank Dominic who wanted to sell the city a plan to put high-powered windmills on the West Mesa to push the dirty air over the mountain."

"To Texas," Lucinda laughed. "What else is in the paper today? she asked apprehensively.

"Dirty politics," Ben answered, handing the paper to his son.

Abrán glanced at the halftones that showed Marisa in the nude. The pictures were fuzzy. The photo showed the outline of her body, but it was difficult to tell if she was in the nude or in a bikini. The figure of the man was a shadow.

"Damn," Abrán cursed. Dominic had sunk as low as possible. Lucinda had forgiven Abrán, but how was he going to explain this to Sara? Juan Oso and Esperanza?

"We don't have to be concerned about these," Lucinda said and took the paper from Abrán and handed it back to Ben.

"You're right," Ben said, folding the paper and tossing it into the trash can. "New Mexico politics can be a dirty game," he said. "I talked to the editor this morning. The paper has been flooded with calls. Half don't think the pictures should have been printed, the other half say they're going to vote for Marisa anyway. Looks like Dominic's plan backfired."

"I don't feel sorry," Lucinda said.

"Good old Frank. He just tried too hard. That obsession he has with being a blue-blooded Spaniard is dangerous. You know, the first Spaniards who came up the Río Grande wanted land, so they could be somebody," Ben said. "They called themselves hidalgos, hijos de algo. To be someone important you had to have land, or royalty. The theme of being sons and daughters of those first Spaniards has persisted in our miserable kingdom. It is Dominic's flaw."

"What *are* his roots?" Lucinda asked.

"We all make history serve our needs, so does Dominic. It's another obsession. He's convinced himself that his father came up from Mexico, instead of from the tenements of New York. And actually there is a story, true or not, of a Domínguez, aka Domenico, a Sicilian from Palermo who married the sister of the Duke of Alburquerque in Mexico. I guess that would be in the early eighteenth century. Dominic latched on to that story, and ever since, he's tried to establish a tie to royalty by tracing his name to that Domenico. He has the sympathetic ear of those nuts who still think that after four hundred years in this land they're still Spanish blue bloods."

"Poor man," Lucinda said.

"The woman he married, Gloria Dominguez, was from Barelas. We grew up together. A poor family, but with a long history here. She's the one with the genealogy, so Dominic tried to make the connection that way. The truth is, I don't even know if Dominic's father was Italian or not. The man did marry an Italian immigrant woman from a good family. He took on the ways of the culture, but for all we know, Dominic's father could have been Egyptian. Dominic knew his mother's clan, but he knew little about the father," Ben paused and looked at Abrán.

"I guess I came to tell you that now you know both your mother and your father."

Abrán reached out and they shook hands. "Thanks," he smiled.

There was a knock at the door. A nurse called "Company!" and pushed in a wheelchair carrying Joe. His head was bandaged.

"Joe!" Abrán shouted and sat up.

"Don't get up, sit still," Joe waved. "How are you?"

"Great! You?"

"Got a headache, that's all. Hey, Mr. Writer Man, so you came. Hi, Lucinda. . ."

"Joe, gracias a Dios you're okay," Lucinda said and kissed him.

"Guess we got banged around by the powers that be," Joe grinned, "but you can't keep a Santo Domingo man down."

"Especially one that runs with Coyote," Ben said.

"You know, we gotta make more use of that character. Maybe you should write a story about him, teach the little Indian kids that Coyote can be a big brother when they're in trouble. Start a Big Brother Coyote Club."

"You know him best, you write it," Ben answered.

"I might," Joe said. "I'm taking your advice. I'm going back to the pueblo. Maybe first I need to get a law degree. Need to know what the high falutin' corporation attorneys are thinking if I'm going to help the pueblo. But the rest of the time, I'm going to pay attention to the old men, get back to the ceremonies and dances."

Joe was finding his way back to the circle of his people, Ben thought, just as Abrán and Lucinda had found each other again. And me?

Benjamín Chávez, a barrio boy baptized by the violence of the city? He had suffered, Cynthia had suffered, and the same violence and fear that was at the core of every city had separated them. In the stories he wrote he would probe the dark center and attempt to bring a healing. Bring people together.

He looked at Abrán and felt proud. Creating was love, but he needed to go one more step. He needed to reach out and love those in his life. Redirect some of that love for people that drove him to write stories.

"I have to go," he said.

"To write?" Joe asked.

Ben smiled. Already they knew him well. His wife was like that. She knew when the nervous feeling came, he had to write. The characters who came to life the day he met Bernie were ready to end their story. Cynthia's story was now told.

"Yes," he smiled. "I think I've found a way to end the novel I'm writing."

"Come tonight," Abrán said. "We can talk. Lucinda and I are going to need padrinos."

"All right!" Joe cried out.

"We want you to come to Córdova and meet my parents, too. When you have time," Lucinda said.

"I'll be there," Ben smiled. "Wouldn't miss it for the world."

He nodded and went out. A soft silence filled the room.

"Kind of all begin with him, didn't it? The day we took him home," Joe said.

Abrán nodded. He pressed Lucinda's hand. The beating he took in the ring, the meal, the relief, or whatever medicine the doctor had given him, suddenly made him sleepy. He closed his eyes.